Fugue in Ursa Major

David Dalton

Fugue in Ursa Major

Acorn Abbey Books

Copyright © 2014 by David Dalton

Published 2014 by Acorn Abbey Books
Madison, North Carolina
All rights reserved
First Edition

ISBN 978-0-9916132-0-5

Edna St. Vincent Millay, excerpt from "Love is not all: it is not meat nor drink" from Collected Poems. Copyright 1931, © 1958 by Edna St. Vincent Millay and Norma Millay Ellis. Reprinted with the permission of The Permissions Company, Inc., on behalf of Holly Peppe, Literary Executor, The Millay Society, www.millay.org.

Acorn Abbey Books
Madison, North Carolina

acornabbey.com

PRO320150221

For Ken and James-Michael

Yet many a man is making friends with death
Even as I speak, for lack of love alone.

Edna St. Vincent Millay

Now the earth was corrupt in God's sight and was full of violence. God saw how corrupt the earth had become, for all the people on earth had corrupted their ways. So God said to Noah, "I am going to put an end to all people, for the earth is filled with violence because of them."

Genesis 6:11

CHAPTER 1

Why is it, thought Jake Janaway, that every time a girl dumps you, you go looking for your telescope and your camping gear? How long do you need for a reboot this time, Jake? Let's see. One day to get over it for every month of the relationship would come to six days. Yeah, six days should be enough, because it was a pretty lame six months.

Jake had been sixteen when he bought the telescope, more than ten years ago. It had taken all his birthday money, plus a loan from his dad. Jessica Stewart had just dumped him, ruining a promising summer and redirecting his attention to the stars, which, unlike girls, were constant. Well, the stars were constant except when city lights washed them out. So that meant that you couldn't have just a telescope. You also had to have good camping gear, and a way to get to the mountains, where the sky was dark.

That summer when he was sixteen his father had driven him west from Charlottesville, scary deep into the hills and forests of West Virginia, and returned for him the following weekend. Dad probably knew somehow, as fathers sometimes do if they get a clue from mothers, about the girl trouble. No doubt Mom and Dad thought that a solo camping trip to the mountains, lugging a telescope, was as good a way as any for an introverted adolescent to deal with a setback in the girl department. And they must have been proud, now that they thought about it, to have a son who wasn't afraid of the dark. Anymore. Or of being alone in the mountains for a week.

Jake thought back, reluctantly, though the hurts do eventually fade: This was, what? The ninth serious dumping since I was sixteen and the ninth I-got-dumped retreat to the mountains, and the stars? And then there was that tenth retreat to the stars, the one that Jake couldn't bear to think about and certainly never talked about and that didn't involve a girl. If he'd stayed in the mountains for a year that time, it would not have been enough. But one must carry on, and one must not frighten the parents too much, no matter what happens. It was that tenth trip on which he had learned to really, truly not be afraid of the dark. Why had it mattered to him so much that he prove to his parents – to Dad, really – that he wasn't afraid of the dark anymore? They always worried too much. Was I ever that fragile?

A sketch pad. Don't forget a sketch pad, Jake. Jake had lots of sketch pads. When the urge to draw struck him, which sketch pad he chose was all about mood. For ordinary daylight moods, for those rare times when he had practical thoughts, there was a little-used sketch pad for things that people might actually build, like little bungalows suitable for the suburbs, with no more whimsy than your average suburbanite could bear. But those sketch pads didn't matter much. It was the fantasy sketches that really mattered to Jake, and it was a half-filled fantasy sketch pad that Jake chose for this trip. There were several Jake originals on the walls of his room. His father had gotten them framed for a birthday once. Towers were a common theme. Above his desk was a drawing of a crumbling stone tower on a starlit night. The tower was overgrown with vines. If there was a door at the bottom of the tower, the door was not visible through the dense briars and creeping thorn vines. All was dark, except that the sky was thick with stars, accurately drawn to include Jake's favorite constellations. The top of the tower was widened and flat, like an observatory. Jake's mother had said that the drawing reminded her of the tomb of Tristan and Isolde. Jake's mother was such a romantic. But Jake hadn't intended anything romantic at all. Those medieval myths, the romantic myths, didn't mean much to Jake. Greek mythology, classical mythology, was more Jake's style. Wait a minute, Jake. Haven't you been in a medieval-style, Dark Age romantic fog a time or two? Yes, Jake, but there's a difference. It's the difference between a mere fling that gets a little mushy and trying to build an entire life, an entire existence, out of mush. Mush makes a nice appetizer for a fling, but too much of it makes a high-maintenance quagmire. Six days, Jake. Get over it.

Damn it, he thought, as he unpiled boxes in the back of the closet. There are not many places where a telescope can hide in a tiny apartment in Charlottesville. And, speaking of Mom and Dad, how smart of them to have a backup plan for their son and to encourage him to be an architect with an entrepreneurial streak. If Jake Janaway wants to take a week off and go to the mountains, then there's no boss other than himself to stop him, as long as he can pay the rent next month on this pathetic apartment. And, thanks to recent events, there's no need even to check with the girlfriend, or to talk her into going camping.

By the time half the contents of the closet had been moved out onto the bedroom floor, Jake found the telescope, still in its original box. Carefully he unpacked it and stroked it. It was still beautiful. He had done his research well that sixteenth summer, and Dad's loan had been generous. What was it his dad had said? "You're going to have to make a lot of money someday, Jake, if you want to afford your own good taste." But taste in girls? Terrible. Why would someone as smart as me, Jake thought, wind up with girls that are so … dumb. A girlfriend lasts two years max. After the ski trips to Colorado, the summer trips to Europe, and spending way too much money to try to keep things interesting, we bore each other. Even the nooky starts to get boring. That's the problem with extraverted girls. They always want to talk. They never stop talking. "You live too much in your head, Jake," they always say, "except when you want you-know-what, Jake." Every one of them had said that. Well, at least I have a head to live in. And a pretty nice body to live in too, if I do say so myself. Anybody who wants one had better want the other. Jake, make a note to yourself. Next time, get intellectually involved with a girl before you're blinded by nooky. And make sure she's an introvert.

Jake started packing up the Jeep. He'd get the packing done tonight and leave early in the morning. Why in the world, Jake thought, do you need a gas-guzzling Jeep, and a fancy one with the heavy-duty drive train, in a college town? Is it because sooner or later you know you'll need to make another telescope trip to the wild mountains? Or maybe you need the symbol of freedom, because between making money and trying to keep a girl happy, you have too little freedom? Is it because Jeeps are complicated, in a simple kind of way (Jake loved paradoxes), and because Jake loves complicated things? Should Jake take a computer? No. He'd just be tempted to email his new ex from some dark mountaintop, with something about stars that wouldn't make sense to her, and the reply would be, "You're too much in your head, Jake. Bye, Jake." And anyway a computer would be too much distraction, too much fiddling with trying to get hooked to the Internet somehow. The point is to get away, remember?

Are you in your head again, Jake? Are you talking to yourself again, Jake? Then again, do you ever stop? Maybe they're right. Maybe I do prefer being in my own head to being with a girlfriend. But every now and then, even an introvert wants to really talk with someone – real talk, not small talk – preferably with someone smart enough to understand. And who has there ever been who I could talk to, really talk to, who could get beyond small talk and who knew the difference between what was worth saying and what was not worth saying? There was Jamie, but let's not think about that now. My old physics professor? I think he got it. Nor did being smart about physics mean that he had to be dumb about everything else. But he had a life, and a wife, and not as much time for ignorant students as some of the less interesting and hornier professors had. Make a note, Jake. If you can talk about Tolkien with a girl, or mechanics, or computers, even about the stars, the nooky will take care of itself. Shut up, Jake. Don't forget to pack water, Jake. Don't stay up all night pecking at the computer, Jake, because if you don't get enough sleep the road trip won't be half as much fun. You'll just get grouchy about people's driving instead of thinking about things that are much more fun to think about when you're all alone in your Jeep, windows out, the warm May air rushing through. OK, one more thing and then go to bed. Print out a map of the area around the coordinates that Dad came up with. He said that's one of the darkest areas in the Appalachians. Then find some satellite images that are up to date. And don't forget to load the right maps into the GPS app. Then go to bed, Jake.

It had not taken much time at the computer for Jake to map out his destination. After half an hour of panning and tilting over some satellite images, checking topographical maps, and thinking about avoiding light pollution, Jake had made a few notes and headed for bed. The next day, as he finally turned the Jeep off the interstate in the afternoon sun toward the first of several secondary roads that he'd need to follow, Jake at last felt like he was getting somewhere. Jeeps are brutal on the interstates, he told himself for the umpteenth time. It just must not be possible, he thought, to build a suspension that truly works offroad that won't beat you to death on the interstate. "Turn right," said the GPS navigator, "and continue 46 miles … southwest, then turn left." Jake had already made the decision to stop driving at dark and find a nice, old-fashioned roadside motel to stay in. There should be a lot of them on these old roads – cheap too. But what in the world would one do in a motel room without a girl or a computer? You're losing it, Jake. Don't give in, Jake. Remember books, Jake? Remember, for god's sake, television, Jake? Remember beer, Jake? Remember your right hand, Jake?

He'd even thought to bring a couple of books, one fiction, one nonfiction, so that he could feed either hemisphere of his brain, whichever was being most demanding at the moment. For his left brain he'd brought a tome on astrophysics. That fit nicely with his plans for stargazing. And for his right brain some classic science fiction by Heinlein. That fit nicely with the classic backwoods terrain. Daytime he could hike up to the ridges and read while he rested. Nighttime he could read with a little headlamp, if he wasn't too tired from hiking and stargazing. Not that Jake got tired easily. So many guys started gaining pounds as they got into their twenties, but not Jake. He still weighed exactly the same as his last year in high school. I wonder why they get fat, thought Jake. No more team sports? Too much time in offices? I bet extraverts get fat more easily than introverts, he thought. Team sports are an extravert thing. Most guys don't know how to get any exercise if they're not in a pack. Gyms are social clubs, pickup joints. Most bicyclists go in packs. As for Jake, he swam, alone. And bicycled and ran, alone. And he actually used the weight machine that took up so much room in the bedroom. If you did it right, exercise time was good thinking time.

Now be honest, Jake. How much of that thinking time is really daydreaming time, most of it about nooky? And what have you been thinking about the whole time you were on the interstate, with the bad pavement bouncing your privates up and down? And since it's going to be just Jake dating Jake for a while, take your time. Make it good. Make it mean something. It doesn't always have to be a quickie on the run. The better you can make it – you know, good fantasies, good memories if you have any, good porn – the longer you can live on it and the better choice you'll be able to make next time, instead of rushing into something with someone dumb just because you're horny. OK, so you're hot. So girls will be falling all over you once they hear you're single again. Play hard to get this time, Jake. No one-night stands. It's never very good, and there are always more complications than you think there are going to be. There's no such thing as free nooky. Not with girls, at least. Find a smart girl and make her wait for it. Make her think you're gay because you won't put out. And then – bam! – fireworks some sultry night after she's decided that she's never going to get it.

Speaking of gay, is that something that's worth re-thinking every few years, Jake? If Jamie was here, he'd understand, wouldn't he? Maybe it would even make him happy, in an odd, Jamie sort of way. It was never hard to make Jamie happy. The way guys hit on you, Jake, you'd never go without, at least not unless you got old and fat. Not that you can't sort of see what it's about sometimes, if you're really short on nooky and a guy is built a certain way and doesn't talk too much. One thing about guys, though. Emotionally they're so simple, so predictable, dogs really. Just feed 'em and pet 'em some and they're fine. No, wait. Jamie was never simple.

Why do you have so few male friends, Jake? There must be some introverts out there who're smart and silent and who know stuff about interesting things. Priorities, I guess. Even good friends will break a beer date in a second if they get a better offer from a girl. Heck, I've done that. What's going on here, Jake? Are you getting sentimental? Are you romanticizing about buddies? Getting too weak and needy to go stargazing in the mountains for a week all by yourself? Yikes. Look at that old tractor. What a beauty. Diesel, too, probably. Watch the road, Jake. There are curves in these old roads. Do you know why introverts don't talk much, Jake? It's because they never stop talking to themselves.

After almost fifty miles on the secondary road, through rain-lush agricultural country gorgeously decorated with hay fields, old barns, and lots of cows, the GPS voice, ever alert, announced the next left turn. And there in the intersection was the perfect roadside motel, clean looking, old fashioned, and not too fancy, with lots of spring flowers around it to make passersby think of nooky. Nowhere nearby to eat, though. Junk food! That would be perfect: some standard American beer, a ham sandwich with chips, and motel television until I pass out. You deserve it, Jake. You've been through a lot lately.

At 9 o'clock Jake fell asleep with the television on, and, in spite of the beer, he didn't wake up until morning, because Jake had a young man's bladder.

For May, it was oddly hot and humid the next morning. "Top down!" said Jake, aloud, as he threw his bag into the Jeep. "Must eat," he said, also aloud, as he started the Jeep. He poked at the GPS screen. I wonder, he thought, if the services data is anywhere near up to date out here among the hicks. Let's see. Food, food, but no backtracking. Hillside Grill. Fourteen miles straight ahead. "Hillside Grill, here we come." Jake, stop talking to yourself until you're out of sight. Why are you feeling so chirpy this morning, anyway? Is bachelorhood agreeing with you? Oh, so that's it. That old illusion of freedom is washing over you again. Remember Jake, the illusion of freedom is exhilarating, but it's only an illusion. You still have rent to pay. You still have student loans. You're still smarting from taxes last month, and the truth is you can't really afford this trip. So enjoy the illusion of freedom, Jake.

The Hillside Grill was a classic roadside diner, Fifties vintage, with homey touches such as flower baskets hanging from the eaves and a big old dog snoozing by the door. Jake stooped to pat the dog on the head. The dog threw back its head, yawned loudly in that silly way that big dogs have, and stood to give Jake a proper greeting. "Whatcha doin', pup? Guardin' the door? Have a good nap, pup? You eat real good, don't you pup?" Jake jerked his head back as the dog, mostly black Lab, tried to lick his face. "No sloppy kisses, pup. Watch it with the tongue, pup. You don't know me that well, pup," said Jake, realizing that it had been months since he'd touched a dog. Jake stood and wiped the silly grin off his face as the front door to the grill swung open and an elderly farmer type emerged. Make a note, Jake. You need a dog.

"Morning," said Jake, smiling toward the old farmer.

"Looks like rain," said the old man, looking at the sky. Jake looked up. I wonder what they see, he thought. All I see is blue sky and big white clouds. Jake was a pretty thorough guy. He had checked the weather forecasts before he left Charlottesville. A cool front was expected to move through, and there was a chance of thunderstorms. But it's always like that in the spring in these parts. And besides it's already so warm today that a cool front is going to feel good and make for better hiking weather. The old farmer got into an old pickup truck and started cranking the engine, and Jake went into the

Hillside Grill. There was a youngish, skinny short-order cook over the grill. A friendly-looking middle-age waitress was putting eggs, bacon, and hash browns in front of the only customers, two more farmer types in a booth by the window. Jake took a seat at the counter. The television mounted on the wall behind the cash register was playing the local news, the sound turned low.

"Good morning, sweetie," said the waitress. "Something to drink?"

"Coffee with half and half," said Jake, picking up the menu from the rack behind the napkin holder. After asking the waitress whether the biscuits were home-made, he ordered eggs and bacon and gravy and biscuits. Jake ate too fast. It was surprisingly good – hick food. When the local weather program came on the TV, the waitress turned up the volume. Everyone else looked toward the TV, so Jake did too. Same thing. Hot today, and a cold front moving through this evening. Thunderstorms likely, rain may be heavy at times, gusty winds. Well, thought Jake, if you have to sit in the Jeep until a thunderstorm passes, that won't be so bad. And if it's too rainy at sunset to make camp, then you can just let the GPS take you to some little motel. You'd have to drive back out of the wildwood, and you'd lose a day of camping, but no biggy. Once you've got a camp set up, a little rain won't kill you, but setting up camp while a rainy front is passing through would be no fun. On the counter, under a glass cover, was a homemade apple pie, with one slice missing. Jake had some. Yum, comfort food, thought Jake. You'll walk off the calories.

Back in the Jeep, Jake poked at the GPS screen and studied the map. He set a winding route, over the smallest back roads he could find, toward the dark-sky destination that his dad had suggested – the mountainous corner where the borders of three states come together – Virginia, North Carolina, and Tennessee. On those back roads, you never knew what you might find by serendipity – fast-moving rocky streams, lush meadows at the tops of ridges, virgin or near-virgin woods and groves, and always the possibility of the perfect campsite near a perfect spot for stargazing. There were no big roads now for miles around. Beyond each ridge was a valley with a stream, and beyond each valley was another ridge, with some of the ridges reaching an altitude of more than 4,000 feet. There would be no moon each night until almost dawn. Jake had done his homework. Maybe he'd camp low, to be near water, and hike uphill to stargaze high. Or maybe he'd find a campsite in a high meadow that was so picture-perfect that it would be worth being stingy with water. But all that was to be determined by chance and serendipity. That was the nice thing about camping. The generalities can be planned in advance, but the final details, the best spots, always come by chance. Jake checked his cell phone. No service. He turned it off. There will be no cell phone service in these parts, so no use fiddling with the phone and keeping it charged.

Jake turned right and drove southwest, past old barns and rolling hay fields. He kept wondering why it was perfectly acceptable for a rural waitress to call him sweetie, though it would have been highly inappropriate for him to call her sweetie. More and more, Jake found himself musing about matters of culture, as though he needed new material to drive the endless internal dialogues. Is it at least partly an age thing? he wondered. Clearly she could call a much younger man sweetie, but would she sweetie a man the same age as she is? And what about a country-girl waitress my age? Would she dare to call me sweetie? I don't think so. Does it mean that she feels safe? Or is it pejorative in that she's saying she regards me as harmless? Does it affect her tips one way or the other, who she sweeties and who she doesn't? Does it imply a touch of dominance, just as "sir" implies a touch of submission?

Wow, what a fine oak tree, thought Jake, admiring a

massive oak, almost but not quite in full leaf, standing alone over a fence between two pastures. That must mean you're a pantheist, because an oak tree like that, well, it moves you somehow, whereas these tacky little country churches are almost always like warts on the full, soft breasts of the countryside. Why does that oak tree move you, Jake? Is it because it's beautiful, in and of itself? Or does it symbolize something? If so, what might it symbolize? A kind of defiant, independent state of full development and maturity, attained in solitude, something related somehow to introversion, kind of a Gandalf among trees? But then again, it had to have sunlight and water. No tree is an island. Maybe it's just that something so massive can be so perfectly balanced. Well, not perfectly. The right kind of storm could take it out, but the odds are obviously good that, even in its hundred-year lifespan, that kind of storm will never come. Speaking of storm, you'll probably have to put the top up before the day is over, considering the weather report and the way the sky is starting to look.

Why Jake, you sentimental old 26-year-old. You're walking through a storm, aren't you, and holding your head up high? How does that song go? Jamie must have played it a million times. Something about a golden sky and never walking alone? Jake, Jake, Jake. You've run off to do your storm-walking, haven't you, so you can get it over with and skip to the never-walk-alone part. You want to lie in the dark under the stars, prove you're not afraid of the dark, sniffle a little when there's no one around to catch you at it, check all the stages of bereavement off your list real quick, then hurry right back to the suburbs, meet someone, and pick up right where you left off. Jake, you are such a romantic after all. Admit it, because you knew all the words to that old song — all of them. That's why you decided to be an architect rather than an engineer. You couldn't see the romance in engineering.

How many strikes is that against you, Jake? You're an introvert, you're an egghead, you're a romantic pretending to be a classicist, you're all wrapped up in yourself, and you're probably a narcissist to boot. Well, maybe not. I guess you like yourself as much as any guy, but no one ever caught you doing it in front a mirror, like that poor guy in college. Two guys, come to think of it. Funny how the ugly ones never get caught in front of a mirror. It's always the hot, athletic ones. You were hot and athletic, too, but no one would ever catch you at something like that, would they, Jake? Unless of course you were so deprived for so long that you were starved for a little variety. No, you're off the hook on the narcissistic thing. Heck, you even went out with a couple of girls because you felt sorry for them. Funny, too, how they started getting dates after you went out with them. Don't you wonder if that had to do with how the girls thought about themselves? Or was it how others thought about them? You hear rumors about girls granting charity dates and even mercy sex to guys, but don't you think it's not commonly known that guys can do charity work too? And make a note of that. Sometimes you can get in a good lick and a gold star without even understanding how it all works. That's a Greek thing, isn't – charity, *charis*, usually translated as grace. To the Greeks, sometimes nooky was a gift of grace and charity from the gods, and that was fine. But to the romantics, charity was only for the poor, and nooky had nothing to do with grace or charity. To the romantics, only god bestows grace, and god never bestows nooky. What a stingy religion.

Charity dates? How did you get on the subject of charity dates? Don't be silly, Jake. No you don't need a charity date. You need to buck up, you need to be patient, you need to learn your lesson, and you need someone smart next time. Smart, but hot too, of course. There are some of those around, yes? Especially in a college town. Jake, you scum. That's why you stayed in Charlottesville, isn't it? Aren't you getting a little old now for the co-ed thing, or are you pretending that you're only interested in grad students? Jake, the more you reveal about yourself, the clearer it becomes what an undeserving fraud you are. You don't even deserve your own right hand.

At that Jake laughed aloud, the warm wind in his face. He glanced at himself in the rearview mirror. Those eyes. That hair. That bod. You like pawing yourself, you weirdo. Take your shirt off, Jake, and give the country girls a thrill, if there are any, because it's starting to look pretty isolated around here. Hold it in the road, now. See there? Just look at those pecs, those biceps, the sixpack, that mysterious little happy trail. You'll do fine, Jake, maybe even for another ten or twenty years. And what will work for you then, old man? When the eyes have wrinkles under them, and the hair is gray – or gone? When those toned muscles have softened and that perfect definition has started to sag? You'll need some grace and charity then, won't you? Better to be a Greek then, not a romantic. Is this what happens when guys see the big 3-0 looming? Will they love you for your mind then, Jake? Or will you have to get married? Will there have to be a contract to keep someone around and get her to put out? Oh my god. She'll be old too. After a certain age, is it always charity sex, helping each other out though the hormones aren't in it? Or are there any hormones left by then? Jake, you're nothing but a poseur, even though you secretly think you're an intellectual. But if you were an intellectual, how would anybody know, since you only talk to yourself?

"Turn left," said the GPS voice. "Continue 26 miles, then turn right." Jake rowed downward through the gears, 5-4-3-2, though he didn't really need to, but just because it was such fun to do in a Jeep. He turned left. Each road was a little curvier and narrower than the one before.

By 5 p.m., after an afternoon of slow driving on winding roads through steep hills, Jake was in the middle of nowhere. It reminded him of how he felt in Ireland, in County Kerry in the northern shadow of Mount Carrantuohill, where he found an authentic old Ireland of a type that he wasn't sure even existed anymore. He'd go around a curve, and suddenly that stone bridge, that hedge, that old cottage, was even more heartbreaking and picturesque than the ones he'd just passed. It just kept getting more and more beautiful, almost like a dream, or a painting of an idealized landscape that doesn't really exist. At least anymore. It was hard to see why these Appalachian roads even existed. For the most part they seemed to lead nowhere – through the woods, across little bridges over small streams of cascading white water, past empty pastures and old fences, and every now and then, but rarely, an old farm, at least half of them abandoned and falling apart. On the old farms that remained in use, the people seemed to live the same way they did nearly a hundred years ago, with pretty much the same technology except for the pickup truck and the power lines. Often the outbuildings were more interesting than the houses – barns with rusty tin roofs, corn cribs, woodsheds, and other outbuildings the original purpose of which Jake couldn't figure out. The roadsides and fields were rarely mowed, and spring wildflowers were everywhere, in profusion. Jake found himself applying the brakes to avoid hitting butterflies.

It's a lot like Frodo's Shire, isn't it, Jake? Makes you want to design a little Thomas Kinkade cottage to tuck up against the woods, doesn't it? Admit it. Where did this weakness for old-fashioned things come from? You, a modern boy, a computer nerd, you whom your dad took to see a space shuttle launch. Is that why your heart is not really in architecture? Nobody wants this kind of traditional stuff anymore, and besides it's not practical, and it costs too much to build. Oh, people *want* all kinds of things, they *like* all kinds of things, but they always end up with a box, even if they stick a dormer on it. And those suburban commercial buildings, meant to last thirty years, max. You're a whore, Jake. How can you stand it? It doesn't even pay very well, and business has been terrible. Why don't you just ditch it all? Go back to nature. Subsist. You could do it. How much stuff do you really need anyway? Oh right. Girlfriends cost money.

All of a sudden Jake felt a distinct chill in the air. He pulled off the road into a patch of daisies to put on his shirt. He'd been so interested in the countryside that he'd forgotten to look up at the sky. There were heavy clouds in the west. There was going to be a thunderstorm. If it rains and then moves on, fine. But if it looks like it's going to storm all night, then don't be too proud to turn back to the nearest little motel. How far would that be? Forty miles at least, I'd imagine. No biggy. There are three good hours of light left, and from the looks of things you're getting close to the right kind of spot. So just take whatever little road looks best, and if the rain goes on too long, then just let Miss GPS take you back to that last motel, the last homely house east of the sea. Except it's west of the sea here, isn't it?

There was a distant rumble of thunder as Jake pulled out into the narrow gravel road, having added a jacket on top of his shirt. "Closer than I thought," said Jake aloud. He backed the Jeep into the daisies again, shut off the engine, and put the top up.

Storm to the west or no storm to the west, west was where Jake wanted to go, because west was where the most promising terrain lay. Increasingly the road ran deep through narrow valleys and crossed tiny bridge after tiny bridge as the road crisscrossed a clear stream in a rocky bed. The late afternoon sun did not reach these valleys. What we need, thought Jake to himself, is a place where the road climbs out of the streambed to cross a gap in a nice, high ridge. Find a place to park the Jeep in the woods about halfway between the stream and the crest of the ridge. You need a meadow or a pasture on the ridge so you can see the sky, with woods close enough for shade during the day where you can put up the tent. Then you can hike down the hill once a day to get water and to wash in the stream. That's how he had always done it, from the time he was sixteen. He had an instinct for finding places like that, and he was feeling really close.

Before long the little road started to climb toward the west and left the stream. The GPS screen showed the altitude rising nicely: 4,200 … 4,300 … 4,400. Then there was a gap between high hills, facing west. For a moment, before a curve in the road blocked his view, with deep woods on both sides, Jake got a glimpse of the western sky. It was dark, very dark. The first drops of rain started to hit the windshield. Jake sighed. Wouldn't you know it. As soon as I find the right spot, with just enough time to set up camp before dark, it rains. "That sucks," he said aloud. And then, as though to punish him for bringing vulgar language to this pristine terrain, the rain began to pour, and the road became very steep, uphill. For a few seconds there was a wave of rain so hard that Jake could barely see the road ahead. He stopped and shifted to four-wheel drive. "Just in case," he said aloud, also turning on the headlights. For a few seconds the blinding wave backed off to a mere downpour, then it was quickly followed by another blinding wave. Jake drove forward slowly, but he followed the No. 1 rule of driving in the dark or driving in fog: Don't drive into what you can't see.

For half a mile he crept ahead, and to his surprise the road suddenly started to descend: 4,500, 4,400, 4,300. At last perceiving danger, Jake stopped. "Think, think." He muttered to himself. The wind was picking up quickly.

"The altitude of that little stream is about what? Forty-two hundred feet? This is flash flood weather in flash flood country. I don't want to be too low." Not too far off, a tree crashed in the woods. "Damn. And the wind will be worse higher up. But I also need to be away from these trees in case the damn things start blowing down. Turn around? Keep going?"

There was another crash in the woods. Another wave of rain, almost impossibly heavy, hit the windshield, along with the painful ringing sound of something hard hitting glass and metal – hail. More out of instinct than anything rational, Jake started driving forward again. He had been able to see west through a gap in the hills. The road must go up again before long. In granny low, the Jeep crept forward at about three miles an hour, its engine strong and comforting against the sound of the violence all around him. Within a minute or so, he started to climb: 4,290 … 4,320 … 4,360. Though Jake couldn't see anything in the rain, suddenly there was a slight increase in the amount of light. He must have come out of the trees. A gust of wind hit the Jeep so hard and pushed it to the right so violently that for a second Jake thought it was going to tip over. Jake stopped. There was now a steady roar so loud that even if the trees were crashing down – were the trees now behind him? – Jake would not be able to hear them. "Tornado?" he muttered to himself. "In the mountains?" He was pretty sure that, in a tornado, a car is not a good place to be. They present too much area for the wind to catch. The Jeep rocked violently to the right again, and, as soon as it steadied, Jake opened the door and pushed his way out against the wind, closing the door with considerable effort.

Instinctively he kept low, but another blast of wind knocked him to his hands and knees. Jake forced himself to go flat against the ground until the wind slowed slightly. "Which way is the water going, which way is the water going?" Jake lifted his head enough to try to see.

It was hard to tell because the wind was blowing every-thing around. But the road appeared to bank slightly, so that the left side was a little higher. Slowly Jake crawled toward the left side of the road to get clear of the Jeep in case it lifted or tipped. The rain was icy cold. Hail was pelting him like marbles, maybe like golf balls. If he was skinning his hands and knees, he couldn't feel it. There was so much water on the ground that he looked up again to make sure he was on the high side of the road. He was pretty sure he was. He crawled. Finally there was grass, and then a bank. Go halfway down the bank, go halfway down the bank, his brain said to him, though he wanted to get up and run, or go back to the Jeep. The lightning and thunder were coming fast and close now, and through the light of the lightning, in spite of the sudden darkness and the curtain of rain, he could see that he was on a grassy bank, not too near the top, not too near the bottom, with no trees dangerously close that he could see. Jake clung to the ground and sheltered his face with his arms. He lay that way for what seemed like forever, unsure which way he was going to die – drowned, struck by lightning, blown up into the sky, or crushed by a falling tree or flying Jeep. He resisted the temptation to raise his head and look every time the roar reached a higher pitch and every time the wind almost lifted him off the ground. If there was something big flying at him, he'd never see it in time, and if he tried to move to avoid a flying object he'd only become a flying object himself. Something was hitting him, certainly. Flying brush? It stung and caused him to go rigid, but so far there was nothing big enough to smash him loose from his tenuous grip on the ground. For what seemed like hours, he lay there drenched, pelted, buffeted, and even pushed around on the ground by the wind for ter-rifying seconds at a time.

Finally Jake convinced himself that the pitch of the storm was dropping. When the speed of the wind seemed safe enough, he raised his head and looked around, trying to guard his eyes with his hand. He tried to wipe the mud from his face on a soaking sleeve. The sky was a little lighter. It wasn't quite night yet after all. The Jeep appeared to be where he left it. The ground was littered with brush and debris. He couldn't see clearly through the rain, but there were dark spots in the road. Trees were down. Lots of trees were down and had fallen across the road. One big poplar had missed the Jeep by about thirty feet. The rain was backing off quickly now, and the sky got a little lighter. Jake didn't know whether to consider himself lucky, or incredibly unlucky. His wounds-licking trip was ruined. But, hey, at least he was alive, and he still had wheels. But with all these trees down he wasn't going anywhere for a while. At last Jake stood up, stiff and shivering. He looked down at himself. He was dripping cold water. All his limbs seemed to be there and working. The shivering became almost violent. He took a few steps, though it was more like hobbling. Teeth chattering, he made his way toward the Jeep. A large pine brush blocked the door. He heaved it aside and opened the door. He had left the key in the ignition. He pushed in the clutch and paused for a second – "Start, baby girl. Start." She did. With the engine idling, Jake turned on the heater and started fumbling in the back for dry clothes. He stripped, dried himself as best he could with a T-shirt, and put on long pants and a soft, heavy shirt. Then he fumbled for the cell phone and switched it on. No service. Frustrated now, he switched it off.

"Of all the goddamned luck," he said aloud. "Now what the fuck am I going to do?" He held his cold hands against the heater ports and tried to think. He was in the middle of nowhere, but they'll get here sooner or later. It depends on how much damage there was in other places, and how populated those places are. If it's bad out there, then this little road is not a priority. But they have to check. They'll know the track of that thing from radar. What the hell was that? A tornado? Do they have tornadoes in the mountains? What will happen next? Let's see. A sheriff's deputy or something will check the road whenever they can be spared from whatever else they've got to do. It could be tonight. But god knows how long it will be before they get these trees up. Hardly anybody lives around here, and anybody who does has enough sense to stash some groceries. You're stuck, Jake. Deal with it. Stay in the Jeep. Stay warm and dry, try to get some sleep, eat something, maybe even read a little. Damned useless cell phone. But who would I call, anyway, and what would they do? What if I'd been hurt out there? Don't even think about it. Will anybody be worried about me? No. Mom and Dad have no idea that I was anywhere near this thing, and the weather here isn't exactly big news in Costa Rica. Unless of course it was a big deal, national news and all that. But surely these storms can't travel very far in the mountains. They hit a hill, make mincemeat of a small patch of woods, and churn themselves out.

Have I got enough gas to stay warm tonight if it gets cold? Yes. But you've got the sleeping bag, dummy. Don't start acting like a super-sized suburbanite who's never been in the backwoods before. Could there be another one? Probably not likely. But you never know. Look around before it gets dark. Figure out where to go. Should I move some of my stuff out of the Jeep? No. That probably would be a bad play on the odds. Start a fire? Would somebody see me? No. It would take too long to start a fire in this soggy mess. Is the Jeep OK where it is? Looks like I couldn't have picked a better place even if I'd had time. Is that a crack in the windshield? Yep. Hail or something. Could have cracked my head, too, but I guess I was lucky. Hurt like hell on my back, though. I'll probably be sore in the morning. It's a wonder it didn't rip the canvas off this thing. But it's on tight, built to take gusts of wind while cruising at 70 miles an hour. The radio! Maybe there'll be some kind of news on a local station. Jake punched the AM button and tuned across the dial. It sure is crummy reception down in here, lots of static. Lightning? Just some bluegrass, some small talk, a preacher. Sounds pretty far away. Hmmm. Abingdon. But some right-wing blowhard talk-show host was ranting away. Nothing local. Jake switched off the radio, switched off the engine, and got out of the Jeep for a look around before darkness set in. There were at least thirty trees across the road, both ahead and behind. There were still lots of trees standing, though, and many of them were blocking his view, so Jake couldn't get any idea of how widespread the damage was. He walked up the hill to try to get a better view, boony-busting his way through fallen trees when he couldn't walk around them. It was getting dark, fast. No moon is out now. You planned it that way, remember? And the sky was so cloudy that starlight was not going to help. It was going to be very, very dark tonight. Frustrated again, Jake turned around and walked back toward the Jeep. Think, Jake, you nitwit. Here it is getting dark and you didn't even bring your headlamp. You're starting to act dumb, Jake. Just get back in the Jeep and sit tight. Someone will rescue your pitiful ass in the morning.

CHAPTER 2

Jake didn't try to count the number of times he awoke during the night. He was stuffed into his sleeping bag in the passenger's seat, with the seat reclined as far as possible. He wanted to stretch his legs, but he couldn't, so he squirmed. But at least he was warm and dry. Each time he woke, he looked at his watch. The night was passing slowly. And each time he looked at his watch he also craned his neck to see both ways on the road, in case there were any lights from either the locals or an emergency crew. Nothing. It must have been a bad one, Jake thought. They're busy somewhere else. Finally dawn came. Jake got out of the Jeep and stretched his stiff and aching muscles. The sky was mostly clear, with fast-moving clouds. The air was cool, probably in the forties. The fallen trees, with brush and litter everywhere, looked even more pathetic in the morning light and the brisk but nonviolent breeze. Jake craved a fire and something hot to eat. Wouldn't you love to be back at the Hillside Grill now? he said to himself. But you've got eggs in the Jeep. You've got bread you could roast. Jake eyed the fallen brush. Easy pickings, if he could just get it to burn. He started to gather brush. In fifteen minutes he had an impressive pile of brush beside the road uphill from the Jeep. A nice fire, Jake, that's just what you need to warm some romance back into your heart. He used his knife – a very good knife – to make a pile of feather sticks from some fallen pine limbs, and he raided the Jeep's litter bag for tinder. In fifteen more minutes he had a pleasant little campfire going. It would be easy to keep it going strong all morning, with all this loose brush around. With the fire crackling, Jake got out his groceries, used the hood of the Jeep as a table, and went to work making breakfast.

With a fire made half from pine, it didn't take long for Jake to scramble some eggs in his tiny pan and toast some bread over the hot coals, dangling it on a stick. Jake sat on the front bumper of the Jeep, waiting for his coffee water to boil and trying to figure out what, if anything, to do next. And then, far up the road, with his 20/15 vision, Jake saw two figures approaching. He focused his eyes, moved his head a bit in the way that people with good vision do, and studied the two figures. It was an old man, and an old dog. The man was old because Jake could see that such hair as was visible under the wide-brimmed hat was gray or white, and on his chin there was a short gray beard. Still, he was lean and moved with springy steps like a man much younger. As for the dog, Jake judged it old because it tagged along at the man's heels, wasting no steps, as though the dog, unlike the man, was a little tired, maybe even lame. The dog was black, probably a Lab. That must be a popular breed in these parts, thought Jake, remembering the Lab at the Hillside Grill. The man had a walking stick. His hat was black, his jacket bright red. As they got closer, Jake stood, no doubt from some cultural reflex that he wasn't even aware of. Funny, thought Jake, he doesn't look like a hillbilly. More like an old professor. Another camper? But how likely is that?

"Good morning," the man said.

"Morning!" said Jake, smiling.

"You OK here? Something's made quite a mess of the road, I'd say."

"Everything's fine," said Jake. "Scared the daylights out of me, though. For a while I thought I was a goner.

I'm kinda stuck now, I guess." The dog walked over and licked Jake's hand, then moved closer to the fire and sat down. The dog was definitely lame. Its right hind foot dragged and made a funny scuffing sound on the ground when the dog walked.

"I'd say you are definitely stuck. Just you?"

"Just me."

"Seen any sign of the sheriff? Any road crews?"

"Nobody."

"I expect they'll be along soon. But they've had plenty to do closer to town."

"What was that? A tornado?"

"Well … the weather people are slow to use that word, but it sure looks like a tornado to me."

"I didn't think tornados happened in the mountains."

"Oh, they do. But they say they don't usually get very far. Sometimes they come in swarms, or they have more than one vortex. But the big ones can climb a mountain if they want to. I've never seen anything like this, though. How'd you manage to keep that Jeep away from the trees? Did you ride it out inside there?"

"No. It felt like it might tip, or worse. I crawled to that bank, over there, with my face in the mud and hailstones hitting my back. It broke my windshield. I was lucky, I guess."

"Looks to me like it wasn't just luck. It looks to me like you made some quick decisions. Do you need anything?"

"A chain saw?"

The old man laughed. "Even if you had a chain saw, it would take you two weeks to get your Jeep out. It doesn't look like a small job, even for the state guys. Lots of firewood here. Somebody will be warm come winter."

"Would you like some coffee?" said Jake. "The water is boiling."

"I'd love some coffee," said the old man.

"Do you live around here?"

"A couple of miles over that ridge," said the man, pointing toward the northwest. "Where are you from?"

"Charlottesville."

"Camping?"

"Yes. Kind of a camping trip and a stargazing trip. You have nice, dark skies around here."

"That we do. Where's your campsite?"

"I haven't really made camp yet. I figured there'd be a good place around here and that I could get set up before dark. Then all hell broke loose. How long do you think it'll take them to clear the road?"

"Hard to say. Even if they started today you'd probably not be out until tomorrow. Probably day after tomorrow at the soonest, considering the size of this mess and the work they've got in other places. The wind took out a couple of houses and a store out on the highway. Nobody got hurt, but it sounds like a big mess."

"Where do you get your news? Was it on TV?"

"No, the radio. Not regular radio. I monitor the emergency frequencies when things like this are happening, and the ham radio bands. They've been talking about it all night. If anything bad happens, you can find out about it fast if you know what frequencies to listen to."

"What do you do out here? You don't seem like a farmer. I mean, not that there's anything wrong with being a farmer, but…"

The old man smiled. "I wouldn't call myself a farmer, though I do a bit of farming, in a small way. I'm retired, I guess."

"Nice place to retire. Though I guess not everybody would think so. I mean, there's not much happening out here. And it's a long way to the grocery store."

"We like it like that, Joan and I."

"Wife?"

"No, the dog." The old man smiled as Jake handed him a cup of coffee. Joan looked up upon hearing her name, but she apparently decided that they were going to be here a little longer since her master now had coffee in his hand, so she moved a little closer to the fire. Jake and the old man sat down on the front bumper of the Jeep.

"Why does she limp? asked Jake.

"She's been that way for several years," said the old man. "She had a stroke when she was eight years old. It turned her into a vegetable. She was paralyzed. But with the help of a good vet, and lots of cortisone injections, gradually her legs started to work again, and she learned how to walk. But the hind leg is still gimpy, and so she walks with a limp. She's a brave dog."

"How old is she?"

"She's twelve now."

The old man rubbed his hand over the hood of the Jeep. "It looks like you got some dents from the hail as well as a cracked window. I didn't get much hail up at my place. I've got an old tree down, and some of my early corn is knocked over, but it could have been a lot worse. It looks like you took the worst of it here. I heard the roar last night. You know the cliché. It sounded like a freight train. It was too late last night to come have a look, though, so I waited until morning. I'd have come last night if I'd had any idea there was anybody out in it. You were probably the fifth car on this road yesterday. There's an outlet when the road gets to the river, about five miles farther on, and not many people have a need to come out this way."

"Yeah, I saw that on the maps. I figured that the best spot for stargazing would be that last ridge running north to south, before the road starts descending toward the river."

"That would be up around my place."

"How'd you pick a place like that? Are you a stargazer

too?”

“Oh, I knew a little about the stars once upon a time, but other things got in the way. I don't have a telescope, but I do like to be out at night, to see what I can see.”

“What got in the way?” Jake asked. “What did you do before you retired?”

“I was an engineer. Among other things.”

“What kind of engineering?”

“Electronics. Control circuits. Telemetry systems. Communications systems. Surveillance systems. Stuff like that.”

“Who'd you work for?”

“The government, mostly. Government projects, anyway.”

“Sounds interesting. Sometimes I think I should have gone into engineering.”

“What do you do?”

“Architecture,” said Jake.

“It's not too late to take up engineering. But in architecture at least you have nicer clients than the government.”

“My clients are not so nice sometimes. They're petty and demanding. They can't make up their minds. They're slow to pay. And worst of all, they have bad taste, but you have to give them what they want. I bet the government has pretty good taste in communications systems and surveillance systems.”

“Extremely good taste. Spooky good taste. And the cost is no object.”

“Secret stuff?”

“Yes. Most of it.”

“Do they still use it?”

“Still classified,” the old man said. “I hope they don't still use it. Except that isn't funny, and I don't know why I'm laughing. Sometimes when you start a project for the government you have no idea how something is intended to be used, and it seems decent enough – you know, defending ourselves from our enemies and all of that. But then eventually there's a regime change, and you hear something that puts things in a whole different light, and what seemed benign at first doesn't seem so benign anymore. But that's the way it is with technology, isn't it? Take your GPS, for example. It can find a lost dog, or it can land a missile on a mosque."

"They didn't do all that development and engineering so that people could find lost dogs, did they?"

"They certainly did not."

"Nice of them to let us use it, though, to find lost dogs. Just think, we wouldn't even know that stuff is up there orbiting the planet unless they let us use it. Come to think of it, why do they let us use it? How often does that ever happen with military stuff?"

"Not very often. But yes, *some* people would know that it's up there orbiting, whether they let us use it or not. As I said a minute ago, it's all about knowing what frequencies to listen to. And as for GPS, I believe it was Ronald Reagan who ordered that GPS be made available for civilians to use. That was in 1983, I believe, or soon thereafter. Do you have any idea why?"

"I'm afraid I don't. I wasn't born then."

"We don't hold you responsible for knowing about what happened before you were born," the old man laughed, "At least not until you're a little older."

"So why did Ronald Reagan make GPS available to civilians?"

"To improve the reliability of civilian navigation systems. Back in 1983, a Korean Boeing 747 flying from Alaska to Seoul went off course and flew into Russian air space. The Russians shot it down. Back then, airliners used inertial guidance systems, and, the theory is, something went wrong with the plane's guidance system. It was on the wrong vector all the way across the Pacific, and somehow that was never detected."

"Theory?"

"It was a huge international event and a very bad episode in the Cold War. Things got very tense, and the standoff went on for days. Shooting down a civilian jumbo jet would be a nasty provocation no matter what country did it. But in this case Russia did it during the endgame of the Cold War, with Ronald Reagan in the White House and Margaret Thatcher, the Iron Lady, firmly in control in Britain. Almost three hundred people were killed. The Russians said the plane was spying for the Americans. There were a lot of American citizens on the plane, including a congressman, and Reagan saw it as just short of an act of war. The airplane's guidance system was triple redundant. It wasn't supposed to fail. So some people claimed that the airplane was spying on a Russian missile test and that the airplane was somehow working with an American space shuttle, Challenger, I believe, that just happened to be in orbit at the time."

"Were the old navigation systems that bad?"

"Do you know how an inertial navigation system works?"

"I'm afraid not."

"It's basically accelerometers – gyroscopes, usually – and a computer. I'm sure you know that, if a gyroscope is spinning, and you try to move it in a certain way, it will resist being moved, and it will also kick back at a 90-degree angle to the motion you force it to make. Inside the instrument, the gyroscope's response to being moved can be measured, and that data can be fed to a computer. The computer knows the equations for modeling the gyroscope's behavior, and the computer just keeps track of the inertial forces acting on the gyroscopes. For example, if the computer felt the gyroscope move straight up, but it didn't feel the gyroscope stop, then the computer knows the instrument is continuing to move straight up, and it knows its velocity. Do a calculation based on velocity and time, and you know how high the instrument is now. So if you track the instrument's movement in all dimensions, and if the computer has a good clock and does some math, then the computer knows where the instrument is, as long as it knew the starting place."

"Sounds funky."

"It's actually very accurate, because instrument makers are that good. It even has some advantages over GPS. Once you start the instrument and input its initial location, it's a self-contained navigation system that doesn't need a signal from the outside and can't be jammed. For that reason, and others, they're still used. And of course GPS and inertial systems used together give you a whole new level of redundancy. And redundancy, you see, is the number one requirement for any system that can't be permitted to fail. If something is essential, you can't have just one. That Korean 747 had a triple redundant navigation system, and those systems were known to be very reliable, so a failure like that is very puzzling, and troubling, to engineers. It makes it harder to believe the official story."

"Human error?"

"Possible, but not likely. Pilots are redundant, and the navigator makes three. Critical cockpit procedures are redundant. It's one of the biggest mysteries in the history of aviation."

"Are you saying it was spying after all? You seem to know a lot about this."

"I don't know if it was spying, and if I did know I wouldn't be able to tell you." The old man smiled and set his empty coffee cup on the bumper. "And everything I just told you is very widely known. But it did change the way we thought in my line of work, about the reliability of technology and how it eventually gets used. For sure, there were a lot of unanswered questions in the official version of the story, and very few people ever knew the whole story. Probably even Ronald Reagan never knew the whole story. The way intelligence systems work, with everything compartmentalized and firewalled, you only know if you need to know. Not many need to know – only those who make the big decisions, and that's not always presidents of the United States or prime ministers of Britain. Or premiers of the Soviet Union, for that matter, though in a democracy, as opposed to a closed society, people are more inclined to blab. And so if you want to build a conspiracy theory saying that the 747 was on a spy mission for the United States, as some people did, then in the end all you really have is circumstantial evidence, because everything else is kept secret. No, to really know what happened you have to have access to some data, authorized or not. But here I am, going on and on, and I must be boring you to death. May I ask your name?"

"My name is Jake, and you're not boring me at all. I could talk about that kind of thing all day. And your name?"

"Phaedrus. Phaedrus Bartholomew. Sorry. I know that's a mouthful."

"That's an unusual name. But believe it or not, I can spell it. The Phaedrus part at least. I'm not sure about "Bartholomew.""

"You can spell my name? How is that possible?"

"I read some Plato, years ago. But how did you get a name like that?"

"I guess my parents were feeling a little whimsical when they named me. My father taught the classics. It was his idea. He eventually apologized, but it was too late. The damage had been done. I was doomed to be an outcast with a name like that. Let's see. What does your generation call it. Nerd? Geek?"

"Nerd, probably. But it doesn't have to be pejorative."

"You know words like 'pejorative.'"

"My dad taught the classics, too. And, gods help me, but I was home schooled, too."

"No kidding?"

"No kidding. So I probably know what you've been through. Though at least my parents gave me a nice, practical name like Jake. I guess Jake's not a nerd name, but I'm a nerd just the same. My mom used to say that the name Jake is the new Jack. In fairy tales, if you were an ordinary boy rather than a prince, you were named Jack. These days, mom says, it would be Jake."

"How was it being home schooled?"

"For a long time, I don't think I knew there was any other way. When I first went to a public school, I felt like a clueless Greek boy from some fishing village who had stumbled into a post-Roman circus."

"I can identify with that," said Phaedrus.

"It was probably worse than you imagine. I could read some Greek, but I had never played a video game. Everything I knew about religion was more than two thousand years out of date. I had to swim pretty fast for a while, but I survived."

"I suspect you're a heck of a swimmer, Jake. You just survived a tornado."

"My parents taught me a lot about culture, I guess. They said just look around and see what everybody else is doing. I thought that was a terrible rule, and I told my parents so, but it was amazing how well it worked."

Phaedrus laughed, stopped for a moment to catch his breath, then broke out laughing again. Then Jake started laughing too.

"Well, Jake, since you and your Jeep here aren't going anywhere, would you like to camp up at my place? I think I can point you to a good spot – nice and high, not too many bugs, nice breeze, and as dark a sky as you'll find."

"That would be great. I would really appreciate that.

But what about the Jeep?"

Phaedrus pushed back the brim of his hat a bit and scratched at his forehead. The resemblance to Gandalf was amazing. "Well, it'll be safe here. Maybe get it off the road as much as possible – over there maybe – and leave a note on it saying you're camping nearby and that you'll be back every day to check on the Jeep and see if the road is open. That should do it, I think. I don't think the cleanup crews will have any trouble working around it if you move it off the road. And I can probably get a message to the sheriff, if he's not too busy."

The fire was dying down. Jake went to the fire to see if there was any dirt to kick over the coals, but there was only mud.

"I wouldn't worry," said Phaedrus. "Everything is so soggy that I don't think that fire will last much longer." Phaedrus got up off the bumper and arched backward to stretch. Joan slowly got up from her moist spot on the ground, shook herself, and then yawned. She moved closer to Phaedrus and rubbed her head against his legs.

"Well, let me grab a few things and move the Jeep, and write that note, and we'll be off. It's so nice of you to offer me a place to camp. Things are looking a whole lot better now than when I woke up this morning."

—▶ ◀—

"This is incredible," said Jake as they reached the hilltop and looked down into a narrow green pasture. "How did you find this place? It's the perfect little farm, though it looks like you've made some additions."

A small house, two stories, weathered gray, sat in the middle of the pasture below the hilltop, surrounded by an old white-washed picket fence. Shade trees hung over the fence. The grass was lush. Dotted everywhere there were roses, irises, and blooming things. On the south side of the house, inside a fence of its own, was a vegetable garden in which onions, cabbages, and several kinds of leafy greens were already well under way. About two hundred yards from the garden stood an old barn, weathered gray like the house but still standing strong. Several other outbuildings stood here and there. There was no sign of livestock, but a rabbit scampered into tall grass when it saw them. Adjoining the house on the north side stood what was clearly an addition. Its design and its wooden siding were in harmony with the much older house. Its purpose was not clear. It reminded Jake of the little community auditoriums one sometimes saw in New England, where town meetings were held and where chamber music concerts were often given during the summer.

"That addition," said Jake, shifting the pack on his back, "Did you build it? It looks like a small auditorium. I've never seen anything like that on a farmstead."

"You can have a look inside shortly if you like," said Phaedrus.

They continued down the hill. Joan, who had lagged behind as they'd climbed, now caught up and scuffled ahead down the footpath. Daisies, violets, and some kind of yellow flowers that Jake didn't recognize lined the path. The grass was tall, and even in May some of it had already gone to seed. There was a small wisp of smoke from what appeared to be the kitchen chimney. As they approached, Jake could see checkered half-curtains in some of the windows. A lush vine – some kind of native grapes, maybe? – grew on the south side of the house around the kitchen chimney. Meandering between the garden and the barn was a line of growth even taller and more lush than what surrounded it. It was a small stream, Jake realized, probably fed from a spring up the hill. The overall effect was so charming that Jake felt as though he was looking at the set of a movie, filmed on location in Appalachia.

"You are so lucky. This is just incredible."

"Thank you," said Phaedrus. "I am … content."

They reached a gate in the picket fence. Over the gate was a rustic wooden arch heavy with roses. Joan waited for Phaedrus to open the gate. Joan went first, followed by Jake, then Phaedrus. Now they stood on a small, shady lawn of tall grass. The grass looked as though it had not been mowed. Stone paths connected the gates and doors. In front of what appeared to be an old well house, a stream of water was pouring from a rusty metal spout into a mossy concrete basin. The only sounds that could be heard were the rustling of the shade trees overhead, the birds in the trees, and the gurgling of the little stream of water. "A fountain?" asked Jake.

"A water spout fed from a spring up the hill," said Phaedrus. "It runs all the time. It's gravity, and the spring water has to go somewhere, so no water and no energy are wasted, if that's what you were wondering. Resources are limited around here. I can't afford much waste."

"It looks rich in resources to me. You've got everything here."

"Well, that's no credit to me. I only bought the place, a good many years ago. What it reflects, really, is how people used to live in these mountains. If they couldn't grow it, or trade with the neighbors for it, they didn't have it. People got through the Great Depression, and two world wars, in places like this. What was that motto in World War II? 'Use it up, wear it out, make it do or do without.' Before the days of textile mills, people around here even knew how to grow flax and weave a lot of their own cloth. For generations they grew all their own food. I can't think of anything they had to bring in, except maybe salt, and coffee if they could get it. A lot of the old timers around here still know how to grow most of their own food. You can put your pack down over there if you like," said Phaedrus, pointing to the porch.

Jake put his pack down, and once again his eyes were drawn to the oversized building that looked like an auditorium. There were no curtains in its windows. It was dark inside.

"I'll show you," said Phaedrus. "The door's around here." They followed the path around the corner of the building, skirting a huge stand of lilacs, and came to a double door. Phaedrus turned the knob on the right-hand side and pulled open one of the two doors. He tilted his head toward the door, inviting Jake to enter. Jake noticed that Phaedrus removed his hat, whether out of respect of some sort or to see more clearly inside out of the sunlight Jake wasn't sure.

The rafters were exposed. The ceiling was high. On one end was a huge stone fireplace. The floor was made of pine boards, wide and roughly finished. It was all a large single room except for one corner, where there was a single square room occupying maybe an eighth of the floor space. The door to the room was closed. There was almost no furniture – three or four chairs. The actual centerpiece of the room, projecting more drama than even the massive fireplace, was an enormous organ console. It sat on a dais on the side of the room opposite the fireplace.

"Incredible," said Jake. "It is an auditorium, I guess. That thing is huge. But I don't see any pipes."

"It's electronic," said Phaedrus. "It has pipe sounds at its command, but they're digitally sampled and stored in its computer." Jake walked toward the console. There were four keyboards, one above the other. There was a large pedal keyboard, with radiating pedals, arching upward on each side.

"I've never actually been up close to anything like this," said Jake. "Do you play it?"

"It belonged to a friend once upon a time," said Phaedrus. "I can play some, or used to. But the computer can play it better than I can. Of course, that takes electricity, and electricity is something I've been short of for a while."

"I don't see a computer," said Jake.

"It's a small, specialized computer," said Phaedrus. "It's that little box underneath the keyboards."

"What are these? Stops?" asked Jake.

"Stops, yes, but more specifically, drawknobs."

"There are so many of them. There are so many knobs and switches and controls that I don't see how one person could manage it all. It reminds me a bit of the cockpit of – a Boeing 747. Not that I've ever seen the cockpit of a Boeing 747, except in pictures, but you know what I mean."

"The organ can help the organist a bit with all that. See those shiny knobs there, above the pedals? They store preset combinations of stops. If the organist presses one of them with his toe, then the stops fly in and out according to the preset."

"Solenoids?"

"Yes, though on a wind instrument it might all be pneumatic."

"Speakers?"

"All around," Phaedrus said, indicating the high ceiling with a sweep of his hand.

As Jake looked more carefully he saw what looked like wood boxes, or chambers, in various places around the ceiling. Each box or chamber was covered with black cloth. He looked more closely at the drawknobs.

"I can recognize what a lot of this means, like 'Viol,' or even 'Diapason,' but what are the numbers? Eight, sixteen. There are even some thirty-twos here in the pedal section."

"The numbers indicate the pitch of the stop. With an eight-foot stop, if you play middle C, then the organ sounds middle C. With a four-foot stop, if you play middle C, then the organ sounds a note an octave above middle C. A sixteen-foot stop is an octave lower, and a 32-foot stop is two octaves lower."

"That must be some pretty low notes."

"The organ can make a lower note than any other instrument. If you pull a thirty-two-foot stop and play the lowest note on the keyboard, then the organ sounds a note that's – let's see – five C's below middle C. That's 16 hertz, and the human ear can't even hear notes that low. You can feel it, though, especially in the diaphragm. It shakes the air in your lungs. It makes some people feel a little uncomfortable. The sound systems in theaters can reproduce sounds that low. That's what you hear in a really scary moment. Or when an Imperial Cruiser is descending toward Tatooine."

"You know your Star Wars! This thing must sound amazing. Are you off the grid?"

"I have been off the grid for about three years now. I have just enough solar for some essentials. There's a generator, but it's been dead for years, and it's not worth fixing. There are other priorities for such cash as I can raise. Being off the grid is no hardship if you don't need it for heat and light. It's one less bill to pay."

"Wow. I admire you for living off the grid. But even if you have better sources of heat and light, you must also have some solar power, since you have computers," said Jake, pointing to the closed room in the corner.

"How did you know I have computers?" asked Phaedrus.

"From the keypad and the lights beside the door over there. I've only ever seen something like that on doors leading to a computer room. It's not exactly something you expect to see on a farm way up in the mountains."

"My solar power is limited. I can run some of the newer computers. And I have some radios. But a lot of my older computers aren't very fuel-efficient. Some of them haven't been booted for many a year."

Jake pointed to the lights glowing above the door to the computer room. "I love this mixture of old technology and new technology," he said. "Speaking of Tatooine, it reminds me of when R2D2 and C3PO are let inside the fortress of Jabba the Hutt. Inside, it's like the basement of a medieval fortress, but here and there are little indicator lights glowing on the wall." Jake laughed. "I don't mean to compare your place to Jabba the Hutt's, but you know what I mean. Come to think of it, when Obi-Wan was living on Tatooine, secretly keeping watch over young Luke, there were little lights in Obi-Wan's place too, though it was only a hut out in the desert. There's an odd magic in that – low tech and high tech unexpectedly found together."

"Though it's probably more about redundancy than magic where old technology and new technology are found together, as we talked about earlier. New technologies can do amazing things, but old technologies are usually much more resilient."

"I had never thought about it like that," said Jake. "But I can certainly see the point. As a matter of fact, there's something kind of profound about that. Most people don't stop to think how … how …"

"How precarious their support systems are?" Phaedrus laughed. "The problem is, redundancy is not cheap. And often old technology costs more than new technology. Jabba the Hutt must have been very rich to afford that much redundancy – a medieval fortress with high-tech security. Most people can't afford much redundancy. I'm hard pressed for redundancy myself, these days especially. People have two cars, a spare tire, an extra toothbrush. But it's hard to have redundancy when having just one of something you need is hard enough. But let's don't get ourselves depressed over dark possibilities. You've come to go camping on a high ridge, and smell the flowers and look at the stars. We can scare the daylights out of ourselves some other time thinking about how precarious our support systems are. Why don't you come down to dinner tonight? I'll give you a tour of the place then. I haven't had a chance to push my cooking onto anyone in a long time. You'll probably be so hungry from going up and down ridges that you might even like it."

"I'd love to come to dinner," said Jake. "And I'd love to have a tour. So I'll wait to ask you what that little green light is about."

Admit it Jake. You wanted to indulge in lascivious self-pity out here where no one could see you. You wanted to commune with other simple creatures like yourself by day and stir up some transcendence and pathos by night, looking up at the stars. A few days of the birds and the bees, the Orion nebula, some mosquitoes and poison oak, some fantasizing, and some playing with yourself, and you'd be as good as new. Funny how things tend to turn out different from what you planned. Instead you almost got yourself killed by a tornado, and you've got two cases rather than one case of post-traumatic stress to deal with – one girl-related and one storm-related. Which one of those almost killed you, Jake? Take a note of that. Girl-related trauma is rarely fatal. And this hermit guy, Phaedrus. What a character. Probably the most eccentric character you've ever met – a stick like Obi-Wan's and a hat like Indiana Jones'. He's a walking encyclopedia. And yet, weird as he is, he doesn't even register on the creepy scale. There's something a little sad about him, too. He must have fallen on hard times. I wonder why he became a hermit. That place cost some money, but now it's all grown up, and he says he can't afford electricity, or the cost of fixing the generator. Why does he choose to live like that all by himself? He doesn't seem like the typical back-to-the-earth type. Maybe he's not as well off as he used to be. But still, it wasn't poverty that brought him here, because it took a lot of money to put together a setup like that. There's some piece of the puzzle that you don't have yet, Jake. Whatever this old man's story is, it's probably pretty interesting. And he's probably not going to reveal very much of it to a dumb young stray like me. But at least you don't have to boil water and pour it into plastic pouches for your supper tonight. And he doesn't seem to mind when I ask questions. He even seems to like it.

When Jake arrived back at Phaedrus' place an hour before sunset, Phaedrus proposed that they do an outside tour before supper and an inside tour after supper. They were leaving the barn and walking back toward the house.

"With such a fine old barn, and all that old equipment still around, why don't you have cows?"

"Several reasons. I'm not always here. I have other … responsibilities, and sometimes I have to be away for several weeks at a time. If I were trying to be as close to one hundred percent self-sufficient here as the older generations had to be, then it probably would make sense to have cows. Cows can use grass, which we can't otherwise use and which is plentiful here, and convert it to milk, which we can use, or meat for that matter. But getting the benefit of the grass also requires a lot of work, which I don't have enough time for, since there's only one of me to do everything. Cows demand a strict daily routine. Milk also has to be used quickly, or preserved somehow, which takes a lot of time and spotless equipment, or it has to be refrigerated, which takes energy. I get on just fine without milk and cheese or butter. Soybean milk makes a great substitute. Soybean milk is fairly cheap and easy to make. It just takes some elbow grease and enough energy to boil it. Or it's cheap enough to buy it commercially in cartons that keep forever but don't have to be refrigerated. So for my situation, cows just don't make sense."

"Do you have a refrigerator?"

"No."

"Of course. What am I thinking? You're off the grid.

It must be harder to do without a refrigerator than anything."

"Not really. What do people keep in their refrigerators? Actually, let me take back the question. It's insane what people put in refrigerators these days. When refrigerators first came along four or five generations ago, what did people put in them, especially rural people?"

"Let me see. Milk? Meat?

"Yes. Butter doesn't even need close refrigeration. It just needs to be kept away from oxygen. Eggs keep pretty well without refrigeration if they're kept cool. As for fruits and vegetables, there are all sorts of traditional ways of keeping them without refrigeration. Refrigeration is more about keeping the foods we buy at the store than about what comes from a farm."

"And so you just do without milk and meat. And soft drinks and frozen pizza."

"Yes. And besides, for almost half the year, you can just set something on the back porch to stay cool. I do that a lot with leftovers. But there's still another reason why I can't justify refrigeration, or freezers as a way of preserving food. Take a guess."

"Hmmm. Well you certainly have room in that big kitchen for a refrigerator and freezer. Oh, I get it. Redundancy."

"Exactly. If you commit a lot of valuable food to something like a freezer, then you have to have a backup. Else if your power source fails – as it often does out here – then you've lost a big chunk of your grub stake. So the redundancy requirement more or less doubles the cost of refrigeration and pushes it even further out of the money on the cost-benefit scale."

"How long have you lived like this?"

"I've lived here for twenty years. I had some money saved and retired early."

"You built the auditorium? Or what did you call it?

The studio."

"Yes. With help from a friend. The old generations that made this farm didn't need a place for the kinds of things that are in the studio, as you call it. They were not likely to have church-size organs, or electronic apparatus, or computers. Or solar arrays. They're on the roof."

"So not everything in the room with the green light has to do with the organ?"

"Not everything. I'll show you after supper."

They ate supper at a small table beside a kitchen window. Joan lay curled up on the floor. Phaedrus had made beans, fresh mustard greens, salmon patties, baked potatoes, and hot homemade biscuits. Phaedrus also had produced a bottle of white wine.

"This is more biscuits than I usually can eat without the risk of gaining weight," said Phaedrus, "but you're young, and you've been riding the range all day. So you need it."

"I sure do," said Jake. "It looks great. Thank you. Nice wine, too. I bet you didn't make that yourself."

"I didn't. Some costs I justify on a curve."

"I wanted to ask you, and I hope you don't mind. The kind of life you have here, and the kind of place you have, it's not like how most people live, to say the least. In a way it seems something like the survivalists one reads about. But you don't seem to have any guns. Sorry. Bad joke. But what led you to this, if I may ask?"

"I don't mind if you ask. An earnest question deserves an earnest answer, though you're probably going to think I'm even crazier than you already thought I am."

"Try me."

"I believe that . . . the world is not as stable as people like to think it is. So I believe in being prepared."

"So you think that bad things could happen?"

"I suppose that's as good a way to put it as any."

"Can you elaborate?"

"I don't mean to sound mysterious, or eccentric. But it's really just a matter of looking at how things are, analyzing the weaknesses, and trying to work out some probabilities. Information on how things really are is surprisingly hard to come by. Let's just say that, as I see it, the probabilities of bad things happening are higher than most people know."

"And the point is to be prepared."

"Yes. To be prepared."

When Phaedrus didn't continue, Jake realized that he wasn't going to say much more, and Jake didn't want to pry. Besides, there was something a little spooky about it, and Jake figured he needed to do some thinking later about whether Phaedrus was totally crazy, or only a little crazy. So Jake changed the subject.

"These are excellent biscuits," Jake said. "What kind of … shortening did you use? That's the right word, isn't it?"

"Yes. Shortening. It's coconut oil."

"Coconut oil?" Jake said with surprise. "Now that you mention it, I think I detect the faint taste of coconuts. Why coconut oil?"

"Coconut oil is saturated, so it doesn't tend to go rancid like most oils. It will last for a couple of years, unrefrigerated. Back in the days when they thought hydrogenated vegetable fats were good for you, they thought coconut oil is bad for you. But coconut oil's reputation has been largely restored, thanks to more modern findings. I try to keep a fair amount of coconut oil tucked away. Olive oil too. But olive oil doesn't keep as well. The old-timers around here used lard, pig fat. It's saturated, so it keeps a long time too, like coconut oil."

When the sunlight through the kitchen window

began to fail, Phaedrus produced two candles. They had dessert under the candlelight. It was fresh strawberries from the garden, with a bar of dark chocolate.

"This chocolate is awesome," said Jake, "and the strawberries too. You're not exactly in a state of deprivation out here, are you? Except from what I've seen so far I do believe you're deprived of television."

"I am in fact deprived of television, and I don't miss it in the least."

"Do you have Internet?"

"I don't. Internet access is not cheap out here when you don't even have a phone line. When I'm in town I stop at the public library. They have computers and Internet access for free. But there are other sources of information."

"Such as?"

"I'm afraid I'm about to answer another question with a question. When this old house was built, how did people get information from the outside world?"

"Radio?"

"That's right. I have radios. And I even have a small satellite antenna under the gable of the studio that you probably haven't noticed."

"Satellite I can understand. But what's on radio anymore? I'm sure you're not talking about satellite radio."

"There's more on the radio than you might think. You do need to know where and when to listen. And you need some equipment, because some of it is data, not talk."

"Data on the radio?"

"Sure. Radio has carried data for years and years. Radioteletype, for example. The protocols that carry data on the radio are pretty much the same protocols that carry your voice on your cell phone. People tend to forget that cell phones are radios first and telephones second. But cell phones are all about radio. The data that I'm talking about though, that comes by radio, is on frequencies that are much lower than the frequencies that cell phones use. Cell phones are close to microwave frequency. They're strictly line of sight and don't go very far. But radio signals down under, say, 30 megahertz, behave much differently. That's what people have long called shortwave radio. Those frequencies bounce all around the earth, and off the ionosphere, in complex ways, and can travel thousands of miles. Those frequencies are still extremely useful and are still used by all sorts of people. To transmit you have to have the right kind of license, at least if you want to operate within the law and international treaties. But they can't stop anyone from listening."

"Radioteletype. That just seems so obsolete. So … quaint. Surely no one has Teletype machines anymore."

"The machines are obsolete, but the protocols are not. The same data protocols that drove Teletype machines are still in use. It's not done with mechanical Teletypes any longer, though. It's done with computers. And the data protocols are much more sophisticated now, because computers can do the encoding and decoding rather than mechanical devices like Teletypes. The newer data protocols use less radio bandwidth and carry farther. Much less transmitting power can be used. Computers and radio make a powerful combination."

"That's amazing. I thought all that was obsolete. Except for cell phones, of course, which as you mentioned is a computer combined with a radio."

"But other forms of computer and radio are not obsolete. Remember the redundancy rule."

"How does that apply here?"

"The Internet could go down. Fiber-optic cables can be cut. The power could go off. Or, for that matter, a government could restrict the Internet or turn it off if they think it's too subversive. That happens in lots of places. But radio signals don't have to rely on anyone's infrastructure. If you've got a radio, and some power, and the right antenna, you can get a signal a very long way, very reliably. Transcontinental communication is actually cheap and easy, if you know how to go about it." Phaedrus smiled and broke off another piece of chocolate. "Of course, most people don't bother, which leaves more bandwidth for the rest of us."

"Do you have antennas? I didn't see any antennas."

"I do have antennas. They're mostly wire, and they're in the trees on the hill up above the house. The connections to the antennas, feed lines we call them, are under the ground."

"You've thought of everything."

"I couldn't possibly think of everything."

"So what kind of information is there on the radio these days?"

Phaedrus thought for a few seconds. "Some of it is completely open source. News, propaganda, things like that. Some of it is harder to find and harder to decode, but it's there. Governments – even big corporations – understand the redundancy rule."

"But what good is propaganda? It's just lies, right?"

"Even propaganda can be useful. If you understand what they want you to think, you can find clues to what they're covering up, or what they're trying to distract you from."

"You listen to secret signals?" Jake grinned.

"I have been known to try!"

"Do you succeed?"

"Even if I did, I wouldn't be able to tell you." Phaedrus laughed.

Jake, with a thoughtful look on his face, said, "I'm really impressed. You've got everything here. At least, you've got everything that someone really needs. Is there anything you don't have that you'd like to have?"

Phaedrus thought for a moment. "A cherry tree," he said. "My cherry tree died of old age. And maybe someone smart to talk with occasionally. Ready for a tour?"

"I'd love to have a tour. But what about the dishes? I don't want to leave you with the dishes."

"Don't worry about the dishes. Joan will do the dishes."

Phaedrus made the last comment in such a straight-faced manner, and this homestead was so strange, that even Jake's quick mind required a fraction of a second to compute that it was a little joke. They both laughed, and Jake couldn't help but think that Phaedrus had perceived, and correctly interpreted, Jake's tiny delay in getting the joke. It was because this place was so strange that Jake wasn't sure what to believe.

"First," said Phaedrus, "you need a headlamp." Phaedrus opened a drawer in the kitchen cabinet and pulled out two camper's headlamps.

"I actually brought mine," said Jake, "for walking back up the hill in the dark. But if it's OK with you I'll use yours and save my battery."

There were five rooms in the main house, two upstairs and three downstairs. One of the upstairs rooms had never been finished off. The exposed framing of the house could be seen in that room. The other upstairs room was a spare bedroom. The house was L-shaped, with a long, roofed porch that wrapped around one corner and sheltered the northern and western sides of the house. A tiny staircase in the joint of the L led upstairs. The staircase made two right-angle turns on the way up. Downstairs was a living room, a kitchen, and a bedroom.

"Some of this furniture looks like it came with the house," said Jake. "It looks authentic."

"Most of it did come with the house."

"I don't suppose that old telephone still works?" Jake

pointed to a crank telephone on the living room wall.

"It hasn't worked in, oh, forty years I'd say. But it's a nice relic and not a bad generation of communications technology, for its time. They must have had a hard time keeping those wires from being knocked down, up here in the mountains, or from being struck by lightning."

"That stove is the main source of heat for the house?"

"Yes. The wood circulator here in the living room, and the kitchen cook stove, supply all the heat. The wood circulator holds enough wood to stay pretty warm all night. But when it's really cold in the winter, sometimes it's best to feed it a couple of logs during the night. The only hardship, really, is that there's no bathroom upstairs. There's only the one bathroom there in the kitchen corner. It was added in the 1950s, I'd imagine."

"I don't see how you keep everything so clean," said Jake. "You must never take a break."

"Joan does all the housework," said Phaedrus. "No workie, no eatie. Teach them well when they're puppies and they rarely go wrong."

The upstairs bedroom was simply furnished and had that spare look that showed that it was for sleeping and not much intended for lounging about. It appeared not to have been used for a long time. Phaedrus did not invite Jake to enter the downstairs bedroom. He only waved his arm toward the open door. But Jake could see some of Phaedrus' clothing hanging on a chair. There was a small table by the window that looked like a writing desk. On one side of the bed was a bookshelf, and on the other was a small table with a lamp. An old rug covered the floor, and what was clearly a dog bed was near the foot of the bed.

Out of the corner of his eye, in an area of the bedroom not lit by the headlamp beam, Jake noticed a dim green light glowing on the wall.

"Another green light!" Jake exclaimed. "So mysterious! Do I dare ask what that one is for?"

"It's for exactly the same thing as the one in the studio. They're actually on the same circuit."

"The suspense is killing me. When do I get to find out what it's for? I hope it's not a letdown. What if the little lights on Jabba the Hutt's walls just meant that the air conditioner was on?"

"How much information can a single light convey, after all? It's either on or off. Two states."

"But there can be a lot of difference between two states," said Jake. "For example, Han Solo is still alive, or Han Solo is dead because something went wrong with his carbon-freeze unit."

As Jake and Phaedrus opened the kitchen door to go outside to the studio, Joan, who had been napping on the kitchen floor, got up to follow them. They walked along the stone-paved path from the kitchen door to the studio door. Inside the studio, everything was dark except for the green light.

"You've seen the organ," said Phaedrus. "Let's have a look in the computer room."

Jake was not surprised to see that the door to the computer room was made of metal and stood in a metal door frame. There was a security keypad above the doorknob. Phaedrus keyed a surprisingly long sequence of numbers. The doorknob clicked faintly, and the green light went out. Phaedrus opened the door, stood back, and invited Jake to enter with a gesture of his arm.

The room was dark except for glowing LEDs here and there of different colors – red, green, and blue. Phaedrus flipped a switch beside the door. Two dim lights lit up on two sides of the room.

"Light!" said Jake.

"Twelve volt lighting, yes," said Phaedrus. "You can turn off your headlamp, if you like, so that we don't blind each other."

There were three floor-to-ceiling racks holding what appeared to be computer equipment. Wires from the backs of the racks went into a wide conduit in the floor. There was a table, a chair, a small bookshelf, a filing cabinet, and an old dot matrix printer on a floor stand. The printer apparently was on. Its LED was lit.

"It looks like a little data center," said Jake.

"That's essentially what it is, with a few extra toys thrown in."

Jake saw that two of the racks were completely dark. But one of them had lights glowing from top to bottom.

Jake pointed to the lighted rack. "May I?"

"Of course."

Jake stepped closer to the rack and skimmed the equipment from top to bottom.

"Computers for sure," said Jake. "But some of these look like radios. I don't think I've ever seen rack-mount radios before."

"Some of the best radios made are rack-mount radios," said Phaedrus.

"May I?" said Jake again, this time pointing to the printer.

"Of course."

Jake picked up the stream of paper about six feet long lying behind the printer and scanned it quickly.

"It looks like … conversations. People talking about their radios, and the weather."

"That's what it is. And I can see that you're thinking, what's the big deal."

"Something like that, I guess," said Jake. "This is a pretty expensive setup for chatting about the weather."

"Let's have a look," said Phaedrus, reaching for the paper. He scrolled through it rapidly, then pointed to several lines. "Have a look at this."

K8JOAN DE IE3OPQ

K8JOAN DE IE30PQ DO YOU COPY OLD MAN 02:12:34Z KK

K8JOAN DE IE30PQ DO YOU COPY OLD MAN 02:12:57Z KKk

K8JOAN DE IE30PQ DO YOU CePY OLD MAN = NOISY TO-NIGHT

02:13:09Z KK

"Radio teletype?" said Jake. "Someone is calling someone? I get it. Someone is calling you."

"That's right. Someone is calling me. But it's not radio-teletype. It's one of the newer data protocols handled by a computer."

"Just to talk about how noisy something is? I'd expect a secret code or something. Something subversive."

"Actually, to encrypt a transmission on the amateur radio bands is illegal. But if you think about it, there might be other ways of working messages into what appears to be chitchat. Can you see a way that someone might work code into something like this?"

"Let's see," said Jake. "The 'de' just means 'from,' and that's part of the calling protocol. So probably no message there."

"Right. And…"

"I suppose you could, by pre-agreement, determine that 'do you copy' stands for something. And that 'old man' stands for something else. Surely you don't let people call you that." Jake looked up for a second and grinned, then went on. "The numbers look like the time of the transmission. The 'Z' probably means 'Zulu,' or Greenwich mean time. I suppose the K's could stand for something, or they may just mean 'end of transmission.' So I could see how 'do you copy, old man' could stand for something that both sides of the communication agreed on in advance."

"Is that all?"

"I think so."

"Look at the numbers."

"Aren't they just times?"

"They are. But who's going to check to see if the times given were correct to the second? No one would bother, would they? Clocks are often wrong, and no one pays much attention to the time stamp anyway. So you could, if you were clever, agree that the numbers in the seconds field stand for something, with sixty possible meanings. And the time is printed out three times."

"But what if there's an error? It's noisy tonight, remember? And that looks like a transmission error here, where it says 'CePY' instead of 'COPY.'"

"Can you see how one might work in an error-checking protocol?"

"Hmmm. Not really."

"What if the seconds, say, add up to a hundred, or multiples of a hundred, if the right numbers were received. Why don't you add them up."

"Let's see. Thirty-four, plus 57, plus 9. That's … a hundred. How sneaky! Is this really a coded message?"

"It could be."

"And I don't even need to ask whether you're **K8JOAN**."

"At your service. That's my call sign."

"And **IE3OPQ**?"

"Someone you've never met." Phaedrus winked.

"Is it really a coded message?"

"It is, actually. And all it means is that he'll call again at a certain time tomorrow on a certain frequency. Nothing nefarious in that, is there?"

"Depends," said Jake, laughing, "On how many other codes you have."

Phaedrus laughed as well. "You're a smart young man, Jake."

"So then," said Jake, some of these are radios and some are computers."

"Yes."

"And the other two racks? They don't seem to be switched on."

"That, actually, is the organ, or a big part of the organ. And as I mentioned yesterday, I haven't been able to power it up since I went off the grid. The first rack holds amplifiers, and the second rack holds computers. It's the computers that hold the pipe sounds, digitally sampled of course. And some very clever programming – for which I get none of the credit – sends the right sounds to the amplifiers when a key is pressed on the organ. The computer itself can play the organ as well, kind of like a computerized self-player machine. The computer has complete control of the organ. It can change the stops, too."

"That thing must draw a huge amount of power."

"Too much for my solar-power system, that's for sure. Three thousand watts or so, I'd say, when it's running full organ in rain-making mode."

"What's that well-machined little gadget on the table?"

"That's a key for sending Morse code."

"So radio teletype is not obsolete enough for you? You use Morse code too?"

"I'm not the first person to say this, but if we didn't have a legacy system for transmitting low-bandwidth, low-speed, highly accurate, human copyable digital data, we'd be compelled to invent such a system. Morse code will get a signal through when almost nothing else will. The human ear is absolutely brilliant at separating signal from noise. That's something machines have a lot of trouble with. Morse code can be done totally without machines such as computers, because we can copy it in our heads. You don't even have to have a radio. I could tap my foot, or flash my headlamp, and send you a signal."

"Amazing. Now, about that little green light."

"As I'm sure you've guessed, the green light just lets me know that everything that's important enough to be redundant is working. Or, more precisely, that both redundant systems are working. I put together a little black box that monitors things. If the batteries are charged and the voltage is above a certain level in both solar power systems, and if certain computers have emitted heartbeat signals within a certain number of seconds, and if certain radios are outputting audio at a certain level, and if the door is locked, then the green light is on. Saves me a lot of repetitive checking."

"What's that on the walls?" asked Jake. "It's unusual, and something tells me it's not for decoration."

"That's copper screen," said Phaedrus.

"Copper screen? What … Oh. I get it. It's to keep interference out. Is it a Faraday cage?"

"It is indeed a Faraday cage."

"Are these signals really that sensitive?"

"No. But what else can Faraday cages do?"

"Keep electrical noise from getting into things? I don't know."

"Well, Jake, at the risk of having you think that I'm even crazier than you already think I am, Faraday cages can stop the radio frequency pulses that sometimes come from the sun, or from nuclear explosions."

"But the Cold War is over!"

"Sure, the Cold War is obsolete. But conflict continues."

"Now you're scaring me! Do you know something I don't know? With communications stuff like this, maybe you do! Or could. I guess it never hurts to be prepared."

"That's the Boy Scout motto, isn't it. We all need to be prepared."

Jake looked at Phaedrus expectantly, hoping that he

would continue, but after a moment of thought followed by a little smile, Phaedrus gestured toward the door.

As they put their headlamps on, turned off the lights, and left the computer room, Jake was pretty sure he saw the outline of a large trap door in the floor. But somehow he figured that he'd already asked enough nosy questions and that he'd better not ask any more. At least not until he'd had a chance to think about everything he'd seen.

Jake found himself drawn to the organ console. He rubbed his hands along with smooth wood top and pressed a few keys. They made a smooth sound, like the sound of wood rubbing gently against felt, but otherwise they were quiet. "May I?" he indicated the drawknobs.

"Sure."

The drawknobs, too, made a smooth, faint sound of wood on felt.

"Why Joan?" asked Jake. "Why did you name your dog Joan? And it's in your call sign."

"Because I've always had a thing about the story of Joan of Arc."

"Why is that?"

"Do you know the story of Joan of Arc?"

"Not really. Everybody's heard of Joan of Arc, but I can't say I remember the story. I haven't even seen the movie."

Joan the dog raised her head and looked at Jake, having heard her name. "She always listens out of one ear, doesn't she?" said Jake.

"She does. Even during the night when she should be asleep. Sometime I'll tell you the story of Joan of Arc."

Jake tried to read the sudden, distant look in Phaedrus' eyes but couldn't. If the old man was crazy, at least he was a nice kind of crazy. Jake turned back to the organ console.

"Contra faggot 32," he read from the letters on the

drawknob. "That sounds like one scary stop. I wouldn't want to run into that one on a dark night."

"That is a very scary stop, actually," said Phaedrus. "I wish you could hear it, though not in the dark of night. It rattles the windows and scares the birds out of the trees. But let's not speak of such fell things until the morning light."

"I see more puns here than I can count. Is this keyboard really called 'Great,' and that one 'Swell'?"

"Yes. And be careful with the eight-foot flute. Don't drop it on your toe." They remained quiet for a while, Jake sitting at the organ console and reading labels on the drawknobs, Phaedrus standing quietly to the side, head down, as though lost in thought.

"Speaking of the morning light, I guess I'd better get back up to my campsite. But thank you for dinner, and the tour. And tomorrow, you must be my guest for supper."

"My pleasure. And I look forward to supper at your campsite. No progress freeing your Jeep today?"

"No sign of them."

"They know about the trees down. I talked with the sheriff on the radio. I imagine they'll have you out by tomorrow afternoon."

CHAPTER 3

The next evening, when Phaedrus and Joan arrived at Jake's campsite for supper, the sun was below the treeline to the west, and the sky was glowing with a golden light. Jake's campsite was up against some woods at the edge of an abandoned pasture. The old fence sagged, and many of the old posts were down, or entangled in honeysuckle. The pasture had reverted to meadow and had grown into a lush showcase for Appalachian wildflowers. The bees were still working hard, making use of every last ray of sunlight. But the birds, which had rioted, hungry, at dawn, had grown quiet now, their little bird bellies full. Huge clouds, heavy but with no immediate threat of rain, glided across the sky toward the northeast. It was a busy, complex sky, with ever-changing shapes, a sky-watcher's Rorschach test. Jake's campfire was now a deep bed of glowing coals, and there was the smell of stew liberally seasoned with onions and garlic. Joan, already perceiving Jake as an old friend, sidled modestly up to Jake to have her head scratched, then lay down not too far from the fire. Jake gave the stew a quick stir and motioned for Phaedrus to sit on some makeshift seats that Jake had fashioned out of some logs.

"I brought some cole slaw," said Phaedrus, "freshly made from cabbage from my garden."

"Wow. Thanks," said Jake. "That will go nicely with the stew."

"What a perfect sky," said Phaedrus. "We get skies like this only in the spring and fall. I like to call it a gothic sky. I've also heard it called a moody sky. There's drama in it. It becomes part of the landscape. It reminds me of Ireland."

"You know Ireland, then," said Jake.

"I do," said Phaedrus. "Of all the places in the world I've ever been, it's Ireland that feels most like home."

"It's funny you say that," said Jake. "I feel the same way. I don't really know why. I don't mean the cities, really, or the pubs, or anything like that. It's the landscape, and the sea. Have you ever stood on top of a high hill and seen the cloud shadows moving across the fields? The light is always changing, and it's never harsh or washed out. The same thing happens near the sea. I could stand on a mountaintop in County Kerry and watch the sea forever when the sky is like that."

"County Kerry," said Phaedrus. "It's one of the most beautiful places in the world. You're so lucky, to be so young and to already have been there."

"And the skelligs," said Jake. "One day I watched for hours as a little boat sailed out toward Skellig Michael. The sea was rough that day, and the boat kept disappearing below the waves. I was a bit afraid that the boat wasn't going to make it. It was hard to be sure in the distance, but I think I saw the boat disappear into the cove, where the dock is on Skellig Michael."

"Have you ever been out to the skelligs?" asked Phaedrus.

"No. But someday I'd like to do that."

"I went there once," said Phaedrus. "I wanted to see the monastery. I wanted to see how the monks lived. They lived out there, you know, for something like 600 years, up until the 12th century. I sometimes wonder if we human beings are still capable of that kind of hard, cold, hungry existence. I wonder if we'd lost that ability even by the 12th century. That period fascinates me. It's what we call the Dark Ages, of course, but it's humbling to think about how hard life was after the fall of Rome, and what some people did to keep a little light in the world."

"Are you talking about the monasteries?"

"Yes. And though life was mostly cruel and hard and short for everyone in the Dark Ages, still a monastery was the place to be. The monks at Skellig Michael were there because they thought that the remoteness and deprivation brought them closer to god, but some of the monasteries were pretty posh. Not as posh as the fortresses of the seigneurs, but they were warmer, healthier, and had better food. Plus the monasteries were networked and in communication with each other. Most abbots had pretty good information about what was going on in the wider world. I think that period is well worth studying. It can teach us something about what kind of infrastructure is truly essential in a simpler world. Those old monks even used carrier pigeons to send each other messages."

"Don't tell me you have carrier pigeons!"

"No. Pigeons are only good for relatively short distances. But if I had a need for redundant communication systems at carrier pigeon range, I'd definitely get some."

"I'd tell you that you're being gloomy again, but . . ." Jake hesitated.

"But you've been a little gloomy yourself lately."

"Does it show?"

"A little."

Neither spoke while Jake served stew in his green plastic campware bowls. They ate in silence for a while except for Phaedrus' compliments on the stew. Joan had already fallen asleep.

"Tell me about your family," said Phaedrus. "You said your dad taught the classics. Did you have a classical childhood?"

62

"You know, it was a kind of classical childhood. I grew up in Charlottesville, not far from the campus. Both my parents taught there. My mother was in the English department. They both retired early. They live in Costa Rica now."

"Do you see them often?"

"They come to the states once a year, usually around Christmas. And I've been to Costa Rica a couple of times."

"Were your parents disappointed that you went into architecture rather than the humanities?"

"A little. But they could see that it was getting harder to make a living with something like the English language, not to mention Greek. So they encouraged me to go into architecture. It was partly, I guess, because of my crazy drawings, and partly because they saw that I liked to work with real things as much as I liked to work with symbols. Not that I ever saw anything wrong with my parents' words and symbols and abstractions. I think most young people feel misunderstood by their parents, but I never really did. If anything, I was annoyed sometimes at how well they understood me. I mean, a guy has the right to keep certain secrets to himself, doesn't he? But sometimes, if we were having a talk – you know what I mean – they'd ask me a question, and if I was slow to answer, they'd answer the question for me. I hate to admit it, but they were usually right. They always knew when I was having girl trouble. That was a little creepy, except that I can't say that they ever pried. My mother would tease me, say things to my dad like, 'The house is going to be awfully quiet for a couple of weeks because Jake is having girl trouble.' They weren't being cruel, really. They knew that there was never anything really serious with any of my girlfriends, and there'd always be another girlfriend soon enough. In a way there is something kind of nice about being between girlfriends. I mean, it leaves me time for doing things that I otherwise wouldn't have found time to do. Girlfriends take up a lot of time. They expect constant maintenance."

"And so you're between girlfriends at the moment?" asked Phaedrus.

Jake laughed. "How can you tell? Either you're just like my parents, or somebody sticks a sign on my back when I'm between girlfriends."

"Your crazy drawings?"

"Yeah. I guess I've read too much mythology, and too many fantasy novels. I don't know how that equipped me to be an architect, because nothing I ever drew was real. But I drew a lot of buildings – ruined castles, ruined towers, little ruined cottages, ruined pagan temples. Always ruins, and hardly ever anything new."

"Do you still draw?"

"Oh yes. I have a sketch book with me. I can show you a few after supper."

They were silent for a while, eating stew and watching the sky. Jake knew that Phaedrus was waiting for him to speak, as though Phaedrus knew that Jake needed somebody to listen.

"Sometimes I wish I was a monk for a while," said Jake at last. "Girls just expect too much. They want to talk to you on the phone at least six times a day. It makes them crazy to go more than a day without seeing you. They don't want you to have any private time. They make all these plans, and you're expected to go along with it. You have to regularly show up to be shown off to your girlfriend's girlfriends, and if you don't behave just so, like the perfect boyfriend, then you get scolded later. You're expected to do all these things that take money, and you'd better not dare ever make any kind of plans without checking first with the girlfriend. God help you if you get caught looking at another girl. You'd better always be freshly showered, and you'd better not ever leave a towel on the floor at her apartment. Break any of their rules, and you're in the doghouse. And if you're in the doghouse, you get all the liabilities of having a girl-friend and none of the benefits, if you know what I mean. That's when a guy starts thinking about the advantages of being a monk."

"What was your last girlfriend's name? What happened?"

"Her name was Amy. I was in the doghouse because I'd broken a date and had done a couple of other things that meant I wasn't being attentive enough. And instead of being a good boyfriend and obediently doing my time in the doghouse, properly following the script for reconciliation by doing all the right little penances and making all the right little romantic gestures, I rebelled. I told her I'd see her in a couple of weeks when she was in a better mood, and she said don't bother coming back."

"Did you have a lot of feelings for her?"

"I liked her as a girlfriend, I guess. I wouldn't say that I was in love, exactly. I mean, I never saw myself getting married to her. But I think that's the key, after a certain age at least. As soon as they see that a boyfriend rela-tionship is not the sort of thing that leads to engagement and marriage, they dump you. Why can't a girl just be happy to have a boyfriend, the way a boy is happy to have a girlfriend? I mean, no one gets married at my age anymore. It's not like they want to get married right now. But they do want what they call a 'serious' boyfriend, and they want a nice, long engagement. It gives them security or something, and status. They want to know that – well, that your theirs. I guess I'm not ready to be under contract. Sometimes I wonder if I'll ever be ready to be under contract. Sometimes I wonder why any guy puts up with all that, except for, you know, the nooky."

"I'm sorry about all that," said Phaedrus. "Maybe it will go better next time. Where did you learn an old-fashioned word like 'nooky'?"

"From my mother, I guess. She had a vast vocabulary

of archaic euphemisms."

They were silent for a while. The wind was picking up, and the sky was starting to clear.

"Are you gay?" asked Jake.

"Did you inherit your parents' intuition, or is it my tidy housekeeping that gives me away?"

"Just a feeling. Plus you're not married or anything. And since I over-disclosed, I thought maybe you could too."

"At my age, it's sort of a technicality anyway," Phaedrus said, "or a matter of history. At my age, things like that don't matter as much. In a lot of ways it's a nice thing to be living on lower doses of testosterone. But you know what I really like about your generation? That you can ask questions like that. When I was your age, people saw it as a dark secret. No one ever would have asked the way you just did. That's progress."

"You changed the subject," said Jake.

"I did?"

"I asked you to over-disclose, and you changed the subject to testosterone and my generation," said Jake.

"I guess I did change the subject. Well, I'm afraid there's a bit of a double standard in this world when it comes to gay people over-disclosing. We hold back a good bit more. Our pasts rarely have much in common with fairy tales. Plus I'm a good bit older than you are, and if I started over-disclosing now we'd be here all night. So for now, would you let me off the hook with a promise? Sometime, if I'm fortunate enough to see you again, you tell me another story about yourself, and then I'll tell you a story about me. But for now, let's just say that I never lived in a fairy tale, and so a monastery – even a monastery for one – started looking like a better and better option."

Jake looked at Phaedrus for moment, then stole a glance at the sky to see if Ursa Major had rotated into sight. There was still no sign yet of Ursa Major.

"How rough was it?" Jake asked.

"Rough enough," said Phaedrus. "Partly, maybe, that's a generational thing, but mostly no doubt it was me. When I was your age, the world was still pretty much like it was in Alan Turing's lifetime. Do you know about Alan Turing?"

"Only a little of the computer stuff," said Jake.

"He and his code-breakers had practically saved the world during World War II, but in the early 1950s he was prosecuted for his sexuality. It was the same charge, actually, that was used against Oscar Wilde – gross indecency. Turing was convicted. Soon after that, he killed himself with cyanide. It seems he ate a poisoned apple, because he had a fascination with the Snow White fairy tale. Anyway, though as I said the world had not changed much, I got out of that era alive. Though, when I think back about it, all of us were damaged, in one way or another. You know what kept me going?"

"What?"

"A dream of rebellion, of undoing about two thousand years of history. I became obsessed with understanding how the world came to be the way it is, why the world had fallen so far since the time of the Greeks."

"Did you find the answer?"

"I think it's clear enough, yes."

"How do you undo it?"

"That's a hard one, isn't it? Because real revolution would require re-inventing and rebuilding our culture all the way down to the bedrock. It would take a long time. And it could only work, really, after some sort of grand calamity. Our world is the way it is now because it was rebuilt out of a calamity – the ruins of Rome. Still, it took hundreds of years. And here we are today."

"I will hold you to your promise to over-disclose someday," said Jake. "And I'll do my best to repay you with a story of my own, but I doubt that it will be as interesting as yours will be. Whatever it was, I hope that things get better. You've still got a spring in your step. You have a lot of life yet to live."

"Thank you."

"Testosterone," said Jake. "We were saying about testosterone, the anti-monk drug. Lots of monks must have been young, though. I wonder how they handled all that testosterone."

"Christianity had all sorts of technologies of repression, but even so I think that their success rates were not nearly as high as they wanted. There are some things that are stronger than religion."

"As hard as it must be," said Jake, "gay guys must have it easier in certain ways. Guys all want the same thing. But there's a world of difference in what guys want and what girls want."

"What girls want," said Phaedrus, "is of course instinctive. And without those instincts it would be very difficult to hold families, or social groups, together. But for males, bonding with females comes with a cost. Males want to travel, to explore, to experiment. They want to go on quests. Girls are not much into going along on quests, even if guys wanted them to. Quests are not weekend outings. Quests are hard. But as for women, I always found that the women I've known improved with age. Men rarely improve with age, but women often do. I think it happens when their wombs shut down, and they have more time for themselves as individuals, without that biological imperative of begetting and rearing children. Their libido often increases, too. When women go on quests, I think it's usually when they're older. Whereas men go questing when they're young. All too often, men are spent by the time they're older and aren't seeking much more than contentedness. Not that there's anything wrong with contentedness. But if I have one piece of advice for you young straight guys, it's this: think about appreciating older women. They'll be there for you when you're older, ready to love you in a way you've probably never been loved before. And give younger women a break."

"I've never heard anybody say anything like that," said Jake. "I doubt that thoughts like that would ever occur to us straight guys. It's funny how 'quest' is not a word you hear very much anymore, unless you're talking about literature. I like that word."

"It's a shame that the word has fallen into disuse, because the instinct is very much alive. But it's frustrated. Once upon a time, when the world was so much bigger, and largely unexplored, that male questing instinct was one of the keys to human survival. It was young men who led the search for new territory, for new and different kinds of lifestyles in new and different terrain. It helped prevent inbreeding, and it kept the gene pool fresh. Questing was a dangerous business, though, and many young men lost their lives at it. But for the species as a whole, those quests yielded great benefits.

"The sad thing is," Phaedrus continued, "the modern world really frustrates the questing instinct. Young men can still travel, to be sure, but that's not the same as exploring unknown places. We humans have been on this planet long enough to have explored the earth, but not long enough to be able to explore the stars. The frontiers are all gone – no more New Worlds, no more Africas, no more Antarcticas. Young men are in a serious predicament. Their questing instincts are frustrated, while the female instinct to tie men down and burden men with families hasn't changed. Men still carry huge responsibilities, but they have less freedom, and no frontiers. They've never known any other kind of world, so they don't really know what's gone wrong and why it seems that every way they turn their dreams are frustrated. No wonder men die younger than women, or commit suicide at much higher rates. No wonder they have midlife crises. They have ancient instincts in a crowded world that's much too far from nature. Oh, they can channel their male instincts into the competitiveness of sports, or the cut-throat corporate world, but those things are a poor substitute for the real thing – you know, a horse or even a boat underneath you, the wind in your face, the stars over your head, the thrill of hope, and danger, and promise. That's what men were made for."

"I wish young women could see that," said Jake. "But even if they never do, what you say makes me proud to be a guy. And I guess I never really realized that gay guys are men too, wired just the same as we straight guys are. Only guys, I think, understand about the stars, or, like you said, a horse underneath you, the wind in your face. And danger. I guess I don't know much about danger. The world seems so safe these days."

"Quests are not obsolete," said Phaedrus. "And there is still danger in the world."

"It's funny. We were talking about monasteries, and now we're talking about quests. Opposites."

"Opposites have this odd way of being found together, though. The questing instinct and the monastic instinct are often found together. It's as though the nature of opposites creates a tension, a kind of energy potential, like the opposite poles of a motor, positive and negative. Opposites make the world go around, pretty much literally, if you've studied your physics."

"Then why does nothing ever happen? I think I've got those two opposites in me – the questing instinct and the monastic instinct. But nothing ever happens. Where's the energy? All I have is routines. And my blueprints. What do you do to make something happen?"

"Maybe you can't do anything. Maybe, instead of finding a story to be in, the story finds you."

"So you wait? Bide your time? Tread water? Cool your heels?"

"What did Luke Skywalker do?"

"He did what he always did – fixed broken evaporators like his stepfather told him to do. Then all hell broke loose. I guess that meant the story found him."

Phaedrus seemed about to speak but didn't. They both sat looking at the sky, watching the stars. Deep in the woods, a barred owl called. The fire was changing to embers. After a while, Phaedrus broke the silence.

"So you came to see the stars," he said.

"I did. I guess I did. Is that some kind of metaphor, do you think?"

"What do you think?"

Jake thought for a while. "Maybe I should have studied something other than architecture. But I learned a few things, I guess, from my English-teacher mother about metaphors. Yes. I think it's a metaphor. Or a symbol of some sort. I think it must have something to do with, you know, the quest. I get so bored sometimes. Architecture is only so interesting, if you know what I mean. I've been in Charlottesville all my life, so what's new to see there? I've traveled some, but that only helps for a while. It wears off, and you have to go traveling again, if you can. Sometimes I wonder if I'll ever be able to pay off my student loans, though I got the faculty discount and my loans aren't nearly as bad as some people I know. And then, of course, there are girls. It's like they keep you on a leash, and when the leash breaks, you run. Then you've got to decide whether to keep running, or go back."

"Have you decided?"

"I always go back. What else would I do? Where would I go? I often get this feeling that I'm in the wrong place, that there's somewhere else I ought to be and something else I ought to be doing, but I don't know where that is or what that is. It's a sort of empty feeling, like when your parents take you somewhere boring, and you don't want to go. You're just there because that's where your parents are, or that's where you were born, or that's just where you ended up somehow, without knowing how or why. When I look at the stars, that feeling doesn't go away exactly, but somehow that feeling lets go a little, and you can think a little better, and dream for a while, and get lost in the imagination."

They were silent as Phaedrus waited to see if Jake would continue. Instead Jake was looking at the stars.

"May I see your drawings?" said Phaedrus.

"Sure," said Jake. Jake threw some brush on the fire to get a bright flame going, then retrieved his sketch book from the tent. They turned their backs to the fire to look at the sketch book in the firelight.

There was a Greek-like ruin of what appeared to be an ancient observatory, perched on a rocky promontory above a rocky sea. There was a tiny cottage in a tiny clearing in a dense forest, and above it a vast sky full of stars. There was a ship with tall sails on a night sea, the ship's mast reaching into the stars. And there was a tiny pasture on a hilltop. On the edge of the pasture was a low wall made of stone, and around the wall was a scaffold, as though this wall, rather than falling into ruins, was just now being built.

"I think," said Phaedrus, "that I recognize this place. It's where we are right now."

"Yes."

"Look at all those stars," said Phaedrus. "They appear to be accurately drawn."

"As accurate as I can make them," said Jake. "And in about two more hours, Ursa Major will be exactly in that position."

"Ursa Major is important to you?"

"It's my favorite constellation. I don't know why. I also use Ursa Major for telling time during the night," said Jake.

"The Greeks, as you know, saw a bear in Ursa Major,"

said Phaedrus. "The Celts saw a wagon. After the Dark Ages, it was sometimes called Arthur's wain. I think I like the Arthur story better, but then I've always had a thing for the Celts."

"I don't know much about the Celts," said Jake.

"No one does," said Phaedrus. "The Romans pretty much wiped them out. But again, let's try not to be too gloomy. I love your drawings. Your drawing of my pasture is wonderful."

"You may have it, then," said Jake.

"What a wonderful gift," said Phaedrus. "Thank you."

"It's my form of the quest," said Jake. "I guess it's all I have. I don't know why everything I draw is ancient and in ruins. I don't know what came over me today. I can't remember ever drawing anything before, like that wall, that was in the process of being built."

As they turned to face the fire again, Jake saw that what he had just said, about something being built, had caused a look of knowing delight to pass over Phaedrus' face.

"I accidentally dropped some kind of symbol, didn't I? said Jake. "My English-teacher mother would have a field day with that."

"Whatever it symbolizes," said Phaedrus, "it seems your gloom is lifting. Your quest may take a new course. To build is good. I bet your mother would agree."

The fire was much warmer now from the burning brush. Joan had moved back a little.

"Do you remember," said Phaedrus, "the scene in Star Wars in which the young Luke Skywalker is giving C3P0 an oil bath, and C3P0 asks Luke what planet they're on? Luke says, 'If there's a bright center of the universe, you're on the planet it's farthest from.' That's the very feeling that draws young men out onto the quest. It's a very painful thing, really, to feel that one is far, far away from the bright center of the universe. Lucky is the man who feels he's in the place where he ought to be. Older men, I think, feel that sometimes, but young men rarely do. It sucks. It's miserable. I'm sorry."

"At least you understand," said Jake. "And you say it better than I would have been able to say it myself. But you make me realize that older men – or at least some of them – have been in the same boat. And now I even wonder if my dad understood after all why I love the stars, or why he wanted me to have such a Greek education, even if I ended up as a pathetic architect. He said something once that made me think that maybe he wasn't such a relic after all. He said that, even though old books were his life, that I should not put too much faith in them. He said that although old books can help keep our feet on the ground, anything new must necessarily come from somewhere else. We were out under the stars at the time, actually. Maybe dad was more of a romantic than I thought he was."

"Your dad sounds like a truly smart man," said Phaedrus. "Though I wouldn't say that's a romantic concept. I'd say it's more Greek. The classical Greeks were always striving upward. The Greeks were open to the new. Whereas romance, I think, is much more sentimental and backward looking. Romance always looks to the past for guidance and meaning. Romance loves old books. But the Greeks, though they cherished their old books by the great poets, knew how to look forward and upward. They were thrilled by the possibility of ongoing philosophical progress. They weren't enslaved to old books. I cringe, to tell you the truth, when I hear the word 'romantic,' because the root of that word is 'Rome,' and for good reason. As Greece declined and Rome rose, the best was lost, and the worst flourished. They were very different worlds, Greece and Rome. Greece I would have loved. But Rome still scares me."

Phaedrus threw yet another log on the fire, as though thoughts of Rome were giving him a chill. Then he continued.

"Rome's religion ties in with this too, you see. If a religion is based on an old book, and if that religion demands obedience to that old book, and if that religion is driven not by a living philosophy but by unquestioning obedience, then the authorities that enforce that obedience need all the help they can get keeping people in line. A living philosophy can see progress. Whereas a religion based on an old book sees only heresy. And so our romantic mythology keeps people looking backward. It causes people to strive in the backward direction that religious authority wants them to strive. If you go back and look at the roots of our romantic myth, you find that it's fatally entangled with religious thinking. It peaked in the 11th and 12th centuries, of course. But you can trace it all the way back to Rome and the ways in which Roman literature started to change after Christianity became Rome's official religion. Rome left a hard legacy."

"But isn't the idea of the quest romantic?" asked Jake.

"That's one of the smartest questions anybody ever asked me," said Phaedrus. "My answer to that would be that questing is a human instinct, as natural a part of us as the instinct toward children. Think of the epic of Gilgamesh. That was a quest, and it's one of our oldest stories, thousands of years before even the ancient Greeks. The Greek poets, of course, wrote about quests. Scholars have been debating for two thousand years what the golden fleece symbolized. Who knows? But the romantic quest, though it has to do with chivalry and relations between the sexes, is ultimately about a holy chalice. What the chalice symbolizes is clear. It refers to a Christian sacrament. So, in my cynical mind, the romantic quest, the Roman quest, the Christian quest, seeks to harness our ancient questing instinct to an agenda. It romanticizes the doctrine of the church. To me, that's creepy. There are a lot of creepy ideas and disguised agendas hidden within that word 'romance.'"

"Like what?" asked Jake.

"For one, a new and untested way of defining human love that was compatible with Christian theology but that crushed a more ancient, much better tested culture of love. But now romance is entrenched. We are all romantics now. I can't say that romance ever worked very well for me."

Jake laughed. "For me either."

"I don't think it works very well for anyone, really. We may find romance for a little while, but it never lasts. We know romance mostly from the outlines of its emptiness, by what's not there in our lives, rather than what is. Though, to be truthful, maybe all quests are about a hole in our hearts."

A shooting star streaked across the northern sky. "Shooting stars probably happen all the time," said Jake, "but we're just not looking. Since you're older, I can't help asking. If the bright center of the universe is out there somewhere, then where are we?"

"That I don't know," said Phaedrus. "But I do know this. The center of the universe moves around. What good would it do to travel a million light years to get to the center of the universe, only to find that it's moved? That's one of the things that stories, or movies, show us – that the center of the universe moves. But Luke Skywalker didn't know that, did he? He was trapped in the story."

The firelight was bright on Phaedrus' face. Jake had to suppress a smile, because Phaedrus looked so much like a wizard when he was talking, especially in the firelight, with stars behind him. Phaedrus continued.

"But at the very moment Luke said what he said about the bright center of the universe, we, the readers, or we the moviegoers, know something that that poor character trapped in the story does not know: that at the moment he said what he said, he was at the center of the universe, that the quest was about to begin. Stories do that. A story can be set anywhere – a shack in Mississippi, a rundown apartment in the Bronx, an ugly house in the suburbs – but if you can tell a story in those settings, a beautiful story, a true story, then that's where the center of the universe is, while that story is being told. Then the bright center of the universe moves again. It's on to the next story."

"So then, you're saying that it's not about where you are, it's about what's happening where you are, the story you're in? If any."

"Yes," said Phaedrus.

"But what if nothing ever happens in my story?"

"What if something did?"

"I think I'd like it if something happened. Something nice, you know. Something not too scary."

"You can't have a story without conflict. And some good stories are scary stories. What if some of what happened wasn't very nice?"

"I guess that's the price you pay," said Jake. "Luke Skywalker certainly paid that price. After all it was Star Wars, not Star Peace, or Star Contentedness. You know, I admit that sometimes when I look through my telescope I think about Star Wars, like I'm looking for something out there."

"Maybe you're looking for the center of the universe."

CHAPTER 4

Back in his little office in Charlottesville, Jake just couldn't get his mind on his work. Not that he had much work at present – just another kitchen renovation from just another suburban client with good credit and bad taste. Jake had almost been insulted that there were only two messages on his answering machine when he got back – one from his dad asking if he'd had a nice trip, and another from his suburban client with yet more trivial modifications to push the cost of a kitchen project a little more over budget. If you're borrowing money to redo your kitchen, after all, why not borrow as much as you can get?

Jake poured himself another cup of coffee from the little coffee maker and went to sit by the window. Back when he was looking for small offices to rent, that was what had sold him on this office – the wide second-floor window with a view of the green hills to the south. No wonder Jefferson liked it here, Jake often thought. Though the poor man would never have lived to be so old if he had foreseen the suburbs, or suburban kitchens.

Come to think of it, that's what Phaedrus' place reminded me of – Monticello. The look was very different, and one is modest while the other is grand, yet they both somehow reflect a similar way of thinking. Both, somehow, are complete, self-sufficient. Both reflect the intelligence and taste of the person who lives, or lived, there. Both, if seen in the right light and in the right state of mind, seem as though the center of the universe could stop there for a while. Both are places where a story could be told.

Let's see. What kind of story would want to be told at Monticello? How about a story about a great mind, independent and rebellious, with a craving for order and beauty? On hot summer days, there would be a passion for life, stuff blooming everywhere, blackberry pies in the kitchen, wine, secret visits in the night from Sally Hemings, even when the master of the house was an old man. Oh dear. Sally Hemings was a slave, wasn't she? I'm forgetting about the slaves that made a lifestyle like that possible. How nice to avoid the dirty work and just enjoy it all, to live the life of the elite. In the winter there would be fires in all the fireplaces, and snow in the garden, but still there would be passion – a passion for order, for good government, for good educations, for good agriculture and good stewardship of the land. Poor man, how awful it would be for him if he could see us now, the land raped by bad agriculture and the soil washing into the rivers, the valleys paved for suburbs, the government sold to the corporations, the descendants of his slaves still not getting a fair shake.

And what kind of story would want to be told at Phaedrus' place? How about a story about being fed up with some of what passes for progress since Jefferson's time, a search for alternatives, an experiment to see if it's possible to go back. Can you get away with picking and choosing your technologies? Can you keep radio, but ditch the power grid? Can you keep good food, but ditch the supermarket? Can you do without the Internet, or even a telephone, and still know what's going on in the world? Can you ditch the crowds, the malls, the traffic jams, the credit cards, the fast food, the mountains of garbage, and keep the stars?

Is Phaedrus a little bit crazy? He doesn't seem to be,

thought Jake, and yet what's all this stuff about bad things might happen? He never did explain. Should I have tried harder to get him to explain? Or maybe he felt like he didn't know me well enough, or trust me enough, to tell me what he thinks might happen. Could it be that if I went back sometime he'd say more?

And it's not Jefferson, really, that the old man reminds me of. He's more like Obi-Wan Kenobi. He even was talking about Luke Skywalker. He's certainly had time to think about a lot of things. Is it because he's old that he's had so much time to think, or because he's all alone there in his own little monastery and has plenty of time for thinking? I envy him that. I wish I had time to think. And it's funny how he thinks about a lot of the same things that I think about. It's like talking with him saves me a lot of time and trouble. He's years ahead of me. If I were his age, and if I had my own monastery, I might have the same insights. But he saves me the trouble.

But why do I feel so … so uneasy somehow. Somehow he seems too smart to be wrong, and too right about so many things to be caught up in some kind of conspiracy theory. I wish I'd pressed him harder to tell me more about the bad things that might happen.

Just then the phone rang – a fairly unusual event in Jake's little office. For some reason, Jake waited until the fifth ring to answer.

"Jake Janaway," he said.

"Mr. Janaway, my name is Mike Marshall. I'm a building contractor in D.C. I've got a client who needs a rush job on some renovations. Nothing complicated. It's all interior work, a couple of bedrooms and a couple of bathrooms to be added to an existing building. Are you in a position to take a rush job?"

"I might be," said Jake. "Nothing I'm working on right now is all that urgent, though I'd need a little something extra, of course, if your client needs someone who'll work nights and weekends to get it done. Is that the kind of rush job you're talking about?"

"Yes it is. There'd be no problem with a surcharge, say forty percent. But I do need the fastest possible turnaround – two weeks, three tops. You'd need to make a site visit before you start, because it's a little tricky how the changes fit inside the existing building."

"Where's the site?"

"It's a mountain place, about 85 miles west, on the edge of the Monongahela National Forest in West Virginia."

Jake made a low whistling sound.

"My client will pay a generous mileage fee, of course."

"I like generosity," said Jake. "Are there any other complications to this job?"

"One more complication. My client has a strict need for privacy. Let's say he's a senator, or something like that. You'd have to sign a nondisclosure. Strictly no talking about the job, or the job site, with anyone. It's not like you have to have a security clearance or anything, but it would be best if you acted as though the whole thing is classified."

"Most of my clients like to show off their renovations to the neighbors, but I certainly get the point that this is a different kind of client. No problem. If you're offering me a contract, I'll take it."

After working out some details and arranging to meet the contractor at the mountain place the following Monday, Jake returned to his seat at the window.

What is it with secret mountain retreats? he thought. But I can get into that. It's almost like a story. Though, what could be more boring than some rich plutocrat who doesn't want anyone to know about his secret weekend getaway and the call girls, or call boys, that he entertains there? Washington really is like Mos Eisley on Luke Skywalker's little planet of Tatooine – you will never find a more wretched hive of scum and villainy. The forty percent extra will be nice. Maybe, thought Jake, I can take a little time off in the fall, go back to the mountains, do a little more stargazing, ask Phaedrus some questions.

Why is it, thought Jake, that when I get into one of these moonstruck moods it's so hard to get out of them? Even the thought of a rich new client can't get me out of it. And it's getting worse. Or is it just that I don't have a girlfriend to keep me distracted, to keep me in a routine? Watch it, Jake. You're thinking about girls again. You'll never give up, will you? You fantasize that you might meet a girl who's interested in the same things that you're interested in, who won't expect you to make chitchat all the time. But enough chitchatting with yourself. Get to work, Jake.

Because the rich plutocrat's building contractor was paying such a generous mileage allowance, Jake was looking forward to a road trip to the West Virginia mountains. Even as he packed the Jeep, Jake wasn't sure how long he'd stay. Should he go take care of business and come right back? Or should he take some camping gear and stay an extra night or two? And come to think of it, there was no great need to decide ahead of time. He could just pack what he'd need for a short camping trip, and if he ended up not using it then it would be no big deal. As he rummaged in the back of his closet for his camping gear, he eyed the telescope. Should he take it? Stargazing wasn't particularly great in the summertime. What the heck, he decided. Why not take it? What else is there to do after dark when you're all alone on a camping trip?

Jake took Interstate 64 west from Charlottesville to Staunton, then U.S. Route 250, which went right through the George Washington National Forest, across the West Virginia line, and on into the Monongahela National Forest. The plutocrat's place was somewhere on the periphery of the national forest, on the western side. The contractor had given Jake some GPS coordinates to help him navigate.

Not until Jake crossed the West Virginia line and saw the signs that said Monongahela National Forest did he finally shake off the taint of city life and all the nagging little everyday aggravations that tend to keep the mind chattering away. What is it about trees? It's almost as though trees, when there are lots of them together, generate some sort of mysterious force field that gets into the human brain and changes its channel to the nature channel. Jobs, rents, bank balances, the constant friction of living up against hordes of people, suburban traffic – it all melted away like sooty, muddy snow piled by a winter roadside. Out among the trees, everything looks different. A guy can remember things that he ought never to forget – that we live on a small, blue planet. That water, though it's ridiculously abundant on this small blue planet, is everything. It makes the trees grow. It's what clouds are make of. It's what our bodies are, other than a few pounds of dry powder. It's the supporting medium of a million volatile chemical reactions that we call life. It may be common here, but it's otherwise rare in the galaxy. And yet we treat it as though it's next to worthless, and the dominant religion sees water, and the rest of nature, as just limitless commodities put there for man to exploit.

Jake stopped at a pullover where the road crossed a small river and took the windows out of the Jeep's doors. He tucked the windows into the back seat, on top of his camping gear. Cars may be evil, thought Jake. They pollute, they're dangerous, they eventually fall apart. But there's nothing quite so exhilarating as driving in an open Jeep on the open road – hardly any traffic, the wind in your hair, your time all your own, nothing to distract you from your own thoughts. And even if they're airhead thoughts, thought Jake, at least they're my thoughts. And there's nothing to distract me from them.

A brown sign by the road, a park sign, suggested tuning to a particular frequency for park information. Jake turned on the Jeep's radio, which he almost never used. As he tuned the radio, he paused, out of amusement, at a quartet of male voices singing a sprightly hymn.

I was sinking deep in sin, far from the peaceful shore,
Very deeply stained within, sinking to rise no more,
But the Master of the sea, heard my despairing cry,
From the waters lifted me, now safe am I.

Love lifted me! Love lifted me!
When nothing else could help
Love lifted me!

All my heart to Him I give, ever to Him I'll cling
In His blessèd presence live, ever His praises sing,
Love so mighty and so true, merits my soul's best songs,
Faithful, loving service too, to Him belongs.

Love lifted me! Love lifted me!
When nothing else could help
Love lifted me!

Souls in danger look above, Jesus completely saves,
He will lift you by His love, out of the angry waves.
He's the Master of the sea, billows His will obey,
He your Savior wants to be, be saved today.

Love lifted me! Love lifted me!
When nothing else could help
Love lifted me!

Fascinating, thought Jake. What was it Phaedrus said about romantic love and how it was compatible with Christian theology? It's almost as though erotic love and Christian love get blurred in their minds. Jake thought of a naughty game he'd heard of when he was around ten years old. You take a hymnal, read the name of a hymn, and append the words "Between the sheets!"

Come Thou Almighty King. Between the sheets!
Touch Me, Lord Jesus. Between the sheets!
All the Way My Savior. Between the sheets!
Have Thine Own Way, Lord. Between the sheets!

After the hymns, an unctuous voice gave a long plea for donations. Doing the lord's work, apparently, took a lot of money. Then came a sermon. The preacher had the rough voice of an ill-educated Appalachian entrepreneur. It was not so much the words that Jake found mesmerizing, it was the rhythms. The words themselves could have been put together by one of the computerized jargon generators that linguists like to experiment with. You feed the jargon generator a big catalog of phrases lifted from actually texts, you give the jargon generator some rules for combining things, and then the jargon generator cranks out something meaningless that sounds entirely original. A jargon generator had once generated an academic paper on postmodern philosophy that got accepted for publication by a scholarly journal. And so it was with this Appalachian sermon. It was a jumble of pious phrases, with particular emphasis on shame and of being afraid of God's wrath. The preacher started out with slow, hectoring rhythms. Then he picked up the pace and got a little more threatening. By the end, he was frothing at the mouth, with aggressive, thrusting rhythms and heavy breathing. And then finally he spent himself in an lascivious orgasmic outburst. Then there was a hymn, while off-microphone the preacher surely lit a cigarette.

"Enough of that," said Jake aloud, poking the radio rudely with an index finger. The next station was talk radio. They seemed to be going on about a conspiracy theory.

"Jim in Conway, Arkansas. You're on the air," said the announcer. Jim in Arkansas sounded young. He also sounded pretty smart, in spite of his accent.

"They're just not getting it," said Jim. "You have to connect the dots. There have been five of these so-called suicides now, all under similar circumstances. If just one Air Force guy tried to tell us they're up to something, and then he jumped off a bridge, or shot himself in the head, and they told us he was just crazy, then I'd write it off, too. But this has happened five times now, in the last six months. Two were pilots. One was a navigator. The others were some sort of logistics guys. They all said the same thing, that they're making some sort of weapons, almost certainly containing nuclear material, in a couple of secret factories in India. They all said they're flying this stuff to bases all over the world. Two of them even had pictures. All of them are dead now. The newspapers and television, they won't touch it. We wouldn't even know about it if the families hadn't spoken up, and the pictures got leaked. Now we have this crash in California. If Travis Air Force Base wasn't so close to Oakland and San Francisco, they'd have been able to cover it up. But even the idiots on local TV figured out that it was something big, and there are lots of nerds out there with Geiger counters. So, do I know what's going on? No. But is something going on? Obviously."

"Frank in Idaho. You're on the air."

"There's no doubt about it," said Frank in Idaho. "It's depopulation. Look, the people who really run things have known for years that there are just too many useless eaters on this planet. They've tinkered with ways of getting the population down, but tinkering just won't do it. Viruses, chemtrails, stuff like that, people get all paranoid about it, but that stuff's too unpredictable, too hard to control. The people that own the world, they're control freaks, you see. If they're going to bring the population down, they're not going to mess around. They're going to just do it. They're going to have a predictable outcome. They're going to have a plan. They're going to have numbers. They're going to do some targeting. I'll tell you where you don't want to be right now. You don't want to be in a city that doesn't produce anything useful to them. You know, Cairo. Delhi. If I lived in Atlanta, or Dallas, I'd get the (beep) out. Now, what kind of technology can you use for depopulation, if you're a control freak? You can't just line up billions of people and shoot them. Look at the Nazis and how much technology it took to eliminate only eleven million people. A technology that can take out billions of people is not something that you just have sitting on a shelf. You have to develop it. You have to test it. You have to build it. You have to move it into place. Can you do that without accidentally losing a few dots for people to connect? Of course not. It's all obvious if you connect the dots."

"Jennifer in Kansas City. You're on the air."

"I'm just sick of all these people playing God," said Jennifer in Kansas City. "Listen to what the lord said, in Jeremiah: 'We are disgraced, for we have been insulted, and shame covers our faces, because foreigners have entered the holy places of the Lord's house.' God doesn't hate Atlanta, or Dallas. It was Babylon that God hated. This country was founded by people who feared God. But we let the foreigners in, the people of Babylon. We let the infidels in. We let in the queers, and the atheists, and all who hate God. God knows his people. He will lift up the righteous and give them a crown of glory. God doesn't need technology. The sword of the Lord is more powerful than any technology we could ever dream of. God made hell for a reason. Vengeance is mine, saith the Lord."

"Take your vengeance and jam it," said Jake, this time poking the radio's OFF button.

Then Jake heard the buzzing, for the first time in years. It was like a swarm of bees. He had first heard it when he was an adolescent, badly sick with a fever after a tick bite he'd gotten on a weekend camping trip. He'd had to miss a lot of school because of that tick bite. He was sure he was going to fail physics class, because physics was hard, and the homework his mother had gotten for him was making no sense at all, though he'd read and reread the chapters on quantum mechanics in his fevered state. The buzzing had come like a vision, like a flash of pure insight. All at once, even though he was sick, what he had read made sense. All the pieces fit together. He had ended up with an A in that class.

This time, Jake wasn't sure whether it was the buzzing or the green wildness of the West Virginia mountains that brought the vision. In his mind he saw an earth that was wild again, green again, clean again, dark again at night, an earth that was back in balance, uninjured. There were people, but not too many, and those people had no power to use against the earth other than the power of their own muscles, or the muscles of domesticated animals, or of wind in the sails of their small ships. Then the buzzing passed, and there was only the hum of the Jeep as it drank its ration of fossil fuel, gliding through the West Virginia forest. Jake tried to hold on to that vision of that earth, but somehow it was not compatible with the asphalt, with the Jeep, with speed, with his suburbanized wants and needs. The vision faded.

Jake's plan was to find a little roadside motel on the western side of Monongahela, have a nice provincial breakfast somewhere at a roadside greasy spoon, and then be at the job site at 11 o'clock to meet the contractor. He spent some time exploring roads around Mill Creek and Beverly, hoping to find a mom and pop motel, something that wasn't part of a chain. But that effort failed, and Jake settled for a chain motel closer to the highway than he wanted to be. But at least he was able to get a quiet room on the back side of the motel.

Jake wasn't even tempted to turn on the motel television. He'd brought some books. Phaedrus had left him curious about a lot of things. Shortly after Jake had returned to Charlottesville after his visit with Phaedrus, he'd gone online and ordered some books. He'd thought about it most of the way back home from that stargazing trip in May. He'd listed in his mind the subjects that he'd become newly curious about, outlined the categories of books that he wanted to read. He'd ended up ordering more than a dozen books. It was June now, and he'd already read almost half of them. At present he was working on *The Fall of Rome and the End of Civilization*, by Bryan Ward-Perkins. The book had been published by Oxford University Press. Jake was finding that he increasingly found himself reading books published by university presses and enjoying them more. He'd also read *The Unsettling of America: Culture and Agriculture*, by Wendell Berry. That book was about industrialization, the migration of Americans off the land, and the steady despoliation of farmland by suburbanization and industrial farming. Jake had read *Collapse: How Societies Choose to Fail or Succeed*, by Jared Diamond. Jake had read a couple of books by physicists, nothing technical, but attempts by physicists to explain to the intelligent public the crazy discoveries in physics during the 20th century and their implications for philosophy. He'd read a couple of books about the usurpation of the economy and the government by private, corporate interests. He'd even read a book about radio communications.

All of this reading had made Phaedrus seem less eccentric. Jake was starting to realize that most people just never bothered to know the things that Phaedrus knows. Most people were distracted by the mass media and assumed that the mass media kept them informed. Increasingly Jake realized that it was all just propaganda, the "official narrative," as Phaedrus had called it. As Jake settled onto the wide motel bed to read, on impulse he got up again and threw a blanket over the television. If I turned the damned thing on, thought Jake, I know perfectly well what I'll see. Since it's summer there'll be stories about shark attacks. Also missing women. Some celebrity gossip, and some scandal or other having to do with a Washington politician caught with his zipper down. There will be shouting heads talking about taxes and government finances, and slimy "experts" giving their expert opinions without revealing whose payrolls they're on. Jake wondered which came first: the ignorant masses creating a demand for ignorant media, or ignorant media making the masses ignorant. They prey on each other, he supposed, like reptiles eating the eggs of their own species. Sometime after midnight Jake fell asleep with a book on his chest.

The next morning, the GPS coordinates led Jake to a narrow but nicely paved road that seemed to lead into the Monongahela forest. He came to a closed gate blocking the road. There was a guard shack beside the gate and a couple of plain-looking cars, both of the same model. A security guy in a brown uniform stepped out of the shack as Jake slowly rolled up to the gate and stopped. Yep, thought Jake. Somebody is rich. And powerful.

"My name is Jake Janaway," he said to the guard. "I'm an architect, and I have an appointment with Mr. Marshall."

"Good morning, Mr. Janaway," said the guard. "Mr.

Marshall said he'll meet you in the parking area. That's about a mile down the road, on the left, before you get to the main house. Park your Jeep in the parking area and wait there for Mr. Marshall. He'll come to the Jeep to meet you and escort you to where you need to go. I'll radio him and tell him you're here."

Jake thanked the guard. The gate opened.

The road wound through enormous old hardwood trees. Jake wondered how many trees had died to make the road. The road reminded him of the roads leading to old robber baron estates, like Biltmore House at Asheville. These roads were always winding, always nicely landscaped.

Jake came to the parking area. There were a couple of identical nondescript cars like the ones he'd seen at the guard station and a couple of pickup trucks with contractor logos on the door. A few hundred yards ahead, through the gap where the road went through the trees, Jake could see a very large house, three stories high at least, built of post and beam and timber. Jake shut off the engine. He saw a tall, lean man wearing a blue hard hat approaching from the direction of the house.

The man reached through the Jeep's window to shake hands with Jake.

"Good morning, Mr. Janaway," he said. "I'm Mike Marshall. I appreciate your driving all this way. The trip wasn't too unpleasant, I hope."

"Not unpleasant at all," said Jake. "I wasn't expecting a chance to get back to the mountains until fall, so it's a treat, actually. I even brought some camping equipment. I thought I might find a spot to set up camp somewhere and stay an extra day or two."

"Well, there are plenty of places around here for that," Marshall said. "Nice weather right now, too. I brought my son up here a few weeks ago, and we did the same thing. I'll say one thing for our client. He's got good taste in terrain."

"And the money to afford it," said Jake. "Isn't this national forest? I didn't think there was supposed to be private property in places like this."

"There are all sorts of exceptions," Marshall said. "There are quite a few old private holdings here and there that are grandfathered in for one reason or another, and they come on the market sometimes. I believe our guy bought this place relatively recently, back in the '90's. The big house hasn't been here for much more than fifteen years. Every summer the senator adds a little something – a barn, new tennis courts, a garage for his vehicle collection. I've worked with the senator for several years, actually. This summer he's making more changes than usual, so it's actually going to be quite a rush to get it all done before winter weather."

So he *is* a senator, thought Jake.

"Post and beam," said Jake. "Now I see what they did with all the timber that they took down to make the road."

"That was before my time," Marshall said, "but I believe you're right about that. It makes sense. This is a long way out to haul materials. That's one of the logistical problems we have here. But to build with timber here you just set up a sawmill near the building site and save yourself a lot of hauling. Saves money too, though with the senator, from what I can tell, money is no object. You may be relieved to know, though, that for the addition on the back of the house, the one you're helping with, we're not using post and beam. It'll be fairly conventional stick built, though with a little structural steel, and brick veneer exterior. Some of the steel is already in place. The structural engineers took care of that. We just need for you to fill in the interior layout and redraw some of the last-minute modifications that the senator's wife has requested. You'll see. It's nothing very complicated, but the important thing is keeping up our momentum and getting that part of the job done before the end of

September."

"You must have checked me out before you called me," said Jake. "You know I'm not the guy for heavy structure, or for post and beam for that matter. Last-minute changes by the wives, and easy interiors, that's my specialty."

Marshall smiled and led the way toward the house. "I don't think anyone checked you out," Marshall said. "But you have a nice web site and some good references."

"It reminds me a bit of Sagamore Hill," said Jake, "but executed in post and beam."

"You're very perceptive," said Marshall. "The senator has mentioned a couple of times that Sagamore Hill was his inspiration for this place. And Teddy Roosevelt was one of his heroes. The senator even secretly sees himself as a conservationist like Teddy Roosevelt, but I believe that senators of his persuasion these days have to keep that a secret from their constituencies. In any case, the senator does admire Roosevelt's home and wanted one like it. And the senator may have presidential ambitions for all I know."

"I'm glad to hear that he's a conservationist," said Jake. "But he sure chopped down a lot of trees for this place."

Marshall chuckled. "Maybe that's why he's going with brick veneer for this addition."

As they approached the house, Jake saw a heavily loaded truck driving slowly up the access road. Before it reached the parking area where Jake had left the Jeep, the truck turned off on a side road to the right and rumbled deeper into the forest.

"Wow," said Jake. "From the looks of the load on that truck, it's not just the house that the senator is adding to this year."

"Yes, that's a little side project," Marshall said. "That job is keeping me up at night. I'm only handling part of that little side project, but it's as tricky as any job I've ever handled. You should be glad you don't have to mess with that one."

"Anything that uses that much steel," said Jake, "is above my pay grade."

Marshall led Jake to his makeshift office, which was on the second floor of a garage big enough for at least ten vehicles. Marshall pulled a tube of blueprints from a shelf.

"Now, before I show you these prints," said Marshall, "what kind of changes do you suppose the senator's wife wants?"

"Let's see," said Jake. "Larger bathrooms and deeper closets."

"I can see you're a man with experience," said Marshall.

Jake found the work that was being requested, even though it was surrounded by an aura of mystery and power, to be pretty much the same boring work as usual. While they were talking about enlarging a bathroom, Marshall's walkie talkie chirped. Marshall picked it up off the desk and answered immediately.

"Marshall," he said. "Yeah … yeah … please tell me you're kidding. OK. I'll be there in about half an hour to take a look at it."

"Confounded concrete and steel," said Marshall as he put the radio down. "There's always some kind of aggravation with concrete and steel. I really ought to keep an engineer on site to sign off on these things. Come to think of it, I think I will. Those guys would rather stay in their nice, cool offices in Alexandria and fly up in their helicopter once a week to savor just how much trouble they caused with the decisions they made the week before. Being up here all the time wouldn't be half as much fun as their little helicopter rides."

After Jake was clear on the changes he was responsible for, he had a look at the existing structure where the addition was to go. He was given a copy of the blueprints to work from, and he signed the confidentiality agree-ment. Then Marshall walked him back to the Jeep. Jake found that he liked Marshall. He was a little gruff with some of his inferiors, but Jake realized that that was an act. All contractor bosses had to act tough. Before Jake got into the Jeep, he asked about camping.

"You said there are good places to camp around here?"

"Do you like camping high up? Young guys like you with strong backs and strong legs usually do."

"I love to camp high up. I don't mind carrying a little water uphill."

"Why don't you come with me, then. I can show you a place I think you'd like. It's where I went with my son a few weekends ago. There's a nice trail up the mountain that follows a little stream, and at the top there's a rocky area with a view for miles. There are plenty of trees up there too, and lots of nice campsites. You can ride along with me to the other project site. It won't take long. But remember, you just signed a confidentiality agreement."

"Understood," said Jake. "Sounds great."

Another heavy truck bearing a load of steel rumbled in and turned into the road that led farther into the forest. Marshall's truck was parked near Jake's Jeep. They got into the truck, and Marshall followed slowly behind the load of steel that was winding its way into the woods. Marshall's radio chirped again.

"I'll be there in five," Marshall said into the radio.

The project area was a place where the trees had been fairly recently cleared. The logs were stacked, apparently to dry, off to one side. The clearing was the size of a football field. There was a dusty area where the ground had been scraped and graded and flattened. There was some heavy earth-moving equipment. An ugly rectan-gular building, built of concrete and steel, was going up. It had no windows. At one corner of the building stood a tall steel antenna tower, about fifteen feet wide at the bottom and much narrower at the top. It looked to be almost 200 feet high. There were stairs about halfway up the tower, then a ladder that continued to the top. On the opposite side of the building was a helicopter pad. Marshall handed Jake a hard hat.

"Wow," said Jake as they walked toward the ugly concrete building. "I'm not going to ask."

"There's not even a lot I could tell you if you did ask," Marshall said, "the one thing I can deduce is that the senator probably isn't going to be a senator much longer."

"What do you mean?"

"I've been around government work for a while, and the senator is not the first VIP I've done work for. When all of a sudden they seem to be twice as rich as before and start to spruce up their getaways and hunting lodges, it means they're about to resign and take a job with some big government contractor or another. You can predict which government contractor just by knowing what committee the senator chaired. This particular senator, I feel sure, will be taking a nice, comfy job with some big defense contractor or another. That's the way Washington works. Guys like us, we're just the hired help, no more important to them than their housekeepers and their cooks. They talk all nice when the television cameras are pointed at them, but the guys who run Washington are in a whole different league than you and me. It's a small club, and, once you get in, you're set for life."

A man in a hard hat approached them from the concrete building, a perplexed and apologetic look on his face.

"I'm sorry to drag you into this again," the man said. "I'd like for you to take a look at the pour in that access shaft. Something or other's not working right with the changes they made last week."

"Dang it, Jim," said Marshall. "Couldn't you have made them use a sledgehammer or something? This is Jake.

Architect."

"Hello, Jake."

"Is there anywhere else ready to pour?" said Marshall, "We have to keep them moving."

"The conduit shaft, maybe," Jim said. "But I'm afraid this is going to cost us some down time."

Jake followed the two into the building. The interior was lit by huge work lights.

"Could you hang out here for a few minutes?" Marshall said to Jake. Jake nodded. The two men then descended a steel ladder near the corner of the building and disappeared below ground.

There were at least twenty or twenty-five workers around, going about their work. None of them paid any particular attention to Jake. Jake felt almost as though he was spying on top-secret government work, but the workmen around him seemed to think that Jake's being there was nothing unusual. Besides, Jake had arrived with Marshall. There did not seem to be any sort of security guy around. The site was awfully remote, after all, and anyone who came in had to come through the main gate. Jake gave in to the impulse to have a look around and satisfy his curiosity as discreetly as possible.

He saw two workmen carrying big rolls of copper through a doorway that seemed to lead into the center of the building. Jake casually moved that way until he was close enough to look inside.

It was as he guessed. The ceiling, floors and walls of the room were already halfway lined with copper. The two workers emerged from the room, apparently going to get more rolls of copper. They nodded in Jake's direction.

"That's a lot of copper," said Jake.

"It's a mighty expensive way to keep the mice and roaches out," one of the workers said.

So, thought Jake. These guys are building a Faraday

cage, and they don't even know what they're building. And what they're building here is just a much bigger and much more expensive version of what Phaedrus has. Jake concentrated on looking disinterested and casual, but he realized that he had a lot of new thinking and rethinking to do. He moved back to where Marshall had left him waiting. Marshall soon emerged from the hole in the ground.

"Are you afraid of heights?" Marshall asked.

"Appropriately scared. Not phobic, though," said Jake.

"Come with me, then," said Marshall. "I've only got a few minutes, but I can show you where you'll find some good camping sites."

Marshall led Jake to the corner of the building with the antenna tower. Marshall started ascending the narrow metal stairs, and Jake followed. They climbed until the stairs stopped, about halfway up the tower. They probably were about a hundred feet off the ground. The stairs opened onto a little platform that filled the center of the tower. There was a railing around the side.

"Wow," said Jake. This is quite a view. We're surrounded by ridges on three sides."

"That's all national forest around us," Marshall said. "I have no idea how you get a permit to put an antenna tower in a place like this."

Jake thought he might as well ask a nosy question, since the question was so obvious.

"What's the tower for?"

"Communications," Marshall said. "We're only halfway up. The tower is 199 feet high, so from the top you have line of site to some other tower somewhere, off in that direction. With line of sight, they'd have the ability to use UHF frequencies, or microwave. And the last time the radio engineer was here, he mentioned that there will even be a shortwave antenna up there."

Jake played dumb. He had learned a few things from

Phaedrus.

"Shortwave? Isn't that obsolete?"

"I would have thought so. But apparently government guys still use it for certain purposes. I think microwave does all the heavy hauling, though. But as far as I know, this is not our tax dollars at work. This is the senator's private money. Those big bonuses from those big defense contractors are probably already coming in."

"The money trickles down some, doesn't it?" said Jake. "Even I am getting a little of it."

"It does. A fraction of it. But you can't count on it. There are fads with the rich in how they spend their money. In the '90s, it was yachts. Now nobody buys yachts. Now they build helipad retreats."

"Are they buying helicopters, too?"

"Not so much. That's a perk they get from their corporations. I also suspect that, more and more, the military is running a kind of helicopter taxi service for their private contractors. The Pentagon outsources something like half its budget to private corporations. That's huge. Not only do those private corporations pull in hundreds of billions of dollars, they also get access to all kinds of classified information, which they can use to their advantage to make even more money."

"Surely you're not implying that our benevolent senator is corrupt," Jake said, having decided to stick his neck out a little to pump for information.

"No more corrupt than any," Marshall said. "But now, the senator's son, that's a different case. When a helicopter shows up with the senator's son on board, then it's time to duck for cover."

"Why is that?" Jake asked.

"You know the cliché. He was born on third base and thought he hit a home run. Arrogant. Imperial attitude. Treats everyone around him like servants, or slaves. Travels with hired commandos that – no kidding – dress in black. Despises immigrants. I once saw him tear into a junior engineer for not speaking English. Apparently the senator entrusts some of his interests to this son, and it has gone to his head. Some people can make a little bit of power go a long way. If I had to deal with people like that, I'd quit. But it's always the security engineers he's after. It's as though he thinks people are out to get him. With a personality like that, it's not hard to see why. Hence the commandos, I guess. But that's human nature, isn't it? If you've got a lot of money, the next thing you want is a lot of power."

"Power and money," Jake said. "The days are over, I guess, when a powerful man could die poor. Jefferson died with so much debt that it took his son a lifetime to pay it off. Whereas now the trajectories of power and money intersect somewhere between the Capitol and the helicopter pads at the Pentagon."

"You've got it," Marshall said. "These days it's hard to tell where the line is between the government and the private sector. It's the same people, and they all know each other and scratch each other's back. A corporation sees a neat new way to make money, they call somebody at the Pentagon, and before you know it there's a new trough to feed at and more free helicopter rides."

"Nice work if you can get it," said Jake.

"And I could probably get it if I played golf," Marshall said. "But I'd rather spend the time with my son. Anyway, see that ridge to the northwest? That's the place. You can reach it from a trail that comes in from the western side. The trailhead is on a public road. The hike to get up there is probably four hours. The views are incredible. This gash in the woods is fairly visible from up there, but it doesn't spoil the view. My GPS is in the truck. I can give you the coordinates from when I went up there with my son. With a Jeep and a GPS and some camping equipment, you've got everything you need. Don't stay up there too long, though. I'll still be expecting those drawings just as we agreed."

Jake took one more look at the surrounding ridges, and they descended the tower.

In Jake's opinion, summer was not the best time of year for hiking. It was too hot. But the way to get around that was to be where there is some elevation. The crest of the ridge he was on was just over 3,000 feet. The temperature was only seventy-two degrees, and there was a steady breeze out of the northwest. Excellent hiking weather.

As Jake worked his way along the ridge, heading toward the rocky promontory that Marshall had pointed out from below, his view of the valley below was mostly blocked by the trees. But Jake knew from the maps he carried that if he was a squirrel in one of these trees he'd be able to see the senator's installation below and to the southeast, about three miles away. His pack was heavy, because he was carrying quite a lot of water. His telescope was strapped to his pack. He wouldn't have wanted to hike all day with a load like that, but three or four hours wouldn't kill him. The stillness was magnificent up here – nothing but the sound of the wind in the trees, and birds chirping. When Jake was hiking in unspoiled forest like this, he often liked to pretend that it was centuries ago, that modernity, and industrialization, never happened. But no matter where he was, it was never too long before the sound of a jet, high above in the stratosphere, would ruin the effect. It was hard to escape modernity. In the traveling he'd done, which was a good bit for someone his age – he was lucky that his parents weren't poor – Jake had never been to a place where there was truly no sign of the modern world. Did such a place even exist anymore? If such places do exist, they must be in awfully harsh environments where you wouldn't want to go without a lot of preparation. Damn the jet engines, he thought.

Jake had to admit, though, that he sure did like his modern GPS. It's hard to get lost on a ridge like this, he thought, but the GPS provides a certain confidence, cuts down on anxiety about being off course, saves time lost in navigation errors. Could those GPS satellites be completely trusted? Jake had heard horror stories of people using GPS units in cars who'd gotten led on wild goose chases. Was that user error and user foolishness? Or does something sometimes go wrong? Maybe, Jake thought, it depends on the quality of the GPS device one is using. Surely they're not all of equal quality. But, as Phaedrus would say, redundancy is a good thing. Jake also had a compass and a topographical map of the area. The map showed him that his promontory destination was less than a mile off. The slope was growing steeper and rockier. The GPS now reported the altitude as 3,128 feet.

Suddenly the trees gave out, and everything was rock. Jake squinted in the sun but was pleased to see that in just moments a cloud would pass in front of the sun, allowing him to relax his eyes and take in the view. Marshall was right. It was quite a vista. To the east across the wide valley was another ridge, higher than the one he was on, more than 4,000 feet. The valley was thick with trees, with signs of small roads here and there. To the southeast, Jake could easily discern the senator's communications tower, beside a clearing that from this vantage point appeared small. The tower, inconspicuous though it was from here, was an insult to the landscape. But nothing else marred the view.

A single stunted pine tree clung to the rocks near the edge of the rocky outcropping Jake was on. He unfastened his pack and leaned it against the tree. Then he sat down to rest and enjoy the silence and the cool air. What the heck, thought Jake. I've earned it. Why not have a little nap. He unrolled his sleeping pad, stretched out in the cool shade, and soon drifted off to sleep.

A sound awoke him. He would have liked to resume his nap, but as his brain came awake he quickly realized that the sound was something he'd half expected. It was the sound of a helicopter, distant, to the east. Quickly Jake unfastened his telescope and stepped out closer to the ledge for a clearer view. After a few seconds, his eyes located the speck that was the helicopter. It was headed toward the senator's helipad. Fixing the telescope on a moving target would be next to impossible, so Jake set up the tripod, attached the scope, and aimed it toward the tower and helipad three miles below. Using the fine adjustments, he soon had the helipad in his sights. He watched as the helicopter hovered and then settled onto the helipad. It was bright blue, a civilian helicopter. That would be the engineer, thought Jake. He could see tiny figures. A vehicle approached the helipad, a pickup truck. That might be Marshall, thought Jake. The helicopter's engine was silent now.

Jake retrieved a snack from his pack. Then he took out a book and lay down on his pad to read. Before long he had dozed again. When he awoke, he gathered firewood and started to set up for the night. About 4:30 p.m., he heard the helicopter start its engines. Soon it lifted off and headed east, back the way it had come.

Jake had the feeling that, somehow, what he was doing was slightly illicit, as though he was spying. The telescope, somehow, had amplified the feeling that he was spying. He reminded himself that he was, after all, on public property, and not breaking any laws. He wondered if this was what was called open source intelligence.

But why, Jake asked himself, do I even think that there's anything going on here that's worth spying on? So what if a rich senator, rather than buying a yacht, builds an underground bunker, a communications system protected by a Faraday cage, and a helipad? So what if he upgraded his wilderness getaway to comfortably accommodate, say, twenty people? So what if he upgraded his kitchen with new walk-in freezers and refrigerators, out here where shopping trips weren't short?

Why have I seen two Faraday cages in the last few months? Jake knew from his reading that natural sources of extreme electromagnetic bursts were pretty rare and probably did not justify such expensive protection. Sometimes, especially during the active phase of the eleven-year solar cycle, the sun's surface would get especially turbulent and stormy, and solar explosions would occur, called coronal mass ejections. These explosions would fling huge amounts of matter and energy out into space. If this matter and energy hit the earth, it could cause serious distortions in the earth's magnetosphere, that is, the earth's magnetic field. The upper atmosphere of the earth would then go crazy, crackling with energy from ionization. Satellites could be knocked out. Radio communications would be disrupted. The northern lights would appear far to the south. If the solar event was powerful enough, there was a chance that the burst of electromagnetic energy hitting the earth could disrupt power grids, causing widespread electrical blackouts. If it was bad enough, sensitive electronic equipment could be destroyed – unless it was protected by a Faraday cage.

But what if the source of an electromagnetic burst was a thermonuclear explosion?

So which of those two ought I to be concerned about? Jake asked himself. There have been coronal mass ejections for as long as the earth has been orbiting the sun. It's not dangerous to human beings. It's only dangerous to electronics, and it disrupts communications for a while. But thermonuclear explosions, now that's something else again.

What if the senator has some kind of inside information? What if Phaedrus does? Since I don't have inside information, how much can I deduce about what might be going on, assuming that something actually is going on?

Would it be possible for me to connect the dots, if I was smart enough? Or can the puzzle only be solved with inside information that I don't have? If I asked Phaedrus point blank, would he tell me what he knows? Do I even want to know?

Don't be silly. Of course I want to know. Maybe even my life depends upon it. But is that fair? What about all those people who don't know, who don't have underground bunkers and walk-in freezers and backup generators?

Then again, Phaedrus doesn't have a backup generator, as far as I know. He's got a big garden, though, doesn't he, instead of walk-in freezers? And he told me that he can get by on so little power that he doesn't need a generator, though it's a shame that that organ can't be played on solar power. Phaedrus, it seems, is doing on a shoestring what a rich senator is doing in grand style. Same thing, different levels of comfort. The senator can support twenty, Phaedrus can support a man and a dog.

What about the senator's underground bunker? Phaedrus may well have an underground bunker, because I saw a trap door. Could that be anything other than a bomb shelter, or a fallout shelter? And if these two guys have fallout shelters, which theory does that fit with for the Faraday cages? That's rather obvious, isn't it? You don't need to go into a bomb shelter if there's a coronal mass ejection.

With dark approaching, Jake realized that these speculations were accompanied by a tinge of fear. If they're expecting something to happen, when might it happen? Phaedrus seemed to be already prepared. The senator, on the other hand, was still working on his underground bunker, so there must be some time. Am I just being paranoid? Or would I be a fool to ignore what I've seen? At the very least, I ought to try to ask Phaedrus some questions. But I can't drop everything I'm doing right now and make another stargazing trip. There must be some time, right? Marshall said that he'd be lucky to have the senator's project finished by winter. I have no choice but to beat down some other responsibilities first, finish the senator's wife's modifications, and suck up a little of the senator's trickle-down money. After that, I can arrange things for another stargazing trip in October.

Jake made only a small fire at dusk and went to sleep early. Around 11 p.m., he was awakened by the sound of a helicopter, this time a heavy helicopter. Jake got up and went to the telescope, which was still on its tripod pointed at the senator's compound. Jake had covered the telescope with his hiking shirt, partly to keep out the dew, and partly to allow his sweaty shirt to dry.

Through the telescope, he could see that the helipad was brightly lighted. The helicopter settled onto the helipad and shut down its engines. This one was black, unmarked, huge, heavy – a Chinook. Suddenly nothing seemed very surprising. Jake threw the shirt back over the telescope and returned to his sleeping bag, which was still warm.

He awoke from a dreamless sleep. He shifted his shoulders away from the pebble that was poking through his sleeping pad. The sky was dark. It was an hour or two before dawn, judging from the constellations. He lay there for a while, looking up at the sky. Perhaps it was curiosity that led him to crawl out of his sleeping bag and return to the ledge, to see if the helicopter was still there and if the helipad was still brightly lighted. The compound was dark. The helicopter must still be there in the darkness. He'd have heard it leave.

The night air was moist and chilled. Jake put his hand on the shirt that covered the telescope. The sweat had no doubt dried, but now the shirt was damp with dew. He picked up the shirt and held it to his face, as guys often do if no one is watching and they're gathering laundry, deciding what to wash. For some reason, in his still-dreamy state, he was conscious of his own scent, something he'd rarely given much thought to in the past. He had showered back at the motel, but he'd forgotten to bring deodorant, and Jake never wore scents. He wondered if people smell the same to themselves as they do to other people. Hadn't Jamie once told him that he smelled like apple blossoms? There was in fact something strangely floral about the natural scent of his shirt, vaguely like an antique rose at an abandoned farmstead, or a blossom on an old apple tree. Pheromones? Maybe that was one of the areas in which the human genome overlaps with the genomes of the plant kingdom. Maybe there actually is something chemically similar in human pheromones and apple blossoms, pheromones made by apple-tree DNA that lingers in the human genome. We humans share lots of DNA even with oak trees, Jake knew. There was even corn DNA still lingering in human DNA. Maybe we have some apple tree genes in us as well. Jake threw the shirt back over the telescope.

As his eyes scanned the sky, he saw a black spot obscuring the stars. He squinted, studying the shape, trying to make sense of it. It appeared to be a large object hovering over the senator's compound. That made no sense. Then the object began to move. It moved slowly, but increasingly it became apparent that it was moving toward Jake. As it approached, Jake could more clearly make out its shape by its silhouette against the stars. It appeared to be triangular. It was enormous, and it was less than a thousand feet above the surface. It was completely silent. As it got closer, Jake could see what appeared to be dim running lights on some of its edges, blue and green. It continued moving toward Jake until it was directly above him: colossal, silent, black, alien, enormously technically advanced and enormously powerful.

Jake stared, head bent backward. He wondered afterward why he had felt no fear. It was as though he forgot to be afraid. Something like this simply could not exist. At least, it could not have come from this planet. From somewhere near its center, a narrow beam of white light shot down through the mist. Jake stumbled backwards, startled yet fearless. But the beam was not aimed at him, it was aimed at his telescope, or his shirt. Then the beam strobed, in a fluttering rhythmic pattern of flashes that Jake was pretty sure he heard as well as saw. It was a low note, musical, reedy, like an organ pipe. It sounded the way he imagined Phaedrus' Contra faggot 32-foot pedal stop would sound. It was not a threatening sound. It almost sounded like a greeting, or a flirtation, with a touch of humor. Then the light went out, and the triangle started to move away to the northwest, as silently as it had approached. As it drifted away, a narrow shaft of bright white light appeared now from the top of the triangle. This laser-like beam pierced upward into the cloudless, starry sky. Again the light strobed, more like a cheery farewell than a greeting, and again the light went out. Jake looked up at the point in the sky where the light had pointed. Was it toward the star Alioth, possibly? Jake stood silent, his mind oddly calm, for long after the triangle had gone out of sight. He picked up his shirt and held it to his face.

It was definitely apple blossoms.

CHAPTER 5

The summer was miserably hot and dry. The Rivanna River through Charlottesville was running at its lowest level in years. The news – Jake found that he was soaking up far more news than he used to do – was full of stories about bad weather. There were floods in Tennessee. Texas was so dry and parched that it threatened to turn to powder and blow back to Mexico. There were tornados in the Midwest and even tornados in New England. The rain in California, which usually came to a halt before June, had continued well into the summer, making a mess of the vineyards and other crops. The Sacramento River was threatening to flood into the endless Sacramento suburbs, swollen by the snow melt in the Sierra combined with the new rain. There were famines in parts of Russia and China. There were food riots in Africa and dust bowls in parts of India. Droughts in Australia had reached disaster levels. In the United States, SUV-driving consumers were angry at Washington because of the price of gasoline , the price of milk, the price of to-matoes for their hamburgers, the price of sugar for their doughnuts and ice cream. Jake regularly asked himself if there were dots that needed to be connected.

Jake had never been much of a TV watcher. He had always been a movie guy. Television got on his nerves.

It moved too slow. It was shrill, a stream of ugly noises that kept Jake from his own thoughts, which were much more interesting to him than television. But television did have one advantage over the news he read on line: video. Whether the disaster *du jour* was a tidal wave, a flood along the Mississippi, a tornado in Alabama, or parched fields and starving cattle in Texas, video added a dimension that was missing in written reports. But Jake, searching for dots to connect, found television to be embarrassingly shallow, as though its target audience had an average IQ of 98.6 or less. On the other hand, if you went on line looking for dots to connect, you could find plenty of narrative to support whatever point of view appealed to you. Global warming? A hoax perpetrated by a vast left-wing conspiracy! Or not. Is regulation and the heavy hand of government strangling the economy? Obviously so! Or not. Are the unions of government employees bankrupting local governments everywhere? It's union greed! Or not. More and more, Jake became aware of the distortion and the disguised agendas that lay behind the noise of the media. Most of the loudest voices, Jake realized, had no real expertise. They were just loud. Those who are supposed to have expertise, like academics, can't always be right, because different schools of thought are always at each other's throats. The best predictor of an academic's views, Jake figured out, is where their funding comes from. Those supposedly academic "think tanks" always seem to have corporate funding. Propaganda tanks would be a better name.

Increasingly, Jake tended toward the depressing idea that ordinary people can't possibly know what's really going on in the world. Those who do know things keep the information to themselves and use it to further their own power and profit. No doubt there exist a few well-meaning people who know things, but they're obscure. How might it be possible to find reliable sources in the chaos of noise, advertising, propaganda, lies, gossip, scandal, and vitriol? No, Jake realized. We're on our own. Something truly scary, truly dangerous, may be happening in the world, or about to happen. But I don't know what it is, and there's no way for me to find out. I can only try to connect the dots as best I can, keep my ears and eyes open, and stay on my toes.

Another thing was nagging Jake – the lack of a girl-friend. There weren't even any prospects at the moment. It's too bad, thought Jake, that modern drug companies can make all sorts of drugs to liberate people sexually – birth control, performance enhancers, and silicone breast implants. But what I need is a drug there'd be no profit in, something for guys like me who ought to be a monk for a while, take some time to get their stuff together, figure out where their careers are going, save a few bucks, find a real friend, really get to know somebody. As far as I know, thought Jake, the only technology ever invented for celibacy was religion, and Jake was pretty sure that there was not a religious bone in his body. I need a bone transplant, thought Jake: a religious bone and a gay bone. Then I wouldn't be such a slave to girls. If every guy was like that, then girls might not be able to set the price so high. Truth be told, the cost of nooky from a call girl is way lower than the price of nooky from a nice girl with a Smith education, all things considered. You'd think more guys would figure that out. But heck, if I went out with a call girl I'd probably end up wanting to get to know her, and then where would I be? Right back where I started. I'd be better off going to church or something.

But just supposing I did find a girl for a while, something casual and temporary. Now where would I find her? Online? No. That's a filthy swamp of lies and deception. No one is who they say they are. That's why I like gyms. They're like cafeterias – you can see what you're getting before you decide to get it. Or maybe you could bump up your age range a little and have a fling with a married woman. She wouldn't demand too much. You could cut and run long before she says she wants to leave her husband and marry you.

Jake, you're no better than a pubescent dog. You have no more self-control than any other American. If food was your weakness, you'd be obese. If beer was your weakness, you'd be an alcoholic with a pot belly. You've already decided, haven't you, Jake? You'll go the gym route. OK then. But just make it a cheap gym, no contract, month to month. Then you can cut and run when her husband starts to get suspicious.

More than once, when Jake got into the Jeep with his gym bag, he ended up at the University of Virginia library instead. The summer was hot. The library was cool. Jake had always loved browsing the stacks. But most of his summer research was done on line in a research room at the library. He was searching for material that was as up to date as possible. He drove to the campus, parked the Jeep near the rugby field and walked up the hill toward the library, talking to himself as usual, though a co-ed volleyball match distracted him for a moment. Lately he had been reading a lot in what he called doomer forums, in which pretty much any unusual event was deemed to be connected with a conspiracy.

"Useless eaters," thought Jake. "They'd never use that term for themselves and their friends, and everybody they sleep with and want to sleep with. But everybody else on the planet is a useless eater. They're all crazy, everybody in every on-line forum I've ever read. But some of them are smart, and some of them cite numbers. 'Useless eaters' might not turn up much academic material, but 'depopulation' might. What else? 'Forced depopulation'? 'Ideal population'? That should get me started."

Jake felt overwhelmed by the amount of material he

turned up. It was August, and the temperature was in the 90s outside, so instead of going to the gym, Jake spent all of a Sunday morning and part of an afternoon reading. One thing in particular stood out, because it was such a good summary of what he'd been reading. It was a talk, on video, by a scientist at a gathering of environmentalists and futurists in Europe. The speaker's name was Henry Snow. He had lush hair and was impeccably tailored. His attitude was casual, though he had the confident bearing of an aristocrat. He stood at a podium and addressed a big room packed with people.

"I've read all your books. They all end the same way. After twenty-some chapters of gloom and doom, each of you includes the obligatory final chapter in which suddenly you become an optimist, and you write out a prescription for what we each can do to help get the planet out of its predicament."

The audience tittered.

"But that final chapter is all bunk, and all of you know it's bunk. Now, 'bunk,' of course, is not a proper scientific word, but I refer you to my own books for my account of the science, which probably differs very little from yours. If you've read my books, you know that I don't end them with that optimistic final chapter – or I haven't for the last twenty years, at least.

"How then, do we get out of our predicament? I'll briefly describe the best-case scenario. By 'best case,' I mean the best case for the planet and for those who survive. For those who didn't survive – and most wouldn't – we'd have to call it the worst-case scenario.

"This best-case scenario requires an immediate – and by immediate I mean within the next five to ten years – an immediate global population reduction to about 500 million people. Why 500 million? I don't have time to explain that number here, but of course it's in my books. Five hundred million isn't an arbitrary number. It isn't even an optimum number. It's the maximum. When

Rome was at its peak, there were only about 200 million people in the world. The population grew slowly during the Middle Ages, and we hit the 500 million mark probably in the 13th or 14th centuries. No one knows for sure. But we do know that, above the 500 million level, the math related to population growth gets more complicated, and consequently technologies beyond Iron Age technologies are required to sustain the population and provide for continued growth. It was during the age of steam – the beginning of the fossil fuel era, of course – when the planet's population first started to rise significantly above 500 million.

"I just referred to the Iron Age. That's not arbitrary either. Iron Age technology is the only level of technology that is sustainable on this planet. That's technology like the technology of the Roman Empire, and it's a level of technology that was not really exceeded during the Middle Ages, because technologies regressed for centuries after the collapse of Rome. Not until after 1700 did sustained population growth begin, and you all now what was happening then. The Iron Age was over, and the age of fossil fuels was about to begin. Humans were getting interested in powerful new technologies using denser forms of energy, like coal and steam. That's where we've been ever since. As technology, there's no great difference – other than degrees of refinement – between an old steam engine burning coal and a modern automobile engine burning gasoline.

"Now, some of you are not merely optimistic. You've gone beyond being optimistic. You're utopians. Some of you are techno-utopians. Techno-utopians think that new technologies will permit us to continue our love affair with dense forms of energy, though that energy will be less polluting – solar, for example. Techno-utopians think we can continue to support a growing population of seven billion or more. That kind of future would be convenient for us humans, to continue to have so much energy at our disposal, to continue feeding that many mouths, and to continue providing private cars for all those people, even if those cars all ran on solar or something. But it would be disastrous for the Earth, and it could never be sustainable, no matter how long the sun continues to shine. That's because we would continue to reshape the earth with all that energy. The earth's resources and biosphere simply cannot sustain that.

"So there are really two kinds of futures for the Earth. Both those futures are futures in which humanity lives with Iron Age technology – Stone Age if we're not careful. And both of those futures are futures in which there aren't nearly as many of us, no more of us than can be sustained with Iron Age technology and its low energy density of muscle power, with maybe a little wind included for transportation.

"We can get to that future in two different ways. We can do nothing, and we can wait for a global catastrophe to take us back to the Iron Age – or the Stone Age – against our will. That would be an uncontrolled calamity, and there would be all sorts of collateral damage. It would be ugly, and its outcome would be completely unpredictable. The unpredictable outcome of uncontrolled calamity ought to terrify you. If an uncontrolled calamity comes, nothing guarantees any continuity of government or even continuity of culture. The word 'dystopia' is a mild word for where an uncontrolled calamity could lead, with the only surviving law being the law of jungle, with the survivors preying on each other and squandering the few resources that survived the calamity.

"Or we can voluntarily depopulate, and we can voluntarily give up our high-density energy. That will be ugly too, but it might be possible to control it, and the collateral damage would be much less. In this scenario, we can have continuity of government. We can have a predictable outcome. Please don't misunderstand me. This process of voluntary depopulation would be terrible. But it would be much less terrible than the uncontrollable alternative.

"Did I hear a question from the back of the room? Yes, go ahead. The question was, 'How do you make a moral case for that kind of scenario?'"

"I don't know the answer to that, though I think the common-sense case is clear enough. But some of my colleagues have made the point that some of our dominant religions already contain such a moral case. That, of course, is the case of Noah and the ark. Noah's god destroyed most of humanity, in order to save the earth. So at least there's a moral precedent. Even God acknowledges that such a thing might be necessary at times."

The audience tittered again. A member of the audience, a middle-age woman who looked rather angry, stood up and made her way to the nearest microphone.

"If we're making a moral case, let's be careful where we get it. It was our dominant religions that brought us to this. They drove all the gods out of nature and redefined nature as something that contained no god, as something to be exploited. They developed the theology of dominionism, and half the people in my country believe in that crap. It was religion that got us into this mess, so some of us are not really interested in religion's moral cases. Instead, how about a moral case for getting rid of religion?"

There were cheers from scattered members of the audience. Someone asked another question: "Suppose you did get the population down to 500 million. How do you keep the world from falling back into the same old pattern of fossil-fuel energy, assuming there's any left, and falling back into a pattern of unsustainable population growth?"

"That's where utopian thinking is useful, I think," Henry said. "In a controlled reduction of population, with continuity of government, you take the necessary steps to see that it doesn't happen again."

Now the audience broke out laughing. Someone shouted, "That sounds more like totalitarianism that utopianism!"

"Yes it does," said Henry Snow. "It's pretty clear that neither the market nor democracy can provide that kind of utopia. Would anyone care to make the moral case for totalitarianism?"

"A new religion!" someone shouted.

"Or that," said Henry. "That could work, too."

Henry was smiling, though clearly he was serious, and again the audience was laughing. There was another question:

"What about a scenario in which we reduce the population slowly, and much more humanely, and try for a soft landing?"

"That's a wonderful idea," said Henry Snow. "We should have tried it fifty years ago. But now there isn't enough time, not nearly enough time."

Jake was getting hungry, so he left the library and walked across campus toward the row of restaurants that lay on the other side of the rotunda. When he crossed the street, he was in front of a church. Someone was playing the organ. Jake went up the steps and tried the front door. It was open. What the heck. It would be cool inside. The church was empty, but Jake caught a glimpse of someone behind the organ console. Someone was practicing, no doubt? Jake quietly took a seat in a back pew.

Jake knew a little about music. He'd taken piano lessons for a few years when he was a boy, but finally his parents had let him quit. His parents had taken him to lots of concerts, but never to an organ recital. So though Jake had listened to a good bit of classical music, he knew little about the musical literature for the organ. He did suspect, though, that the piece the organist was practicing was by J.S. Bach. He had played some easy Bach on the piano and actually had been intrigued by the form of harmony that his teacher called counterpoint. In counterpoint, nothing stood still. Everything was moving. There wasn't just one melody, there were several. The music and the harmony are kind of woven together in a complicated, moving pattern, like a Celtic knot. It took a lot of mental exertion to follow the motion of all the threads of the music. To do it on the organ must take not only mental exertion, but also physical exertion, because the feet had to play all the lowest notes, and Jake knew that the lowest note is always critical to the harmony.

The organist was trying to get through a particularly gnarly and dramatic section of the music. He'd start, move along nicely for a while, then blunder. He'd start again. Sometimes he'd play the pedal part alone, then put it all back together and try again. Again he blundered and stopped, and Jake knew from the sound, though he couldn't see the organist or the keyboards from where he was sitting, that the organist had brought his fists and forearms down on the console to create a mighty discord, expressing his frustration. Then the organist peeked around the side of the console. Apparently he had noticed that he had a listener.

"Don't just sit there!" the organist shouted from the front of the building. "Help me!"

"I'm afraid I can't help you," Jake shouted back.

"Yes you can. You can turn pages."

Jake took that as an invitation to go up to the console, which pleased him, because he was curious. Lugging his stack of books, he walked to the front and stepped up onto the platform that supported the pulpit, the altar, the seating for the choir, and the organ console.

"Hi, I'm Jake."

"I'm Martin. Do you read music?"

"A little. I'm rusty."

"Great. I'll start here." Martin pointed to the music. "You turn the page about two beats ahead of me. OK?"

"Sure."

Martin started again. Jake's presence, not to mention his page-turning, must have had a beneficial effect, because this time Martin got all the way to the end of the piece with only a few minor blunders, none of which was bad enough to cause him to stall.

"That was a little better," said Martin. "Thank you."

"You're welcome."

"From the beginning. Here we go."

Jake had never watched an organist at work. It was impressive, even intimidating. Martin was wearing shorts and a T-shirt. On his feet there were only tennis socks. He was lean and muscular, with strong, athletic legs. Something about him reminded Jake of Jamie. Isn't it sad, thought Jake, that the gay boys who're always screwing up in gym class, who seem to be complete klutzes when it comes to sports, secretly play the organ. Their skill and coordination is as good as the best of athletes, and yet they get nothing but grief and are treated like outcasts. No wonder they take refuge in music. The tradeoff is probably a good one, because what they missed out on in high school doesn't amount to much in the long run. And organ-playing is an extraordinary skill, as any athlete can see.

"You're good!" said Martin. "We're making progress. One more time, and when I get to this part … here … do me a favor and pull these two knobs, here and here."

"OK," said Jake. "I can do that."

Two pages into the piece, Jake pulled the knobs as instructed. The sound of the organ increased threefold. Jake could feel it in his chest. It was breathtaking. The score took a lot of organ breath too – an endless run of sixteenth notes that hardly ever changed to eighth notes. The pedal part was a little less busy, but not much. Jake was pretty sure he could feel a draft from the direction of the organ chamber, as the organ's strong lungs inhaled and blew, inhaled and blew, in response to Martin's instructions. Martin sat surprisingly still as he played, his motion as efficient as an athlete's, no drama, no histrionics, no attempts to make it look hard, which it certainly was. Though Jake sensed that Martin enjoyed his closeness, while he was playing he was focused only on the music. The piece ended with a colossal minor chord. Jake had been right. It was Bach.

"Very good, Martin," said Jake.

"Thank you. Are you a student?"

"No. I just came to the library."

"To the library, and you're not a student? There are so many other things that you could be doing."

"I'm a nerd," said Jake.

"So am I."

"Let's see, let me think of something nerdy to say. Does this organ have a thirty-two foot stop?"

"Wow. You are a nerd. No, it's not that big an organ. We've got some nice sixteen-foot reeds in the pedal, but that's it. When you pulled those drawknobs there, on page three, you were adding those sixteen-foot reeds, among other things."

"Amazing footwork," said Jake. "You'd be good at soccer."

"I am good at soccer. Too hot for that today, though. It's much cooler in here."

Jake pointed to an extravagant vase of flowers on top of the organ.

"Do you always have roses like that when you practice?"

"No. They're left over from a wedding they had in here yesterday." Martin stood up, on the pedals. There was a low, booming, reedy discord from the organ. Martin took one of the roses and handed it to Jake.

"Here. Have one. They'll just go to waste."

"Wow. Thanks. No one ever gives me flowers."

"That's a pity." Martin lowered his eyes. His taste was much too refined to push the flirting any further. And Jake didn't want to tease him, or lead him on. That would be cruel. Neither of them spoke. There was the faint sound of moving air. Jake wasn't sure whether it was the air conditioning or the organ blower.

"Thanks for the concert," said Jake. "I'd better be going."

"Thanks for turning pages," said Martin. "I can see you're experienced at turning pages." Martin pointed to Jake's stack of books, which Jake had left on the floor beside the organ bench.

"I've got a lot of reading to do."

"I see you do. And pretty heavy reading at that, from the looks of some of the titles. Stop by again sometime if you're at the library. I'm often here on Sunday afternoons."

"Thanks," said Jake. "I might do that. Your pages make for much more interesting turning than mine."

Jake blushed. Was that a Freudian slip? Had he just popped out with an accidental, disguised, flirtatious compliment for this deserving but probably lonely young man? What was it about straight guys that made them tease gay guys like that? Jake glanced at Martin to make sure that Martin hadn't taken it wrong. Jake was pretty sure that the look on Martin's handsome face was a kind of sadness, a resignation, a letting go. It was because Martin knew that he would never see Jake again.

"Bye," said Martin, with a warm but weak smile that Jake understood perfectly. The smile meant that Martin wished there could be more, but he understood.

"Later," said Jake. "Thanks again."

Jake did not look back, but the organ was silent as he left the church. He knew that Martin was watching him.

Jake stepped outside, and the wave of grief for Jamie hit him harder than the suffocating August heat. Why did gay boys always have to be so charming, so sweet, so damned lovable? And yet I wouldn't know how to give them what they want. It could only lead to breaking his heart. In a better world, there ought to be a way.

From the organ came the sound of a quiet but majestic hymn. It had been a long time since Jake had been to Jamie's grave. Why not? He even had a rose to leave there.

CHAPTER 6

Summer wore down Jake's defenses, as he knew it would. His thoughts and daydreams increasingly tested his weaknesses and tempted him back into refining the guy-seeks-girl game. To be honest with himself, he had to admit that he actually was plotting, approaching the problem like a nerd. What strategy would hold the best chance of success and quality with lowest commitment, the lowest price to be paid? He even thought about a period of bottom feeding – just hitting the bars periodically and getting by with a series of girls whose phone numbers he would lose. But eventually he decided on his usual strategy – a change of gym. By adding a few miles of extra driving to his gym days, he could go to a gym that had a new assortment of hot girls and good odds, and maybe end up with a girl who might be worth keeping for a while before he had to repeat the cycle. He'd be patient like a fisherman, give it time, play it smart.

So, Jake, is the plan all clear? You'll make no sudden moves, blow your cover, and get yourself mowed down. Be patient. Aim high, and don't settle for less than you deserve. Let the girls do the work. Refine your shy-boy routine. Don't try to talk your way into it. Be coy, make use of those eyes of yours, especially during those all-important first encounters. If you move too fast, or set your sights too low, or don't pay attention to quality, then it won't last a month, and you'll have to start all over again. But if you get it right, you'll be set for a while. Of course, the longer it lasts and the better the rewards, the farther you have to fall, and the longer you have to mope, when the inevitable happens. Or maybe you'll wake up and realize that she's raised the price of everything to more than she's worth and more than you can pay. That is, she starts demanding commitment. But that's the risk you always run with the ladyfolk. They're trying to play the game just as smart as you are, except that they have their own rules, and they're playing for a different endgame.

It took almost a month for Jake's patient strategy to pay off. She made the first move, according to plan. She seemed to be on the same gym schedule – or she had figured out his – and after a week and a half of drawing Jake into little chats, she had invited him to lunch, which went OK, and he reciprocated by inviting her to dinner.

She worked for the foundation that operates Monticello. She had a love of architecture and a certain familiarity with American architectural history. She had an artsy flair. She loved to take photographs and paint in watercolor. She thought Jake's drawings were "precious." Lots of her friends were artists, and most of her social life seemed to have to do with artsy circles. Jake thought this was promising, since it implied that she was not as materialistic as many girls are and had different ideas about what constituted merit and social status. She was tallish and naturally lean, had great hair, which was cut in a kind of timeless, classic style, and she seemed to have good taste in most things. Her name was Alexandra. Her friends called her Al. She had grown up in Washington. She had a certain sense of entitlement, a risk to watch out for. Al's mother apparently had a lot of power. She had some sort of high muckety-muck position in the State Department or something. Al was vague about that.

After the third date, she invited Jake into her apartment, and that made it official: Jake now had a girlfriend again. The few weeks that immediately followed the thrill of making it official was always one of the most bittersweet parts of a relationship. Sweet, because you were getting laid again. Bitter, because it's when you found out what the price was going to be now that you'd had your free sample. Alexandra's price was high, but it was about what Jake had estimated. He would be expected to attend art openings with her. He would be expected to be in attendance with her at least a couple of times a month for gatherings of her social set – mostly her girlfriends – to be displayed and to be exercised and trained in the social duties of being the boyfriend. He was forewarned that he would need more blacks in his wardrobe by fall. Meeting the parents in Washington did not seem to be on her radar screen at the moment. For that Jake was grateful and optimistic, because he knew that when a girl gets to that stage of her strategy, the price of what he was already getting was about to go way up, and that it would be more than he could pay. He was much too young for the commitment thing, had far too much exploring to do. Girls his age are too young for that too. Why is it that they're always in the market for something "serious," even though hardly anybody these days gets married until close to thirty or even later.

But Jake never puzzled too long or too hard about these mysteries. He just assumed that that's the way females are wired and that there's nothing that can be done about it. He'd heard some guys sing the praises of older women, young divorcées, maybe, who wouldn't demand so much, who'd offer a roll in the hay – or even ongoing rolls in the hay – without wanting to get a guy under contract. Maybe the goods weren't as fresh, but they were free (and experienced), leaving a guy unencumbered to enjoy his precious youth, writing his own script, playing his own role rather than the eternal, unvarying, domesticated, pathetically common role that all of society – especially feminine society – would ultimately compel him to play when he was too old or too tired to fight it anymore. And depending on how much money he was making, eventually age would depress his bargaining power. But for the time being, he could probably look forward to six to twelve months of a reasonable deal with Alexandra before she upped the price, a deal that he hoped would leave him with enough of himself left over to be young, to do a few of the things he wanted to do, to try to figure out some of the hard things about life, and about the state of the world, that really needed to be figured out.

As for figuring out the state of the world, Jake could not shake the feeling that, ever since the day back in May when he'd met Phaedrus, he was up against the dark borders of a mystery that might be important. If he let his imagination run – and it sometimes did run to some pretty dark places – then "important" might be too mild a word. "All important," might be better, or "life or death." Jake just couldn't get it out of his head that Phaedrus, that eccentric but brilliant old man living like a hermit or a monk up in the mountains, knew something that he couldn't talk about – or something that he didn't know Jake well enough to talk about. And why was Phaedrus' place so oddly equipped, and in a way so oddly similar to the way the rich senator's place was equipped? How serious, or how imminent, would a threat have to be to justify that kind of preparation and precaution? If you're rich, like the senator, maybe you can afford to be prepared for all sorts of things that aren't likely to happen. But Phaedrus wasn't rich, and it appeared that pretty much all his resources were focused on preparation – redundant preparation, even – for some sort of dark event.

Jake began to understand why some people are so attracted to conspiracy theories. No doubt, in many cases and probably most cases, there was a touch of craziness involved – fear or even paranoia. And in other cases, no doubt, conspiracy theories were colored – or discolored – by a person's ideological or psychological biases. But what happens if a rational, skeptical, but deeply curious person sees certain evidence that something really is going on? The evidence will be incomplete, of course. And one is working against opposing forces that are actively trying to keep something secret or to disguise the truth about what is really going on. Under such circumstances, one has no choice but to try to connect the dots. Suddenly that metaphor of connecting the dots seemed very apt. And Jake also realized that this is exactly the kind of work that spies and intelligence services do. They try to gather and verify as much information as they can – information that someone doesn't want them to have. Then they try to connect the dots and build a picture, as accurate as possible, about the significance of what is being hidden from them.

Jake recalled what Phaedrus had said about trying to decode secret signals that could be heard on the radio. He had used the term "open source" to refer to information that is available to anyone and which might be useful for the analysis of intelligence. He had mentioned how radio was used for propaganda.

Jake began to see how most people know only what someone wants them to know. Maybe everything that is put out as "news" isn't necessarily propaganda, but it's still stuff that powerful interests want people to know about.

And so, if governments find spies and intelligence analysts so important to their operation, where did that leave ordinary people? While searching the Internet for concepts that might be useful for this kind of thinking, Jake came across something an old newspaperman had said back in 1976. He had said, "Newspapers are an intelligence service for the common man." Jake knew that that was no longer true, even if it ever was true. Back when newspapers still had real power, there was a saying "Never argue with a man who buys ink by the barrel." But today, newspapers no longer matter very much, and such a saying sounds almost like a joke. Jake was smart enough to know that what is passed off as "news" on television and cable has almost no value. It was at best "infotainment," or even a deliberate attempt to mislead and distract people.

So where did that leave the common man who wants to know what is really going on in the world? That, Jake realized, is a serious problem with no easy answer. And it was a whole new way of thinking about the idea of conspiracy theories. If something secret and nefarious really was going on, then, almost by definition, any person who tried to connect the dots was a conspiracy theorist.

Were there still people in the world who acted as spies or intelligence analysts for ordinary people? Whistle blowers, and those who leak government secrets, would certainly be in that category. But as soon as they're caught, their spy career is over. Their access to secret information is cut off. Upon reflecting on this, Jake realized that, if there really are people who have an ongoing mission of spying for the common people, then they have to fly below the radar. That means that a limited number of people have access to what they've learned through their spying and how the dots connect. It has to be kept within small circles, else they would quickly be shut down, and their access to information would be cut off. That's why, Jake realized, spies become useless if their cover is blown.

And Jake realized that, if he had ever in his life met one of these spies for the common people, it was Phaedrus. He fit the profile perfectly: smart, nosy, well connected, discreet, motivated. Increasingly Jake was confident that he wasn't just being paranoid, and that Phaedrus wasn't just an eccentric old man. It seemed pretty possible – probable even – that there might really be something going on and that Jake had connected one or two of the dots. Am I brave enough – or stupid enough, or smart enough – thought Jake, to try to connect more of those dots? And what about that black triangle? Had he really seen such a thing? There were no other witnesses. No one would believe him. He had not mentioned it to anyone. And if the black triangle was real, was it just a coincidence that he had seen it where he had seen it? Or did it somehow fit into the larger mystery? Sometimes Jake felt like Sherlock Holmes. Sometimes he felt like an idiot.

Jake made a list of the dots he had gathered. Using the list, he tried to pretend that he was an intelligence analyst trying to make sense of an incomplete set of data. Some of the dots came from Phaedrus, the others came from his visit to the senator's private compound up in the mountains and some of the things that Mike Marshall, the senator's engineer, had said. Jake tried to list not only possible points of fact, but also principles to keep in mind that might be useful in interpreting what little information he had. He suspected that he was reinventing the wheel, that real spies and intelligence analysts had pretty standard methods of doing this kind of work. That might be worth some research, he thought – spy techniques – but for now he'd approach the problem as best he could, by simply trying to be rational, skeptical, and as scientific as possible.

First Jake listed the guiding principles:

1. The principle of elite secrecy. Phaedrus told a story about how a Korean 747 was shot down by the Russians over Russian air space, where the plane was not supposed to be. Russia said one thing; the United States said another. The public never knew the truth. It seems highly likely that only a few well-placed individuals in both governments knew the full, true story. The principle is that governments, and elites, can and do keep secrets and that the common people normally have no

means whatsoever of getting at the truth.

2. Sources of information. First, there is spying. My good luck in being able to visit a powerful senator's secret compound was a form of spying. Second, there is eavesdropping. Phaedrus spoke of the possibility of listening to, and decrypting, radio transmissions that we were not meant to hear. That would be eavesdropping. Third, there is information passed on by knowledgeable parties who can be trusted. If Phaedrus shared some of what he knows with me, that would be this type of information. Mike Marshall, the engineer, also knew important details about the senator's secret compound. If he had told me those details, that would be this type of information. Fourth, there is what Phaedrus called "open source" information. This is information available to everyone – from newspapers, for example – that may reveal little on its own but which may help connect the dots when combined with information gotten from other sources. Fifth, there is background information. Background information could never be too broad or too deep, because other forms of intelligence cannot be reliably interpreted without broad knowledge and expertise. For example, the 747 incident could not be interpreted without an understanding of how navigation systems work. The significance of Faraday cages cannot be interpreted without knowledge of what Faraday cages are useful for. The significance of radiation shielding cannot be interpreted without an understanding of what the potential (or expected?) sources of the radiation are.

3. The principle of propaganda and disinformation. Phaedrus mentioned that much of what can still be heard on the radio is propaganda. Clearly, much of what is presented as news actually is propaganda. In the 747 incident, both the American and the Russian governments were almost certainly lying in what they told the public. It is, therefore, necessary to be skeptical of everything we're told. It also is necessary to keep in mind that infor-

mation captured in spying operations could be planted, to intentionally mislead anyone who is investigating.

4. The principle of redundancy. If lives and property are at stake, elites require redundancy. Redundancy was a big deal to Phaedrus. Redundancy probably would make the job of a spy or an intelligence analyst easier, because redundancy creates more things to detect. But redundancy might also create ambiguity: Has one found the target, or only a backup, or a decoy?

Then Jake tried to list what he knew about the mystery at hand:

1. Though Phaedrus would not say why, everything that was strange about his place had to do with two factors: protection against radiation, and long-distance communication using his own infrastructure. He didn't even seem to have a telephone, and he certainly didn't have the Internet. But he had radios, with systems for both transmitting and receiving. These radios had the ability to encrypt and decrypt. They were redundant, and they were solar-powered.

2. Phaedrus was interested in breaking through the secrecy of others (as in decrypting radio signal), and he himself was secretive. He would not tell me what his secrets are. Even his remote location implies a need for secrecy.

3. Whatever danger Phaedrus is concerned about is serious enough to effect him where he is, remote or not. That trap door probably led to some sort of radiation shelter. He does not seem to be hardened against bombs, only against radiation.

4. Phaedrus clearly was using his radios to communicate with someone. That person might be far away. He implied that this communication was coded. It is unlikely that Phaedrus would have such a stealthy and redundant system unless he was receiving high-value information from it. Phaedrus did not reveal the location of that person, but Jake realized that, had he been

attentive enough to ask, or to remember the radio call sign he saw on the printout, then the approximate location, or at least the nationality, of that person would be known. It seems likely that this person has some sort of insider knowledge. Was it also possible that Phaedrus might have access to inside information that he could transmit and share?

5. The rich senator was upgrading his secret compound to make it resemble Phaedrus' place in important ways. The only difference, really, is scale. The senator's place is built for multiple people, with many luxuries. Phaedrus' place accommodates one person and a dog, with no luxuries.

6. The rich senator presumably is close to the very center of American power, including military power. He too sees a need for hardened communication systems, but surely it can be assumed that the senator is an insider and that Phaedrus most likely is an outsider. The senator knows what he knows because he's in on it. Phaedrus knows what he knows because he's spying on them, or getting information from someone who is spying on them. Therefore Phaedrus probably knows much less than the senator knows.

7. The one essential difference between Phaedrus' place and the senator's place is that the senator has an important need for transportation, while Phaedrus puts very little emphasis on transportation. Didn't Phaedrus have a vehicle in one of those outbuildings? Surely he does, though it was not visible. But the senator has a helipad.

8. Whatever the senator is involved in involves the military. That was a military helicopter that arrived in the middle of the night.

9. Though very little information is available on the time line for whatever is happening or is about to happen, the senator's project is a rush job. Phaedrus would only say that he believed that bad things are going to happen

and that information on those bad things is difficult to get. If Phaedrus knows anything about the time line, he didn't say anything about it. Still, Phaedrus clearly liked me, and clearly his invitation to come back any time was sincere. He had not said, "Come back in less than three months or it will be too late." Tentatively, the time line looks like more than four months but less than a year.

10. Does the black triangle have anything to do with all this? Or is an alien spaceship over the senator's compound just a coincidence and a red herring?

Having summarized what little he knew, Jake also thought about a scheme for increasing his portfolio of knowledge. It would mean doing more research so that he'd have more background knowledge against which to analyze his intelligence. He'd need to find out everything he could about the rich senator. He'd need to read up on the effects of electromagnetic bursts and what sort of forces produce them. He'd need to read up on radiation shelters for human beings and what kind of forces produce dangerous radiation. In particular, he needed to understand what kind of force produces both electromagnetic bursts – which damages electrical gear but is not really dangerous to human beings – and the kind of radiation (ionizing radiation, as in radioactive fallout) that can kill human beings unless they have shelter. He needed to know more about radio communication, in particular how radio signals can travel long distances. He needed to pay attention to political events to see if there was any freely available open source information that might help connect the dots. He needed to be alert to possible disinformation and distraction.

And, most of all, he needed to see Phaedrus again. It would be difficult, because of Jake's work load and his need to make money, to make a trip to Phaedrus' place before October. The new girlfriend had increased his need for spending money. But that gave him more than two months to do some homework. The next time he saw Phaedrus, he'd be much better equipped to get information out of him. And he'd be much better equipped to figure out whether Phaedrus is a genius and a spy or just an eccentric old man. Or something in between.

Jake was cooperative – occasionally even enthusiastic – in paying the price that Alexandra demanded. There was an August art event having to do with *plein air* painting. At least once a week there was a gathering of her friends at a local bar and restaurant. There seemed to be regular gatherings on Sunday afternoons at the place of one girlfriend or another. They were all extraverts, every last one them, including Alexandra. Jake endured regular teasing about being "quiet," or even "shy." He'd try to find a quiet seat away from the center of social action when he could, but Alexandra had a tendency to come and squeeze in beside him, resting a hand on his leg or putting her hand behind his head and ruffling the back of his hair, things she rarely did when they were alone. Jake would participate in the small talk as best he could, would try to laugh when everyone else laughed, would occasionally even insert a brief witty comment if something occurred to him and his mind wasn't wandering too much. But mostly he was bored. But that was a price that a boyfriend had to pay. Nooky is never free.

In September, the concert season started. Jake asked Alexandra if she'd go with him to an organ recital. The recital was to be on a Skinner organ built in 1906, though the organ had been restored.

"Organ concert?" she said. The look on her face was sour, as though he'd asked her to help him shuck oysters.

"Sure," Jake said. "I've never been to an organ concert. It's something I'd like to know more about. From what little I do know, organs and organ music are kind of neat."

"I didn't know you were interested in things like that.

It's kind of passé, don't you think? Nobody listens to organs anymore. Even churches are getting rid of them. Isn't there something else you'd rather do?"

"But Alexandra, this is one of the few times I've ever asked you to go somewhere with me. I've done lots of things that you wanted to do. I thought you like art. Isn't organ music art?"

"OK. You got me there. Have you always been into organ music? Or is it something new?"

"It's something new," I guess. "Phaedrus has one. It's huge. But he's off the grid now, and so there's no electricity to play it. I thought it was interesting. They're beautiful machines, really, very complicated. He told me some interesting things about how they work."

"You're such an antique lover, Jake. Anyway, can I think about it? Sarah's cookout is that same Sunday afternoon. She'd kill me if we don't go."

"If you want to go to Sarah's cookout, that's OK. I can go to the organ concert by myself."

"But Sarah …"

"Sarah has lots of friends."

"But what about…. Anyway, never mind. Let me think about it."

A week later, when the plans were settled and their calendars sync'ed, Jake scolded himself for not just going to the organ concert alone. For several weeks, Alexandra had been lobbying him about going with her to Washington in early October for the wedding of a college roommate. It was to be a rich girl's fairy tale wedding, with full costumes. Alexandra would go to the organ recital, but Jake would have to go to the wedding. Alexandra kindly offered to help him plan his wardrobe.

In the nooky department, Jake supposed that he was getting as much value for his investment as he ever did, though the adventure he'd hoped for, the kid-in-a-candy-store experiences that he'd been imagining, had not happened. Alexandra's passions seemed to lie outside the bedroom, and though she was good when she was in the right kind of mood, she also had a tendency to be stingy at times. But that was not unusual. What guy ever gets everything he hopes for? But Alexandra probably wasn't getting everything she hoped for either. Fair is fair.

—▶ ◀—

Early fall was a busy time, and not at all disagreeable. Jake had a new girlfriend, even if she wasn't the girl of his dreams. He had some compelling new interests, and he was onto something that he thought might even be important. The ominousness of what he was onto added a bit of thrill and mystery, he had to admit. He also was not sure whether he really took it all seriously or whether he was just letting his imagination run free, as an alternative to boredom. Of course he couldn't mention his mystery to anyone, including Alexandra. She'd think he was crazy. He had told her a little about Phaedrus – superficial things – but the mysterious parts were more than she'd be able to understand or handle. And so Jake continued his research in private, in the little free time he had left after making a living and keeping up with girlfriend maintenance.

What he learned about the rich senator didn't surprise him. It was pretty much what Jake expected. The guy had been in office for more than 15 years. He was rich, probably a billionaire, and his family had financial interests in energy, banking, big agriculture, and high tech. There had been a brief conflict-of-interest scandal a few years ago about his financial stake in a big defense contractor. One of his grandsons had once gotten arrested on some sort of date-rape charge. But there seemed to be no more dirt on him than the average senator. He was on committees having to do with banking, defense, and foreign policy. He did a lot of foreign travel, sometimes at taxpayer expense if it tied in with his senatorial responsibilities, and sometimes paying his own way. He was said to be friends with a couple of heads of state, and he seemed to attend lots of high-level "retreats" in foreign capitals or at the gathering places of the global elite. Jake read as much about the senator as he could find, even if it seemed to have no immediate bearing on the mystery at hand.

As for the massive and dangerous bursts of electromagnetic energy, the Internet was full of talk about that, much of it coming from people who identified as "survivalists." The science of these electromagnetic bursts was pretty straightforward. The bursts would induce electrical currents – potentially strong electrical currents – in wiring and in any kind of electrical device. If the induced current was strong enough, then the device would be damaged or destroyed. There are, as Jake already knew, two kinds of events that produce these bursts – one natural, the other man-made. The sun can cause it, and it has happened before. The most powerful event on record was the Carrington Event, which occurred in 1859. The world was much less dependent on electricity and wiring then, but telegraph systems all over the world failed, and telegraph operators got electrical shocks from the induced currents in the wires. The Carrington Event was caused by an enormous solar storm with a "coronal mass ejection" from the sun that hit the earth's magnetosphere. In the man-made department, an electromagnetic pulse also is a byproduct of a nuclear explosion. Such a man-made event would have an effect similar to the Carrington Event, though on a smaller scale. Jake found that there are even nuclear weapons designed to inflict their maximum damage from an electromagnetic pulse. These weapons are designed to detonate high in the atmosphere, allowing the pulse to cause damage anywhere in its line of sight. It is possible to protect electrical equipment from electromagnetic pulses by completely enclosing the equipment inside a metal box or screen.

Jake also read books and articles on surviving the radioactive fallout that occurs after a nuclear explosion. He found a rich literature on this, because, during the Cold War, the American government actually encouraged people to build fallout shelters, and the government maintained a system of public fallout shelters stocked with food and water. During the Cold War, and probably today as well, the government maintained well-equipped shelters for high-ranking government and military officials. As with electromagnetic bursts, the science is straightforward. A nuclear explosion vaporizes large quantities of matter, and this matter becomes radioactive. This radioactive matter is carried by the atmosphere and gradually falls to the ground. At first this fallout is intensely radioactive, but luckily fallout radiation loses its intensity pretty rapidly. Two weeks inside a shelter probably would be sufficient. The shelter must have the right kind of shielding – three feet of earth or the equivalent. Obviously it must have provisions for air and sanitation. It also must be stocked with food and water.

Jake found the science of radio signal propagation to be a good bit more complicated. Most of the helpful literature on this was from amateur radio operators. Jake came to the conclusion that it would be nearly impossible to master this subject merely from reading. Rather, it seemed to be all about knowledge combined with experience. But if you boiled it down, some generalizations could be made. How far radio signals will travel depends on the frequency. Signals at certain frequencies, the so-called "short wave" frequencies, could potentially travel thousands of miles. But it depended on many factors – the time of day or night, the time of year, and conditions in the earth's upper atmosphere. Conditions in the earth's atmosphere, both for better or for worse, were closely related to the activity of the sun. It also depended on how much transmitter power was used, the quality of the antennas on the sending and receiving end, and the quality of the receiver. It also depended on how the radio signal was "modulated." Phaedrus had mentioned digital forms of modulation handled by computers, using low transmitter power, with data sent at a very slow rate and with protocols for detecting and correcting errors in the data. Some of this was very clever and even seemed to be fairly new technology. But this much was clear: If atmospheric conditions were fairly normal, then an experienced radio operator who wanted to send a signal to someone a few thousand miles away probably would be able to do that. It probably was not possible to do continuously, but if you chose an appropriate frequency for the time of day, then at some point during a 24-hour period you'd have an excellent chance of success. And fortunately, Jake found that there is a symmetry to radio propagation. If someone can hear you, then odds are very good that if they transmit back on the same frequency, you'll also hear them.

But the part of his research that Jake found most disturbing was the aftermath of man-made events that could cause electromagnetic pulses and kill people with radiation. It depended on how localized the destruction was. If only a small area was affected, then the rest of the world might carry on pretty well. But if it was widespread, there would be cascading consequences that could even effect the entire planet. This was another area that "survivalists" as well as scientists had written about extensively. The electrical grid would almost certainly go down, and problems with the electrical grid had a tendency to spread like dominoes over a large area. Communications systems would go down. Even if the situation otherwise returned to normal, it might take a long time to repair the electrical grid – months, maybe longer, not least because there were very few spare parts for repair. Without electricity and communication, money would stop flowing, except for what people happened to have in their pockets. Transportation would be severely crippled. The grocery stores would soon be empty. Water systems and sewer systems would stop working. People would suddenly find themselves in the Dark Ages.

And then Jake thought about Phaedrus' setup there on his little mountaintop. The electrical grid going down wouldn't effect Phaedrus much, because Phaedrus was already off the grid and had some solar power. Phaedrus had his own communications systems that operated off of solar power. Jake was pretty sure that Phaedrus had a fallout shelter. Did Phaedrus have stores of food and water? Jake guessed that he did, and, if so, that was not the sort of thing that he would keep in plain sight. Jake guessed that Phaedrus also had seeds and a plan for getting back into production if something bad happened.

It all made sense, and it all fit together. Jake chuckled, though, when he thought of a flaw in Phaedrus' plan. There was only one Phaedrus. He was not redundant.

There was one other important part of Jake's reading. He even already had a copy of the reading material, though he had never read it. That was a volume of Plato, containing the dialogue from which Phaedrus had gotten his name. What a peculiar name to pick for a child, Jake thought, even for a professor of the classics.

Jake read Plato's "The Phaedrus" dialogue.

■▶ ◀

Almost from the beginning of the organ concert, Jake could see that Alexandra was having to exercise considerable control to keep from squirming. But Jake was intrigued, particularly by the Bach fugues that started the program. He had done some reading on fugue form and had listened to a few recordings, but never before had he heard a fugue played live. The sheer intelligence of it was humbling. How could a composer take four separate and independent lines of melody and weave them together with such cleverness and complexity? Nothing ever stopped moving, including the harmony. It was completely unlike a song or a ballad, in which the melody rests atop an accompaniment that provides the harmony. Each of the four voices accompanied the other voices in a rapidly moving chase. Jake knew that the organists' two hands were playing the upper three melodies (or "voices," as they are called in a fugue), and that the feet were playing the lowest voice. Jake knew that the word "fugue" had a second, nonmusical meaning. It was used to describe a kind of disturbed mental state in which a person was doing something that appeared to be under conscious control, but the person actually was not conscious of what he was doing, or at least was later unable to recall what he was doing. Actually playing a fugue must feel a bit like that, Jake thought, because the organist couldn't possibly think fast enough to consciously play something so complex. It must require long training and considerable talent to perform such a feat. It was breathtaking.

And speaking of breathtaking, Jake realized that he was at times holding his breath, and at other times he had a tendency to hyperventilate. He became conscious of this because he didn't want Alexandra, or anyone nearby, to think that he was breathing strangely. He quickly realized that he was somehow feeling a tendency to breath in sympathy with the organ, as though it had lungs, and as though it became breathless at times and needed to catch its breath. It was clear to Jake why someone with Phaedrus' intelligence was drawn to an instrument like the organ. Jake thought that, rather than calling the organ the king of instruments, the *nerd* of instruments might be more descriptive. Though the violin, for example, contains centuries of evolution and may be a work of art, the organ is almost outrageously complex and might weigh many tons. Jake knew from his reading that, these days, digital systems had made the control mechanisms inside of organs a great deal lighter and easier to maintain. But the wonder was what organ builders were able to do with mechanical systems centuries ago. Jake knew that the organ he was now listening to was over a hundred years old. He wondered if any of the control systems were now digital.

The organist ended the first half of the program with a piece called a passacaglia. Jake did not know what the technicalities of passacaglia form might be. He made a mental note to read up on that. But the piece was slow, poignant, and very, very contemplative – Bach's high intelligence in a very different mood from the mood of the fast-moving fugues.

When intermission started, and Jake and Alexandra filed with the rest of the audience toward the lobby, Jake could tell from the look on Alexandra's face that something unpleasant awaited him in the lobby. She wasted no time.

"That was boring," she said. At least she said it very quietly. "You've heard enough, haven't you? We don't need to stay for the second half?"

"I really enjoyed it," said Jake, looking not toward Alexandra but through the auditorium toward the organ, where the organist, an attractive middle-aged woman, was shaking hands and chatting with members of the audience. A few people had approached the organ console and were looking it over, though they kept a respectful distance and didn't touch it.

Jake reflected for a moment and decided that it was best to let her have her way. She smiled at him in a certain beaming, seductive way that Jake didn't recall having seen very often since their first chats at the gym.

"It's still not too late to get to Sarah's cookout," she said. Jake suppressed his reaction, smiled weakly, and gestured toward the exit. Jake was pretty sure that she was a little more giving than usual in their bedroom activities that evening. Perhaps she had remembered that she had not entirely honored the deal they made about his going to the wedding in Washington.

—▶ ◀—

October came. The wedding was everything that Jake had feared it would be. What girl doesn't want her wedding to be like a fairy tale – she a princess, her groom a prince. This bride had taken the fantasy a little farther than usual. She had designed her wedding around the cult film "Princess Bride." The bride and all of her attendants, male and female, were more in costume than in wedding attire. The best man was in the costume of Inigo Montoya, complete with sword. The groom was tall and blond, though not nearly as handsome as Cary Elwes. His shirt was laced with a string, and he wore leggings and a tunic. The church was large and lavishly supplied with flowers. The wedding clearly had cost a fortune. And how could all these young people packed into the church afford to fly in from all over the country for this? There was quite a grand organ in the front of the church, but it was not played. Instead, the music was recorded and played through a sound system – fairy tale music, plus lush, sentimental strings, and some pop songs. Jake had to admit that it was pretty amusing, and Alexandra thought it was fabulous. But Jake was eager for it all to be over so that they could get to their hotel room. He was expecting Alexandra to be more amorous than usual tonight. She owed him for this, and attending weddings was a powerful aphrodisiac for young women. Plus the hotel room had cost a fortune. Jake hoped to get as much value as possible out of his considerable expenses. At least it was only a hop and a skip to Washington from Charlottesville. He hadn't had to spend vacation time and fly in from Seattle, like some of the guests.

Jake was right. Alexandra was all over him when they got back to the hotel room.

"What's got into you?" he said, as she sat astride him on the bed, unbuttoning his shirt.

"What do you mean? Nothing's got into me. But you just looked so *good* today at the wedding. I was so proud to be seen with you. Of all Amber's friends and their husbands and boyfriends, you were the hottest. You even behaved. I didn't hear a single groan out of you."

"Maybe I was amused."

"You devil. You did laugh a few times, now that I think about it. What was so funny?"

"Oh, I guess it reminded me of 'Princess Bride.'"

"The best movie ever made."

Now Alexandra was unfastening Jake's belt. Jake emitted an involuntary little gasp when he realized what she was going to do. This would be only the second time she had ever done it. But first she teased him, complimented him on the hardness of his pecs, on the tightness of his abs, on the cuteness of his little belly button.

"This is called a happy trail, isn't it?" she said.

"I'm happy. I'm happy," Jake said.

And then suddenly there was a shrill electronic sound like a tiny siren, coming from across the room.

"What the hell?" said Jake, startled, rising up onto his elbows. Alexandra was climbing off him.

"Don't worry about it," she said. "It's nothing. Just my mom."

"Your *mom*?"

"Yes. Just a second." Alexandra went to her bag, which was sitting on the desk, and took out of it a device that looked like a little pager. She read something on the device's tiny screen, then picked up her cell phone.

"Mom?" she said into the phone. "What's up? You picked a terrible time."

Jake could hear her mother's voice well enough to follow the conversation.

"I figured it was a terrible time, dear," she said. "And that's why I called. Drills are more effective when they're at terrible times."

"OK then. Drill over? I called you right back, just like I promised I always would."

"You did, dear. Thank you. Are you having a good time?"

"It was fabulous. I'll tell you all about it later."

"OK dear. Call me Monday. Thanks for calling back so fast. I'm impressed."

"Sure thing, Mom." Alexandra put the phone away.

"What the hell was that?" said Jake. "What the devil is that little squawk box?"

"It's nothing. It's just a D.C. thing that my mom is a real hardass about."

"Some sort of pager?"

"Yes. People with jobs like hers, and their families, have to carry them. It's for terrorist alerts and stuff. If Washington goes on alert, some kind of security plan kicks in. I have to call my mom, and she tells me where to go. Every now and then she does these drills to make sure I'm paying attention."

"The price of power," said Jake.

"Perks of power is what my mom says. Poor you. Look at you. Your happy trail doesn't look so happy. It's amazing how fast that happens."

"It's reversible."

"How long does it take? I've never really understood that."

"Start up here again," said Jake, "and see what's changed by the time you're down there again."

"Oh look!" said Alexandra. "It's already happening."

—◆ ◆—

For months, it had been Jake's plan to make a second trip to Phaedrus' place in late October, as close as possible to the new moon. This was not the sort of trip that Alexandra would want to make, nor would he have considered inviting her. But he was experienced enough with girlfriends to know that he would catch plenty of flak. She would never be able to understand why he wanted to visit that old man, as she called him, and girlfriends can never think of any good reason why a boyfriend might want to go anywhere alone. If he had been thinking more clearly, he would have made it part of the bargain for going to the wedding, instead of settling for half an organ concert. But it was too late now. Jake realized that it was a strategic mistake to have waited to tell her until four days before he planned to leave. But he'd just have to buck up, break the news to her, and put up with the fallout. The fallout would be compounded by the fact that, several times, she had mentioned a Halloween party at the apartment of one of her friends. Jake had been noncommittal, but of course she had assumed that they would go to the Halloween party. When Jake told her about his plans to spend a four-day weekend on a solo hiking trip to the mountains and a visit with Phaedrus, they had their first serious fight.

She berated Phaedrus. Her unkind words, spoken a bit too loud, sounded almost jealous. She scolded Jake for wanting to be alone too much, for reading too much, for not being very sociable with her friends, who, she said, were good friends and far more interesting to spend time with than some old man up in the mountains. Jake held his tongue, but he walked out of her apartment and closed the door very, very quietly – though he realized that she would not grasp the meaning of the quietly closing door, that the meaning was ironic, that it was meant as a slam. This relationship was right on schedule. The list of his failings as a boyfriend was usually delivered around month four to six. His phone was silent for a good four hours, then the calls and messages started coming in. He waited half an hour to respond, then sent a text message: "I'm sorry that you're angry, but I really want to do this. No, I'm not mad. Let's talk about it when I get back."

Jake remembered what Phaedrus had said about the romantic myth. That made him feel sad for Alexandra. Certainly there were young women who set exceedingly high goals for themselves – playing the cello in a major orchestra, or excelling as a Rhodes scholar, or becoming secretary of state someday, or president of the United States. But for most young women, their highest striving seemed to be directed toward that fairy tale of romantic love. From this Jake derived an important insight. When and if the time comes to marry, it mustn't be a girl whose main goal in life is to get married. There must be some other centerpiece in her life. That really narrowed the field. Could Alexandra ever grow into that? Could her art ever be that important to her? Jake wasn't sure. Maybe. She had more going for her than a lot of girls. But for now, Jake was letting Alexandra down. Jake was being a sorry Prince Charming.

But look in the mirror, Jake. What fairy tale are you living in?

CHAPTER 7

On an fine, golden morning in late October, Jake packed the Jeep for the trip to Phaedrus' place. The Jeep itself was all spiffy; he had washed it carefully the day before. The windshield broken during the storm had long ago been replaced. The sky was almost unnaturally blue with huge low-flying clouds, the kind of clouds that children see all sorts of mythical creatures in if they lie in the grass on a hillside looking upward, the way Jake had often done as a boy. The morning light had that magical golden hue that can happen only in October. It had to do, Jake supposed, with the clear autumn air and the angle of sun when it is a bit north of the equinox. Why, Jake wondered, did the world sometimes seem to be full of promise, full of magic, when other times the world was so dreary. Jake was smart enough to realize that it was not the world that uras any different. Rather, it was our own state of mind, but we perceived it as though it was out there in the world, through the miracle of psychological projection. When the world looks this beautiful, thought Jake, when the world looks as though anything is possible, when one almost would not be surprised to catch a glimpse of a unicorn in the woods, then it is a sure bet that one feels happy. So distracted was Jake by the pleasure of his good mood that he almost forgot the telescope. He had to stop the Jeep, dash back into the apartment, and rummage in the closet for the telescope. He scolded himself. What if he'd forgotten the telescope? So pay attention, Jake. Don't get into such a fugue inside your own head during this drive that all of a sudden you realize you can't remember a thing about the last fifty miles. You need the thinking time, that's for sure. But you need the road trip, too – you know, scenery, new vistas. So pay attention.

But while you have some freeway miles to get behind you before the mountains loom, how about dealing with the first order of business, then let go of it so that your mind can wander the misty mountain passes and all that. How are you doing in the girlfriend department? Does she understand you? You never spend much time on that question, do you Jake? Do you need to be understood? Or is that a luxury? But no, she doesn't understand you very well, though there may be signs that she's getting better. If you think that being understood is important, then keep that in mind next time. But, overall, how is Alexandra working out for you? Pretty much average, in all departments, wouldn't you say? It's too bad that you didn't do better, but at this point in your life you don't want anything serious, do you? In other words, you've adjusted your expectations for your stage of life. You've even tried to keep the door open to other forms of existence. So then, is there anything else in this department? Or have we covered it all? Look's like we've covered it all. Move along.

Now then. All this theorizing you've been doing about conspiracies, all this half-paranoid dark research. Are you just trying to find some excitement because your life is so … so average? You have your average side, too, you know. Are you just trying to find a better story to live in? Or is there really something ominous going on?

You can't possibly know. You have no way of knowing, because you don't have access to any more information or any more knowledge than the average TV-watching, god-fearing American. To think that you can reach some sort of conclusion is a complete waste of time. It can't be done.

There is only one possibility: Phaedrus. You just need to ask him the right questions this time. So have those questions ready to ask when the time is right. List the questions in your head. And what better stimulus for question-listing than fugue-listening? Jake had brought recordings of fugues – his new passion, fugues for his fugal state of mind – and he played them loud as the Jeep's hard suspension bounced mercilessly and he endured the punishment of the freeway miles. By mid-afternoon, Jake was approaching mountainous terrain, and he turned west off the freeway onto winding secondary roads.

Jake wanted to see if he could find his way back to Phaedrus' place without any GPS assistance. He did. There were many turns on many winding country roads as Jake made his way up to the higher elevations, but other than a couple of spots where he wasn't absolutely certain, he nevertheless made the right choices and soon found himself on roadways that he knew he had seen before.

When Jake was here before, it had been May, and the hills and slopes and streambeds were lush with the vigor of spring. Now the undergrowth of summer was yellowing and dying back, and the trees at some elevations were in their full fall color. There were tacky Halloween decorations in some of the yards – plastic pumpkins and an occasional real pumpkin, ghosts and goblins hanging in trees, and every now and then a witch on a broomstick, all of it made of cheap plastic or cheap fabrics and bought at roadside dollar stores. The air was growing chillier here in the mountains, and some of the older houses had smoke rising from their chimneys and big piles of firewood on their porch, or stacked in outbuildings. The people here must be pretty poor, and yet many of them had new, expensive vehicles.

At last, on a narrow, winding road overhung with deep forest, the pavement ended, and Jake knew that he was now less than ten miles from Phaedrus' place. Soon he noticed the stumps of trees that had been blown down in the storm that had caught him last May. The mess had been cleaned up, and the forest growth was so dense that in most places the loss of trees was barely noticeable. Jake had not been using GPS, but now he checked his location against a topographical map and noted the altitude. The terrain was rough here and of three basic types. Either the road was running through a narrow valley right beside a stream, or it was clinging to a steep mountainside, or, more rarely, it followed the crest of a ridge for a while. The streamside valleys were too narrow and too dark for human settlement, so the only potential homesteads were on the ridges. But these tended to be rocky and narrow. Somehow Phaedrus had found the perfect spot, if it was isolation you wanted. As the Jeep wound nearer to Phaedrus' farm, Jake could remember it clearly. There was a lower ridge that was unusually flat, providing about five acres of land suitable for the gardens, orchard, house and outbuildings of the farm. From this area, a rough road wound up a steep slope – though not too steep for a mule or tractor – to another ridge top with an elevation about 400 feet higher. This ridge top also was naturally flat, providing about eight more acres suitable for pasture and fields. That was not a great deal of farmable land, but it was enough for the tenacious settlers to subsist on and raise a family. It was another great stroke of luck that there were springs near the upper pasture, providing a gravity-fed stream of clear water to the house, the barn and the chicken house below. Phaedrus' driveway, if that was the right word for it, was almost two miles long and connected to the gravel public road just above a hairpin curve. The driveway was very rough and not well maintained – no problem for the Jeep but inaccessible, no matter what the weather, to the average suburban vehicle, including heavy SUVs. Jake could only imagine how hard it was to get in and out in bad weather, with mud or snow or ice.

Phaedrus probably had put a lot of work into finding this place. Even two hundred years ago, when the settlers were moving into these mountains, there were plenty of people who thought that ten miles to the nearest neighbor was too close. How different Phaedrus is from those early settlers, thought Jake. He is educated. He is urbane. He is isolated and yet knows what is going on in the outside world. He has technology. He has an almost wizardly knowledge. He has a walking stick and a floppy hat. Did he really want this? Or did he turn his back on the world for some reason?

Jake steered the Jeep into the rough road leading up to Phaedrus' place and stopped to shift the transmission into low range. The engine whined, operating at freeway speeds, but the gearing of the Jeep's transmission was so low that the Jeep ascended at less than ten miles per hour. The ride jostled so much that some of Jake's camping equipment shifted and fell in the back of the Jeep. Sometimes a wheel would come to a rock, one side of the Jeep rising as the wheel climbed over and down the rock. Other times a wheel would dip into a rut. The ground was moist, but there was no mud. Though the slope faced southwest toward the sun, and though the afternoon sun was bright above the trees, still it was dark here under the trees. The leaves were a thousand shades of green, yellow, red and brown, but they had not yet begun to fall. The density of the foliage was impressive. Some of the trees were nut trees – oak and hickory. Occasionally Jake would see a squirrel turn toward him to bark and scold for the intrusion, then turn tail and run up a tree. Jake came to a slippery part in the road where water from a spring in the overhanging rocks ran into the roadway, but the Jeep rolled on without complaint.

At last the ground began to level out as Jake approached the top of the ridge. Here the road curved through the orchard. A few apples still clung to some of the trees. The grass under the fruit trees was still lush and bright green from the autumn rains. Grass loves cool weather. Jake passed the barn. The big barn door hung open. As the driveway approached the house, Jake glimpsed through the fruit trees an old pickup truck parked near the kitchen door. And then there was Phaedrus, in his floppy hat as usual, with Joan, the black Lab, at his heels. Phaedrus seemed to be loading things into the truck, which looked to be at least forty years old. As the Jeep slowly approached the house, still whining along with its transmission in low range, Phaedrus stood smiling. Joan remained at his side, leaning against Phaedrus' legs. Jake turned the Jeep out of the driveway and stopped between two apple trees. As he shut off the engine and stepped out of the Jeep, Phaedrus and Joan were there, Joan wagging her tail. Phaedrus shook Jake's hand warmly as Joan waited patiently for her share of the greeting.

"Jake, my friend!" said Phaedrus. "It's so nice to see you. I had hoped you'd come back someday." Jake reached down to scratch Joan between the ears.

"I hope you don't mind my dropping in like this," said Jake. "But I really didn't have any way of forewarning you. Between your stars and your conversation, I really wanted to come back again. I hope you'll let me use that camp site again for a couple of nights."

"It's an honor," said Phaedrus. "And well timed, too. This is one of the best times of year up here – clear skies, fresh air, wood smoke, pumpkin pie, apple pie, all that. How have you been?"

"Good," said Jake. "It was a busy summer. I made a little money. I worked too much. But it gets tiring being so responsible and living the suburban life. I needed to see some trees and sky. And it would be nice to talk about something other than building codes for a while."

"Good. You can help me decide whether apple pie is best with a little nutmeg mixed in with the cinnamon. And you can help me argue with the squirrels about how we're going to split the walnuts."

"Now those are conversations I could really get into," said Jake.

"You almost missed me, though," said Phaedrus. "I've got to make a little expedition. It should take only four or five hours. If you had arrived even thirty minutes later you'd have found me gone until after dark. So you timed it well. Why don't you come along on my expedition?"

"Would I be in the way?"

"Not at all. I could use some help setting up an antenna. Radio propagation has been pretty poor for almost a week, so I need a little more altitude. I can explain on the way. And don't worry about having to set up camp in the dark. I have a spare bedroom. The dust in there may make you sneeze, but it's comfortable enough. Then you can bring that tent and stuff out of the Jeep tomorrow."

"That sounds great," said Jake.

"Are you hungry? Would you like a quick snack before we head out? I have some of my usual sourdough bread, and there's cheese, and onions, and probably some blackberry preserves."

"You have no idea how good that sounds."

Soon they were winding their way through unpaved mountain roads in Phaedrus' rattly old truck. Joan was between them in the middle, sometimes lying with her head against Phaedrus' leg, sometimes sitting up as though she was enjoying the scenery. Occasionally she'd give Jake a little nudge or a little lick.

As they drove, Phaedrus explained that they were going to a place on a high ridge where he could put up a temporary antenna in a position greatly superior to what he could achieve back at the farm. Under more normal conditions, Phaedrus explained, the farm's antennas were adequate. But every now and then, Phaedrus said, when conditions were tough, he'd make this trip. Phaedrus did not say anything about why it was so important that he get a signal in or out. But he did say that he'd been in radio silence for a week, implying, Jake realized, that whatever the nature of Phaedrus' radio communications, a week of silence was at the upper limit of what was acceptable. Jake did not find this surprising. It could easily be made to fit with Jake's dot-connecting.

They drove, Jake guessed, for about forty miles, all of it on winding roads in mountainous terrain. There was almost no other traffic, and they passed only a few dwellings. Phaedrus mentioned that much of the land was owned by timber companies. But it did not seem as though much timber harvesting was being done, because the forests on both sides of the narrow roads were deep and dark, and rarely, in the distance, did Jake see any areas that had been cut.

The old truck rumbled along the relative flat of a ridge crest, and a couple of miles away Jake saw a more or less round mountain whose crest rose at least five hundred feet higher than the surrounding ridges. Phaedrus announced that they were almost there. A side road turned off toward the round mountain. The road was blocked by a metal gate. Phaedrus stopped the truck and opened the gate, which appeared to be locked with a combination lock. Jake asked no questions, and Phaedrus offered no information about why he had access to the road leading up this mountain. The road was perilously narrow. It made almost a full revolution around the mountain as it wound upward toward the top. The old pickup truck, with its high suspension, handled the rough road pretty well. Jake found himself admiring Phaedrus' clutch technique. As a Jeep driver, Jake knew that to handle a clutch well in steep terrain took experience. When they reached the crest, Jake saw that the more or less flat area of the crest was no bigger than a baseball field. It was dominated by a steel fire tower. The tower was obviously decades old. Its tired silver paint was half stained with rust. Inside the tower frame, but clearly visible, were metal steps that reached the top in about five flights. Jake guessed that the tower was sixty feet high. He was relieved to see that it had steps rather than a ladder. It was about an hour and a half before dark. Phaedrus stopped the truck in a small parking space beside the tower.

"Wow," said Jake. "You let that tower be a surprise, didn't you? Is it climbable?"

"Very climbable if you watch your step," said Phaedrus. "Are you up for that?"

"I think so," said Jake. "I've never been on one of these things, and when I've seen them in pictures I always thought they're so cool. Is it still in use?"

"No. It was decommissioned as a fire tower more than thirty years ago. It's still in good shape, though. It belongs to a friend. He gives me access to it when I need it for radio work."

"What's our mission?" Jake asked.

"Would you like the quick version, or the nerd version?" replied Phaedrus.

"The nerd version, please."

"Our mission is to both transmit and receive a low power radio signal. We need about ten minutes of good reception and ten minutes of good transmission. The signal we want to receive is scheduled to be transmitted in about forty minutes. It will be in the 20-meter band, just above 14 megahertz. If we are unable to receive that signal, we have the option of trying again an hour later on a different frequency. That's the 30-meter band, just above 10 megahertz. These two bands have somewhat different characteristics of propagation, so the odds are pretty good that if one band won't work, the other will.

"I have some antenna equipment that I leave stored here. It's up there, in the cab of the tower." Phaedrus pointed, and Jake did a little mock shiver as he regarded the steep stairs and the height of the cab.

"But don't worry. We're not going to have to climb around on the roof of the cab or anything like that. We're going to just let some antenna apparatus hang out over the side, working behind the safety railing. I have a small-ish radio transceiver with me and a little tablet computer. All of it runs on batteries. Any questions?"

"Yes," said Jake. "This signal that we want to receive. Where is it coming from?"

Phaedrus thought for a moment. Finally he said, "If I told you, I'd have to shoot you. But I can tell you that the signal is not coming from inside the United States." Phaedrus chuckled, noticing the wide-eyed look on Jake's face and Jake's barely contained curiosity.

"And I also can tell you that I am a loyal citizen of the United States, that I'm not involved in any conspiracy, and that I am not seeking the overthrow of the U.S. government."

"I don't know how loyal a citizen I am, but I'm ready when you are," said Jake.

Joan hobbled over with her usual shuffling gait and lay down under the steps. Apparently this was routine for her. The climb to the top of the tower was not as spooky as Jake had feared. Jake noticed how fit and springy Phaedrus seemed to be as he climbed the steps. He moved like a much younger man. But Phaedrus slowed down when they reached a section of the steps where a weld had broken, allowing the steps to sag slightly under their weight. At the top, a trap door led from the last step of the stairs to the floor of the cab. It opened onto a small uncovered porch, or observation deck. Jake and Phaedrus climbed onto the observation deck, and Phaedrus lowered the trap door. There were two padlocks on the door of the cab. They were keyless, combination-type locks. Phaedrus unlocked them both. But before they went into the cab they paused to take in the view.

They were surrounded by forest in all directions, as far as they could see. Here and there, miles off, could be seen signs of human activity, but mostly they were in a wilderness. The sun was behind clouds at the moment, sinking into the west. The light was slanted, golden, perfect.

"The light is amazing," said Jake. "This would be beautiful in any light, but you can't do better than low-angle evening light in the month of October, with about fifty percent cloud cover, which is what we have now. I think I could live in a place like this."

"Ah yes," said Phaedrus. "That's a common fantasy for an introvert, living in a fire tower, or a lighthouse."

"Was this place ever occupied for long a time?"

"A ranger might be stationed here for several months at a time during fire season. You'll see a bunk inside, a tiny kitchen, fairly primitive sanitation facilities."

"What about water?" asked Jake.

"Water had to be trucked in. Normally the place was resupplied about once a month with water and food and provisions. There's a spring below the ridge if the water runs out."

"There doesn't seem to be much space for storage, though," said Jake.

"Most of the storage is below. There's an underground water tank. There's also an underground storage area. That made the storage area more secure, and it kept things from freezing. If there was anything urgent, they could always send in a helicopter. But that was probably rare, because it was expensive." Phaedrus pointed to the landing pad below, which was now so littered with grass and loose gravel and weeds that Jake would not have immediately recognized it for what it was. The landing pad occupied almost all of the small peak that wasn't occupied by the tower itself and the small parking area.

"At this altitude," said Jake, "it must get pretty cold up here in the winter."

"Normally this place wouldn't have been occupied in the winter, because fire risks are lower in the winter. Fire season starts in the spring, depending on rainfall, and continues through summer and fall. Again, depending on rainfall."

"How did the ranger communicate with the outside world?" asked Jake.

"By radio," said Phaedrus. "But it was VHF radio – that is, very high frequency radio, in the range of 130 megahertz or so. Radio at that frequency is strictly line of sight, but thirty, forty, fifty miles is all you needed to stay in touch with headquarters. And because of the height of the tower, the ranger here also could act as a relay if there were any men on the ground in the woods below who needed to get a signal out to the edge of the forest."

"Was everything solar powered?"

"There was some solar power," said Phaedrus. "But there also was a generator – and even a backup generator – down below. They didn't need to run the generators all the time. But they started one up as needed. The power was used only for electronics. Cooking used what they used to call 'white gasoline.' It was the same for lighting, that or kerosene. You could even operate a small refrigerator off of kerosene."

"Books," said Jake. "I hope they trucked in books."

Phaedrus laughed. "We'd better get started," he said.

The antenna, Phaedrus explained, was a Yagi. It was made of very light aluminum tubing. It had been partly disassembled for storage. Phaedrus slid the parts together as though he'd done it a hundred times. They used screw drivers to lock the parts together. The antenna attached to a kind of boom. Using the boom as a lever and handle, they slid the antenna out over the side of the observation deck. Jake saw that there were brackets, already installed, into which the boom fit and locked into place. The job took less than fifteen minutes.

"So it's a directional antenna," said Jake.

"That's right. Point the antenna in a particular direction, and the signals in that direction are four or five times stronger than they otherwise would be. Plus, any noise or unwanted signals coming from other directions are similarly dampened. The directional nature of the antenna, plus our altitude here, makes for much better operating conditions than I have back at my place. My place, and the antennas I have there, are fine in normal conditions, but when the atmosphere – or more specifically the ionosphere, or the sun – is not cooperating, then so far I've always found that this place has worked for me."

"Your determination is impressive. And you realize of course that, in spite of your secrecy, you're giving away a piece of information."

"The azimuth?"

"That's right. I'd say your antenna is aimed more or less northeast."

"Right you are," said Phaedrus. "Now I'll give away even more information. If we can pick up the signal, I'll let you listen to it."

Jake felt a brief thrill until he remembered that the signal would be in some sort of digital format. "Let's hear it!" he said.

Phaedrus attached a coaxial cable to the antenna and took the other end of the cable into the cab, explaining that it was quieter in there and easier to concentrate. He screwed the cable into the radio, then attached the little computer to the radio as well. Soon there were static sounds, followed by some Morse code. But Jake already understood that it was not Morse code that Phaedrus was looking for. Phaedrus was still tuning the radio, making small adjustments in several buttons, no doubt working on optimizing the signal.

Soon Phaedrus pointed to the speaker. "Listen," he said. "What do you hear?"

After listening for a while, Jake heard mostly static, but he also could hear what sounded like a funny little tune played with only a few musical notes.

"Is that it?" Jake asked. "Those funny little tones?"

"That's it," said Phaedrus. That's our station. Right now it's only transmitting something generic so that we can hear the signal and tune in. The real transmission will start in (Phaedrus looked at his watch) eight minutes."

For eight minutes they were silent. Phaedrus listened carefully, occasionally making tiny adjustments on the radio. The eight minutes passed. Jake could still hear the tones, barely audible in the static. Phaedrus obviously was capturing the signal in the little computer, or perhaps decoding it. Jake could see letters and numbers scrolling across the screen of the computer, but Jake couldn't read it. That took about ten more minutes. Then Phaedrus typed something into the computer, a few words at most. An acknowledgment? And then because the sound stopped, and a red light on the radio came on, Jake assumed that Phaedrus was transmitting. In less than five minutes that was over.

"That's it," said Phaedrus. "We're done. We succeeded. I really appreciate your help. And now we can pack up this stuff and get home for some supper."

After they made their way down the steps to the rocky ground, Jake saw Joan sniffing at an area under a shed-type roof ten or fifteen yards from the base of the tower. Jake was pretty sure he saw what appeared to be an entrance to some sort of underground installation. There was a heavy metal door on it, and the door appeared to be very solidly locked. Under the roof were some rusty tubs, probably for washing clothes. Between two of the posts on the far side of the shed were two strands of clothesline, the clothespins long gone. Farther on, near the edge of the woods, was a small shack that appeared to be a privy.

Phaedrus' spare bedroom was on the second floor of the little house. Though Phaedrus had brought fresh sheets, the blankets and quilts were musty and old-fashioned. One was even an old patchwork quilt, which might have been an antique. Phaedrus had made the bed, then returned downstairs to his own bedroom and left Jake with a candle. Jake was charmed at the idea of sleeping in such a rustic house with only a candle for lighting. It helped to know that the candle wasn't just an accessory added for the sake of atmosphere. It was the most practical form of light here. Phaedrus had said that he preferred not to use oil lamps, though they were cheaper than candles. Oil lamps could be overturned or broken, and start a fire. Whereas candles, Phaedrus said, rarely got out of hand no matter what kind of accident they met with. Jake explored the room by candlelight. The room seemed to be a receptacle for an assortment of objects that there wasn't room for elsewhere. There were books, all of them old, mostly classics of English literature. There were dictionaries for French, German, Latin, Greek, and Italian. There were several old clocks that either didn't work or that were not kept wound. There was a small stringed musical instrument that Jake thought was an autoharp. There was high-quality laboratory glassware where vases might have been expected. There were several laboratory instruments, decades old, that appeared to be expensive and of high quality. One was a magnetometer. There were three Geiger counters.

There was an oscilloscope, a frequency counter with a Nixie tube readout, and a radio frequency generator. All were dusty, but all appeared to be in excellent condition as though they'd work as good as new if Phaedrus only had electricity.

And there were photographs. Most appeared to be family photographs. But there were two photographs of a quite handsome young man. He appeared to be in his mid- to late 20s. He had dark hair and a noble profile. In one photograph he was standing on a green slope above a rocky coast. The sea, with rock formations that looked like the Irish skelligs, were behind him. The sky was heavy with clouds. In the other photo he was seated at an organ console. And what an organ it was. It must have been in a very large church, possibly a cathedral. The young man was dressed in formal dark clothing, almost a tuxedo. This was not a casual situation. The young man might well have been giving a performance. Based on hair styles and such, Jake guessed that the photo was thirty years old. The young man's look was intriguing and sophisticated. He had a poet's eyes.

There was something poignant about the two photos of this young man, even to Jake's strong straight identity. There was charisma, androgyny. It made Jake realize how little he had really done in his life, certainly nothing exotic, nothing that expressed the kind of individualism and accomplishment that this young man seemed to possess. Jake assumed that Phaedrus had once loved this young man. Was Phaedrus loved in return? If that was the case, then perhaps Phaedrus had led a rich life. Though Phaedrus was an engineer, it was clear that his life had been touched by art, and by artists. Jake found himself wondering if, when he was Phaedrus' age, he would be able to look back on a life that rich, with people who were smart, and complex, and who did unusual things. Jake felt ordinary, somehow. He wondered if someone like Phaedrus could really find him interesting.

Before Jake went to bed, he found himself in front of a small mirror in the candlelight. He raked back his dark hair and looked himself in the eyes, which were green. Do you have a poet's eyes? he asked himself. Jake decided that he just might, that it might be the quality that people were referring to when they teased him about being dreamy.

Then Jake heard the buzzing sound. He took hold of a nearby bookcase to steady himself, but he continued to look into the mirror. The room was dark except for the candlelight on his face and chest and shoulders. The buzzing rose, more intense than he'd ever known it to be. He closed his eyes for what must have been only seconds, but during those seconds a thousand thoughts scrolled through his mind. The thoughts were all woven together in the way that only the buzzing could weave, everything clear, concise, consistent, harmonious – like the parts of a fugue. As always with the buzzing, it wasn't so much a flash of insight; it didn't occur in an instant. Rather, it took time, and it played itself out in a perfectly ordered way, like a song.

The buzzing faded. Jake opened his eyes and looked at himself in the mirror again. No, it probably wasn't narcissism. It wasn't about how Jake sees himself, or how Jake loves himself. It was about Jake as others might see him and as others might love him. Though the room was cool, Jake removed his flannel shirt, then his undershirt. Jake, you are a fraud, he said to himself. You manage to simulate modesty, but you're really part peacock. Yes, I can see resorting to poetry to try to capture the peacock in the mirror. It's something mysteriously timeless and transcendent, and not just in the eyes. I won't look like this forever, but I do look like this now. Whatever that is in the mirror, it's only partly me. I didn't make it. I'd have no idea how to make it. It doesn't even belong to me. I'm just the formless ghost who lives inside it. Nature did this. Nature made this. Maybe it's true what the mystics say, that creation wants to experience itself, every object, from every possible perspective, even from the perspective of a caterpillar hiding on a dandelion leaf, or of a wolf, or of an old dog, or of an old man. What can he see that I can't see?

— ➤ ◀—

Jake spent much of the next day setting up his camp and doing a little hiking. Phaedrus had excused himself for the day, saying that he had a lot of work to do in the kitchen. Supper was to be at Phaedrus' place that evening, and tomorrow Jake would have Phaedrus up to his campfire.

When Jake arrived for supper just after sunset, Phaedrus' kitchen was in perfect order. There was not one pie but two pies – one apple, one pumpkin. There was a bottle of wine, no doubt from Phaedrus' mysterious stash. There was trout. Phaedrus had caught it himself that very morning, apparently when he'd hurried out right after breakfast with Joan and his walking stick. There were potatoes and cabbage that Phaedrus had grown. The mixture of wonderful smells in the kitchen – cinnamon and garlic, fish and onions in the oven, potatoes in a pot, cabbage and bacon in a skillet – doubled Jake's appetite with the first whiff. Phaedrus had even baked fresh sourdough bread. The loaf was cooling on a rack beside the stove. The bread's scent also lingered in the warm kitchen. The kitchen was so warm, in fact, that Phaedrus had opened the window slightly, and a light breeze ruffled the curtains beside the little table. Phaedrus poured them each a glass of wine and held his glass aloft.

"To your return," said Phaedrus.

"I'm honored," said Jake. "But I don't think I deserve all this. I have never been in a kitchen that smelled so wonderful and in which everything looked so good. Two pies! I don't know how you did all this in one day."

"I was going to bake today anyway, and catch a trout today anyway, so your timing was perfect. I can't wait to hear what your stars have brought to you since May. So what have you been up to?"

"Some interesting things have happened … kind of mysterious, really. I don't know what to make of it. I was hoping you might be able to help me make sense of it."

"Now I am truly intrigued."

"I saw a UFO," Jake said.

"You saw what? You mean you saw lights in the sky, or something?"

"No, no. I saw a lot more than that. It was huge, and it was directly above me. It shot a beam of light down at me. Well, not directly at me, but right in front of me."

"What did it look like?"

"It was dark. It was shaped like a triangle, and it was as long as a football field. That sounds silly, doesn't it? People always say that it was as long as a football field."

"And this light?"

Jake described the triangle and the light, with as much detail as he could recall.

"And tell me again where this was," Phaedrus said.

"West Virginia, a job site I was checking out."

"I think I'd like to know more about that job site," Phaedrus said. "But can you recall any other details about this black triangle?"

"That's about it," Jake said. "But it's strange how I felt. I mean, I wasn't afraid or anything. For some reason it didn't seem threatening. It almost seemed like it was trying to communicate with me, joking with me."

"Joking?"

"It's hard to explain, but that's how I felt. I know it sounds like a paranoid delusion or something, but it was as though it somehow knew things about me, and it was teasing me. There was something playful about the light rather than threatening. And when the light shot up into the sky, it was into one of the constellations that I know best. I think I could even name the star it pointed at."

"Really? What star was that?"

"Alioth, I think."

Phaedrus didn't say anything, but he looked unusually thoughtful.

"So, what do you think? Jake asked. "Do you believe in UFOs?"

Phaedrus laughed. "After a story like that, how could I not?"

"Seriously."

Phaedrus seemed almost troubled now, as though Jake had asked a question that Phaedrus didn't want to answer. They were quiet for a while. Jake waited, as though determined to get a serious answer.

"I propose a deal," Phaedrus said. "If you'll give me a pass on that question tonight, you can ask me again in a year. Maybe sooner."

"You're killing me!"

"A year. Meanwhile, I think you should trust your feelings."

"My feelings? About what? About the black triangle, or whoever was on it, knowing things about me?"

"Maybe things happen for a reason."

"You're being mysterious again!"

"Just for a year."

"What choice do I have. I accept your deal, but it's going to cost you more pie and more sourdough bread. At least, as long as you promise that you're not teasing me, that you're not putting one over on me."

"Never," said Phaedrus. "But this job site and this place up the mountains, can you tell me more?"

"You must think I have an overactive imagination,"

said Jake.

"There is no such thing as an overactive imagination."

"I got a contract for a rush job. I'm not supposed to talk about it, but somehow it seems OK to talk about it with you, since you clearly know how to keep secrets. Anyway, the contract is with a senator. No need for me to name him, but he's rich, has lots of military and energy connections, that sort of thing."

"In other words, it could be almost any senator."

"You're probably right. Of course, I'm not dealing with the senator myself. I was hired by an engineer who works for him. This senator has a private compound up in the mountains west of Washington. Clearly he's had this place for years, but he's expanding it and adding some new frills. He's in a hurry. So, the stuff they want me to do is ordinary stuff, things like drawing up the layout for new living quarters inside a larger building. But this is not just any building. It's … how would I say it … hardened. They're using huge quantities of steel and concrete, hauling it in from who knows where. There's some kind of underground work going on. There's a new helipad, military grade. They're putting in some kind of new communications center or data center, and the walls are lined with copper." With that Jake paused to observe Phaedrus' reaction. Phaedrus didn't respond, didn't so much as lift an eyebrow.

Jake continued, "I camped one night on a ridge within sight of this place, several miles off. There was military traffic. A Chinook helicopter flew in during the night. The engineer who hired me said I should not talk about what I've seen there. I don't know. Maybe it's just the way that rich senators normally live. But I couldn't help but think … but think that this senator's place was a lot like your place, only scaled up. You don't have the helipad and visitors in Chinook helicopters, of course. I suppose." Here Jake paused to see what kind of reaction he was going to get from Phaedrus. Phaedrus thought for a while, long enough to reach down and scratch Joan between the ears (she had approached the table, maybe to beg), but Phaedrus, as usual, responded with a question.

"What do you make of it?" Phaedrus asked.

Now Jake wasn't sure how to proceed. He had hoped that Phaedrus would help him out, give him some kind of signal about whether it was OK to even have this kind of discussion. But Jake was already in pretty deep. He'd mentioned the similarities between Phaedrus' place and the senator's place. So there was no turning back now, or Phaedrus would take him for a coward, or for someone who was afraid to make connections between things that he had seen with his own eyes. So Jake decided to double down.

"Well," said Jake. "Obviously I can't know anything for sure, because I don't have much information to work with. But I did spend some time thinking about it, trying to figure out what, if anything, can be reasonably deduced, and if there are any dots that can be connected." Again Jake paused, hoping for some sort of feedback.

"And?"

Now it was Jake who reached under the table to scratch Joan between the ears. She was snuffling along the floor, looking for dropped crumbs.

"I think he's adding some kind of fallout shelter," said Jake. "And please pardon my nosiness, but I think you might have one too. And he's building a big Faraday cage inside his data center, or communications center, or whatever it is. Now maybe military specifications call for all new data centers or communication centers to be shielded against electromagnetic interference. But your place is not military spec, and you have a Faraday cage, too. As for the senator, obviously he's very well plugged in. He has sources of information that I can't even begin to imagine, secret sources. Again, please pardon me for doing such a poor job of minding my own business, but you seem to have sources of information too, sources that you don't, or can't, talk about. But maybe I'm just … meddling in the affairs of …" Jake began to stammer now.

"I think I know that line," said Phaedrus. "I think it was one of the elves, Gildor. He said, 'Do not meddle in the affairs of wizards, for they are subtle and quick to anger.' I'll take the wizard reference as a compliment. But you have nothing to fear here. Now, rich senators with military connections, that may be different. I admire you for noticing these things and making the connections. I commend you for being curious about it. And I even commend you for bringing up the subject."

"I'm relieved. I was afraid you'd be annoyed."

"I'm not annoyed. I'm impressed. Are there other things you've noticed? Any other dots you've connected?"

"Well, not really. There's a limit to how much I can make out of so little information. But I admit that I boned up on the some of the background. You know, how fallout shelters are constructed and how they're used, what they can protect you from, and what can cause the events that they can protect you from. Electromagnetic pulses are pretty interesting too. But if you ask yourself what kind of event can cause both radiation and an electromagnetic pulse, then the answer is not very … comforting. If you, as a rational person with private sources of information, need protection against such things, and if the rich senator with all his resources feels a similar need, then it seems to me …" Jake paused.

"Yes?"

"Then it seems to me that any rational and sensible person – which I would like to think I am – would wonder whether … whether there is some kind of risk or danger in the world that a rational and sensible person would want to know about."

Now Jake felt that he had gone far enough and that he should stop and see what Phaedrus would say.

"Jake, I admire your curiosity and your resourcefulness. And I sense that you haven't even told me yet about all the dots that you've connected, or about what kind of stories you've imagined that would explain what you've seen. You seem to be concerned that I would discourage you from this pursuit, but that is not the case at all, as long as you realize, as I'm sure you do, that you shouldn't talk about the senator business. Senators can be dangerous. But as for me, I am not dangerous at all. But as you already realize, there are things that I can't say, things that I can't talk about. Short of those things that I can't talk about, we can talk about it as much as you'd like.

"Now, I don't want to keep you on pins and needles, wondering whether there is something ominous in the works or whether, as you say, you just have an overactive imagination. No, you don't have an overactive imagination. Furthermore, it seems that you are careful to discipline your imagination by seeing how it compares with the real world.

"But I'm beating around the bush, because I never thought to have a conversation like this, and it's not something I'd thought about how to handle. But yes, there could be – is – something ominous in the works, and as you've guessed from connecting dots, it may be – is – dangerous. So I'll say this, and please forgive me if I blunder about and measure out my words too much. Nothing is exactly … imminent, as you no doubt deduced from the fact that the senator's project is still under construction. But I guess it depends on how you define 'imminent.' If – when – something happens, there will be – should be – some warning. A day, maybe. Two days, maybe three. As for the warning, you would recognize it. And if you do recognize such a warning – am I still beating around the bush? – I would like for you to come here. Come as quickly as you can. But I should stop for a minute and make sure you understand that you must not discuss this with anyone. That's for your protection. And for mine. There is nothing you could gain from discussing it with anyone, but there could be much to lose. Can we agree on that? Can we agree that everything that is said in this room tonight is between you and me?"

"I agree," said Jake. "I understand. It scares me a little, but I understand. You have my word."

"Good. Excellent. As I was saying, come as quickly as you can. For the next few months, keep your outdoor equipment handy. Keep the gas tank in your Jeep as full as possible. Make yourself a kind of 'go bag.' It would be best to keep it in the Jeep. It should contain water, dried food, survival clothing, things like that. You'll also need a battery powered radio – but store it in a metal can. With luck, if you start quickly, the Jeep should serve you. But you won't be able to count on that. That's why you must waste no time if you perceive a … warning."

"Can't you give me some hints? What sort of warning?"

"I'm sorry. No hints. But you'll know. Then move, quickly."

Jake realized that he was squirming. He tried to control it. His hands were cold and sweaty.

"I think I can guess what you're thinking now," said Phaedrus. "What about other people. I know how that feels. But if you said something, broke your promise not to talk about it, it would serve no purpose, help no one. Because no one would take you seriously, and they'd worry about your mental state. And unfortunately you can't help them. I think you'll realize that, after you've thought it through. I can't help you much with that process except to repeat that nothing releases you from your promise not to talk about this. You will need some time to see if you can live with it. It will feel wrong, thinking only of yourself. But that's the reality of it."

"Can't something be done?" Jake said. "Whatever it is we're talking about here, can't something be done to stop it? If enough people knew? The right people?"

"Nothing can be done, and there are no right people. I can't explain that. But nothing can be done, no matter how clever or how heroic. To try would be suicide."

The room felt cold to Jake, though the fire was crackling. The warmth in his belly from the food and wine was gone. He was afraid he might start shivering.

"Yes," said Jake. "I don't know what we're talking about, but I think I see who we're talking about. And we are nothing to them. At least, I am nothing to them."

"You are on the right wavelength," said Phaedrus. "And we've probably said just about all that can be said on the question. We might talk about generalities, but we can't talk about specifics. I've already said too much. But it does seem to me somehow as if the stars brought you here. I apologize for saying things that sound airheaded or mystical. Let me take that back and retreat to a metaphor. It is as though the stars brought you here."

"I think I know what you mean," said Jake. "And what you say about retreating to a metaphor reminds me of things my English-professor mother used to say when arguing with my father. He'd say, 'How do you know that is the case?' And she'd say, 'I don't. But it is as though that is the case.' And of course it was much harder to argue with that. But you mentioned generalities that we might talk about. I can think of some generalities. Is it government?"

"Can you clarify the question?"

"Is it government behind this? The military?"

"No," said Phaedrus. "It's power. Governments always answer to power. If you're lucky, governments answer to the power of democracy. But we're not that lucky anymore. There are other centers of power."

"Why?"

"Can you clarify the question?"

"Why would anyone do such a thing?"

The question seemed to perplex Phaedrus. Finally he

said, "Maybe they believe it is for the best. Do you know the population of the earth?"

"Around seven billion."

"Right. And what do environmentalists and ecologists say about the earth's carrying capacity and the state of the earth's climate. But, again, I've said too much."

"Yes," said Jake. "It's not only too much to talk about, it's too much to think about. But it sounds as though power, whatever power is, is smarter than we think. The public are allowed to think that they can go right on doing what they're doing forever – consuming, wasting, driving their heavy trucks and living in big houses, as though there's always more stuff wherever stuff comes from."

"Power is definitely smarter than we think," said Phaedrus. "And, for better or for worse, power always has a plan."

There were a few moments of silence as Phaedrus saw that Jake was searching for words.

"I'm honored, you know," said Jake. "Truly honored."

"How so?"

"If we're not just two crazy people, and if there is some kind of truth behind all these ellipses that we've been exchanging with each other tonight, then you have done me a great honor, and I am flattered. I mean, why should you care about me, or what happens to me? No matter what the reality is, or what happens, I thank you for that."

"Maybe I have secondary motives."

"Secondary motives?"

"Sure," said Phaedrus. "One is a hermitage. Two is a monastery. Monasteries tend to be far more productive and viable."

"I see what you mean," said Jake. "But I'm afraid my monastic skills are lacking."

"You can learn. But the important thing is that you're smart, and you think for yourself. You're young, and healthy, and probably pretty fearless. You know how to use your imagination, as well as how to put your nose to the grindstone. You'd end up as abbot someday."

"Abbot. What a strange old word, obsolete. It expresses a certain kind of power – a smaller, local power to be sure, nothing like the big kind of power that we've just alluded to. And 'abbot' also expresses some kind of … I don't know … kindness and caringness. You'd make a good abbot, Phaedrus."

"I would try," said Phaedrus. "And search the stars for guidance."

"And the radio waves as well," said Jake.

Phaedrus reached for the apple pie.

➤ ◄—

Jake's original plan had been to spend the next day hiking the ridges and streams of the thick forest around Phaedrus' place. But instead, after a cold and fireless early breakfast sitting in the morning sun outside his tent, he presented himself at Phaedrus kitchen door. Phaedrus was washing dishes, and a kettle of water was whistling on the wood stove.

"Is there anything I can help you with today?" Jake asked. "There must be plenty of projects that need done around a place like this."

"How nice of you," said Phaedrus. "How much time do you have?"

"All day," said Jake, "Until it's time to light a fire and start making supper."

"Then I have just the thing," said Phaedrus. "I had a farmer haul in a load of composted horse manure. It needs to be tilled into the garden. And then the garden needs to be sown with winter rye."

"That sounds like a nice, monkish job," said Jake. "You mean you have a tiller?"

"I do," said Phaedrus, "Powered by fossil fuel. It's old, but it gets the job done. And don't let the word 'manure' scare you. It's composted and smells as sweet as a forest floor."

"Then I'm ready when you are," said Jake.

"Have a seat and have some pumpkin pie while I finish these dishes."

— ◄—

Jake started his campfire for cooking supper a couple of hours before dark, to allow time for a good bed of coals to form. He had put some thought into what to make for Phaedrus' supper. He had settled on omelets with cheese and mushrooms, fried potatoes, and a loaf of bread brought from the city, rewarmed near the coals of his campfire. He'd brought two bottles of wine, one red, one white. Phaedrus arrived about half an hour before sunset, with Joan, of course, scuffling along behind. Jake had even brought cheap wine glasses. He poured the first glass of wine while the potatoes were still sizzling. Phaedrus proposed a toast, to the simple life.

"We got into some strange topics last night," said Phaedrus, "and I haven't yet had a chance to hear a full report on what you've been up to in Charlottesville these past few months."

"Let's see," said Jake. "I have a new girlfriend." Phaedrus raised his glass.

"Her name is Alexandra. I am ashamed to say that I met her at the gym. She's pretty. She's nice. She's sort of a social butterfly. She runs with an artsy crowd. She's pretty high maintenance. That's the downside of having a girlfriend, I guess – the maintenance. It's not anything serious, but it's fine. It's good. She wasn't exactly thrilled about my coming here this weekend, though."

"She doesn't like camping?"

"Not really. She'd rather go to art openings, or to cafes

with nice patios."

"Do you spend a lot of time with her?"

"As much as I can. Not as much as she would like. I've had a lot of work to do, and sometimes I work at home. I have a drafting table at home. But she'd always rather I come to her place. It works out. I mean, we don't fight about it or anything, but I suppose I don't play the boy-friend role as well as she might like me to."

"Do you talk a lot? Do you have good rapport, good understanding?"

"Hmmm. I suppose it's gotten a little better. But conversation is not her thing, really. She's an extravert, and her friends are extraverts, and she's never had an introverted boyfriend. But I gave her a couple of articles to read about introverts, and she's definitely making an effort. But sometimes I think that there is no such thing as an extravert who really understands about conversation. I mean, they talk. And sometimes they even all talk at once. But it's as though they … it's as though they lack a sense of what's worth talking about, or how many words a particular topic is worth. Or, god help me, they tell endless anecdotes. I think that's the default conversational style of extraverts, actually. I call it the anecdotal style. They tell each other these small, stupid stories – sometimes long stories, but small stories just the same – and they laugh, and they even seem to be into each other's little stories. After somebody tells a story, that will remind someone of something, and then that person will tell a similar story. But … I don't mean to sound like I'm complaining. You know how these things are."

Then Jake realized that his social life didn't make for high-quality anecdotes. So he changed the subject.

"I've been reading a lot," said Jake. "It's always a struggle to find enough time to read, but I'm pretty good at reading in snatches. I even read on the stationary bicycle. I read a book on organ building."

"Organ building?"

"Yep. I guess the subject was just too nerdy for me to resist, because I've always had a weakness for things that complicated."

"Have you worked through the complications of organ building?"

"Well enough to satisfy a dilettante, I suppose," said Jake. "At least with the wind instruments. But with the digital versions, which apparently regularly fool people who think they can easily distinguish between a wind instrument and an electronic instrument, I'm not so clear on how that is done."

"That would make a nice show and tell sometime," Phaedrus said. "We could take the back panel off the console in my studio, and I could point to what's what. Even if I don't have the electricity at present to light it up."

"That would be interesting," said Jake. "And I also read a couple of books on the theory of espionage and intelligence analysis."

"Now that's an odd topic. What led you in that direction?"

"Connecting the dots, of course. I figured there must be some pretty well developed theories on espionage and how to build the largest possible picture out of the smallest set of available facts. I was frustrated, I suppose, because I had so few facts. So I suppose I tried to make up the difference by resorting to theory."

"Did it help?"

"Not much. Maybe a little. But it did cause me to realize a few things, I think. One is just how little people really know about what's going on in the world. The people who run things, they have these vast intelligence systems to suck in information and analyze it. They're completely paranoid that something will slip past them, that there might be something going on that they don't know about. So they know a lot, and they keep it secret.

But what about the common people? Clearly they know nothing. They know worse than nothing, really, because the people who run things, in addition to their vast intelligence systems, also have vast propaganda systems for the very purpose of making sure that the common people know nothing and that they're kept distracted and pacified."

"I'm sorry you've had to learn these things, Jake. But also I'm impressed."

"And so I figured, what hope is there for a common person who is stupid enough to want to know what is really going on? There is no such thing as an espionage system for the common people, or intelligence analysis for the common people. Oh, there might occasionally be leaks, and leaks are good. But otherwise the common people are like cattle, who don't even think to ask what truck they're crowded onto, or where that narrow walkway down the ramp leads, or even what that banging and mooing sound is up ahead of them. They just keep walking on down the ramp, even without a cattle prod to their flank, because they're … cattle. But this is depressing. And I don't really mean to try to go back to what we were talking about last night, because I think we said everything that can be said. But it's depressing. It's not a thing that's easy to accept. But let's not discuss such things in the dark of night."

Jake added logs to the fire and poured wine. Phaedrus was thinking.

"And I read 'The Phaedrus,'" said Jake.

"You read Plato?"

"I did."

"And what did you think?"

"It's not exactly easy reading. I had to read parts of it more than once. And I had to read a little commentary, too, I admit, so that I was confident that I was on the right track. First of all I suppose it made me realize how much I don't know about the history of our own culture. Hardly anyone does. No one bothers. My dad – the classics professor, you remember – used to complain about that all time. Though I don't remember ever hearing him talk about 'The Phaedrus.' Perhaps he thought that 'The Phaedrus' is not a thing that young boys, and one's son in particular, need to know about, even if he thought that a good dose of the classics would do me good. And second, the history of our culture notwithstanding, it is striking how drastically some things have changed. I mean, I don't think I'm a homophobic person, and I thought I was pretty up to speed on realizing how some people's lives – and loves – aren't as easy as other people's lives. But I think I realize that it's even worse than I thought, just because something that once stood at the apex of culture, or the apex of the hierarchy of loves, now stands at the bottom. I don't entirely understand it. But then, I wouldn't, would I? Because I have always been immersed in a culture very different from the Athenians' culture." Jake paused, slowly turning his wine glass in his hand. Phaedrus was looking into the fire.

"And so," said Jake, "I wanted to ask you what you think. I'm sure you've been familiar with 'The Phaedrus' for as long as you could read, since you're named for it. And I'm sure you've thought a lot about Plato's world. Or, rather, Socrates' world. How did we get from there to here?"

Phaedrus reached for the bottle of wine and tilted it toward Jake. Jake extended his glass. Then Phaedrus refilled his own glass.

"The shortest possible answer to that question," said Phaedrus, "is one word: Christianity. Though, to be sure, during the last centuries of the decline of Greece there were sects and systems with views a good deal more prudish than Socrates'. And those views became pretty well established in Rome, though it was never the big deal that the church made of it. My belief is that it was all part of the project of stamping out the pagan religions. That had to happen before the Romans could establish Christianity. Much of the territory that Rome Christianized – France, the British Isles, Ireland – were Celtic. Many people don't realize that the Celts had very open minds – and open beds, for that matter – on the matter of love. Monotheism has had some strange effects on the human mind, both the individual human mind and the mind of the masses – the cattle mind, as you say. If there are many gods, then there are many ways of looking at things, multiple ways of understanding the same phenomenon. Different gods might have different points of view, and any individual human mind could shift its point of view, as appropriate, with support from the appropriate god. With monotheism, it was one size fits all, and anything else was of the devil.

"The pagans did have some big gods, of course. The Greek gods that lived on Olympus are an example. The Celts also had some big gods, gods that were known and worshipped wherever you found Celts. But there also were local gods, little gods. This idea of local gods is completely foreign to us today. It would be fair to say that it has been beaten out of us. But to the Celts, a hill or a tree might have its own little god, or a spring, or a well. The Celts could acknowledge a kind of exuberance in the world around them, because a god could spring up anywhere. And so differences of any sort – I like to call that exuberance, the exuberance of nature – were not as threatening. It could simply mean that a person was under the influence of a particular god. Not only that, but a person could be under the influence of one god on Monday, and another on Tuesday."

"That had all sorts of consequences, didn't it?" Jake said. "If there are no gods in the natural world, then attitudes toward the natural world change drastically."

"That very true," said Phaedrus. "There are those who say that it's religion that made possible the exploitation of nature, first by removing god from nature, and then by telling humans that the earth is there for humans to use and to have 'dominion' over. Soon enough, humans have dominion over a dying planet."

"I've heard them on the radio," said Jake. "They think the earth is not a problem, because earth's resources can never be exhausted."

"Or because," said Phaedrus, "they think they'll be raptured up to heaven in the end times, and the mess we've made of the earth won't matter."

"Who'd miss them?" Jake said.

"Some of my old friends have criticized me," said Phaedrus, "for focusing too much on the church's crimes against human love rather than the church's crimes against the earth, which they regard as far more serious crimes. I can't argue with that. But it's all the same thing, really, and they go together – a deep distrust of what is natural and an obsession with some sort of divine purpose from some sort of invisible world. It's amazing, really, that the church became one of the richest and most powerful forces on earth, by selling something invisible."

"Surely threats helped, too," said Jake. "You know, hell. That's quite a product line: heaven or hell, take your pick. Both are free, but leave the money in the basket on the way out."

"That's monopoly power," said Phaedrus. "It took a long time to chop down all the sacred groves and get rid the pagan competition, but the church built a monopoly."

"Sacred groves," said Jake. "That's a nice thought. Would the pagan gods come back, do you think, if we invited them?"

"I suspect not," said Phaedrus. "Not unless the rapture whisks all the monopolists away to their invisible world. But with the monopolists gone, yes, I do believe the old gods could be enticed into coming back."

"Nature would have dominion over us, rather than the other way around," said Jake. "Exuberance returns. I can see the profit in subduing nature, the better to exploit it, but what's the profit in subduing love? And sex?"

"I have never been able to properly answer that question," said Phaedrus. "Sex and love, I suppose, distract people too much from invisible things. If what you're selling is invisible, sex and love are too much competition.

"But it took centuries. The old religion held out in remote places of the Scottish highlands as late as the 18th and 19th centuries. But what is impressive, if you think about it, is just how much repressive energy was required from the church to get human sexuality into the small bottle they wanted it in. Now, keep in mind that repression takes work. It costs money. It requires troops of people to do the work. No centralized power is going to waste such a vast amount of repressive energy where it isn't needed. The point is that the love lives of our ancestors were much richer and much more varied than the love lives of people today. And their love lives were almost certainly happier."

"But they missed out on all that great invisible stuff," said Jake.

Phaedrus laughed. Jake reached for the wine bottle and poured for them both.

"But the forces of repression never gave up. They succeeded. As I've often said, we are all Puritans now."

"But let's keep pretending," said Jake, "that the Puritans never happened. Can we go back to the Greeks? Do you understand 'The Phaedrus,' Phaedrus? I found it to be pretty rough going."

Phaedrus laughed.

"I think I do, yes. If only because my life has been everything 'The Phaedrus' is not. My life has been the un-Phaedrus, the complete opposite of 'The Phaedrus.' It's my life in reverse, and I was unfortunate enough to see what was missing, and to see how things might have been, but weren't. A short piece of writing from the past, like 'The Phaedrus,' can shed a tiny light on how things have changed. But the change is bigger than we realize, and we are forced to use our imaginations to think what people might be like today if it weren't for Rome and Rome's religion.

"So sometimes I ask myself, 'What is the opposite of 'The Phaedrus'?' And then I think of Oscar Wilde. Rome's religion managed to turn Socrates' highest form of love into the lowest form. Do you remember what Oscar Wilde called it? 'The love that dare not speak its name.' Here was a great man, one of the great artists of his century, but the radical changes introduced by Rome reduced Wilde to whimpering and pathos. I'm referring to one of the last things he wrote, his *De Profundis*. Almost everyone abandoned him. He was ruined. He died in squalor. Though he had at one point in his life the strength and power to lash back, in the end he was defeated. Many people know what this defeat is like, have felt it and endured it in their own lives. But many don't even see what they have lost. In the last fifty years there has been progress, there is no doubt about that. But we are nowhere near where we were in the time of the Greeks or the Celts, nor will we ever be again, as long as the Christian era lasts.

"In short, to understand 'The Phaedrus,' all you really need to know is that it is the opposite of *De Profundis.*"

They sat quiet for a while. Jake threw some logs on the fire. Then Jake spoke, his eyes on the sparks flying up from the fire, one hand scratching Joan's head. She had come to lean against him.

"You know, Phaedrus, you don't have to always be so academic and abstract about it. It's been hard for you, I can see that. I think my inner Puritan is a wimp. I mean, I'm not freaked. I've been around a gay person or two."

"I wouldn't want to bore you, Jake. And I know that you're not freaked out. It's not that. Instead, it's like it's confidential or something. I know that doesn't make sense, but it's the best I can do right now."

"OK, but I won't forget your promise."

"About secrets? Stories?"

"Yes," said Jake. "You still owe me one."

"And you owe me one, too," said Phaedrus.

"It's still a deal," said Jake. "Oh. I have a little present for you."

Jake went to his tent, rummaged in a pack, and returned with a sheet of heavy drawing paper.

"I made this one for you," Jake said.

It was Phaedrus' little farm. Everything was drawn very much as it actually had appeared in the spring, but all the buildings were of stone, with gothic touches. Nothing was decaying, but everything was old and covered with ivy. It was lit by starlight and a tiny crescent of a setting moon. From one window, Phaedrus' bedroom window, a dim yellow light glowed. The fences, now made of stone, were covered with vines and blooming things. The studio, now of stone, looked more like a chapel, with a steep gothic roof. In the yard there was a puppy, like Joan, but young. The puppy sat on its haunches, looking at the moon. There were two cows in the pasture. Overhead was Ursa Major.

Jake was pretty sure that he saw Phaedrus' hand shaking. Phaedrus nodded silently, as though he did not trust his voice to speak. They were silent for a while and let the fire die down. Joan was asleep at Jake's feet, near enough to the coals of the fire to catch some of the heat in her old bones. After a while Jake reached for the wine and for what remained of the bread. He poured them both more wine, and, using his hands, tore the bread in two. He handed one piece of the bread to Phaedrus and kept the other. Phaedrus took the bread, easily picking up on the pun. They raised their glasses, but neither of them said anything.

CHAPTER 8

In mid-December, it snowed, and for about half a day, before traffic turned the snow into a mess, Charlottesville looked like Christmas. It was the fluffy kind of snow, big flakes falling in still air, and it made the suburbs look almost livable. It was a Sunday morning, and the traffic was light, so the snow wasn't much disturbed. The pavement was obscured and had been transformed into fields of white. Trees sagged. Rooftops glistened. Christmas decorations sparkled. Jake had spent the night at Alexandra's. He'd left early while Alexandra lingered in bed, saying that he wanted to get some shopping done while there weren't many people out. The truth was, he wanted to drive in the snow in the Jeep before the afternoon traffic turned everything ugly.

He drove through the university campus just to appreciate the wintry scenes. The trees were majestic. Most of the students were gone, but a few were out, building snowmen and hitting each other with snowballs.

Admit it, Jake. You've been feeling more Christmasy than you've felt in years. Why is that? Is it that you've had a glimpse of the fragility of the world? Is it that Christmas is one of the best things left, something ancient and pagan? Is it that Alexandra is coming around and is taking you more seriously, that she's more willing to meet you halfway? She even wanted to go to San Francisco with you for the parents' annual visit from Costa Rica. And you'd have taken her. But Alexandra's imperial mom wouldn't let her go, wouldn't hear of the idea of Alexandra not being home for Christmas. It was the one time of year, Alexandra said, when her mom could really break free of her duties at the State Department. Or was it the Senate? Alexandra never really made it clear. Maybe her mom was a State Department liaison with the Senate staff, or some similar Washington-type power thing. Even though he had been home schooled, Jake had been given a lot of freedom as a boy. Alexandra, not so much. Her family had kept an eye on her, kept her close to home. Alexandra had wanted to go to school in Massachusetts, but her mom had insisted on Charlottesville, a short train ride from D.C. Alexandra was on the phone with her mom at least once a day. And Alexandra had said that her mom's clinginess actually was getting worse, which made no sense, because Alexandra was on her own now, making her own living, trying to figure out what kind of life she wanted.

And what about Jake's parents? Their years of worrying about Jake were pretty much over. You're doing just fine on your own, aren't you, Jake? Plenty of young people these days are still living with their parents, even at the age of thirty and older. It was a screwed-up world, when so many people that age couldn't get a start in life. And except for the few who got a shark-in-training job on Wall Street or an elite-in-training job in Washington, young people weren't living nearly as well as their parents did. What twenty-something or even thirty-something can afford to get married, let alone have a $50,000 Princess Bride wedding? Only a few. But as for Jake's parents, these days he worried more about them than they worried about him. It was a huge relief that they were in Costa Rica. If something bad was going to happen, they'd almost certainly be safe there.

A particularly fine specimen of holly tree on the campus reminded Jake of Phaedrus' place. In Phaedrus' upper pasture, at the edge of the woods near Jake's campsite, there stood a similarly grand holly tree. Holly trees looked so Christmas-card Christmasy when loaded with snow. Jake wondered what Phaedrus did at Christmas. Did he feel lonely? Then again, Phaedrus, a pagan at heart, would most likely ignore Christmas. No wait. That can't be right, because all the good parts of Christmas are the pagan parts. Phaedrus had asked for his phone number. There was no way that Jake could call Phaedrus, because Phaedrus didn't have a phone. But certainly Phaedrus could get to a phone if he wanted to call Jake. If Phaedrus ever calls, it won't be just to chat. It will be because something is up.

Speaking of pagan, Jake, did you decide what to get Alexandra for Christmas? You'd better make up your mind quick, and get into the mall first thing when it opens, before the throngs get there. But first Jake needed to stop and get some gas for the Jeep. Then he needed to make one of his rare trips to a box store to get household things like detergent and toilet paper.

At the gas pumps, a middle-aged man with a huge belly and greasy hair got out of an enormous SUV across from Jake. The man cursed and growled as he started the gas pump.

"Look at that," the man said to Jake, who really wasn't in the mood for conversation. "It's up sixteen cents since the last time I filled up. It just keeps going up. It's those idiots in Washington. What the hell do they think armies are for?"

"Maybe you should use less of it," said Jake.

Clearly that wasn't the expected response.

"You seem to be using it too."

"I'm not complaining, and I haven't said anything about armies. And besides, it's not Washington. It's the oil companies."

"Are you some kind of tree hugger?"

"Yes."

"Liberal?"

"Worse."

"The problem is, Washington won't let us drill for it. It's all those damned regulations."

"Where'd you hear that?"

"On television."

"Maybe you watch too much television."

"What do you watch?"

"I don't watch anything."

The man seemed puzzled by that, as though he assumed that all information comes from television. But luckily Jake had finished filling up the Jeep, and he drove away without saying anything else. It could have gotten out of hand, because all of a sudden Jake's Christmasy mood was gone.

All the way to the box store, Jake fumed. Cheap gas – that's an entitlement to some people. Ensuring cheap gas – that's what governments and armies are for. But it was the way the man looked, more than anything else, that had disgusted Jake. It wasn't just the man's weight. It was the pinched, hateful look that seemed to be permanently fixed on his face. Inside the box store, Jake's mood only got worse. Everyone moved so slowly, as though merely pushing a cart and deciding what stuff to buy taxed the limits of their capacity. And always there was that pinched, miserable look – mouth in a frown, shoulders sagging, bellies hanging low.

Don't these people ever have orgasms? thought Jake. How do they breed? Or are only the teen-agers capable of breeding? Surely what I am seeing here is sexual poverty – grinding, miserable, self-perpetuating sexual poverty. What this country needs is a poverty program for sexual poverty. How might that work? How about a Sexual Social Security program. You pay in when you're young, and you draw on it when you're old. It would be a kind of sexual Marxism – to each according to her need, from each according to his ability. And by no means would this be oppressive to women, because women are just as needy. It would be up to young guys like Jake to put some smiles on their faces. That man at the gas pump. Could he possibly be a decent lover? His wife must be as miserable as he is. They surely must live in a state of abject, soul-killing sexual poverty. Then something in the culture converts the sexual misery into hatred and political rage.

What crazy ideas you have, Jake. Sexual Marxism would be like pushing mercy dates and mercy sex to the outer limits. But one thing is for sure. If a politician ever proposed a Sexual Social Security program, he'd get lots of votes. All the old folks would vote for it no matter how many sermons were preached, as long as the secrecy of their ballot was protected. And the young people, if they had any sense, would vote for it, because they'd have so much more to look forward to when they got older. Then again, young people rarely think ahead that far. Sexually, it's hand to mouth, month to month, paycheck to paycheck, minus a tithe to pay the fines for the preachers' sex. Such are the wages of Puritanism.

Jake's mood had changed again, thank goodness. He had to stop himself from laughing out loud. Then he heard a ruckus from the direction of the electronics section – a sudden outburst of angry shouting and a crash like a heavy box being dropped. Jake hurried that way to see what it was about. He couldn't see very well past a shelf of children's furniture, but it appeared that people were fighting over some televisions in the aisle that led toward the grocery section. Two security guys rushed past him. The scuffle didn't last long and had ended by the time Jake got close enough to see. But he saw two guys hurrying away with a cart loaded with two or three televisions and two women talking angrily with the security guards. The woman and security guards were standing beside a sign promoting a super-good deal on wide-screen televisions, limited quantity. It wasn't hard to figure out what had happened. Jake had heard of this sort of thing before, but probably the stores were usually able to hush it up before it got into the news, unless somebody got hurt, or somebody got it on video.

Jake moved on to get his toilet paper and detergent, staying well clear of the electronics section. It was amazing how a little Christmas shopping could reveal so much about America. If the whole damned country was wiped out, who'd miss us? Not yet, though, thought Jake. I've got to make a trip to San Francisco.

━ ◂ ━

That same evening, Phaedrus went up the hill to the upper pasture, just to look down and have the view of his little house covered with snow. Joan wanted to go, but the cold and the snow would have been too much for her. Phaedrus left her indoors to lie by the fire. In the snow, especially at dusk like this, the place looked so self-contained, so complete. But it was a deception caused by the perfect, if accidental, composition of the picture. It had never been complete. Even those few months, years ago, when Colin had come to stay for a while, Colin's impending departure had hung over the place like the lingering next-to-last notes of choral symphony. The notes are rich and poignant while they last, the chorus filling the hall with its full choral power. But the ear and the mind are preparing for the final chord, which is inevitable, and the ear knows full well what that chord will be. Then there is silence, and the silence goes on and on. This spot, from here near the holly tree, was the angle from which Jake had drawn it, though Jake had drawn it in the spring. It's too bad he can't see it now, thought Phaedrus, in the fading gray light, with that same yellow glow from the same window.

Phaedrus returned to the house. He had an appointment with Colin on the radio. The words streamed
slowly across a computer screen, having traveled all the
way across a turbulent North Atlantic. The turbulence,
though, was only a turbulence of sea and air and mois-
ture. Electromagnetically the atmosphere was unusually
clear, giving Phaedrus and Colin a chance to talk longer
than usual.

How's the weather in your mountains today, Mr. B. Are you
having a storm too?

**A snow storm, yes. The finest and prettiest we've had in
years. Are you getting winter weather too?**

The wind is up, and the deluge will arrive during the night.
I hiked out to the coast today just to see the waves hitting the
skelligs. And then I came home for my wee Irish supper —
cabbage and potatoes. The cats are curled up by the fire. The
wife has gone to bed.

Any news?

Finally, yes. I was able to get in touch with Johnson. Are
you copying OK? I have a paragraph ready to send you.

Clear copy. Send away.

I ran into our old friend Johnson in Dublin yesterday. He
was pretty down. It seems he's in a bit of a rough patch with
his health. The diagnosis is still up in the air, but Johnson has
got it in his head that he's not going to get any better. He says
Dublin is getting to him. He says that if the doctors there can't
do anything for him by his birthday, which I think is around
January 10, he's going to quit Dublin and go back to the family farm, see what fresh air and the country doctors can do for
him. He asked about you. I told him you are fine. He said to
tell you that you've got a good life and a good plan. Just stick
with the plan, he said, and make every day count, because
we're all on our own. Poor guy. I had this funny feeling that I
won't ever see him again.

**Clear copy on your last paragraph. I'm so sorry to hear
about Johnson. If you talk with him again, please give him
my best. What I'd give to raise a glass to the old times.**

Since the band is so strong and quiet today, maybe we can talk for a while. Is everything in good order there?

As good as one might hope for. I'm feeling old for such a hard winter, but life goes on. How about you? Are you ready for the worst of winter?

Same as you. We've got a good woodpile, and the barns are as full as I've ever seen them.

Good. I'd love to see those Irish barns of yours, full of wheat and potatoes. Don't forget the ale.

Don't worry. I never forget the ale. Have you heard anything lately from your young friend?

Not since he was here in October, no.

I haven't had a chance to ask you. Is he like his father?

There are moments when they look so much alike that I'd have a hard time telling them apart in poor light. But there's something very modern and contemporary about the son. He has traces of his father's classical style, but otherwise he's fully his own person.

What's it like, communicating with someone so young and contemporary, and so much like John used to be?

It's as though he's bilingual. He speaks fluent archaic. Would we expect anything else from a young man home-schooled by those two?

He's an architect, you say?

Yes. But his heart's not in it. So many young people these days, I think, have to make some hard choices to make a living. The new motto, I think, is "Do what you hate and the money will follow."

Very sad and very true. And it's even worse here, especially for our young people. They may be leaving the country again, for all I know. Though I don't know where they would go. Do you think he'll be coming back, this young man?

Impossible to say. He knows he's welcome. I think he likes it here. But he has a life out there. A place like this makes a nice retreat when a young man needs a break, but what young man would want to live the way I live?

Don't sell yourself short, Mr. B. There are a few people in this world who can appreciate the likes of you.

You are too kind.

Will you call him, at least, when it's time?

Yes. I will call him.

Next month is going to be a busy month. Things may move fast.

He's only a few hours away. If he wants to come here, he'll probably know when it's time. But I'll call him.

Sounds like you had a pretty good talk.

I think I got the point across, yes.

Well, if he does return, I hope he treats you more thoughtfully than his father.

That was a long time ago. We were young. We were all different then, Colin.

And some of us, when we're young, are not very sure about who we are. Like Jake's father. But I worry about you, Mr. B. You never really had anyone, not like the rest of us did.

I had good friends. You were always there, Colin. You never let me down.

You know what I mean. And I did let you down a time or two. I took you for granted, like everyone else did. Somehow you never made a big fuss over your devotion, Mr. B. It was easy to take for granted. I always thought that I'd make it up to you somehow, that I'd find someone who was just right for you, and introduce you, or something. But you're a tough case, Phaedrus. You're one in a million. So it follows that the right person for you also is one in a million. There were those who said you'd turned your back on the world. But I always knew that it wasn't like that. You just gave up after so many years of trying. You didn't have to give up, Mr. B. For that one person in a million, you are pure gold.

It's a little late, I'm afraid.

Don't say that! Maybe what we need when we get older is a little different from what we needed when we were younger, but the basics never change.

It was the endings that always did me in, Colin. There were always some good times, before the endings.

My dear Mr. B., I know you, and I'm ordering you to try again. No matter how badly it goes, you always manage to fill up your heart again — from what bottomless reservoir I have never understood — and carry on. And besides, you need help, and someone to look after you the way you look after that old dog of yours. How is Joan, anyway?

CHAPTER 9

Jake's parents always returned from Costa Rica at least once a year, at Christmas. They had given up on the East Coast, though, saying that they just couldn't take the cold weather anymore. For the past few years, Jake had joined them for Christmas somewhere in California, and this year it was San Francisco.

Two days before Christmas, they rented a car. The plan was to drive across the Golden Gate Bridge to Marin County, then drive up the coast through Point Reyes National Seashore. They stopped at a little dockside cafe in Sausalito to enjoy the view of San Francisco across the bay. Each year, when they sat down for the annual interview on how the year had gone, his dad started with a similar question:

"How's work?"

"Not bad," Jake said. "Busy. I've even been pulling in some extra money. I had a rush job from some rich people. It was dull work – big bathrooms and big bedrooms and big closets in a luxury living area – but they paid me well. And before you ask, I put almost all of it in savings. I've been too busy to spend much money anyways."

"I hear there is someone new in your life," said his mother.

"Alexandra. Yeah, I met her during the summer."

"Well?" said his mother.

"I know your next question, Mom. No, it's nothing serious. Alexandra's nice, but I'm too young for anything serious. Every guy deserves a few good earnings years when he can still spend it on himself."

"What is she like?"

"Pretty. Kind of artsy. Likes to go to gallery openings more than anything in the world. We hang out a few times a week. Usually with friends. Her friends."

"But you never did have a lot of friends, Jake," his mother said.

"I've heard that before. How many friends does a guy need?"

"Speaking of friends," said his mother, "What ever happened to that nice young man from high school, Ben. Didn't you say he moved out to California?"

"Yeah, he's somewhere here in the San Francisco area, or down around Palo Alto. I haven't heard from him in a year or more. He turned out to be gay and upped and moved to San Francisco. Who'd have thought."

"Sounds like you were the last to know," his mother said.

"But you didn't think …

Both of his parents laughed. His father spoke first.

"No, we never thought that. But sometimes we were afraid you'd break his heart. He was such a nice boy – smart and introverted like you. We always liked him. Your mother and I were always a little befuddled about why you never saw the stars in his eyes."

"I think he was as clueless then as I was," said Jake. "Stars in his eyes? Nah. But I think he has a nice boyfriend now, so these things work out in the end, and they're living happily ever after in San Francisco."

"San Francisco is not your sort of place, is it? I think you got a bigger thrill out of Arcata and Humboldt County last year. California's hick places."

"San Francisco is beautiful, and all that. And there sure are a lot of smart and good-looking people here – people who'd cut your throat for a parking space. But I don't think I'm much of a city person. Even Charlottesville seems crowded sometimes."

"Maybe you got that from my side of the family," said his mother. "My grandfather was a farmer, and it was farmers all the way down, as far as I know."

"Actually, I'd take a city over the suburbs any day. Charlottesville at least tries to disguise its suburbanness. It's smart enough to at least be ashamed of it. But sometimes I wonder if you two – and your generation – didn't get a much better deal. You both did what you loved and made a living at it."

"But it was getting more difficult," said his dad. "After the eighth budget and staff cut we got the message. It was cowardly of us, I suppose, to take our pensions and cut and run, to a place where we could stretch out the money and stretch out retirement."

"But I don't regret it," said his mother. "I couldn't take the politics anymore. Or the students' attitudes. It all changed so fast. It was terrifying. We miss you, Jake. We miss you all the time, but we like being in Costa Rica. We would have loved to see you follow in our footsteps, in the liberal arts or the humanities. We tried not to pressure you either way. But we saw years ago that it was going to get harder and harder to make a living."

"I don't blame you at all," said Jake. "Costa Rica was smart. It was the right thing to do. But people my age, we don't have a chance. The only option is to pick an empty career, whatever gags you the least, then try to make enough money to pay off the student loans. I thank y'all for that, though – that my loans aren't nearly as bad as other people's. But architecture? I'm supposed to find meaning in that? All I do is draw up big bathrooms for rich people. No, you two are lucky. You got to do what you love, and then you were able to get out when the money people took over and it all started getting ugly."

"What would you rather be doing, Jake?" his dad asked. "You never seemed to be all that clear about that kind of thing, at least at college age."

"I don't know. Be a slacker, I guess, until I have time to figure it out. Read. Learn some alchemy. Take up whittling. Study the stars."

"Speaking of stars," his dad said, "I brought something for you."

"Yeah?"

"I brought you my telescope."

"What? The Celestron? Why?"

"It's just too foggy and rainy on our mountainside. I figured you'd get more use out of it. It's back at the hotel. You can take it with you on the plane, or I'll ship it to you, whichever is easier."

"Incredible. Thanks, Dad. No one of my generation would ever be able to afford one like that. Not unless you got a business degree and work for a hedge fund or something. I'll put it to good use, I promise."

"I knew you would."

"Speaking of stars, I met this cool old guy up in the mountains. It was last May. I was going for a hike in one of those little zones with low light pollution that you listed for me, and a storm – probably a tornado – blew a bunch of trees in the road and I was stuck for a while. Anyway, I camped on this old guy's place, and he had some funny things to say about the stars."

"A farmer?" asked his dad.

"I suppose he's a farmer now. But he's more like a professor. He could hold his own against you two. He was an engineer, but that didn't keep him from reading everything in the Western canon. Anyway, he was amused by my stargazing. He said that, symbolically, it is as though – there's your simile, Mom – I'm searching for the center of the universe. He says that the young hero – that would be me – always feels as though he's stranded in the middle of nowhere. 'Well, if there's a bright center to the universe, you're on the planet that it's farthest from.' Do you know that quote, Mom?"

"Of course. C3PO. Star Wars."

"That's right. Anyway, this old guy has a mind that just won't slow down. Every time I talk with him – I've been there twice – I'm exhausted, like I've been trying to keep up with a pack of coyotes all night, and the moon is full."

"What does he do out there?" Jake's mom asked.

"He has a little farm, chickens and such. He's off the grid. He's a hermit. We still have hermits these days. Who knew? I feel sorry for him in a way, out there by himself, so smart, but nobody to talk to. I have to say I admire the way he lives. And he has room for a dog. An old dog, though."

"I get it," said Jake's dad. "Help me out with the metaphors here, Anne. There was something in the stars, and a storm blew you onto this old hermit's shores. And the stars are saying that the monastic life just might beat the suburban life and drawing up bathrooms for rich people. I'm not criticizing, mind you. Those sound like pretty good insights to me. After all, we fled to Costa Rica."

"Something like that, Dad. I accept my fate, though. The suburban life is my lot, at least for now. But the wise have always studied the stars, and we have to bear witness to what we see on the other end of the telescope. You taught me that, both of you."

"So we did," said his mom.

"How are things on your tropical mountainside?" asked

Jake. "Is it still quiet, and safe, with bananas hanging in every tree and fresh water pouring from every rock?"

"Yes," said his mother. "Paradise."

"Good," said Jake. "I'm glad you're where you are. It's a good place for you. You're out of the suburbs. Maybe someday I'll get out of the suburbs, too."

— —

A few days later, when Jake took leave of his parents at the airport, Jake pressed a sealed envelope into his mother's hand.

"Mom, I want you to hang on to this, but don't open it. If anything ever … happens, if you can't get in touch with me for some reason, then open it. Now don't ask a lot of questions, and don't worry, because I don't mean to make you uneasy. It's just a little … insurance, that's all."

"Jake, what is this? Have you written a will or something? At your age?"

"Mom, please. Don't ask. But just humor me and hold on to it, OK?"

"OK. And now you humor your mom. If there's something else we need to talk about, you call me. Right away. OK?"

"Always," said Jake.

CHAPTER 10

On a Saturday morning in late January, Jake and Alexandra took the early train from Charlottesville to Washington. It was Alexandra's idea. There were a couple of art galleries that she wanted to visit, and they were to meet some of Alexandra's friends for a late lunch near Dupont Circle. The plan was to take the evening train back to Charlottesville. Alexandra had agreed not to let the lunch run too long, because Jake wanted to have time to visit the Air and Space Museum and the planetarium. Alexandra had never been to a planetarium. Jake was hoping that the experience might help her understand his fascination for space, and for the stars, without her having to endure the inconvenience of being outdoors in the cold night air. Alexandra had been paying a lot more attention to Jake's interests lately, so the time seemed right. It was a fine winter day for a visiting the tourist sites in Washington. For January, the weather forecast was not too harsh – clear skies with a high in the mid-40's – so they also planned to do a little strolling on the Mall.

As soon as they emerged from the Metro station, it was clear that something was going on. Three military helicopters flew overhead at low altitude, heading west. Jake even felt the wash from the rotors, and he and Alexandra had to shout to hear each other. Looking around the Mall, Jake could see two other helicopters sitting silently on the ground in the direction of the Capitol. There also were small groups of soldiers here and there. The soldiers were milling around casually, but some of them were holding rifles. Jake approached a couple of park service security people, who were less threatening than the soldiers, and asked them if they knew what was going on.

"Just some military exercises," said the security person, who was armed with a radio but no weapon. "Very routine."

The security person looked as though he might say more, but he was drowned out by the sound of another helicopter, this one approaching the Capitol from the southeast. Jake was pretty sure that Andrews Air Force Base was in that direction.

The sound of the helicopters caused Jake to think back to that day last summer, when he had camped on the ridge overlooking the senator's mountain retreat. Jake realized that he had let his mind wander too much since Christmas, that he had not maintained his focus on connecting the dots in whatever dark events might be under way. It was as though the weight of his suspicions had fatigued him, and he had fallen back into the routine of work. Not to mention, Alexandra had been a lot more fun lately. That was distracting, too. Now he felt like kicking himself for taking his eye off the ball, because something felt weird about all this military activity in the center of Washington.

"Let's go over to the White House," Jake said. "I want to see what these military exercises are about. Did your mom mention military exercises?"

"No," said Alexandra. "I don't think that sort of thing is on her radar screen."

As they made their way to the White House, two

more helicopters approached, these from the south-west. Jake kicked himself again for not having done the homework on some basic military matters. He realized that he was unable to distinguish an Air Force helicopter from a Marine helicopter, and he was not absolutely certain of the location of the two military bases closest to Washington – the Quantico Marine base and the Andrews Air Force Base. But he was pretty sure that the helicopters were all Black Hawk helicopters. He also guessed that they were VIP transport helicopters, not gun ships. But whether the helicopters approached from the southeast or the southwest, almost all seemed to be departing toward the west.

Soon they reached the park that faces the White House. There were no helicopters visible near the White House, and all seemed quiet behind the iron fence. Once again Jake approached a park service security person, hoping to get some information.

"What's up with all these helicopters?" asked Jake. "Is the White House in on these military exercises too?"

"All's quiet here," the security person said. "The President's in Alaska."

Yet again Jake wanted to kick himself for not having paid enough attention to the news for the past few weeks. He had almost forgotten that the President had made a trip to Seattle, followed by some kind of visit to military bases in Alaska. There seemed to be no unusual military presence around the White House, just the usual guards at the gates. So then, it appeared that all the helicopter traffic and other "maneuvers" were focused around the Capitol.

Jake wanted nothing more than to sit down and think for a while. But here he was, in Washington, many miles away from the Jeep. And he was with Alexandra, and he had a good six or seven hours of socializing before he could even get on the train back to Charlottesville and gain some thinking time. He looked at his phone to check the time.

"We'd better get to the planetarium," he said to Alexandra. "We should try to catch one of the next shows. What time are your friends expecting us?"

"At 2 o'clock," said Alexandra. "And I promised them we wouldn't be late."

Sometimes in a good planetarium Jake felt as though he actually was outdoors at night. The effect was just so real, even if the clarity of the stars was greater than in the out of doors. He even suspected that planetariums intentionally keep the place a little chilly, to enhance the outdoors effect. Soon Jake was lost in a fugue, carried away in his imagination, as he usually was while under the stars. He tuned out the people around him, Alexandra included, though she cuddled against his shoulder in the chilly air. Even when the planetarium's projector sped up the passage of time, and the stars wheeled overhead, Jake stayed in the fugue, as though he was an ancient tree anchored deep in the soil, measuring time in eons rather than hours and days. He had seen planetarium shows many times before. But this time he watched with a new question: Where is the center of universe? How would we recognize it if we saw it? What a slow story I've been in, thought Jake. I've never been in love, and nothing truly wonderful or truly terrible has ever happened to me. Well, some stuff was terrible enough, but not by any cosmic standard. Jake had never been in a war, or witnessed a holocaust, or a plague. He was like a hothouse plant, raised in a hospitable environment. He'd seen others suffer, yes. But he had gotten off easy.

As the stars slowed their wheeling overhead, and as Jake saw from the position of Ursa Major that dawn was approaching on this virtual Earth, suddenly he was aware of Alexandra snuggled against him. He snuggled back. Jake had realized that, though he had spent many hours out under the stars, he couldn't recall ever watching Ursa Major roll into view or fade out in the morning light with a girl cuddled against him.

When the lights came on, Jake felt as though he had been awakened from a trance. Alexandra was saying something. He wasn't sure what she had said. He searched backward in his fugal memory to recover her words.

"Another hour to kill," she had said.

As they filed out of the planetarium, Jake turned his phone back on. He had turned it off to silence it during the show. He had a voice message. It was from a number he didn't recognize, with the area code for far western Virginia. Many times, Jake had imagined such a message. He was eager to listen to it, but he needed to be in a quiet place, somewhere he could concentrate. When they reached the lobby, he proposed that they take a bathroom break. Alexandra gladly assented.

The men's room was empty. Jake could hear himself think. The message was from Phaedrus, and it was about forty seconds long. Jake played it back:

"Hello, Jake, this is Phaedrus. I'd like to talk with you for a minute if you're going to be available. I'll keep this message brief. It's very important. Things are happening fast all of a sudden. If you would still like to come here, it had best be right away. I'm sorry I couldn't give you more … notice, but we can't control events, can we? Please remember the suggestions I gave you last time you were here about equipment and such. If you can be here before dark tomorrow, that would be ideal. Actually, it's more than just ideal, it's urgent. I'll try to call again in two hours, but after that I won't be near a phone. I'm really hoping to see you tomorrow. If you aren't prepared for a little trip right now on such short notice, don't worry. I've got everything you need. I hope to talk with you in a couple of hours."

Suddenly Jake had a case of butterflies in the stomach. So now the moment had come when he was forced to make a decision. Are the dots really connected? Was there a way to hedge, to go to Phaedrus' place but to come back to Charlottesville as quickly as possible if it turned out to be nothing? Tomorrow was Sunday. That gave him one day. He did not have any important appointments or deadlines next week. To be away for a few days would not be the end of the world. And what about Alexandra? If he thought this was for real, how could he just leave her? And how could he possibly explain anything to her?

When he met Alexandra back in the lobby, she looked serene, still glowing, probably, from the long cuddle. Jake did his best to hide his nervousness.

Back outdoors on the mall, the helicopter traffic seemed to be subsiding. Jake tried to think it through. What kind of significance could there be in military maneuvers and heavy helicopter traffic near the Capitol? Were they ferrying members of Congress out? They couldn't possibly evacuate the whole Congress. That many people – the House of Representatives was like a mob – couldn't possibly be allowed to know what was going on. If that mob knew, then the secret would be impossible to keep. No, Jake figured that the majority of the members of Congress were just as up the creek as the rest of the population. Only a few key members, like the rich senator, would know what was really going on. It would be easy enough to invent a cover story for the congressional losers. For example, they could be told that the maneuvers were to practice an evacuation of the Congress, should such a thing ever be necessary. And for purposes of the maneuvers, it was not necessary for everyone to take a helicopter ride. Just a few key members as proof of concept would be sufficient. Those lower in the hierarchy would never be the least bit suspicious, because they were surely accustomed to some members of Congress being VIP's and others being congressional nobodies. But what about the White House? The president was said to be far away, in Alaska. That was a good story. It got the president out of the picture.

As he had these thoughts, Jake knew that he was taking this seriously. And if he took it seriously, then he had to get back to Charlottesville. The train was due in Charlottesville in the late evening. He'd get everything ready, load the Jeep, and leave Sunday morning at dawn. If it all turned out to be nothing, if Phaedrus didn't have a convincing story when he saw him, then Jake could be back in Charlottesville by Tuesday or Wednesday, with no great damage done. He'd get Alexandra to go with him, and he'd think of some way to explain it to her.

Jake asked Alexandra if she'd like to spend the next hour in one of the art museums rather than the Air and Space museum. She quickly assented. Jake calculated that, because she would be less bored in the art museum, he'd have more time to work out a plan. And besides, she'd been awfully nice in the planetarium, so she deserved an art museum.

An hour and a half later they were in a restaurant bar near Dupont Circle with Alexandra's friends. They were all talking and laughing. Occasionally the roar of a helicopter would intrude, and the conversation would go on hold while everyone nursed their drinks. Jake left his phone beside his drink on the counter, where he'd know immediately if it rang. It did. The call was from the same number in western Virginia. Jake answered it immediately.

"Hello, this is Jake."

"Jake, this is Phaedrus. Do you have a few minutes to talk?"

"I do. But I'm in a noisy place. Give me thirty seconds to go outside." Jake told Alexandra that he was going outside to take the call and that he'd be right back. She nodded.

"OK," Jake said, as soon as he reached a quiet spot beyond the door of the bar, behind a concrete column to help mask the noise of the traffic. "Phaedrus. It's great to hear from you. What's up?"

"Jake. I'm so glad you answered. I'm sorry I can't explain everything right now. You listened to the message I left earlier?"

"Yes."

"Would you like to come? I can explain everything much more easily after you're here."

"Yes. Yes, I want to come. But I'm in Washington right now. I took the train. The Jeep is in Charlottesville. I'm taking the train back to Charlottesville tonight. I can get there by tomorrow evening. Will that work?"

"Yes. That will work, though I think we … need to hurry with this. I'd say you should plan on being here tomorrow before dark, at the latest. Don't put a lot of time into preparing. Just bring warm clothes, good boots, that sort of thing. I'll have everything you need. I'll fill you in when you get here. This is probably not the best time to be in Washington. I think you should get out of Washington as soon as you can. Is there any chance of an earlier train?"

"I'm afraid not. There's only the evening train. It's an interesting day in Washington, some kind of military maneuvers, lots of helicopters."

"I see. Yes. I think you should leave as soon as possible."

"I have a thousand questions, but I'll save them until tomorrow. And Phaedrus. I'm with Alexandra. What should …" Jake paused to try to figure out how to say it.

There also was a pause on other end of the line. But Phaedrus spoke first.

"I understand," Phaedrus said. "By all means bring her. But she'll need warm clothes too, hiking boots, things like that. How much have you explained to her?"

"I haven't explained anything, really."

"Events are moving fast," said Phaedrus. "We no longer have to be so coy. You can tell Alexandra whatever you need to tell her, as long as it's only Alexandra."

"Great. That will make it easier," said Jake. "Can I reach you on this number?"

"No. It's a store, a good many miles from home. I don't plan to be back here for a while."

"OK, Phaedrus. I'll see you tomorrow."

"OK, Jake. Be careful. Watch the sky. You did a lot of good research. If you see anything, you'll know what it is."

Jake spent the next two hours in the noisy bar and restaurant squirming. He couldn't yet get out of Washington, and he had to be sociable. The women were talking about galleries. The guys were talking about sports. Jake pretended to be interested in a soccer game that was playing on a television screen above the bar. That at least gave him an excuse for being distracted, and he could try to think while his eyes were on the television. He couldn't say anything to Alexandra now. Later, when they were on the train, he would think of some way to explain to her why they needed get to Phaedrus' place in the mountains as quickly as possible. Should he hedge? Should he maybe try to make it sound like a lark, an impulsive romantic trip to the mountains? She'd probably find a story like that much more compelling.

Jake was amazed when the party broke up early. Everyone seemed to have somewhere they needed to be. And the noise of the helicopters was interfering with conversation. It was not quite 4 o'clock, and the light was still good outside. That meant that Jake and Alexandra had some time to kill before the train.

"Why don't we go back to the Mall?" said Jake. "I'd like to see what's up with all these helicopters. Then we can head for Union Station early and find a nice cafe, and maybe warm up with some hot chocolate."

"Good idea," said Alexandra, "as long as we don't stay on the Mall too long. It's starting to get cold out there."

As they approached the Mall, they passed a black

Humvee parked between the Lincoln Memorial and the Reflecting Pool. Armed troops in back uniforms stood beside the Humvee.

"What the devil?" said Jake. "Those look like private soldiers."

There weren't many people out now. Jake couldn't tell whether the soldiers were eyeing them suspiciously or merely checking out Alexandra. Jake took Alexandra's hand. He shivered, whether from the cold or his ever-increasing nervousness he wasn't sure.

"You're shivering," she said. "You need some hot chocolate."

"I do," said Jake. "But first I want to see what all that activity is about up around the Capitol."

It was rapidly growing darker. As they hurriedly along beside the Reflecting Pool, suddenly there was a siren sound from somewhere inside Alexandra's coat. Jake had heard that sound before.

"Damn," said Alexandra. "Mom always does this at the worst time. And how does she always seem to know if I'm in Washington?"

"Maybe there's a tracker in that thing," said Jake.

They sat down beside the Reflecting Pool so that Alexandra could call her mom. Jake cuddled up against her. Alexandra fished her cell phone out of a coat pocket and called her mom.

"What now, Mom? It's kind of cold for one of your drills. I'm outside. I can't talk long."

"This is not a drill, Alexandra." Jake could easily hear Alexandra's mom's voice.

"What do you, this is not a drill?" said Alexandra.

"They've called an alert. Something's up. It's real. I need to have you picked up, immediately. There's no time to waste. You have to hurry."

"But I'm in…"

"I know where you are. There's a helicopter waiting near the Capitol. Two men in dark uniforms are coming to meet you. Go with them. They'll get you to the helicopter."

"But, Mom, I'm with Jake. I can't just dump him. What's going on? A helicopter? Why?"

"There's no time to explain now, Alexandra. Just do as I say."

"But Jake…"

"I see. Fine. Bring him then, and we'll sort that out later. But there's no time for questions. Just go with those men. I have to go now, but I'll see you soon. OK?"

"OK. But what's going on?"

"No time now. I'll explain when I see you. I'll see you in an hour or two."

Alexandra put the phone back in her pocket.

"You heard?" she said.

"I heard," said Jake.

"We'd better go," said Alexandra. "I don't know what this is all about, but we'd better go. Suddenly this all seems really scary."

Alexandra grabbed Jake's hand, and together they started to jog toward the Capitol.

"Alexandra," said Jake. "We need to talk. There are some things I need to tell you."

"Now? What do you mean? We can talk on the helicopter."

Jake's mind was roiling. Running made it even harder to think. And then, to add to Jake's confusion, there was the sound of an approaching jet engine, at low altitude. It was coming from the south, as though it had taken off from Washington National Airport but for some reason was failing to gain altitude. Just before the plane broke into view above the Mall, terrifyingly close to the tree-tops, a much louder jet engine could be heard streaking in from the north at the same low altitude. The first jet was not a big one. It was some sort of private jet, an executive jet. The second jet, however, was a military fighter jet, probably an F-16. It was headed straight for the executive jet. The executive jet, apparently seeing the threat, suddenly banked into a sickening high-speed turn to reverse its course, losing altitude as it did so. Jake was afraid it was going to fall somewhere near the Jefferson Memorial. The panicked jet was trying to turn south, back toward the river. Somehow it remained aloft, completed its turn, engines screaming, and gained a little altitude. Now it was heading south, toward the river, running from the F-16. Then the F-16 fired its guns. A shell hit the wing of the executive jet with a dull pop that arrived at Jake's ears two or three seconds after he saw the flash. Then the little jet began to roll, spewing flames and smoke, lighting up the darkening sky. Jake never heard it fall. It had probably gone into the river.

Jake and Alexandra had stopped running now, staring upward, bewildered, terrified. But things only got worse. Now there was the sound of machine-gun fire from the direction of the Capitol. There were a few short bursts from one gun, then much longer bursts from several guns.

"That was machine guns," said Jake. "Which way do we run?"

"Mom said…"

Suddenly two armed men in black uniforms were on top of them.

"Alexandra Brantley?" said one of the men.

"I'm Alexandra Brantley."

"Come with us," the man said.

"Jake?" said Alexandra, twisting in the man's grip and turning toward Jake. She looked like she might scream.

"Come with us," said the man. "You'll be safe."

Alexandra took Jake's hand and pulled. Jake hesitated.

"Jake, what's wrong? Let's go," she said.

Jake took her hands. If only he had time to think. It was all happening too fast. He stood there for a second, looking at the sky. Then he looked back at Alexandra. Now both men had their hands on her.

"Alexandra, I can't."

"What do you mean you can't? They'll take us somewhere safe until this is over. My mom will tell us what's going on."

"It's more complicated than that, Alexandra. I don't know where they're taking you, but I don't think it's where I belong right now." He held Alexandra's hands tightly. The armed men were pulling her away.

"Jake, that's just crazy talk. Come on. Whatever this is, it will be over soon. Then we'll go back home."

"I can't, Alexandra. You go on. You'll be safe."

Jake let go of Alexandra's hands. The men were dragging her away now, toward the Capitol. She was crying.

Jake stood and watched as they dragged her away. If only he had been able to explain. She deserved to know.

"I'll call you," he shouted after her. "I'll call you and explain." But Jake was not sure that Alexandra had heard him. Soon they disappeared into the twilight.

Jake turned south. It wasn't far to the bridge. He needed to get across the bridge and get back into Virginia. Once he was across the river, he could figure out how to get to Charlottesville, to the Jeep.

As he sprinted back toward the Lincoln Memorial, Jake saw an abandoned bicycle lying against some shrubbery. No one was around. He stopped and set it upright, bounced it to check the tires. It seemed to be serviceable. Jake mounted the bicycle and sped south, toward the Arlington Memorial Bridge.

"What the fuck!" shouted Jake. He shouted it into the sky, like an idiot, but he couldn't really hear himself over the sound of the sirens and helicopters. He pedaled hard, jumped the bicycle over holes in the pavement, leaned dangerously into turns hoping that there was no loose gravel. He swerved dangerously close to a pair of joggers who seemed to be arguing about which way to run. He needed to pee, bad. But he kept pedaling.

The Arlington Memorial Bridge, which should not have been busy on a day like this, was crazy with cars, all of them honking and going too fast. Everywhere there was the sound of sirens and helicopters. Jake was in the pedestrian lane on the upstream side of the bridge, going dangerously fast. There were no pedestrians to get in his way. Jake wasn't sure why just getting across the bridge into Virginia would make him feel safer. Maybe it was because he'd feel farther away from people. It would be easier to avoid being seen. That was Jake's strongest feeling as he flew across the bridge – not wanting to be seen, and finding somewhere to piss. It felt like being in an alien invasion movie. One of the things he'd learned from those movies was to get the hell out of the city, to get as far away from people as possible. Bridges were a major red flag. That's where the aliens caught up with everyone in "War of the Worlds." As Jake approached the Virginia end of the bridge, suddenly everything around him went dark. All the lights had gone out. The stars were a thousand times brighter all of a sudden. He slowed the bicycle to let his eyes adjust.

He reached the traffic circle at the end of the bridge. He stopped well away from the traffic and got off the bike. He pissed against a bush. As long as the bicycle was up to it, he now had a plan. There would be no train. He bounced the bicycle again, felt its tires, explored the cables with his hands. The bicycle seemed to be in good shape. It was more than a hundred miles to Charlottesville. If there was no trouble, the bicycle would get him to Charlottesville well before morning. He'd take the straightest course possible but try to steer clear of densely populated places and the main roads. The route should take him through Manassas and Culpeper, roughly the route that the train takes.

And now that he had a plan, as he rode he could try to figure out some other things. What the hell had happened in Washington? Alexandra's mother was a powerful person – obviously much more powerful than Jake had realized. If that was the case, then Alexandra's mother might have known what was happening. If so, then her family were among the lucky few with a ticket out. As for those who didn't have a ticket out, what would they do? That might explain the machine guns. And the jet? It was almost certainly a private jet. It was impossible to figure it out, but it might be that things weren't going very well for low-level functionaries with no golden ticket out.

What about this blackout? Was it temporary? Or were the lights not coming back on, for a long, long time? In any case the darkness was a boon. Jake was still able to see the roadway pretty clearly. He'd be better hidden in the darkness. With no competition from artificial light, the stars were perfectly legible. Jake would navigate southward to Charlottesville by the stars.

If only he could explain to Alexandra, make sure that she was alright. Jake took his cell phone from his coat pocket and called her number. There was no answer, not even a prompt for leaving voice mail.

Jake got back onto the bike and sped south into the dark.

CHAPTER 11

Jake arrived at his apartment about an hour before dawn. His legs ached. He needed sleep. He was sweaty and thirsty. He was tempted to take time for a shower, but there was no water. Everything was dark, and Jake had to use a camping headlamp to load the Jeep. At least he had followed some of Phaedrus' suggestions. He had a go bag prepared – actually two go bags – and he threw them into the back of the Jeep. The go bags actually were backpacks. They contained everything that Jake could think of that might be useful off the grid – matches, first aid kits, a wind-up emergency radio, dehydrated food, energy bars, a water filter of the type used by hikers to drink safely from streams, lots of warm socks, rain gear, knives, basic tools, even some lightweight fishing gear. The packs were heavy. Jake carefully stowed into the back of the Jeep the Celestron telescope that his dad had given him at Christmas. Almost as an afterthought, Jake found an old wooden chest containing some heirloom silver. His mother had given it to him before they left for Costa Rica. That was worth keeping, Jake reasoned. He also came across a frayed Virginia Cavaliers baseball cap that Jamie had given him years ago. Jake took that too.

As Jake started the Jeep and headed for the Interstate, the first glow of dawn appeared in the sky. The people in his apartment complex had seemed restless though not yet panicked. Some had been out fiddling with their cars with flashlights. Candlelight showed through some apartment windows. A guy who didn't even seem to have a flashlight had asked Jake if he had any coffee to spare. For the eighth or tenth time, Jake tried to call Alexandra. Again there was no answer and no voice mail prompt. Jake also tried to call his parents. Nothing. Cell phone systems had either stopped working or were hopelessly overloaded. As he drove, he saw no sign that there was electrical power anywhere. But everywhere there were confused-looking people, even at this hour, as though some people had been up all night. They were wandering back and forth across their yards, clustering with their neighbors, packing things in their cars. They were arguing. Some were rushing. Some were dawdling.

"Just look at them," Jake said to himself. "They're like fucking zombies. They're all so fucking stupid that they'll all drive into the cities, go wherever there are the most people, wherever they see some kind of light or smell something frying. They don't have a television, or a cell phone, or even a radio to tell them what to do. And so they just stand around and argue about what to do.

"And just how are you doing any better, Jake? Why is it so hard to keep the gas tank full, Jake? Phaedrus told you to keep the tank full, you dumb-ass zombie, and you've barely got more than half a tank. So what are you going to do about it? How do you pump gas when the fucking grid is down? If you had a hose, could you siphon some gas? See there? See the slippery slope you're on? You're already thinking about lawbreaking and disorder, because you didn't fucking think ahead, even though you knew. Ah. You weren't sure. Brilliant.

"Just drive. Just get the fuck away from people. They're zombies now, but as soon as their kids get hungry, they'll be criminals. Drive Jake. But don't outrun your head-lights, Jake. Better yet, hold it down to fifty-five. It'll be much safer and save a lot of gas. You'll get much closer to Phaedrus' place before you run out.

"What the fuck? Why did they shoot down that jet? Why would there be machine-guns at the fucking U.S. Capitol? But stop worrying about Alexandra. She'll be fine. Clearly her mom has power. Just look out for your-self now, Jake. Hold it in the road. Watch out for the fucking zombies stumbling across the fucking highway in the dark. Think."

Jake tried the Jeep's radio again. Once again there was only static. About fifty miles south of Charlottesville, the suburbs were behind him, and he was in more open country. Jake felt a little safer from the suburban zombies and decided to have a go at buying gas. He saw a sign promising gas and food eight miles ahead.

The exit was a small country road. There was little to be seen other than a cinderblock building with rusty signs advertising gasoline, milk, bread, and lottery tickets. Two cars were parked in front of the store. Jake stopped the Jeep in front of the gas pumps. When he tried to activate the pump, there was no response, just silence. The pump's display was dark. As Jake fiddled with the pump, then tried the other pump, an older woman with disorderly white hair and wearing a man's coat stepped just outside the door of the store and called out to Jake.

"The power's out," she said. "I can't pump any gas."

"Is there another station around here?"

"Which way are you going?"

"South."

"There's another one at the second exit, about ten miles. But they won't have any gas either."

"How about snacks? Can you sell some snacks with the power out?"

"If you've got cash."

Jake followed the woman back into the store. It was dark except for the light through the front glass windows and a small window in the back. Jake selected a ready-made sandwich, a bag of chips, and some vegetable juice. He wanted to buy more, but he was afraid the woman would think he was hoarding.

"How much?" Jake asked, trying to sound calm.

"That'll be thirty dollars," the woman said.

"What?"

"This could last a while," she said. "Others may want it as much as you."

"How much for just the juice, then?"

"That'd be ten."

Jake set the sandwich and chips back on the counter and threw down a ten. He was starving, but there was no time to do anything about it now. He got back into the Jeep and was soon on the Interstate again.

What happened next was so unexpected and so quick that Jake really wasn't sure whether he only imagined it. He thought he saw a flash of light in the rearview mirror, to the north. It was something like far-off lightning, but this was January. At the same time, the Jeep's engine seemed to misfire. For a second, no more than two seconds, the engine ran rough, and the Jeep lurched, then everything returned to normal. Jake turned up the heater. He felt cold. His palms were sweating. He tried to think of an explanation for what had just happened other than a distant nuclear detonation and its attendant electromagnetic pulse. But he couldn't think of any other explanation.

Now he started to pass stalled cars. Most of the drivers had managed to coast out of the roadway, but some had stopped right in the middle of the Interstate. Confused drivers were raising the hoods of their cars. A couple of people tried to flag Jake down. One man made an obscene gesture as Jake kept moving. The Jeep had felt that pulse too, but the Jeep had misfired and kept running. Jake pondered the possibility of trying again to get gas. He decided that it was hopeless, that it would only cost time and expose him to people whose cars had stopped running and who were obviously getting increasingly agitated as they transformed into zombies and criminals. Jake tried to make some rough calculations about how far he could get. Give or take a gallon of gas, he figured he could get within twenty to sixty miles of Phaedrus' place. That meant that saving fuel was more important than haste. The speedometer registered seventy miles an hour. He was letting himself get addled, letting himself get scared.

"Slow down, Jake! You'll kill yourself, and even a Jeep won't keep running if it hits one of the obese ones at seventy miles an hour."

Again he backed off to fifty-five. It was the only smart thing to do, because getting more miles out of the Jeep meant fewer miles he'd have to walk.

The fuel gauge was down to a quarter of a tank when he finally got a station on the radio. It was on the AM band, and it was weak. Jake was pretty sure it was a Cuban station broadcasting in English. The announcer was speaking in grave tones. There were occasional crashes of static that drowned out the voice, but Jake could follow most of what was being said. It was grim.

Nuclear detonations had been reported by the hundreds all over Asia and parts of Africa. The detonations were concentrated in cities and densely populated areas. These detonations had continued for the last four to five hours. This information apparently came from the Cuban and Russian military. No reports were available on what actually was happening on the ground in those places, and no information was available from civilian sources. But much could be deduced from the military's information, the announcer said, and it seemed a near certainty that casualties must be heavy. During the past hour or two, there were reports of a few detonations in the United States – in southern California and roughly in the area of Boston and New York City. Military sources were working to confirm those reports. Cuba, the announcer kept emphasizing, was not threatened, nor had there been any detonations within 1,200 miles of Cuba. Cubans citizens were instructed to listen to their radios and to remain alert, because there might be a danger of fallout in coming days. Listeners in the United States were told that they should take cover, with a supply of food and water. The announcer said that Cuban military sources were doing their utmost to determine the reason for the detonations and who was responsible. It seemed likely at this point, the announcer said, that American weapon systems had been accidentally activated, for unknown reasons. Only the United States, the announcer said, had such a widespread nuclear capability, and only an accident seemed likely to explain detonations on American soil, which were now confirmed.

So then, thought Jake. The flash that I saw in the rearview mirror must have been New York or Boston. That's not close enough to be threatening, at least not unless the fallout comes this way, but that will take a while. But there is no way of knowing where, or when, the next detonations might be. Again Jake felt the need to talk with his parents, and with Alexandra. But when he looked at his phone, it said "No Service." At this point, thought Jake, that probably is not going to change. The phones are going to stay dead. He tried the GPS app on his phone. It was still working. Thank goodness for military technology, thought Jake. Those GPS satellites are probably shielded. But by now he knew how to get to Phaedrus' place without help navigating.

About ninety miles from Phaedrus' place, Jake turned off the Interstate and headed west. The sun was now low in the west. The air was getting colder, and again Jake turned up the heater. Jake's arithmetic showed that it was now time to find a place to hide the Jeep. The terrain was good for hiding a Jeep. Jake started looking for little trails or logging roads into the woods, at the lower elevations. The gasoline gauge was well into the red zone. The sky was increasingly growing dark. Rain started to fall. Jake switched on the wipers and suddenly remembered the storm he'd been caught in last spring. How fortunate for him that, on that day in May, that he was stranded within walking distance of Phaedrus' house. But now he was at least 45 miles from Phaedrus' place, rather than just down the hill. He'd have no choice but to walk it. Until he got there, there would be no fire, no coffee, no Joan, no promise of a nice dinner, no Phaedrus to explain everything and to decide what to do. Jake was on his own, and safety was 45 miles away, through forested terrain that was constantly uphill and downhill. It would take two miserable days to get to Phaedrus' place.

Jake spied what looked like a logging trail leading into a ravine. He quickly braked the Jeep to a stop and backed up to have a closer look. It was promising. He shifted the Jeep into low range and four-wheel drive, then crawled the Jeep slowly off the road into the ravine. There were small fallen trees and rocks as big as soccer balls, but the Jeep rolled over them with no complaint. The trail continued for several hundred yards, more or less level, bending gently to the right.

The Jeep was in the gear that Jake called granny low, moving at only two or three miles per hour while the engine whined at more than 4,000 rpm. The ravine narrowed. Its banks grew higher and its sides steeper. The Jeep had gotten Jake to the top of many a remote ridge and many an ideal stargazing spot. But just now Jake wanted to be low, not high. The trail through the ravine was now approaching the southern side of a steep bank. There were a number of rocky outcroppings. Jake looked at the odometer. He was seven-tenths of a mile from the road, deep enough into the woods to avoid casual detection by wandering zombies.

Most of the pulses, Jake figured – and there surely would be more – would come from the northeast, because that's where the population centers are. This bank would provide considerable electromagnetic cover from that direction. With the Jeep's headlights off, it was apparent that darkness was early here, deep in the woods. Jake had not worked out a detailed plan for what to do next, and it was useless to think about that tonight. At least he had gotten out of Washington safely, and he was now within walking distance of Phaedrus' place. There was no chance of his continuing tonight. He was exhausted and had ridden a bicycle for most of the previous night. He'd spend the night in the Jeep. Jake hated sleeping in the Jeep.

"And why," said Jake, "considering all that has happened, are you feeling so damned horny? Do you get off on this kind of stuff? Is it only the adrenaline? Just do it, then, you animal. But use the light to clean up and don't make a big mess, because you're going to have to wear these shorts for a while."

◆—◆

Jake was up before daylight. He had been so exhausted that he'd slept even though he was cramped half upright into the Jeep's passenger seat and couldn't stretch out his legs. He stuffed his pack as heavily as he could bear. For Jake, a 45-mile hike over two days, even in mountain terrain, was nothing to fear. Jake's fear was of other things: desperate people mostly, and whatever perils might erupt from the sky. He felt sentimental and worried about leaving the Jeep. He was leaving many valuables behind, including his dad's telescope and his mother's silver. But, with luck, no one would discover the Jeep here for a while, and he'd return for it when he could. If there was any fuel available in the aftermath of this, a Jeep might be a good thing to have.

A light rain was falling when he set out. The main danger was traffic, so Jake always kept an eye on the woods and the quickest way to dash into hiding. The temperature at dawn had been in the low 20s, but by late morning the temperature was in the mid-30s, and Jake removed his cap. He'd seen only one truck all morning. He had heard it coming and had easily scurried out of sight.

Around noon, the flashes began. They came from the north and a little east. They looked like distant lightning, but they lingered longer and were constantly shifting hue. They'd start bright white, then turn blue, and then slowly fade into red and yellow. There was no sound, no shock wave, just the usual rustle of the winter wind in the trees. Jake had no idea how to estimate the distance to this silent mass extermination. He guessed that the detonations could be as close as Washington or Baltimore or as distant as Philadelphia or New York.

Radiation-enhanced weapons, Jake new, were detonated high in the atmosphere, so the flash would be visible much farther away than a Hiroshima-type blast close to the ground. At the distance of these flashes, radiation from fallout would not be an immediate threat, even if the wind was blowing this way. Prevailing winds were toward the east, so the fallout from cities along the Eastern Seaboard would most likely drift out over the Atlantic Ocean, posing no danger here in the Appalachians. It was the western and midwestern cities that most likely would cause fallout here. Jake doubted that he'd be able to see flashes from as far as away as Denver. But Chicago was probably upwind, depending on the jet stream. Certainly St. Louis would be a danger here, and flashes in St. Louis probably would be close enough to be visible. What about Charlotte? Fallout from Charlotte probably could be substantial here. Asheville! Asheville wasn't so much a city, more like a large town.

It was a beautiful, civilized town and deserved being called the San Francisco of the South. Jake hoped that Asheville would be spared. Still, anything could be happening, anywhere. And probably the detonations were just getting started. Anyway, it wasn't the flashes that mattered. It was the wind, carrying fallout. Jake had no instrument for detecting that. Geiger counters were not exactly standard camping equipment, but Phaedrus had them.

When he crossed a ridge in early afternoon, Jake lingered for a while to watch the sky again. There was a word for his state of mind right now. What was that word? Dissociation – the mind just refuses to go there. This is what depopulation looks like, Jake thought, seen from afar. This is what it looks like to be bombed back into the Iron Age. This is how the global elite rids the world of useless eaters. For a moment Jake found himself making a mental list of the people he knew who lived in those cities to the north, their lives being wiped in a flash of radiation. For most of them, it might not be an instant death. It might take days, one organ after another failing, yet the knowledge that death was certain. Then dissociation kicked in again, and Jake thought only of Alexandra. Alexandra, at least, was probably in a safe place, in a bunker somewhere stocked with food and wine, enjoying the perks of her mother's job. For all Jake knew, they might even be at that rich senator's place in West Virginia. Then again, the very rich and very powerful probably had plenty of refuges ready to shelter them in luxury when this day came. They had money and power, therefore they were among the few who were allowed to know things. They had the resources to be prepared. Ignorance and death, propaganda and deception – those things were for the little people. In out-of-the way places, a few hardy people would survive. They would be the new peasantry for a new Iron Age. Jake would be among the lucky few, but he would be a peasant. He had found a monastery to take him in, and he would learn to live the monastic life. But first he had to get there.

All afternoon Jake hiked, stopping only to fill his water bottle from mountain streams. He ate while walking. He had plenty of energy bars. As dusk approached, Jake was on the lookout for a place to camp for the night. Earlier, he had resolved to walk all night, but he was just too tired. The terrain was steep here, and even walking downhill was tiring. As he descended a steep, winding stretch of road toward the next stream and the next bridge, he heard an engine approaching. It sounded like a diesel engine. It was probably one of the heavy pickup trucks that the locals were so fond of. Jake sprinted into the woods and hid in a laurel thicket. From there he'd be able to see the truck as it passed.

As it approached, Jake saw that it was a large white pickup truck, the type with four doors and a large passenger cab. There were three men inside. The back of the truck was loaded, but it was impossible to see what the load was because it was covered with a tarpaulin and secured with rope and bungee cords. The truck roared past, dangerously fast, Jake thought. But Jake had already learned from traveling these roads that the locals drove very fast up here. Maybe it was because they knew the roads. Maybe it was because they were careless. Someone threw a can out a window. Or maybe, thought Jake, it's because they are drunk.

The truck disappeared around the next curve, but Jake heard it slow and stop, probably less than half a mile away, and in the direction that Jake was going. Jake emerged from the laurel thicket and stood in the roadway the better to listen. The men in the truck had looked like the sort he wouldn't want to tangle with – big, ugly, bearded – so he waited, ready to scramble back into the thicket. He heard a dog barking. Then there was a gunshot, and the dog was quiet. Jake dashed halfway to the thicket and stopped again to listen. For about five minutes, there was silence. Then he heard two more gunshots. Jake felt a strong urge to get back into the thicket, but he stood still to listen, knowing that he'd hear the truck in plenty of time if it returned. After twenty more minutes, it did return. Jake took cover, lying on his stomach in the laurel thicket peering out toward the road. This time the truck sped by even faster than before, scattering gravel and leaving the lingering smell of diesel. Jake crept out of hiding and returned to the road, always keeping as close to cover as possible.

Now he smelled smoke. It wasn't the clean smoky smell of a wood fire. Rather, it smelled dirty, like trash burning. Jake was in a creek bottom now. The road went over a little bridge, with pure mountain water gurgling across the rocks below. He saw a house, a typical, humble frame house, probably seventy-five years old, of the type that older people around here often lived in. Smoke was lazily drifting from one of the gables of the house into the evening air. The smoke was definitely not coming from the chimney. The house, or something in it, was burning.

Jake thought about creeping by, getting to the next ridge, and setting up camp for the night. But what if someone needed help? He wanted to know what had happened, and he knew that it couldn't be good. Making as little noise as possible and sticking close to the trees, he stole forward until he came to a muddy driveway. Halfway down the driveway lay the body of a dog. Jake approached the house, trying to make himself clearly visible by standing in the open, near the middle of the driveway, and called out.

"Is anybody there? Do you need help?"

There was no response. Jake passed the corpse of the dog. It was bleeding from the head. Again Jake called out. There was no response.

Heart pounding, he stepped slowly onto the porch of the house, called out again, and knocked on the door frame. The door was standing open. He pushed the door open a little wider and tried to look inside without actually going in. Some smoke came through the open door, but it did not appear to be dangerously thick, and no heat poured out the door. There was only the smell of dirty smoke and burning plastic. Slowly Jake stepped inside. But only a couple of steps were necessary. The house was small. The door led straight into the living room. An elderly man and woman lay sprawled on the floor in sickening positions. They were lying in pools of thick blood, and their clothing was bloody. Jake stepped back and closed the door. He felt like retching. Clearly the old couple were dead. Apparently whoever had robbed them had tried to set the house on fire, but the fire had fizzled out. He'd tell Phaedrus as soon as he got there, but otherwise he couldn't think of anything to do. Walking as quietly as he could and listening, he returned to the driveway and headed toward the road. He paused over the corpse of the dog. It was a hound of some unknown mix, big and black. Jake knelt and stroked its shoulder. Jake was shaking with anger. There was another emotion too – a hatred of humanity. Whatever was happening out in the world right now, many kind and innocent beings were dying. But some were going to get exactly what they deserved.

CHAPTER 12

The first glimmers of dawn were in the sky when Jake reached the familiar hilltop and found himself in Phaedrus' orchard. The silhouette of the barn, the house, and the building that Phaedrus called the studio were outlined clearly against the morning sky. It was peaceful, quaint, homey. To Jake it even looked safe, the first safe place he'd seen in days.

Jake had no idea how to announce himself in a way that would not alarm Phaedrus in the darkness. Should he lie low and wait for more light? But Jake couldn't bear to wait, and besides, Phaedrus wasn't the jumpy type. Jake decided to turn on his headlamp and stand in such a way that his face was lit. He decided on the kitchen door. Jake knocked, softly at first, then louder.

"Phaedrus? It's Jake."

There was no response, no sound from inside. Jake knocked and called again. Surely Joan would have heard him, but still there was no response.

Jake called again outside the studio. Again, there was no response. Then he called again outside the barn. No response. The shelter was the last place to look.

The outside door of the studio was locked. Jake swore and pulled off his headlamp. The sky was much brighter now. He could see clearly without the headlamp. Jake tried to think. It was completely possible that Phaedrus had gone into the shelter days ago. But surely, as thorough and thoughtful as Phaedrus was, he'd be on the lookout for Jake's late arrival and would have made some sort of arrangements.

Jake returned to the kitchen door. Once again, Jake knocked and waited, but there was no response. He turned the knob. It was not locked. He opened the door and called again. Then he stepped slowly into the kitchen. Just because it was the spot he was most familiar with, Jake went to the little table beside the window. It was dark in the kitchen, although through the window he could see a lightening sky. Jake took his headlamp from his pocket, put it on his head again, and switched it on. On the table was a brown envelope. On the front of the envelope in bold black ink was written "Jake." Jake seized the envelope and opened it. Inside there was a note, or a letter, typed on white paper on an old mechanical typewriter.

Jake,

Joan and I had to leave temporarily, but we will be back. Exactly when we will be back depends on conditions, but my guess is that I'll be away for two to three weeks.
Everything is ready for you and Alexandra. You need to get into the shelter immediately. You probably know where the shelter is. It's underneath the studio. The combination for the studio door is 11-22-36. You'll see the trap door in the floor. Everything you'll need is inside the shelter. I have left a packet of instructions there explaining how the shelter's systems work and how to keep safe. There also are instructions on how to use the instruments and how to interpret the readings you get from the instruments. I've done my best with the available time to anticipate what you might need to know and to leave instructions. You'll find

everything in a binder inside the shelter. There probably are things I've overlooked, so do be cautious, and always leave yourself the largest possible margin of safety. After the instruments confirm the all clear, I should back here within three to five days.

I apologize for not being here to greet you. I had not anticipated the need to be elsewhere, but something came up.

I hope you enjoy the reading material.

Phaedrus

A hard blow of ice and emptiness hit Jake in the stomach. Phaedrus had left home to make room for Alexandra in the shelter. Phaedrus' fervor for redundancy surely meant that he had a place to go, but clearly there was not enough room, or enough supplies, for three here. Jake realized that he probably had put Phaedrus at risk, because a backup plan is rarely as well provisioned as a primary plan.

Then Jake felt, suddenly and unambiguously, what he'd been trying to deny for the past few hours – another wave of dizziness, much worse this time. The room was spinning. He leaned over and put his hand on the table to steady himself. As the room spun faster, his nausea grew. He staggered out the kitchen door and threw up on the frosty ground. A wave of panic made the spinning even faster. Could this be radiation sickness, so soon? Surely it was only bad water. The water wouldn't be fatal. He leaned against the kitchen wall and tried to steady himself. Now his teeth were chattering. He had to get somewhere warm and safe.

Soon Jake was in a small, dark, underground room lit only by his headlamp, leaning against the ladder that led up to the studio. Right by the ladder was a switch. Jake flicked the switch, and three dim lights inside the shelter glowed. All he wanted was to throw up again and then to lie down. The room was about twelve feet long and eight feet wide. One side of the room was filled with cabinets and shelves for food, water, and other supplies. The other side of the room, near the steps leading down from the trap door, had shelves holding instruments. In one corner, on the side with the steps, was a privy, equipped with a curtain for privacy. On each of the other two walls was a fold-down cot. Each cot was in the sleeping position, with a generous stack of blankets and two pillows for each cot. On one cot there was a stack of books.

With his hands against a wall, Jake made his way across the spinning room to the privy. He fell down on his knees like a drunken student and threw up. After a few dry gags, he crawled toward the nearest bunk. The stack of books was in the way. He pushed the books onto the floor and crawled onto the bunk. He reached almost desperately for the blankets. He almost fell in the floor while reaching for more blankets from the other bunk. He pulled the blankets around himself and curled up into a fetal position. With his eyes closed, the world was spinning even faster. He groaned and rolled onto his back, trying to get the spinning to stop, dreading having to leave the warmth of the blankets and the softness of the cot to throw up again.

What are you doing here, Jake? Is all this real? Is the world really getting torched out there? Is there anyone left but you? How much longer are you going to last, if you've had a fatal dose? If it was just bad water, and you pull through, then where will you be? This isn't your home. You don't belong here. You don't really know this old guy who's looking out for you. Why is he looking out for you, you of all people? You don't know how to live like this. Maybe you can get to Costa Rica somehow. It's probably safe there. Don't be ridiculous. How would you get to Costa Rica? Walk? Are you stuck here? Do you have any options at all? Will you ever be your own man again? You'll be nothing but a useless eater, a pathetic refugee, dependent on someone else, for everything.

Jake was shivering. He felt too exhausted to fight the spinning. He gave up, no longer caring enough to fight even the cold. The shivering slowly subsided, as Jake fell deeper and deeper into blackness.

He was on skis on a high, steep mountain. The snow was fresh and deep. He was flying downhill at a reckless speed, so reckless than the slightest error of lean or flex would send him against a tree, or into a bank of snow. The snow was so deep and so heavy that an avalanche could start any time. He stole a quick glance behind him at the looming mountains of snow and rock, then quickly redirected his attention to his course again. To stop would be impossible. Even to slow down would be impossible. It was dusk. As he skied, always at the edge of panic, it was getting more and more difficult to see what was ahead. For terrifying seconds at a time, in the dark shadows of nearby trees, he was skiing blind. Then he'd emerge again into the vanishing golden light, steering frantically to avoid the trees and to stay on his feet. Then suddenly the slope was twice as steep, and he was moving so fast that it felt like falling. Then there was nothing beneath him, and he *was* falling. He fell into a canyon of blackness and whiteness lit faintly with a golden light. Then he hit something soft, and he stopped moving. He was cold, too cold to move, too cold to want to move.

He didn't fight it. This is death, he thought. When struggle is useless, it's better not to struggle, to seize a last few moments of peace. He felt a faint warmth on his face, like warm breath. He didn't move or open his eyes. It was useless to fight. Death always wins. Better not to look. Lie still. Be eaten.

Something soft and warm touched his neck, then his chest. It was gentle, sensuous, admiring, slightly erotic. Still Jake didn't move or open his eyes. Then the softness and warmth made a little whinnying sound and poked him in the stomach, then in the crotch, rudely but playfully.

Jake, still flat on his back, opened his eyes and looked up. It was a horse, huge and silver gray. It stood over him, looking down at him with wise, bright eyes that were beautiful and silver blue.

"Are you feeling up for it now?" asked the horse. It was a stallion. Jake blinked. He tried to clear his head. He was cold, though his crotch still felt warm from the horse's nudge.

"But it's so big," said Jake. The horse was definitely a stallion. Why bother to ask for it so politely when Jake was so helpless? The warmth in his crotch was embarrassing, but he couldn't hide it.

"Not that, silly. You don't deserve that yet. I meant, are you feeling up for being on our way? We've got miles and miles to go."

Jake struggled to pull his eyes away from the stallion parts and back to the horse's face. There was an amused twinkle in the horse's eyes. Jake felt unbearably embarrassed. He totally would have done it, somehow, if that's what the stallion had wanted.

"Sorry," said Jake. "I guess I'm confused. I think I've been sick. Go where? Who are you?"

"There will be plenty of time to explain," said the horse. "You're far from dead. But we need to get going. Get on. I'll keep you warm."

Somehow Jake got onto the horse's warm back and lay forward. There was no saddle. There was only a strange cord for Jake to hold on to as he clung to the horse with his arms and legs. The cord was intricately woven, perhaps with Celtic knots. It was looped around the horse's neck. Jake shivered one last time as the horse's warmth spread into his body, though his chest, his stomach, his crotch, and his cheek. Jake's legs were clamped tightly around the horse's ribs and flanks. His arms were around the horse's neck, firmly holding the cord. He was sure the horse could feel his erection. The horse walked.

They seemed to walk for days. Occasionally Jake would open his eyes and look around him, but he saw only things that he didn't want to see – burned-out houses, corpses, fields in ruin, felled trees, poisoned streams, broken machines. Once he thought he saw Jamie, as Jamie had looked when they were fourteen. Jamie stood on the opposite side of a wide, slow-running stream, wearing a shabby jacket and shivering in the cold. Jake wasn't sure that Jamie recognized him. Jake tried to call out to Jamie, tried to figure out how to get the horse to stop. But Jake felt paralyzed, and he was unable to make a sound.

The horse walked on. Jake was still cold, and the horse's back was warm. Somehow he felt welcome on the horse's back. He felt protected, a rare feeling that he could faintly recall from childhood. Jake clearly was a bother and a burden to this magical beast, and yet for some reason Jake must be worth the bother, worth rescuing and taking to wherever they were going. At times, Jake slept, but he never worried about falling. Holding the horse, their bodies so snug together, was such a comfort. It was as though the horse was wise, invincible in its maleness, and as though the entire mission of all that maleness at present was to protect Jake. They walked and walked. Eventually they seemed to be coming into warmer country. Then they were climbing. They were on the slopes of a high, conical mountain, and their destination seemed to be its top. After hours of winding upward through the trees, they stood at the crest. They were in a round opening in the trees. There was a fire. Around the fire was a group of men and women, some elderly, all in dark robes, seated on rough wooden stools. The horse stopped by the fire and turned its head to look back at Jake.

"It's a pity you didn't study harder," said the horse.

Jake climbed down from the horse's back. This was a

good-bye. The horse winked, gave Jake a gentle swat on the buttocks with its tail, and walked into the trees. Now Jake felt suddenly alone and small, missing the protective power of the horse's warmth and strength. Jake stood near the fire, facing the men and women. They were going to administer an examination, Jake knew. They looked serious, but they did not look threatening. Behind them, at the edge of the trees, was a young woman about Jake's age, very pretty. Jake knew that she had just been examined, and that she had passed. She, too, winked at Jake, then she, too, slipped quietly into the trees. Jake's eyes tried to follow her.

"Jacob," said one of the men, clearing his throat. "We will begin. Name the forty brightest stars of each of the eighty-eight constellations. Order the constellations as you might see them from the promontory at Whitrock, starting with the winter solstice."

Jake took a deep breath, then he started to call out the names of stars.

The examination went on for hours.

Consciousness returned slowly. His body felt impossibly heavy, and Jake felt too weak to move. So he lay still on the cot in the fallout shelter, struggling to remember where he was and how he'd come to be here. Gradually he put all the pieces back together. The intense emotions of the dreams lingered, adding to Jake's confusion. After what seemed like hours of struggle in which consciousness faded and returned, he felt a little better oriented as his fever broke. He was underground, in a shelter. He had been sick. He was at Phaedrus' place, but Phaedrus wasn't here. He was warm except – except for a cold, creepy feeling in his lower body. Startled, he turned on his side. He touched the bed and felt his clothing. He had wet himself. The surge of shame caused him to jump to his feet. He staggered and steadied himself against a shelf, dizzy again.

"It's OK, Jake," he said. "You've been sick. Nobody will

know. Don't dwell on it, Jake. It's what happens when you're sick, with no one to look after you. How will I ever wash this stuff?"

He rested for a few minutes. Then he stripped the bed, tried to hide the wet things near the privy, and found fresh linens. By the time everything was clean and dry, he was exhausted and fell asleep again.

When he awoke, his mind seemed clear. He wasn't sure how long he'd been sick. Two days? Three? He looked around the little underground bunker.

There were two chairs, two small bookcases, and two storage areas for personal items. There was a reading light above each cot. It was all very tidy and very organized, a well-planned, if far from extravagant, hidey hole for two people stocked with at least three weeks' worth of supplies.

On the floor was a heavy stack of books that he had knocked off the bed. In the stack was a binder. Jake opened the binder. There were some typewritten notes written by Phaedrus, and there also were manuals for some of the equipment. The topmost note from Phaedrus was about monitoring radiation. Jake sat down on the bed to read. As the after-effects of his sickness started to fade, he felt desperate to know what was going on out there and what had made him sick. Phaedrus' instruments, no doubt, would help him. And Phaedrus' notes would tell him how to use the instruments.

The notes revealed that there were instruments for detecting radiation located outside the shelter, with their readouts located on the wall near the ladder. There also were portable devices and wearable devices for measuring total radiation exposure. The first thing Jake did was to locate one of the portable devices and use it to check himself for contamination for fallout. He had followed the instructions in a note that Phaedrus had left by the trap door and had wiped himself down before entering the shelter. He had left his clothes above. He ran the probe through his hair, thinking that hair would be the most likely sticking place for fallout. As far as he could tell, the radiation level was only slightly above the level of normal background radiation. Next he tried the outside instruments. There were four outside instruments, partly for the redundancy and partly because each sensor was slightly more sensitive to radiation sources in a certain direction. All four instruments showed similar readings, and all four instruments registered decidedly above the background level, though not high enough to be very dangerous. Gradually Jake became satisfied that he had not been exposed to significant levels of radiation, that it was only bad water that had made him sick. Next Jake turned his attention to the shelter's radio receivers. His brain was starting to function again, and his brain was desperate for information.

There were four receivers, all with antennas located outdoors, outside the shelter. The antennas were disconnected so as not to conduct electromagnetic pulses into the shelter and damage the radios. The connecting cables for the antennas were located in a heavy metal box mounted on the wall. Phaedrus' instructions were to connect only the antenna needed, only when it was needed, and to otherwise leave the antenna cables inside their metal box. Two of the four receivers were for redundant monitoring of the ordinary broadcast bands. A third receiver was for monitoring the ham radio bands. This receiver was connected to a small tablet computer capable of decrypting data signals. Phaedrus' instructions for this looked pretty complex, but Jake was confident that he'd be able to work it out. The fourth receiver was only for higher frequency UHF and VHF transmissions. Jake knew that UHF and VHF frequencies did not travel far, probably 25 miles at most. That receiver would be able to pick up transmissions by local law enforcement, if any local law enforcement remained. There was only one radio capable of transmitting as well as receiving. That was a VHF radio that was meant to be used for two-way communication with two small walkie-talkies. If anyone had to go outside the shelter, the walkie-talkie would permit communication with the inside of the shelter. Jake figured that the first place to listen was the AM band on which he had heard the Cuban station. Jake was not surprised to hear nothing but static. It was morning, and AM signals would not travel far at this time of day. Not until after dusk would there be a chance of hearing Havana.

Jake found something to eat, then he lay down on one of the cots to read and wait for dusk. But again he fell asleep. He awoke and looked at the clock. He had slept for four hours.

There were three clocks. Two had digital readouts. One displayed the local time, to the second. The other displayed Greenwich Mean Time, also to the second. Both gave precisely the same time, to the second. The third clock was a large mechanical clock, the type of clock that requires regular winding. It was of such high quality that Jake thought that it might more accurately be called a chronometer. The mechanical clock displayed the local time and exactly matched the digital clocks. Phaedrus must have wound the clock and set it before he left.

Jake went to other side of the room to check the instruments. The radiation level had risen. It was more than 10 percent higher than when he had fallen asleep. Jake opened the metal box on the wall that housed the antenna terminals. He found the antenna cable that was labeled "AM broadcast" and connected it to one of the receivers. He slowly tuned across the AM band, paying close attention to the frequency on which he had heard Radio Havana. But he heard nothing but static. He switched off the receiver, re-coiled the antenna cable, and put the cable back into the metal box. Then he found the cable labeled "HF ham bands." He connected that to the receiver for ham radio frequencies. Jake had no experience with such receivers and had never listened to shortwave broadcasts. But he had done some reading on radio theory, and now the time had come to see how much of that reading he could remember.

Slowly and patiently Jake twiddled the dials. For twenty minutes he heard nothing. Then he heard beeps. It was not a strong signal, but it was clear enough in spite of the static. It was Morse code.

Jake had no idea how to understand Morse code. He knew that it was composed of dots and dashes. He hit on the idea of getting a pencil and paper and trying to write down the sequence of dots and dashes, so that he could decode them later by looking at a chart of the alphabet in Morse code. But he found this to be surprisingly hard to do. Partly it was because the code was coming in too fast. And partly it was because it was difficult to maintain the concentration needed to record what he heard with a minimum of errors. He knew that there were many gaps in what he had written down, and probably many errors. His hand quickly tired, but he kept writing. After a few minutes, the transmission stopped.

Jake got the Morse code chart from the binder and a fresh sheet of paper. He tried to do the translation, then quickly realized that, when he was trying to write down what he heard, it had not been at all clear when one letter stopped and the next began. Consequently he had written it as a continuous stream, not as chunks of separate letters. He could make no sense of what he had written. Occasionally he would see two or three groups of letters that appeared to be typical of English, such as "TH" or "AN," or even "SOM," but it was hopeless. He gave up, resolving that next time he would try to hear each letter separately and write it down separately for decoding.

Again Jake tried to find Radio Havana. He heard nothing.

The books were still on the floor. One by one, Jake picked them up and checked the title, then stacked them on the cot. There was a volume of Plato. There were several Civil Defense-era books on surviving nuclear fallout. There were books on gardening, building and masonry. There were a couple of books on ham radio, one of them thick and quite technical. There were three books on astronomy, two books on meteorology, and several books on medical diagnostics and first aid. There were books on British and American history. There were no fewer than six books on the fall of Rome and the Dark Ages, not including the two books on monasteries and monastic life.

"Dang," thought Jake. "How long did he expect this bunker stay to last? Will there be a pop quiz?"

Near the bottom of the stack, Jake found a surprise. It was a thick book, published by a university press, with the title *Rome's Church: How It Changed Us, What It Cost Us.* The author of the book was Phaedrus L. Bartholomew. So then, there were many things about Phaedrus that Phaedrus had never gotten around to mentioning. Phaedrus had said that he was an engineer, but the jacket copy on the book revealed that Phaedrus also had credentials in history and philosophy. Jake examined the table of contents, then flipped quickly through the book. The book appeared to be a thorough indictment of Rome and the Roman religion, Christianity. There were several chapters on Rome's destruction of the Celtic cultures of France and the British Isles. There were chapters on the persecution and Christianization of Ireland and the centuries-long repression of pagan religion and culture. There were chapters on the monasticism of the Dark Ages. There were several chapters that appeared to be an analysis of Christian theology, followed by a sharp condemnation of that theology.

Though Phaedrus had never mentioned this book, Jake was not surprised. It all fit together. All of it was consistent. It also revealed a certain modesty. Phaedrus was a man who could talk about a subject without mentioning that he had written a book about it. Phaedrus had always been so intellectually modest with Jake, had always treated Jake like an intellectual peer. He was always Socratic. Jake realized that he never felt ignorant, or even young, when he was with Phaedrus. Rather, Phaedrus made him feel smarter somehow, and intellectually braver, more willing to take on subjects that he previously would have thought were too hard, or too far beyond him. Phaedrus made Jake want to stretch.

When Jake got up to search for a snack on the kitchen side of the room, he realized that it wasn't just Phaedrus he had displaced. There was a dog bowl, and two large bags of dog food. He also had displaced Joan.

Jake wanted to read Phaedrus' book first. But some of the material touched on his survival. He would read those first and exercise enough discipline not to cheat. He fell asleep reading. When he awoke, it was 3 a.m. He connected the antenna and switched on the receiver for the AM broadcast band. Almost immediately he found a station in the lower part of the band. It was weak but clearly intelligible, and it was English. The station soon identified itself as the Bermuda Broadcasting Company. A male voice and a female voice were speaking alternately, and in very somber tones. Jake, wearing headphones, took notes on what he heard:

Over four days, nuclear warheads numbering in the hundreds and possibly thousands had been detonated over almost every population center on the planet. Bermuda had not been affected. All civilian communications systems appeared to be down. Power grids were down on all continents. Some military communication systems were operable, and the information on which the broadcast was based was being relayed to the Bermuda government by the British military. Citizens of Bermuda were not in any immediate danger. All, or almost all, of the nuclear warheads that had been detonated appeared to be of a type optimized to release maximum levels of radiation with a minimum of blast force. That is, the warheads were designed to kill people while leaving infrastructure largely undamaged. The warheads were being detonated above the surface of the earth, causing severe electromagnetic pulses but reducing the levels of fallout. Casualties were impossible to estimate, but government officials were saying that because of the vast number of detonations and their proximity to population centers, it was likely that billions of people had died or had received fatal doses of radiation.

The British government said that it had no reliable intelligence at present on who was responsible. Government officials said that, though clearly the American military had been involved, it seemed unlikely that the American government alone was capable of so many near-simultaneous strikes on all continents. There was speculation about whether the destruction was caused by some kind of accident, or a series of technical mishaps, or a political showdown that somehow had gotten out of hand. There was speculation that terrorists had somehow hijacked global military systems. If the destruction was intentional, then the motivation was unclear, though it seemed undeniable that drastically reducing the population was a possible motivation. If it was a colossal accident, it was difficult to explain the ongoing coordination of the detonations and the inability to stop it after four days. There had been no communication with the United States government or its military.

Jake had included a sketch pad in his backpack. When he wasn't reading, he drew. He had cheated and started reading Phaedrus' book. The book made him want to draw while he digested what he read. He drew a detailed scene of Phaedrus' little farm. This time the setting was winter. It was night, with a clear sky full of stars. Everything was covered with snow. Icicles hung from the eaves of the house and barn. At the edge of the woods stood two small figures in dark cloaks. One of them held a lantern that emitted a faint light. They were looking upward, watching the descent of an enormous square-rigged galleon descending from the sky. The galleon's prow pointed downward. It was just above the treetops. The galleon was so brightly lit with lanterns and torches that the treetops glowed. In the far background, a silver-gray horse peered out of the woods.

Days passed. Jake read and periodically checked the instruments and listened to the radios. The radiation outside was at levels dangerous enough to avoid and certainly high enough to cause long-term damage to health. It was high enough to make a person sick and no doubt to kill a certain percentage of those exposed. But it was not nearly as high as it would have been if more conventional nuclear warheads had been used. However, just because radiation levels were moderate here in the remote mountains did not mean that it was that way everywhere. It all depended on the weather and one's location relative to the detonations. Jake dared to hope that, locally at least, the survival rate of wildlife would be high. When he realized that he was thinking of wildlife rather than the local people, he wondered if he should feel more guilt. But Jake didn't really know whether there were that many people around here. Would they be a threat? Did Phaedrus have a plan for that? Jake began to realize that he had been so focused on getting to Phaedrus' place and into the shelter that he had not started thinking about the dangers outside the shelter. It would be winter. Most people would not have much food. Surely Phaedrus has a plan, Jake thought.

Jake never heard Radio Havana again, but twice he was able to hear Bermuda. Earlier reports were being confirmed. The detonations had stopped. The speculation by Bermuda's sources was that it was over, since the detonations seemed designed to kill and since that job already had been accomplished, globally, with grim efficiency. The sources on the radio expressed hope that, once the fallout had cleared in another one to two weeks, there would be no further danger.

Jake had never read anything as compelling as Phaedrus' book. In normal times in a normal world, and if he had never met Phaedrus and been swept up in what was happening, such a book might seem superfluous and academic. But the book explained everything. It was now much easier to understand why Phaedrus was content to live so far from civilization. It was because he had a very low opinion of this civilization. There had been other civilizations in history that were much more to his taste. And though Phaedrus allowed for individual exceptions, it also was clear that he did not think highly of the type of person this civilization generally produced. Although all the book was written in concise language, it was dense and heavily footnoted. It was the summaries that followed each section that Jake found particularly helpful, because in those summaries Phaedrus spoke less guardedly and allowed more of his personal views into his writing. Jake would have liked to underline many parts of the book, but he dared not write in the book. He did, however, mark many sections with sticky tabs of paper in the margins. These were the parts that Jake wanted to read again, or that he would like to discuss with Phaedrus sometime, when better times had returned.

He read these parts for the third time:

And so it is clear that the primary mission of the religion of Rome, from the beginning, was to serve earthly power and the hierarchies of earthly power. This was clear not only from its theologies as they developed over the centuries (and similarly clear from which parts of its own texts the hierarchy scrupulously chose to ignore), but also from the worldly actions of the church in the political and cultural arenas, the pretensions and pieties of its rhetoric notwithstanding. The heads of the church must be given the status of kings, and its cardinals must have the status of princes. The wealth and power of the church must be great enough to at least compete with, and when possible to dominate, secular power. Competition from any competing religions must be ruthlessly persecuted and eliminated, no matter what the cost and no matter how many centuries were required to do the job. The one exception was Judaism, which because of its access to wealth was useful to the church hierarchy, and which was not a proselytizing religion that sought to compete for the church's clients. It was the Celtic civilization of Gaul and the British Isles, with its pagan gods, that was the first competition to be eradicated — torn out by the roots — by the Roman religion long after the armies of secular Rome had gone.

But the Celts were not the last such civilization to be thus destroyed. The attitude of the church, from the time of the first Christian emperor, was imperial. What is remarkable is that the imperial attitude of the church has not changed in two thousand years of history. Secular Rome with its armies and aristocrats was forced, in the end, to eat humility as it fell, having dished out so much domination and genocide to so many others. But the church of Rome was never humbled, either by the weaker outside forces with which it came into conflict and which it was able to dominate, or by its own sometimes inconveniently meek theologies. Once the church got its hands on the levers of imperial power, starting with the emperor Constantine, it never hesitated to use that power. Some critics of my position may argue that it is not true that the Roman church has not been humbled, and that the church no longer holds the all-powerful position that it held in previous centuries. But those critics forget that, in spite of the secular influences that have forced changes upon the church in all centuries including our own, those changes have always been minor. The culture in which we live is the creation of the church. Possibilities for life and thought that lie outside the boundaries of that culture are rarely available to most people, the doomed, dogged work of heretics notwithstanding. The fact that we are unconscious of how this culture contains us, restrains us, and limits even the thoughts that are available to us to think, changes nothing. We are creatures of a culture created by the church of Rome, and the vast majority of us cannot see outside this narrow creation. If a Celtic Druid remained alive today, this narrowness, this shriveling of the possibilities of life and thought, would be starkly apparent to him or her. A Druid might be able to remind us of what is missing, to tell us about some of what has been driven out of the world by the domination of the church of Rome. But there are no Druids alive today. The last one has been dead for centuries. And of the Druids' knowledge almost nothing remains. The church's efficient methods saw to that. The Druids were hunted down and exterminated.

I also am arguing that, in our time, it is the religion of Rome and the constraints of its culture that more than any other factor hold back human progress. Of course I do not mean here technological progress, as it obvious that Christian culture has been peculiarly successful at promoting technological progress, and for unflattering reasons that I have described elsewhere. But for those who define progress differently, human progress is blocked in all directions by constraints put in place by, and still enforced by, the Roman religion and the culture it produced and sustains. I should hasten to add that the Roman religion is not uniquely guilty here. All political and religion systems, though they may start with the purest of intentions, have a tendency over time to be usurped by elites and to serve entrenched power. Christian and non-Christian systems of power obviously have much in common. But it is the Roman religion, I am arguing, that developed the richest set of theologies and methods of social control to put into the service of hierarchies and elites. Indeed, I believe this fact is at the root of the Roman religion's superior results in producing and retaining wealth and power for those groups and nations whose elites learned to use this power. After all, how many empires has the Roman religion assisted? There was Rome, the Carolingian empire, two incarnations of British empires, a Spanish empire, an American empire. Would any of these empires have been possible without the Roman religion?

But no empire lasts forever. Surely it also is true that no imperial religion lasts forever, though the Roman religion is still very much with us. Are there any signs today that the Roman religion may be waning? Its cultural grip is strong, even if its religious grip has weakened in some quarters. I have argued that the signs of any weakening are scarce, especially culturally. I also have argued that, if change is always incremental, as it has been for the last two thousand years, then we are likely to see another two thousand years of domination by the Roman religion. This is because of its ability to subsume, to crush, and, if it is forced to, to even adapt to opposing trends. The Roman religion learned centuries ago, starting with the Gauls, that if a competing religion or competing culture could not be converted, then its people must be eliminated. Since the elimination of so many clients of Christianity is unthinkable, and because those clients and their nations dominate the planet (for now, at least), then it seems likely that the religion of Rome will be with us for a long, long time. ...

However, of all the types of repression and control enthusiastically pursued by the church of Rome, one form of repression stands out for the unrelenting zeal with which it was practiced: sexual repression. We examined some of the motivations of this repression, some of which were rational (an emphasis on an unbreakable marriage contract and the rearing of children) and some of which were irrational (here we must throw up our hands and turn to Freud). We examined how this policy of extreme sexual repression was consistently sustained for centuries, though the emphasis of the repression might vary slightly from age to age according to the perceived threats of that age and to counter any popular resistance encountered during that age. No one escaped this repression, though some categories of people felt it more sharply than others. Its strictures were imposed, though not necessarily equally, on both men and women, the married and unmarried, the heterosexual and the homosexual. It even was imposed on children, particularly on boys and their universal practice of the rites of Onan.

Starting in childhood, both males and females were trained that sex was a duty and privilege of marriage and that the sole purpose of sex was procreation. The less pleasure involved, the better. Celibacy was the ideal. Marriage was the only refuge for those too weak for celibacy. For females and their families, for centuries, no shame was greater than the shame of bearing a child outside of marriage. Adulterers must be severely punished. Those who secured divorces — that is, if divorce was even available — must be stigmatized, and life must be made as hard for them as possible. Though, of course, the church might grant a divorce or an "annulment" if the right amount of cash found its way to the right places. Loose women were marginalized. Male indiscretion, if heterosexual, might be winked at if it was appropriately discreet, though this certainly was not always the case, especially for those men who could be made into useful examples of the wages of sin. Though it might seem that such language is an overstatement or unfair to the intentions of the church, nevertheless I defend my claim that the church's goal was to make sexual misery as near universal as possible. Sexual misery was a goal, a good. Sexual misery would help keep the minds of the church's clients focused on the divine, on the rewards waiting for the chaste and virtuous in heaven.

It is often argued that these arrangements are in the best interests of children. I have pointed to work by anthropologists that call into question this argument, since so many cultures, in the present as well as in the past, have had distinctly different arrangements in which the welfare of children was a shared responsibility of a tribe, a community, or an extended family, and in which the welfare of children was not dependent on the stability of sexual arrangements between only two adults.

In the church's sexual system, all human sexual energy not directed toward procreation must be either repressed or sublimated. For the church's priesthood (as for the sexually mature but unmarried), sublimation and chastity were prescribed. If sublimation failed, repression would have to do, and the church made a science of repression. The church clearly recognized the large proportion of human resources required for child rearing, especially for those who lived in a state of subsistence (as so many did). The church also recognized the potentially large fund of human resources available for the tapping if a certain number of men and women were relieved of the responsibilities of child rearing. Hence the policy of celibacy for priests and nuns, who if celibate could devote all of their time and labor to the church's business and who were expected to give up for a lifetime any hope of sexual happiness. Many priests (and nuns) found other sexual outlets, to be sure, but it is doubtful that sexual activity under the weight of so much shame and furtiveness could lead to anything approaching sexual happiness.

Many have been mystified by the church's extreme emphasis on the repression of homosexual activity. These theorists tend toward a more Freudian, as opposed to historical, explanation. I have argued that the church would not be likely to waste perfectly good repressive energy where there was nothing to repress. The Celts of France, Ireland, and the British Isles were known for their frank and unabashed sexual expression. Even Greek historians remarked on the sexual freedom of the Celts, who did not stigmatize homosexual practice. It was said that Celtic soldiers frequently took other soldiers for lovers, that chieftains often had boys as well as wives (and that all three slept together), and that Celtic youths would offer themselves to older men and were offended if they were turned down. To wipe out a culture in which men had sex with each other so freely and to replace it with a system that all but guaranteed universal sexual misery was not a small project. It took centuries of repression, and that repression continues to this day. So the church was up against not only the powerful sexual legacy of the Celts (and to a lesser degree the Greeks) but also the sheer exuberance of human sexual behavior, especially male sexual behavior. I have argued that, in the absence of repression, incidental homosexual behavior between human males is almost universal, even though the majority of human males prefer women. The sexual energy behind such exuberance is so great that centuries of repression by the church could reduce homosexual activity only to the high level that Kinsey found in the 1940's. The church at least was able to drive such behavior into the darkness, to make it furtive and shameful. Genuine relationships supported by homosexual bonding were made almost impossible.

Some have argued that the true purpose of the stigmatization of male bonding was to produce a certain type of male more useful to imperial elites — highly competitive males who could easily be trained to violence against each other. There is a quotation attributed to soldier Leonard Matlovich in 1975: "They gave me a medal for killing two men and a discharge for loving one." At the very least, the universal tendency of elites toward moral hypocrisy is exposed. Whether the more effective breeding of violent males was part of the intent I cannot say. But considering the love of Greek and Celtic males for war, such work hardly seems necessary.

Some of the church's zeal in persecuting homosexuality might also be explained by how common it was inside the church, especially after celibacy for priests and nuns became the rule. Thus the repression could be seen in a more Freudian light, as an expression of the church's own guilt and denial.

Why should we care very much about sexual repression, in a world in which other forms of repression, and other forms of misery, are of greater concern? This is a reasonable question. One answer is that the many forms of human repression — political, economic, sexual — tend to be found together, rather than in isolation. If there is rebellion against one form of repression, then other kinds of rebellion are likely to follow. If there is one form of repression, then other forms of repression are likely to go along with it. This is because, to elites, particularly religious elites, the control of a population is understood to require limiting that population's options in all areas of life. If history contains examples of peoples who were politically and economically repressed but whose sexual freedom was unchallenged, I cannot think of them.

Some may argue that the Reformation brought some improvements. I would not agree. Protestant hierarchies have been no less zealous than Catholic hierarchies in maintaining systems of sexual repression, and often they have been worse. The sexual freedom of the flock was never on the table for reform.

Some may also argue that brief flowerings of sexual liberation have brought the masses some relief from sexual repression, citing, for example, the United States in the 1960's. I would argue that the degree to which a sexual revolution occurred in the 1960's can largely be attributed to birth control, which did indeed bring a measure of sexual freedom to both men and women, while giving married people the ability to choose how many children to rear. This was probably the greatest achievement in the liberation of heterosexual sexuality in the entire Christian era. But we must not exaggerate its benefits, because the entire system of shame and limited possibilities remains very much in place. It is like increasing a prisoner's ration from three crumbs a week to five and calling it liberation.

It also is true that in recent decades substantial gains have been made by those who identify as homosexual. Even same-sex marriage has become a possibility, though some might argue that this constitutes sharing the yoke rather than an increase in exuberance and freedom. But what modern men — all men, not just men who identify as homosexual — are unable to perceive, because knowledge of other possibilities have been purged from the culture, is that all men have lost the possibility of freely expressing their surplus sexual energy with other men. By the surplus sexual energy of men, I am referring to the fact that men seek more purely sexual activity than women, and the fact that men, during much of their lives, do not have access to a female who is willing to provide them with sex. Many cultures have, without shame or stigma, channeled this surplus sexual energy into the relationships that men have with each other. A Greek or a Celt transplanted into our culture would perceive this barrier immediately. We can no longer perceive it, having internalized the narrow strictures on male sexuality that have been imposed by the church's system of sexual repression.

The church of Rome understood that what we now call "incidental homosexual behavior" between males — it was everywhere in Rome, after all — is natural and is very prevalent in cultures in which it is not repressed. When analyzed, the templates that support this repression bear a close resemblance to the templates that were used for so long to deter boys from practicing the rites of Onan (and which still are used today in some quarters). For example, it was said that masturbation inevitably leads to a slippery slope of greater temptations and ever more perverse practices; that it is unhealthy, emotionally or otherwise; that it poisons one's suitability for marriage; etc. This repression has cost all men, not just those who identify as homosexual. This cost is paid not just in the loss of sexual release and bonding between men. Men also pay in another way. If the rules permit males to have sexual alliances only with females, then women are empowered to better monopolize and better control male sexuality. Women can demand more for what men want from women, and offer less in the bargain. In those cultures that grant freedom and respect to the sexual possibilities between men, women's bargaining power with men is reduced. I will leave to women the question of whether that is good for women. But men win in two ways if they are free to bond sexually with other men: Men's exuberant sexuality can be expressed with other men; and at the same time sexual expression toward women also can be more exuberant, because men have greater power in sexual bargaining with women. Now, some may argue that it is a good thing (as the church does) that male sexual exuberance is thus restrained, that men should be kept in sexual yokes. But such a view implies that there is something pathological and excessive about male sexuality. Yet it ought to be self-evident that male sexuality is what nature made it, and that its natural exuberance cannot be repressed without a price being paid. Simply because we can no longer imagine a society in which the free expression of male sexuality is permitted — a society which also respects the interests of women and children — does not mean that no such society is possible or that no such society ever existed. I am arguing that such a society did exist, that it was dominant in Western Europe for centuries, and that Rome and the Roman religion all but extinguished it. That society, of course, was the society of the Celts. The Greeks, in spite of strong cultural threads that lionized sublimation and asceticism, also achieved substantial sexual freedom for men. But women, by today's values, did not fare as well in Greek society as they did in Celtic society.

To Socrates, says Plato, love and sexual expression were a kind of divine madness. In particular, Socrates was referring to love and sexual expression between males. To a religious elite with a population to control, nothing could be more dangerous than this divine madness, whether that divine madness is heterosexual or homosexual. To the Roman church, this divineness of love and sexual expression had to be redefined as diabolical. It had to be replaced with shame. ...

And finally, given where we find ourselves after so many centuries of domination by the church of Rome, is there anything that can be done to get the church of Rome out of the private lives and intimate relations of those whose cultures have been dominated by the church of Rome? I am of the view that the possibilities are limited and that history shows that change will occur in tiny increments. Once a culture has fully internalized strictures that at first had to be externally imposed, repression is self-sustaining and is faithfully passed on from one generation to the next. History strongly implies that any major and rapid change in a culture is possible only as a follow-up to subjugation and humiliation by violence. Furthermore, the process cannot be left to casual or random forces. The conquering elite must impose a program of sustained pressure to eradicate the unwanted previous modes of thought and behavior and replace them with new modes. Even then, the process may move much more slowly than elites would desire. The subjugation by Rome of the pagan population of western Europe took centuries, despite a well-designed and well-financed program of repression.

My own view is that the slowness of this process should be attributed not to a lack of zeal by the Roman church but rather to the strength and stability of the cultures that the Roman church sought to crush. Consider Christmas. The church's efforts continue to this day to convert Christmas into a pious and joyless religious observance, but the folk memory of a profane and indulgent midwinter festival has persisted. This ongoing problem that the church has had with Christmas actually exposes a major miscalculation made centuries ago. If the church of Rome had put its resources into simply stamping out all memory of the pagan Yule celebration, it might have succeeded. To instead try to redefine the holiday and superimpose Christmas on top of Yule had the unintended consequence of keeping the memory of Yule alive. The lesson learned: That it is safer to purge unwanted elements of culture than to try to convert and co-opt them.

The corollary is that Western culture is unlikely to ever throw Christianity off its back unless cultural destruction on an apocalyptic scale forces a cultural reboot, after which a new kind of elite systematically ingrains a new kind of culture.

CHAPTER 13

By the seventh day in the shelter, the radiation level outdoors had peaked and was starting to decline. At least twice a day, Jake would try the radios. One evening he was able to tune in the Bermuda station again, but there seemed to be little new information. Several times on the ham bands he heard weak Morse code, but he was never able to decode anything useful from it. Phaedrus had left detailed instructions for monitoring a particular frequency for low-power data signals of the type that Phaedrus used to communicate with his distant source. But as far as Jake could tell, he was receiving nothing but noise. On the tenth day inside the shelter, Jake caught the last minute or so of a conversation between two ham radio operators who were actually talking rather than using Morse code. Jake did not know their location, but wherever they were, both men were saying that conditions outside were almost at the safe level. One said that he planned to go outside briefly tomorrow. He promised a report to the other ham on what he found. There was life out there. Jake felt a little less alone.

Phaedrus' instructions said that when the radiation had declined to a certain level and had remained there for 48 hours, then it would be safe to leave the shelter for an hour or less a day. Jake had a fantasy of finding Phaedrus and Joan, back from wherever they had gone. But surely, if Phaedrus returned, he could simply knock on the shelter's trap door. That gave rise to a new hope – that there would be a knock on the trap door, that Phaedrus would be there. But there was no knock on the trap door. On the twelfth day, Jake decided to go out and have a look around. His plan was that he'd check the house, the studio, the driveway, and the orchard and garden to make sure that everything was secure and that there was no sign of unwanted visitors. Then he'd return to the shelter.

Jake climbed the ladder, unlocked the door, and emerged into the side room of the studio. A gray light came through the window. It was raining. He was prepared for that. He had worn a rainproof jacket. Jake tried the door to the computer room. It was locked. Phaedrus had left no instructions for getting into that room. Either Phaedrus didn't particularly want him in that room, or there was nothing in there that Phaedrus thought Jake needed. The two green lights near the door were glowing. Apparently all was well in there, at least.

Next Jake tried the door to the main room of the studio, the room with the lofty ceiling and the organ. It was not locked. Jake went in. On the opposite side of the room was the organ console. The organ had been wrapped in metal foil. Jake smiled when he realized why. It was a quick and dirty way of protecting the organ's electronics from electromagnetic bursts. Jake smiled at Phaedrus' thoroughness and his desire to protect the organ when so much had been lost. Jake wondered if it was because Phaedrus valued the organ or because he valued the memories of the person it had belonged to. In this room too there was a panel on which two green lights glowed. Jake opened one of the wide double doors and went outside. An icy rain was falling. Mist and fog hovered here and there, particularly near the edge of the woods.

Jake had decided to check the barn first, where the truck was kept, then the driveway. If there were no tracks in the driveway, then they'd probably had no visitors. It would take some time to go all the way to the bottom of the driveway and back, but Jake had decided that it was the only thorough way to look for tracks. He also had a small hope that he'd see Phaedrus' truck down there, parked below the fallen trees blocking the roadway. But the first step was to see if the truck was in the barn. The barn door was latched but not locked. Jake swung the wide door open far enough to step inside. The truck was not there. Jake closed the door and secured the latch. As he walked to the driveway, the rain fell harder. The roadway was muddy in places, and Jake slipped occasionally in the mud as he made his way down the steep drive. He passed each of the fallen trees. None of them had been disturbed. When at last he reached the bottom of the driveway in pouring rain, there was no sign of Phaedrus' truck, no tracks, and no sign of recent traffic on the gravel road that led to the outside world. Jake was pretty sure that that was a good thing, that anyone who came this way now probably would be up to no good. Jake wanted to see one person only: Phaedrus.

Jake struggled up the steep drive, trying to avoid the muddy spots. He'd probably been out of the shelter now for nearly an hour. Next: the house. The kitchen looked the same as when he'd arrived. There were two green lights. He checked each room. In Phaedrus' bedroom, the bed was neatly made. On the wall glowed two green lights. In the corner was a desk, and on the desk were about a dozen small photographs, nicely framed. Jake was drawn to the photographs. He knew so little about Phaedrus and what his life was like – or at least what his life was like before he became a hermit. The photos were all portraits, all of them old. One must have been

Phaedrus' mother. Another showed a young Phaedrus sitting at a Teletype machine. There were several photos of young men, all of them handsome. One of these young men was the same young man in the photos in the other bedroom, the one who was clearly an organist and probably Irish. Jake picked up one of the photos for a closer look. This was a different face, and he knew that face. Suddenly, with a great inrush of breath, he felt as though a black hole had opened underneath him and he had fallen into an unreal world. This made no sense. This could not be. How could Phaedrus not be here to explain this? It was Jake's father. The photo must have been taken at Oxford, when his father was a grad student. There was no time to think it through now. Whatever the explanation might be, it would have to wait, and it would have to come from Phaedrus. For now, there was too much to do. Distractions and preoccupations could be dangerous. Jake pulled himself away from the photographs, fighting with his feelings, which he knew were irrational. Was it some sort of deceit, some sort of betrayal? But how could that make sense, with two people who care about him as much as his father and Phaedrus care about him? Did it explain why Phaedrus always seemed to be holding something back, always saying less than he knew? But it was useless to speculate, useless to let his feelings make the situation harder than it already was. He should stay focused, stay on his toes, be patient, wait until he could ask Phaedrus.

Next Jake went to the chicken house. He remembered six chickens from his previous visits. There was a fenced lot for the chickens beside the chicken house, but normally they were given the run of the place, and they usually kept to the orchard area, wandering together as a flock sometimes into the edges of the woods. The door to the chicken house was closed. The chicken lot was empty. Jake opened the door and looked inside. Three chickens came rushing toward the door. It was dark inside. The shutters had been closed on the chicken house's one window. As Jake's eyes adjusted to the light and he looked around, he saw vessels of food and water set here and there. Apparently Phaedrus had given the chickens a big supply of food and water because he expected to be away for a while. The water looked dirty. Jake saw one chicken stretched out ungracefully on the floor. It appeared to be dead. Two hens were huddled together in a corner, looking lethargic and possibly sick. And though Jake was no expert on the behavior of chickens, it appeared that three of the chickens were healthy and normal. Jake emptied the chickens' dirty water containers, rinsed them, and filled them with fresh water from the ever-running water spout. There were icicles, but the water was still flowing. The chickens seemed to still have plenty of food. Jake found an old rag and used it to pick up the dead chicken by the feet. He carried it out and threw it into the woods. Jake assumed that radiation had killed the chicken and had made two of the chickens sick. Considering what had just happened on the planet, that was not a bad casualty rate. Jake returned to the shelter.

That day at dusk, for the first time since he'd been in the shelter, Jake picked up a signal from Phaedrus' far-away radio contact. It was the same short sequence, repeated many times over a period of ten minutes, and amounted to nothing more than the distant station calling Phaedrus' radio call sign, identifying itself, waiting for a response, then repeating the call when nothing was heard. The last call included a few words indicating that he would try again tomorrow at the same time on the same frequency. Jake had no transmitter for this frequency. He could only listen.

The next day it was still raining. The radiation level was dropping fast. Jake assumed that the rain was washing away the fallout. He figured that he'd stay outside the shelter for three or four hours today. Tomorrow he'd probably be able to leave the shelter for good. The house was much colder than the shelter and, without a fire in the kitchen, was anything but cozy on a dark February day. But a fire in the cook stove, Jake knew, would change everything. Phaedrus' wood shed was well stocked. Soon Jake had a respectably hot fire going in the kitchen stove. Figuring out the stove's draft controls was no big deal. Jake was good at fires, though he had never been a Boy Scout. Fire-starting and fire maintenance was one of the things his dad had taught him well, something that all boys should know. There were two big kettles. Jake filled them with water and put them on to boil. The main source of hot water was a reservoir built into the stove. It would heat enough water for the bathtub. Jake felt a kind of guilt, having a warm bath in Phaedrus' kitchen. And what about Joan? Did she have a dry place and a fire to warm her old bones, wherever they were?

After Jake's bath, he went to the chicken house, to check on the hens again. One of the sick chickens had died. He found its corpse in one of the nests. It looked as though it had felt cold before it died. It was settled into the straw, its wings drooped around its body, its head tucked under one wing. Jake picked up its cold, stiff body. It was shocking how light the chicken was, as though it was all skin and feathers. Its eyes were closed. Its oddly big feet were clenched. Suddenly a wave of sadness and grief seized Jake, and a sob convulsed him with so much power that he almost dropped the body of the chicken. He leaned against the wall, shivering with grief and with the cold he suddenly felt, until the worst of it had passed. This time he could not bring himself to throw the chicken's body into the woods. He put it down tenderly in one of the nests, went to the barn, and found a shovel. He buried the chicken under an apple tree. He refilled the little grave with mud. Rain water puddled in the hole. The rain wet Jake's face and ran down his forelocks, into his eyes, rinsing away the warm, salty tears.

He returned the shovel to the barn. It was dry inside and smelled of the hay that Phaedrus kept for the comfort of the chickens. Then Jake returned to the driveway, to check for signs of visitors. Nothing had changed since yesterday. Water was washing across the gravel of the public roadway, but there were no tracks and no sign of any recent traffic.

The next day Jake moved out of the shelter and into the house. The rain continued, though with less intensity. Jake built fires in both stoves. He made a big pot of soup, imagining Phaedrus returning to a warm house and hot soup. Jake worried. What if Phaedrus' truck had stopped running? It was only 40 miles to the tower, which is surely where Phaedrus had gone. Phaedrus was in shape. He could walk home from that distance in two or three days, though for Joan it would be a big problem, especially in such cold weather, given her crippled leg and her arthritic old bones.

Jake waited three days. He told himself that he was being rational, that Phaedrus would have returned by now unless something was wrong. Right after dawn on a clear, cold morning, Jake set out with six days of food in his backpack. When he reached the public roadway, he stopped and listened for signs of anyone approaching. There were always woods near the road that he'd be able to dash into. He recalled a couple of dwellings on the way to the tower, but he could skirt those by temporarily taking to the woods. So great was the distraction of his emotional turmoil that he hardly felt any discomfort from the harsh pace he set for himself. Several times he scolded himself for not paying attention to where he was, for not listening more and being more watchful. But all day the emotional storm inside of him just would not subside. Luck was with him, and all day there was no sign of any traffic on the road. He came to a dwelling in late afternoon. From a distance he could see no sign of people or of any kind of recent activity. He skirted the place anyway, keeping inside the woods on the opposite side of the road even though it slowed him down and took him through a rocky stream bed treacherous with ice in places.

Dusk came. A young moon was in the sky. There was more than enough moonlight to keep walking. He did not feel tired. The moon would not set until early morning. He walked on. The air grew colder, though the wind settled down a bit. He was startled by two deer as he crossed a small bridge. He was pretty sure he saw an owl, moving through the trees like a ghost. He heard the sound of distant coyotes. Clearly here in the remote mountains, there were many wild survivors of the fallout. It could have been much worse. As the moon moved toward the western horizon, Jake marveled that he did not feel tired. He had not even eaten, though he had stopped several times to drink water. He scolded himself. This was not sustainable. Emotional turmoil is no fuel for a long hike, especially now that it was night.

He was high on a ridge when the moon set. He stopped to watch. As the sky darkened, the stars shone bright in the clear winter air. Jake moved off the road and followed the ridge through the trees, looking for an isolated place to sleep. About half a mile from the road he came to a rocky area where the trees thinned out. From there he could see most of the sky. He sat on the rock and devoured three energy bars. He had a small tent, but he decided to sleep in the open, so that he could see the stars. He spread his sleeping pad on the flattest spot he could find and laid out his sleeping bag. After he crawled into the sleeping bag he unrolled his tent and used it as a tarp to cover the sleeping bag, to keep the frost off.

Lying on his back facing north, he had a clear view of the sky. He knew most of the constellations and many individual stars, but his eyes always went first to Polaris, the North Star. Its fixed position provided a sense of stability, a reference. It kept him from feeling lost in that deep sea of stars, stars which were always moving, always wheeling overhead. Ever since he was a boy, when he lay like this under the sky, he felt a certain anxiety that gravity – whatever gravity might be – was arbitrary, delicate, and even unreliable. It was easy to imagine that he was looking down into the sky, not up. What then was to stop him from falling into that sea of stars? If he fell, would he fall helplessly in a straight line? Or would he somehow be able to steer, to fly among the stars, using Polaris as his guide? There was a line in the film "Peter Pan" that had made a great impression on him as a boy, and he always thought about that line when he was looking down into the stars. It was Peter's directions for how to get to Never Never Land: "Second star to the right, and straight on till morning." If I fell right now, Jake thought, and if I fell straight down, where would I go? Into the constellation Lyra, probably. What would be the second star to the right? Vega, probably.

When Jake awoke there was frost in his hair and frost all around him. The air was clear. Jupiter was setting near the western horizon. He reckoned that he had only about ten miles to go. He should reach the tower before noon. He scanned the horizon in the direction he thought Phaedrus' tower should lie, hoping that he might be able to catch a glimpse of it from here. But he saw no sign of the tower. This ridge was probably too low. He made his way under the trees back to the road. He checked the roadway carefully for any signs of fresh traffic. There were no such signs. The road now started to wind down the ridge. Jake unwrapped an energy bar as he walked. He was almost out of water. He probably would have to crack some ice to refill his bottle at the next stream in the next bottom. That was a wonderful feature of this mountainous terrain. There was a stream of some size in every valley. One was never far from water, just as one was never far from a ridge from which to watch the sky and to scout the terrain. Jake always felt at home in the mountains. He must have gotten that from his dad, who had grown up in the mountains of Virginia. And though Jake had never thought of it before, he thought he understood now why a mountainous place like Costa Rica had appealed to his father, and to his mom, who also had enjoyed their mountain trips for hiking and stargazing. The downside to mountains, the price one had to pay for beautiful ridges above alternating with lush streams below, was the steep slopes that connected them. But either because he had been born with his dad's mountain-friendly legs, or because he had earned them from so much hiking as a boy, Jake's legs never seemed to mind the steep slopes. His mom had once compared him to a mountain goat, leaping from rock to rock with no effort even while wearing a backpack. His legs bore him rapidly toward the tower in the cold morning air.

All morning Jake saw no sign of people or vehicles. This area was all forest, too steep and too rugged for even the most determined settlers. Jake walked fast, faster than was sustainable, but he knew that he was close. By noon the tower was in sight. Jake made his way up the narrow access road and climbed the two fences with their keep-out signs. His palms were sweating. A thousand scenarios for what he might find had run through his mind. He tried to dismiss them, to clear his mind, to slow his racing pulse, which he knew was from apprehension, not from the exertion of the hike. He broke through the trees and caught his first close-up sight of the tower. Sure enough, there was Phaedrus' truck. When Jake was in hearing distance of the tower, he called out, then stopped to listen. He heard no response. Jake picked up a rock and went to the bottom of the tower. He used the rock to bang on the metal frame of the tower, then called again. Again he heard no response. The truck was unlocked. It offered no immediate clues. But underneath the truck, where there was shelter from wind and rain, was a nest of old blankets that clearly provided a bed for Joan. It was difficult to tell how recently the nest had been used. The privy was empty. Under the shed roof near the tower was the small shack that Jake assumed contained the steps leading to an underground shelter. The door was padlocked, from the outside. Almost hidden, folded over the side of one of the washtubs, was a pair of heavy work pants. The fabric was torn near the left knee. There were heavy bloodstains on the left leg of the pants, at and below the knee. It appeared that Phaedrus had tried to wash the pants but had given up. Jake's heart was pounding. This was serious, but it certainly did not seem to be fatal.

There was nothing to do next but to go up the tower and look for signs. Was Phaedrus hard of hearing? Jake didn't recall ever detecting any sign that he was. Certainly Joan was not hard of hearing. Jake called again and heard no response. Then he started up the steps. His backpack was awkward, and he had to be careful not to snag it on the railings in the tight turns. He was prepared this time for the creaky spot where the steps sagged slightly, but still it unnerved him. He reached the last few steps. The trap door leading onto the observation deck was not locked. Jake pushed the trap door open and climbed onto the deck. The observation deck was empty except for a small covered pail. A chamber pot? He saw no one inside. The door was not locked. Jake went in.

The cab of the tower had clearly been recently occupied. There were books and a water bottle, almost empty, on the table. On the cot were a pillow and some blankets neatly folded on top of a sleeping bag. Jake felt a wave of anxiety at what he saw on the counter top. A first-aid kit was open, its contents spread about. There was a bottle of painkiller medication, almost empty; a bottle of antiseptic, three-quarters gone; a pair of scissors; and a roll of bandaging, also almost gone. In a way this was comforting, because it offered fragments of an explanation. Clearly Phaedrus was alive and taking care of himself. The tiny dresser contained items of clothing. There were a few tins of nuts and some dried milk in the pantry. On a shelf was an open box that contained Phaedrus' radio. It had been partly disassembled. Another box contained the computer that Phaedrus used for decoding radio transmissions. Its screen was broken. It too was partly disassembled. Something had gone wrong.

There was a pair of binoculars on a shelf. Jake took the binoculars and returned to the observation deck. Slowly he scanned the edge of the woods, working his way around 360 degrees. He saw a couple of spots that might be paths into the woods. Jake was tempted to go down and explore the paths, just to be doing something, but he reasoned that the best course was to wait, because Phaedrus' things were here.

CHAPTER 14

Jake fidgeted, alternately studying the terrain around the tower with the binoculars and studying the state of the interior of the cabin, trying to build a story out of the clues. There must have been an accident, a fall, maybe. Phaedrus had injured his leg. His radio, or his computer, or both, had been broken in the accident. Phaedrus' ability to walk and move around must have been impaired for a while, but he must be better now, since he has gone out. But why didn't he just drive the truck home? Jake thought about trying to see if the truck would start, but he had no idea where the key might be.

Then he heard a bark. Joan! Jake dashed for the door and went out onto the deck. At the edge of the woods on the west side of the tower, Joan had emerged from a path into the woods. Not far behind her was Phaedrus. He was limping, leaning on his walking stick. He was wearing his wide-brimmed hat. He was carrying some-thing heavy. A jug of water? Jake waved his arms and called out. Phaedrus looked up. Joan barked again. Jake had to force himself to go slowly down the steps. He had a bad feeling now about those steps. Phaedrus and Joan had stopped to wait for him. Jake was young. Let

Jake do the running while while an old man and an old dog wait. They both looked older than before, but happy. Phaedrus had set down his jug of water. Joan stood patiently, smiling her doggy smile and waiting for the humans to have their hug, then she had hers.

"Phaedrus! What happened?"

"I fell," he said, shaking his head as though in shame.

"The tower steps?"

"The tower steps. It was the day I was planning to go home. The steps were wet. I was carrying things down. All of a sudden there was no friction, none. My feet flew out from under me. I bounced down a whole flight of steps. My knee caught a railing. It made a mess of my knee, bruised me all over, broke my radio and my tablet computer. I'm just lucky I didn't hit my head."

"How bad is your knee?"

"Bad enough that I had to sew it up. Twelve stitches. But that was nine days ago. Tomorrow the stitches come out. I'll be ready to start home, I think."

"The truck?"

"Dead."

"So you were going to walk?"

"How else? But it's not myself I'm so worried about. It's Joan. It's going to be hard for her. You walked here?"

"Yes."

"Everything is OK there, back at home?"

"Yes. Except that I was worried sick about you. And there was a message on your radio. Your friend is worried too."

"Yes. I thought my friend would be worried. Where's Alexandra?"

"I left her in Washington. It's along story, but I'm sure she's safe. Her mother had more power than I knew."

"We have a lot of catching up to do," said Phaedrus. "We should go up. I'd offer you supper, but I'm almost out of food."

"I have some extra. I'll cook. Here, let me have the water."

They reached the tower steps. Joan looked up longingly.

"She hates staying down here alone," said Phaedrus.

"Would she let me carry her up?"

"I don't know. Let's ask her. Joan, would you let Jake carry you up the steps?"

Joan smiled.

"You go first," said Jake. "Just leave the water here. I'll come back for it."

"No, it's OK. The pain and soreness are much better now. And for some reason it's safer going up than coming down. I can carry the water. I need to practice for the long walk home. And for that matter, you do, too, because I'm afraid Joan will need your help. But you stay a flight behind me, OK? That way, if I fall, I won't take you and Joan down with me."

Slowly they made their way up the steps. Joan did not protest, nor did she even seem to be afraid as Jake scooped her up, cradling her with her legs partly folded under her tired old body.

"She peed just a few minutes ago," said Phaedrus, "but you'll probably have to repeat this process before bedtime."

"We can handle it," said Jake. "She's the best old sack of potatoes in the world."

When they reached the observation deck, Phaedrus pointed at a kind of swing-out crane and hand winch affixed to the side of the tower.

"Before we settle in," Phaedrus said, "how would you feel about loading some wood onto the freight elevator, and let's have a fire up here tonight. It gets really cold in there when there's no sun through the windows, and I haven't hard a fire up here since I came out of the shelter.

There's even some wood down there already split and ready to go."

"Sounds cozy," said Jake.

Soon they had a fire in the tower's little pot-belly stove. Jake started a supper of soup, rice, rehydrated vegetables, and hot chocolate. Joan fell asleep on a rug by the fire. Phaedrus sat near her, enjoying the warmth and a cup of hot tea.

"Where shall we start?" asked Phaedrus. "Have you been able to use the receivers? As for me, I've been in total isolation, no radio, for almost ten days."

Jake told him what little he knew from the few signals he'd been able to pick up on the radios.

"So what has happened, Phaedrus? I don't suppose you have to be so mysterious now."

Phaedrus frowned, and leaned down and scratched Joan behind the ear.

"I can't confirm much," said Phaedrus. "Partly it's too early for much to be known about the state of the outside world, even if I had a working radio. But the odds are that it all went according to plan, and everything has radically changed out there. Three weeks ago the population of the earth was about 7 billion. Now it's probably about 500 million, or will be once the dying is over." Phaedrus paused to give Jake time to think about that.

Jake didn't say anything, but he sat down on the rug beside Joan.

"Jake, I'm really grateful for your looking out for me. I'm sorry that you have to turn around and hike the other way, but Joan and I will be really glad to have the company on the way back. We'll slow you down, I'm afraid."

"It will be a nice stroll," said Jake. "But it's crazy out there. I ran out of gas on the way from Charlottesville, had to ditch the Jeep and walk. It was totally stupid of me. People are killing each other. I'll tell you about that later. But no one came around your farm."

"And no one probably will. The sheriff and I are good friends. He keeps an eye on things. Did he come by?"

"No. Not while I was there."

"He's a wily one, smarter than he seems. He'll come out to check soon, if he hasn't already. Once the locals, or as many of them as are left, know that the sheriff is still alive, and I promise you he is alive, they won't mess around, not in our end of the county."

"Who did this, Phaedrus? Why? And how did you know what was going to happen?"

"It's going to take some time, Jake, for me to fill you in. It's complicated. Plus I've been out of the loop with a broken radio. For now let's make do with a short version. It's going to sound like a bad screenplay, but there you have it. There was plan, a conspiracy, put together by some people who are very rich and very powerful, working with some people who are very smart. It was an international thing, though it depended largely on the resources of the United States. It took more than ten years to unroll the plan. These people knew that the world was on course for calamity. Calamity is almost too mild a word – there are too many people, too much consumption. The environment is on the edge of disaster. The climate is teetering toward runaway changes. The hope for any kind of political solution was zero. All trends were pointing toward uncontrollable disaster, with virtually no predictions possible about the post-disaster conditions, simply because there were too many wild cards. So these people, these billionaires and these smart people, decided that a controlled disaster was the only hope, to bring the population down. They used what they call radiation enhanced weapons, to kill people while keeping physical destruction to a minimum. They focused these bombs on population centers all over the planet, pretty much all the densely populated places. Rural areas, isolated areas, they left alone. They figured that if you were hardy enough to survive the bombing and resourceful and independent enough to survive the aftermath, then you're their kind of citizen, and welcome to the new world. They'll give no one any help. It's a test, you see. That's it in a nutshell, Jake. Welcome to the new world."

"How did you know about all this?"

"I've known, for years, some of the smart people who came up with the plan."

"But you didn't …"

"No. I wasn't involved. But I had some sources for leaks. They seem to want me alive."

"That's good. But why?"

"We have a lot to talk about."

"Are we the lucky ones? Or were they the lucky ones, the ones who're gone?"

"In my opinion, Jake, we are the lucky ones. But much depends on how smart we are, every day, every hour, every year, from here on out."

"You're the smart one, Phaedrus. You had a plan. You had a place. I have nothing. I'm just young. And dumb. And undeserving."

"You're young. And you're deserving. And you're not dumb. I know it must be hard, Jake. It's survivor guilt. Everyone who's alive now must be feeling it. But we have more surviving to do. And we have to build a new world."

"I'm afraid I don't have much experience in building worlds."

"But you will before long. I know that must sound flippant, but I believe it's true. We can't just be passive and let the new world be like the old one, or let other people make all the choices, or just leave it all to chance. We have to use our imaginations. We have to exert ourselves, re-invent, rethink, rebuild. Our place is tiny, but there's a lot we can do."

"I'm flattered that you say 'we.' But I don't even know

how to hold a hammer. I certainly don't know how to re-invent the world, or rebuild it."

"I can show you how to hold a hammer."

"Phaedrus, again I can only thank you. Without you, I wouldn't be here. But I don't know how to earn my keep."

"You do yourself too little credit. I know how things must look right now, but just give it some time. Jake, I need your help."

"You know I'll help any way I can."

"Good. But let's deal with all that some other time, OK?"

"OK. But Phaedrus, I have another question that I need to ask you."

"Yes?"

"How is it that you know my father?"

"Oh. You know."

"I found a photograph in your room."

"I see. Well, then. I knew your father at Oxford. I was a grad student. It was his first year. We became good friends."

"So when my dad gave me the coordinates for your place, the part about the dark sky was just a cover. Why did you keep that secret?"

"Your dad asked me to. I wish he could explain it to you himself. He thought that you and I would get along. He thought that if you saw me as your father's friend, it wouldn't be the same. I assumed that you might visit once, if you were looking for a dark sky, and that would be that."

"But I came back."

"Yes."

"And then I came back again."

"Yes."

"You could have told me."

"I thought it best that your father tell you. And now, of course, he has no idea where you are. I wish he could know that you're safe."

"I think there is a way."

"What's that?"

"When I saw them at Christmas, I gave them a letter. It was sealed, and I made them promise not to open it unless something bad happened. I was afraid that they'd worry, or think that I'd lost my mind, or that I was suicidal, if I told them that I thought something terrible was about to happen. Anyway, I told them in the letter to find a ham radio operator and to listen on a certain day of the week, at a certain time, on a certain band."

"You're brilliant!"

"I was just trying to take advantage of your radios, that's all."

"So you played a little trick on them. A nice trick, but a trick just the same. Just as your father played a little trick on you. I guess that makes you even."

"Maybe. Still, he has some explaining to do."

"I'm sure he will do that."

"What was he like? You say you were friends? How long did you know him? When did you last see him?"

"I knew him for four years. The last time I saw him was when he left Oxford. He had met your mother by then. They were engaged. They were in love."

"Was he a good student?"

"The best. We always said that he was a classics student with the soul of an engineer, and that I was an engineer with the soul of a classics student."

"Did you know my mother too?"

"Not really. She … she ran in different circles, and she drew your father into those circles, I suppose."

"And did you see them after Oxford?"

"No. There were letters from time to time. And obviously we kept track of each other's coordinates. But I haven't seen your father since the Oxford days."

Jake, who had been sitting on the floor with Joan, got up and put wood into the pot-belly stove. It had grown dark outside, and much colder, while they'd eaten their supper and talked.

"We should turn in early," said Phaedrus. "You must be exhausted, and we should get started early tomorrow, if my stitch-removal surgery goes well. I think I'm up to it, though. It's Joan I'm worried about. She's been getting weaker. This winter has been very hard for her. She's thirteen years old, you know. That's old for a dog her size. She may slow us down some. She will need your help on some of the steeper slopes, especially if she's cold and her joints are hurting. I have some pain medication for her in the first-aid kit. That should help some."

Joan had looked up and yawned when she heard her name. Now she got up, limped toward Jake, and leaned against him.

That night, Jake bedded down on the floor of the tower cabin, in his sleeping bag. Joan cuddled against him, between Jake and the stove. It was a long time before Jake fell asleep. He was pretty sure that Phaedrus, too, was not sleeping. Joan seemed to know that, because she got up periodically, nuzzled Phaedrus in his cot, then returned to her warm spot between Jake and the stove.

Jake and Phaedrus reckoned that at their slow rate of travel, it would take three days and two nights to reach the farm. They loaded their packs, trying to keep them as light as possible, though they packed all the remains of the food. Phaedrus anguished over whether to leave some of his books behind, but in the end he left them, vowing to return for them whenever that was possible. Phaedrus' stitches had come out cleanly and painlessly.

He declared himself as ready to travel as he was ever going to be.

Again Jake found himself admiring Phaedrus' youthfulness. His hair was almost white, but his skin still looked young, and he was remarkably free of wrinkles. He neither moved like an old man nor spoke like an old man. Phaedrus was spry. He did not seem to have any hearing loss, and he didn't even wear glasses except to read. Jake had often noticed the bad habits that older men almost always fall into. They talk too much, they listen too little, and, even if they ask a question, they're not interested in the answer. They forget things, and they tell the same stories over and over. Their stories are too long and rarely interesting enough to justify their length. Even Jake's father, fifteen years younger, had started to develop these tendencies. But Phaedrus had somehow avoided the old-man habits. Socratic was the word that always came into Jake's mind.

They left everything tidy inside the tower. Phaedrus locked the trap door securely, and they made their way down the steps, Jake carrying Joan. Phaedrus secured the truck as best he could and made sure that the underground shelter and the storage area were locked. By an hour after dawn, they were on their way.

Joan was valiant in her efforts to keep up her pace, but she could muster less than half the speed that Jake was capable of. Occasionally, when they came to a particularly steep hill, Jake would carry her for a while. She sat patiently in his arms, though she could not have been comfortable, and occasionally she gave Jake a lick.

"You once promised to tell me the story of Joan of Arc," said Jake. "I'm curious about this saint that Joan is named for. I think Joan may take after her."

Jake had never heard Phaedrus talk at length the way he did that afternoon in telling the story of Joan of Arc. Was it simply a way of passing the time as they walked, or did the story of Joan of Arc really mean that much to Phaedrus? He told the story in detail, citing multiple sources. A source that Phaedrus frequently cited was Jules Quicherat, who according to Phaedrus had set down the complete historical record on Joan of Arc during the 19th century, including all the records of the Inquisition. That, explained Phaedrus, was the mother lode of the story of Joan of Arc. He cited several other French historians, and an English writer named Vita Sackville-West. It was as though Phaedrus had read all those works yesterday. The story continued all afternoon as they walked, and the story didn't end until they were sitting by their campfire, which they built far up into the woods so as not to be seen from the road. Phaedrus concluded by citing from memory some lines by George Bernard Shaw, from Shaw's preface to a play about Joan of Arc. It went like this:

And since neither Church nor State, by the secular necessities of its constitution, can guarantee even the recognition of such self-chosen missions, there is nothing for us but to make it a point of honor to privilege heresy to the last bearable degree on the simple ground that all evolution in thought and conduct must at first appear as heresy and misconduct. In short, though all society is founded on intolerance, all improvement is founded on tolerance …

Then they sat silent for a while, Joan leaning one shoulder against Jake as she often did, with her other side toward the fire. Phaedrus quietly got up and added logs to the fire, then resumed his seat, looking thoughtfully into the fire. It was as though both of them were in a trance, transported for a while by Phaedrus' storytelling into the medieval world of Joan of Arc. How could this simple peasant girl have nudged the course of history? How could she have known what she knew? How could her simple and honest words have confounded the learned men of the universities and the church? Were her voices real? How could the church have burned her?

For the first time, Jake saw Phaedrus for what he was.

Like Joan of Arc, Phaedrus was a heretic.

"I read your book," said Jake.

"Oh? Which one?"

Jake laughed.

"You're a constant surprise, Phaedrus. The book about Rome. I found it on a shelf when I was looking for reading material for the shelter."

"I see. Would you like to talk about it? I hope I didn't shock you. I dumped the book on you and never really prepared you for it."

"I thought it was brilliant. Try not to get yourself burned at the stake, though, Phaedrus. OK?"

"They'd have to find me first. And besides, hermits aren't always dangerous. Those are the only two choices available to the heretic, really. Either try to change the world, or try to get away from it."

"Then why not try to change the world?" said Jake. "Do you remember what you said to me yesterday about that? Have you changed your mind?"

"Back then, my calculating side told me that changing the world would be completely futile. I could as easily turn a battleship by whacking it with my walking stick."

"Are things different now, now that we've been bombed back into the Stone Age?"

"Maybe. Very possibly. And I'd say we're more in the Iron Age than the Stone Age," said Phaedrus. "Greece, and the Gauls. My favorite time."

CHAPTER 15

When at last they reached steep driveway to Phaedrus' little farm, Joan was too worn out to make the climb. Jake carried her, teasing her for being a sack of cabbages. The fallen trees blocking the road had not been disturbed, but there were signs of footprints that were not very fresh, and there also were signs that a vehicle had parked off the roadway where the drive began.

"It was probably the sheriff," said Phaedrus. "He probably came to check on me. And to find out what supplies I've got stashed."

There was a note on the kitchen table. They read it together, Jake leaning over Phaedrus' shoulder.

Phaedrus,

I came around to check on you. I figure you went to your other place for some reason. I'll be back on Wednesday. There are quite a few things we need to discuss.

– Mike

"How about you start a fire in that stove while I get a radio set up," said Phaedrus. "It'll soon be time to see if we can hear Colin."

Jake started a fire, and soon the kitchen was warm

and smelled of onions. Phaedrus went out to his radio room. Joan went to sleep on her rug near the stove. Jake had rummaged through the pantry and was making a pot of soup.

The soup was almost ready when Jake heard Phaedrus enter through the kitchen door.

"It smells wonderful in here," said Phaedrus. "And it's so warm. Thank you."

"Any news?"

"Quite a lot of it. Let's have some tea, and I'll fill you in."

Water was already boiling, and soon the tea was poured into Phaedrus' ancient porcelain.

"There are still a lot of unknowns, as you might imagine. But all the evidence so far is that the population of the planet is now between 400 million and 700 million. Colin favors the smaller number. And it will decline even more if there are widespread epidemics, which is likely. Colin's guess, and I'd agree, is that before the population starts to grow again – who knows when that will be – we'll reach a level as low as 350 million, which is about the population of the earth in the year 1400, after the plague. Colin has far less information about North America than about Europe, but it seems our North American cities are dead, and that was the plan. The survivor estimates are largely based on the size of the rural populations. The elites are in their enclaves, of course, and are starting to regroup and re-establish communication, but everyone else is on their own. The new masters of the universe have already started lighting up the control centers, but that will take some time. But that means very little to us, because we won't see any government activity for a long time, except for our sheriff."

"The power grid?"

"That will never come back, really. It's much too big

and much too decrepit to bother with. When electricity returns, it will be much more local."

"The Constitution?"

"Suspended."

"Communications systems?"

"Everything is down, of course, and much of it will never come back," said Phaedrus. "The military, and the elite, have their own communications systems."

"What about all those power plants?" said Jake. "What about the nuclear generators? What's keeping them from boiling over?"

"That was not really a problem. The military for years has had its way of getting all those dangerous systems off line. It took them years to prepare for this, Jake. They knew what they were preparing for – at least, the ones in the inner circles."

"The smart people and the billionaires."

"That's right."

"So Phaedrus, I don't exactly know how to put this, but what's our situation?"

"We have a lot of talking and thinking to do. We're not entirely alone. As I said, our sheriff – and I hope you get to meet him tomorrow – is a wily one. We have enough staples for between two and three years. Though of course we need to supplement that as much as possible with what we can grow, and with what we can trade for with our neighbors."

"Neighbors?"

"We'll hear more about that tomorrow, when the sheriff is here, I suspect."

"So we're farmers now, I guess."

"Yes. But I hope you won't feel humiliated by that. We're not just farmers. We're also a sort of outpost, a hub of communication and – dare I say – a hub of smarts, in a world that's suddenly pretty primitive. We're kind of a monastery. Now shall we go try to reach your parents?"

"Yes!"

Not since Jake's first visit to Phaedrus' place had he been inside the radio room.

"Now let's see," said Phaedrus. "You told your parents to listen on 20 meters, at dusk. Is that right?"

"That's right."

For half an hour, Phaedrus scanned the band, alternately listening and calling stations in Costa Rica. There was no response. Phaedrus assured a dejected Jake that they would try again tomorrow.

—▸ ◂—

Phaedrus had said that they should expect the sheriff the next day around 11. The sheriff arrived with a passenger, a sad-looking young man of about 16. They were flushed from walking up the hill. Phaedrus and Jake went out and met them in the orchard. Phaedrus introduced Jake to the sheriff. The sheriff introduced the young man to Phaedrus and Jake. His name was Mark. The sheriff was not a great deal younger than Phaedrus, and he was almost as lean. Mark was strong and wholesome-looking, though he had a provincial look about him and a bit of pout mixed in with the sadness.

"You might as well saw up those trees in the road now," said the sheriff to Phaedrus, "and use them for firewood. I can't say that I blame you for taking precautions, but you know I don't allow any hanky-panky in my county."

Jake decided that he'd wait a few minutes to tell the sheriff about the hanky-panky he'd seen on the way in. As for Mark, it was clear that Phaedrus was expecting him, that he and the sheriff had discussed the situation on the radio.

"Mark," said Phaedrus. "We'd be glad to have you here, if you'd like to stay. I'm so sorry to hear about your parents. They were good people. We'll all miss them. They could have done a lot to help us all get through the times we're facing. If you'd be willing to stay, we'll frame up a room for you upstairs. I have some materials in the barn. It shouldn't take long. I'd really like for you to stay. We could use a hand around here. There's a lot of work to do."

Mark only nodded, looking at the ground.

They all retreated to the warm kitchen, coffee for the sheriff, tea for Phaedrus, and hot chocolate for Mark and Jake. Mark got acquainted with Joan. Phaedrus and the sheriff needed to discuss supplies.

"No, no," said the sheriff. "You keep all that. You've got two boys to feed now. But I'll for sure take some of that powdered milk off your hands. Let me know when you've got those trees sawed up and I'll have one of the guys stop by for the milk. Now what about those two upper fields of yours that are going to waste? If I can get somebody over here with a tractor, and if I can find some seed sets to lend you, can you grow potatoes in 'em, now that you've got these strong boys to help you?"

"We'll grow you bushels and bushels of potatoes," said Phaedrus, "if Mark and Jake are willing. I've got a couple of small fields that would be perfect for peanuts. Do you know where I can get some seed?"

"I'll ask around," said the sheriff. When can you let me know about these messages?" The sheriff pointed to a neat stack of pink forms on the kitchen table. They actually appeared to have been typed up with a manual typewriter.

"I'm afraid I'll need a little time on that, Sheriff. As you know, I've been out of the loop for a while. But just from the little bit of listening I did yesterday, the nets are starting to shape up, and they'll be getting the traffic organized pretty soon." The sheriff nodded, but Phaedrus noted the puzzled look on Jake's face.

"One of the things that amateur radio operators have

always done, Jake, is handle communications in emergencies – getting people in touch with their families and things like that. The sheriff is collecting queries of that sort, and I'll be passing them into the radio networks that hams are setting up to handle that sort of thing. Before long we'll be able to relay messages from one end of the country to the other, and even farther, if need be."

"Phaedrus is a handy man to know," said the sheriff.

"And I've been saying the same thing about you," said Phaedrus.

"Sheriff," said Jake, "I have a question. I came here from Charlottesville, in my Jeep. Idiot that I am, I ran out of gas. I hid the Jeep in some woods, about forty miles east, and walked the rest of the way. Do you know of any way I can try to get my Jeep back?"

"In good shape, was it?"

"Perfect, if nobody's found it. Less than two years old."

"One more Jeep could come in handy around here. How much gas would you need? Would five gallons do it?"

"Five gallons would be more than enough."

"Forty miles, you say. That's probably one county over. I'll get you there, even if we have to relay you. Phaedrus says you're an architect?"

"I try to be. Nothing big. Nothing fancy."

"Well, the day may come when that will come in handy. Looks like that room upstairs will be your first project."

"We'll make it all nice for Mark, and it'll meet all the building codes," said Jake.

The sheriff and Phaedrus chuckled. Mark even managed a weak smile.

"I'd better get going," said the sheriff. "When will you be monitoring my channel, Phaedrus, in case I need you?"

"Every day at sunset. I'm almost always in the radio room then."

➤ ⬅

A few days later, the sheriff picked up Jake in a squad car. As they drove, Jake told the sheriff everything he could remember about the old couple and the fire. When they reached the rough trail leading to the Jeep's hiding place, the sheriff stopped the car to let Jake out and popped the trunk so that Jake could get the five-gallon can of gasoline.

Jake picked up the gasoline can, waved his thanks to the sheriff, and headed into the woods. The can was heavy. He had to keep shifting the weight from arm to arm. He was afraid that both arms would be pulled out of their sockets by the time he reached the Jeep. After forty miserable minutes of lugging the gasoline can uphill and down over rough terrain, Jake came to the Jeep. It looked undisturbed. He unlocked the door, put the key in the switch, and turned it, to see if the panel would light up. It did. He switched it off again and poured some gasoline into the tank, spilling less than he'd feared he would. He left about two gallons in the can. Three gallons should be enough to get home. Then he put the key in the ignition again and turned the starter. There was no hesitation at all. The Jeep started. It was like being reunited with an old friend.

"Woohoo!" shouted Jake. "Way to go, girl!" All the items stowed in the back seemed to be just as he'd left them. Jake turned the Jeep and slowly crawled out of the woods. He reached the road and turned toward town, toward the hardware store, toward home.

The hardware store was in the county seat, a town so small that it had only one stoplight. The stoplight was now dark, which didn't really matter, since there was no traffic. The store was still open. It was dark inside, since the only light came from the front windows and a couple of small windows near the back. The owner had a kerosene lantern on the counter for looking into dark corners. A couple of farmer types were wandering the store, as though taking inventory and dreaming about what they might possess, if they only had something to trade. Jake said good afternoon to the owner, endured the inquisitive look, and wandered the store. Sure enough, there was not one small generator but two, one a little bigger than the other. Jake wandered back to the front of the store."

"How much for the generators?" Jake asked.

"You're the fifth person to ask that today," said the owner from his stool behind the counter. He was a large, overweight man with an honest look about him. "How much do you want to pay?"

The owner chuckled when he saw that Jake was taken aback and had no idea how to respond.

"I'm not real interested in cash," the owner said. "I'd rather trade for tangibles. Got any tangibles you'd like to trade? If that's your Jeep out there, I'll trade you for that." One of the browsers heard the owner's comment and laughed.

"How about some silver?" said Jake.

"Silver? Now we're talking." But the owner had a puzzled look on his face, and the browser stole a little closer to listen.

"Are you from around here? I don't think I've seen you before."

It took only a fraction of a second of reflection for Jake to realize how it must look to the locals, so he came back with a solid answer.

"I'm new here, but I'm staying up at Phaedrus Bartholomew's place. The sheriff will vouch for me. In fact the sheriff dropped me off to pick up my Jeep. I ran it out of gas a few weeks ago and stashed it in the woods."

"Then if you can come up with silver, I'm sure we can do a deal. You won't be offended if I mention it to the sheriff, though?"

"Not at all. How much silver would it take to get you interested in a trade?"

"Sterling, or bullion?"

"Sterling."

The owner looked at the dark ceiling, doing some calculations in his head.

"Well, I'll be honest with you," he said. "The sheriff would shoot me if I wasn't honest, and Bartholomew too, for that matter. The price of silver is probably pretty good at the moment. A mere ten ounces and the small generator is yours. Twelve ounces for the bigger one. They run on gasoline, though, you know. No gas comes with that."

"The smaller one should do," said Jake. "Also, I need some paint. And some of those wool socks. And a couple of pair of work gloves, and some finishing nails."

"Paint!" said the owner. "I hadn't expected to sell any of that for a while." He looked at Jake with a new respect, especially after the request for finishing nails. But the fact was that he had already heard of Phaedrus' new residents, from the sheriff. He'd heard about the city boy who had just showed up mysteriously. He knew Mark, and he knew about Mark's new home. He guessed easily enough what Jake's goods were for, except for the generator, though that didn't surprise him at all, knowing Phaedrus. And though this Jake was clearly a city boy, he had a nice honest name and a certain charisma about him – healthy, well-spoken, nice looking, and as strong looking as any farm boy.

"Good deal," said the owner. "Silver for all that? I'll add it up and see what it comes to. You tell Phaedrus that I'm figuring sterling at fifty dollars an ounce. If you hear – and I know Phaedrus has his sources – that I'm far off from what they're trading for in Richmond, you let me know, and we'll work out some adjustments next time you're in. There are two people you don't cross in this county. One's the sheriff, and the other is Phaedrus Bartholomew."

Soon Jake's Jeep was lighter by a few ounces of silver and heavier with a new generator and a bag of hardware and dry goods. In a way he felt guilty about the generator. The plan he had in mind for it didn't have much to do with survival, but somehow it seemed important. And besides, Phaedrus would find other uses for it, as long as there was a little silver to trade for gasoline. Jake realized that the silver was worth a small fortune now but that he'd better hoard it and make sure that it was used not just for the benefit of the three residents of Phaedrus' little farm, but also for the community. It already was becoming clear to Jake that, though the farm felt isolated, it also was part of a community. The sheriff's respect for Phaedrus was clear enough, as was the respect of the owner of the hardware store. Already, no one seemed to question that Jake belonged here. Little by little, the complexity and brilliance of Phaedrus' plan was making more sense. Jake knew that he'd probably be encountering new elements of that plan for a long time.

It was an hour before dark when Jake got back to the farm. Phaedrus and Mark had just come down from the upper fields. Phaedrus had wanted Mark's opinion on the plan for the spring planting. They both admired the Jeep, ran their hands over its fenders, marveled that Jake had been clever enough to hide it not only from the pilferers but also from the electromagnetic pulses. Jake had covered the generator with a blanket. That was to be a surprise for later. But he handed out new socks and work gloves, and proudly showed them the paint and nails. Phaedrus gave Jake an odd look but didn't ask any questions about how the bill had been paid. But Phaedrus had a radio. He'd know by dusk.

At dusk, Jake and Phaedrus went to the radio room to try again to call Costa Rica. This time someone answered. It was a ham operator in Costa Rica, who said that Jake's dad was there with him. Jake's hand was trembling when he took the microphone. Phaedrus discreetly left the radio room and returned to the kitchen.

"Jake, son," said his dad's voice, which broke on the word "son," then recovered. "I'm sorry your mother's not here this evening. She has been here most days, but tonight it's just me. It's such a … such a miracle that you're alright. We've been dying to know where you are, how you knew something was going to happen. Where are you?"

"You gave me the coordinates, Dad."

"Are you OK? I can't imagine…"

"I'm fine, Dad. Phaedrus is fine. Everything is fine. Well, everything is not fine, but you know what I mean. But we're OK. Tell Mom not to worry. Phaedrus had a plan. And somehow I just fell into it. It's a long story. Maybe next Christmas we can catch up on all that."

"I understand. I understand. And wouldn't we be lucky if anyone can travel even five Christmases from now. But at least you're OK. That's what matters."

"Dad, I need to ask you some questions. I know this is not the most private way in the world to talk, but I really need to ask you some questions. OK?"

"OK, son. I haven't had a chance to think about the answers, but I'll do my best."

"Just being honest is all that matters. I just need to know why didn't you tell me."

There was a pause, as though Jake's father was taking inventory of the things he had not told Jake, trying to figure out where to start.

"Well, son, there are a number of things I haven't told

you, things we've never talked about. But I think you're right. We should try to cover the basics now and save what we can until some future Christmas. Where should I start?"

"Why didn't you tell me why you gave me his coordinates?"

"Because I thought you needed somebody to talk to. Sometimes your mother and I … we saw you grappling with existential questions. But you were always so secretive. You didn't want to talk with us. Somehow I just thought that you and Phaedrus … that Phaedrus was somebody you'd be able to talk with. But what young man wants to talk with his father's friends? So I didn't want to make it impossible for you to see Phaedrus as who he is, with your own eyes."

"Existential questions?"

"You know your mother, Jake. To your mother, everything is an existential question."

"Dad, I don't know what to say. We'll talk next Christmas, then. Can Mom be on here tomorrow?"

"She'll be here tomorrow, Jake. She'll be so relieved, and she can't wait to talk with you. And would you give a message to Phaedrus? Knowing Phaedrus, I'm guessing that he left the room."

"Sure, dad."

"Please tell him that, if possible, I'd like to talk with him tomorrow, too."

➤ ◄

The next morning as Phaedrus, Jake and Mark were finishing breakfast, Jake said that he had a surprise, a surprise that he hoped would bring a little entertainment to the place. Mark, who was gradually becoming more talkative, spoke up.

"Video games!" he said.

"That's maybe not out of the question eventually," said Jake. "But I think the first piece of entertainment will be more to Phaedrus' taste. It's out in the studio. Come see."

Joan had developed a cough during the past few days. She was lying near the stove for warmth and got up to follow them, but she sat down again with a sigh, seemingly out of breath. Mark, who was bonding with Joan very quickly, stooped over her.

"Need some help, Joanie?" he said. "Want me to carry you?"

Joan gave him a lick, indicating the affirmative. Mark gently scooped her up, and they made their way through the cold late-winter air to the studio. Jake pulled the blanket away with a flourish to reveal the generator.

"Would that be enough power to make this beast of an organ breathe again?"

"Glorioski!" said Phaedrus. "Four thousand watts!"

The organ was still wrapped in metal foil. While Phaedrus carefully lifted the foil from the organ, Jake and Mark folded the foil in neat squares to preserve it. Soon the huge organ console sat proud and silent on its dais, like the king of instruments that it was. Mark was impressed.

"I've never seen anything like it," Mark said. "It's so big. And so complicated. Who knows how to work it?"

"It will play itself," said Phaedrus. "That is, if it's still working. It has been years since it was played, but the last time it was used it worked great."

"How can it play itself?" asked Mark.

"See this box?" said Phaedrus, pointing to a device attached below the keyboards. "It's a kind of computer. And old friend of mine used to play this organ. This box recorded all the keys he hit. With luck, if everything still works, the box will replay my friend's playing just like his original performance. It will be coming from the box's memory, but my friend will be playing the organ."

"Unbelievable," said Mark. "Almost as good as a video game."

"Why don't you two build a fire in the fireplace while I check everything out," said Phaedrus. "I can't remember when this room last had a fire, and music. It would be a shame to have one without the other."

Soon there was a large and cheery fire in the large and cheery fireplace. Phaedrus, having checked the electrical connections and the wiring to the organ's many speakers, pronounced the organ ready for a test. Phaedrus had moved the generator outdoors so that its noise and exhaust would not be a problem. Joan was watching from a place near the fire. Jake noted with pleasure how excited Phaedrus seemed when he gave Jake the word to start up the generator. Jake returned to the studio and stood beside the console. Phaedrus opened the bench and retrieved a key. He placed the key in the switch.

"Cross your fingers," he said. "Here we go."

He turned the key. There were clicks and thumps inside the console, and suddenly it lit up, looking very much alive. Mark gasped at the impressive display of lights. There were lights everywhere – lights on the music desk, lights on the pedals, lights over the keyboards, lighted knobs, lighted buttons.

"That's incredible," said Mark. "I've never seen anything so complicated.

"And what shall we hear?" said Phaedrus, opening the bench again and removing a box of old-fashioned looking floppy disks.

"That's easy," said Jake. "We must have a fugue."

"A fugue it is," said Phaedrus. "And I know just the one. It was my friend's favorite. I don't even need to mention that it's by Johann Sebastian Bach. It's the Fugue in D minor, number 565 in the Bach works catalog. Here we go."

Phaedrus put a disk into the box and pressed a button.

There was a moment of suspense as the box made a low clicking and buzzing sound. Then Jake and Mark were startled when suddenly there was a great clatter of light and noise and activity on the console as the drawknobs for the stops flew into position, just as Colin had set them many years ago. Suddenly the studio seemed as vast as a cathedral as the organ seemed to take a deep breath, then began to sing. No one moved. They stood and watched the console as Colin played the fugue. Jake occasionally glanced at Phaedrus, who almost seemed to be having trouble breathing. And Jake understood that Phaedrus was experiencing what he himself had experienced at the organ recital a few months ago. It was the irresistible tendency of a lover of the organ, when moved by its music, to breathe in sympathy with the instrument, to hyperventilate as a piece of music reached its crisis. One identified with the instrument, rode the instrument and its wind as though sailing a clipper ship through high winds and rough seas. Phaedrus stood silent. Jake discreetly looked away. Finally, the fugue ended, leaving only the sound of the crackling fire. No one spoke. Joan, who had been listening, put her head down again as though to return to her nap. Phaedrus seemed deep in thought, but after a minute or two he spoke.

"Guys," he said. "This place is alive again. I never thought I'd see it, but here we are. It's an honor to have the two of you here. The world out there is pretty screwed up. But with your help we'll hold this little farm together. Monasteries helped bring people through one dark age. They might help bring us through another."

Suddenly Joan, despite her breathing trouble, jumped to her feet, alert, and made a low growling noise. She had heard it first. Then, in the distance, they all heard a sound, rapidly approaching. It was the unmistakable sound of a helicopter, and a big one at that.

CHAPTER 16

Jake and Mark were ready to run, thinking only of destruction raining from the sky. They looked toward Phaedrus for an indication of what to do. But Phaedrus calmly raised a hand in a soothing gesture.

"It's nothing to worry about," he said. "I think I know who this might be. Let's go out and meet them."

Jake and Mark exchanged looks of anxious incredulity, but they trusted Phaedrus. When had he ever been wrong? The helicopter set down in the field behind the house. Phaedrus, followed by Jake, followed by Mark, followed by Joan, walked toward the field. Joan was panting, but in her excitement she insisted on traveling under her own power. The helicopter's engines and heavy blades slowly wound down. Jake recognized this type of helicopter. He had seen them often enough around Washington. It was a Black Hawk, with the markings of a VIP transport helicopter. A door opened. A man in dark civilian clothes emerged, followed by a man in uniform. Jake and Mark stood where they were while Phaedrus walked ahead to meet them. The three of them shook hands. Jake was not close enough to make out the conversation, but it was apparent that Phaedrus knew the man in civilian clothing. They talked, looking grave, as they walked toward Jake and Mark, both of whom assumed a posture of awe as it became clear that Phaedrus knew someone this obviously powerful and that they were to be introduced.

"Jake, Mark," said Phaedrus. "I'd like for you to meet an old colleague of mine from Oxford, Henry Snow. And this is his military escort, Lieutenant Vasquez."

They all shook hands. Phaedrus continued.

"We have a few things to talk about, so maybe you guys could excuse us for a while? Henry, Lieutenant Vasquez, we just happen to have a fire out in the studio. Why don't we go there. Would your pilot like some coffee or something?"

"He'll be fine in the ship," said Henry Snow. "I think that's his protocol. But I'd love some."

Jake and Mark scurried off to make a show of resuming work on Mark's bedroom. But they were too excited to do much more than look out the window at the huge helicopter and speculate about what was going on."

"Are we in some sort of trouble?" Mark asked.

"I really doubt that," said Jake. "Phaedrus said that man's an old colleague from the university. I know it sounds weird, but I think I may even know who he is. I knew that Phaedrus had connections, but until recently I had no idea that he has connections with so much power. I just hope that he can tell us, that it's not something he has to be secretive about. That's the only thing in the world that Phaedrus is brutal about – secrets."

"You know who that guy is?" Mark said, eyes wide. "Who is he, then?"

"I'm not sure yet," Jake said. "But I think I listened to a talk he gave once. It was about the collapse of civilization."

Half an hour later, Phaedrus came looking for them. Jake and Mark were making a show of putting up drywall in Mark's room, though they weren't making much progress.

"Jake, Mark," said Phaedrus, "Henry wants to take me on a little reconnaissance mission in the helicopter. Mark, how would you feel about staying here and looking after Joan? And Jake, would you be interested in coming along?"

"You'll never get me up in that thing," said Mark.

"Sure," said Jake. "Yes. That would be amazing."

Soon they were strapped into the luxurious passenger seats of the Blackhawk. It was surprisingly quiet inside as the helicopter lifted off. Through the big windows, Jake could see Mark and Joan in the orchard, watching them go. The helicopter turned east into a clear sky. Phaedrus looked thoughtful. Lieutenant Vasquez' presence seemed to be a formality, or something to do with protocol, because he looked casually out a window and didn't appear to be listening to the conversation. The helicopter rose to an altitude of only six or eight hundred feet from the treetops and sped eastward. Henry spoke to Jake.

"Jake," he said, "Phaedrus tells me that you witnessed a little disorder in Washington."

"I did," said Jake. "Do you know what that was all about?"

"A no-fly was in effect. The Air Force was under orders to shoot down anything that was in the sky without authorization. Some private jets and small planes tried to push it. It seems you saw one or two of them being taken out."

"There was shooting at the Capitol. What was that about?"

"It would take a long time for me to fill you in on all the background," said Henry. "Phaedrus can answer a lot of your questions later. But the short version of what happened at the Capitol is that not everybody had a ticket out. When some members of Congress and their staff figured that out, they got rowdy. The military had orders to use whatever force was necessary to protect those with tickets out and get them onto helicopters. I'm sure it was ugly. I hope you weren't too close."

"No. I was halfway across the Mall. My girlfriend had a ticket out, I think. Or at least I think her mother did."

"What's her mother's name?"

"The last name is Brantley. I don't think I ever heard her mother's first name."

"I think I know who that might be," said Henry. "I don't think you need to worry about your girlfriend. I'm sorry you had to witness all that. You did good – getting out of town and getting to Phaedrus' place. Phaedrus, young Jake must have a thousand questions. We should at least give him the high-altitude version. Would you like to have a go at it?"

"There was a twist of events that I was not aware of until now," said Phaedrus. "Remember how I told you that some very rich people were working with some very smart people to reboot civilization with a controlled calamity? It seems the smart people pulled off a coup. Who needs billionaires now? Billionaires would expect to make all the decisions, and they're not nearly smart enough for that. They'd think only of their own wealth. So as of today, there are a lot fewer billionaires in the world. We are now living in an intellocracy. For better or worse, a bunch smart people are in control of the world. Some ruthless smart people, I'd say. But smart people nonetheless. Don't hold Henry responsible, though. The coup against the billionaires was a surprise to him, too. Henry is on the culture team. Actually Henry is on lots of teams, but he's not on the team that offs people."

"The culture team?" Jake asked.

"That's a good name for it," said Henry. "The smart people are smart enough to know that, if we reboot the world, then we have to reboot with a whole new operating system. That new operating system has been only partly written. A lot of work remains to be done. It would be hard to get that work done without minds like Phaedrus.'"

"Or minds like yours," said Jake. "I saw a video of a talk you gave once. The talk was about controlled calamity, to borrow the term that Phaedrus just used. It must not be easy to control a calamity. But I can see the nerds won, if you don't mind my calling you that, because you ended up with the helicopters."

Henry smiled and glanced at Phaedrus. Henry looked impressed. Phaedrus looked proud.

And Jake looked at Phaedrus with an ever-increasing respect. Jake felt small. What had Jake ever done to earn a place on a ride like this, with people like Henry and Phaedrus? But Jake was beginning to see what was going on. He was starting to realize that, whatever the new operating system for the world might look like, Phaedrus' thinking was going to be a part of it. The nerds were going to come up with better ideas.

"Nerds," said Jake. "Or Druids, same thing. The revenge of the Druids."

Henry Snow smiled.

"Maybe the nerds have been avenged," said Henry. "But the revenge of the Druids is likely to take a bit longer. I see why you like this young man so much, Phaedrus. He sees the long view of history. But, as Jake also sees, it's ironic, but it's not funny. Rebooting the world is an ugly business. Jake, I'd like for you to understand that, in a broad sense, I plead guilty for what has happened. All members of a conspiracy must be held responsible for the actions of any of its members. But most of my influence is with the culture team. My job is only to help come up with a better operating system for a rebooted world. Other teams did the ugly work. And as for Phaedrus, he had nothing to do with any of it. He was only spying on us. As we intended."

Henry laughed again. Phaedrus rotated his chair away from the window to face Jake and Henry.

"The reason I'm here, of course," said Henry, "is that I want Phaedrus on the culture team. He has spent years thinking about this kind of thing."

"What do you think, Jake?" said Phaedrus. "Can we spare a little time away from our fields and orchard and garden?"

"We?" said Jake. "You flatter me. But I read your book, Phaedrus. Go for it. Mark and I will mind the fields."

A chime sounded. Henry picked up a headset, listened for a moment, and gave an acknowledgment.

"The pilot says we're near Blacksburg," he said.

Soon they were flying low over the campus of Virginia Polytechnic Institute. There were a few small signs of life and activity below – a moving vehicle and some people standing in front of buildings, looking up at the helicopter.

"They did everything they could," said Henry, looking toward Phaedrus, "to spare the research centers. That can't have been easy with Boston. I'm not sure how they handled Boston. But I do know that the Palo Alto suburbs were spared, all the way from San Jose to Berkeley, and including San Francisco. They wouldn't have dared to endanger Stanford University. Many members of the teams came from there. Palo Alto may now be the only living American suburb."

"It's hard to imagine a world with no suburbs," said Phaedrus. "How do you re-wild a suburb?"

"People are working on that," said Henry. "It will take time, I'm sure, and a lot of recycling. But with luck this poor beaten-up planet will never see anything like the suburbs again. Maybe you can imagine how much an intellocracy, as you called it, hates the suburbs, except of course for Palo Alto. You should have seen them in some of the meetings I've been in. It wasn't just the physical reality of the suburbs and the environmental desolation of the suburbs, it was everything the suburbs stood for, everything the suburbs symbolized to them. Yes, the suburbs will be erased and will never happen again if a certain group of nerds has anything to do with it.

"Anyway," Henry continued, "I wanted you to see that the university is in good shape. They'll be getting some military support soon, to help them get back up and running. And since you're only half an hour from here by helicopter, Phaedrus, you'll probably be seeing more of this place."

The helicopter still sped eastward, over the rolling Appalachian hills. Occasionally there was a small sign of life – smoke curling above a small house surrounded by dense woods, or a couple of people in a barnyard, looking up. They passed over Roanoke. Even at the helicopter's low altitude, there was almost no sign of life. They flew over a suburban shopping center. Nothing moved. Lieutenant Vasquez had binoculars. He handed the binoculars to Henry and pointed. Jake's young eyes soon saw what they were looking at. Two men had furtively crept out of what appeared to be a grocery store. They were hiding behind a car, looking up at the helicopters.

"Looters," said Henry. "It looks like a few people made it. But notice how the streets and public places are empty. Most people just went home to die."

Their destination, it seemed, was Lynchburg, and soon another chime from the pilot let Henry know that they'd arrived. There was something else that Henry wanted Phaedrus to see. Henry pointed out a large church, then a college campus. The campus was Liberty University, Henry said. Jake knew that Liberty University was a training and indoctrination center for evangelical Christians. The helicopter approached what appeared to be a football stadium and flew lower, only a hundred or so feet above the ground.

"Not everybody went home to die," said Henry. "It

looks like Jonestown, doesn't it?"

There were bodies sprawled everywhere, mixed with litter, tents, tarpaulins, filthy blankets and the ashes of burned-out fires. Jake had once seen photographs of a mass suicide by members of a cult. It had happened in the 1960s, in Guyana. The cult members had drunk poisoned Kool-Aid at the instructions of the cult leader.

"They were waiting for the Rapture," said Henry. "This actually happened in a lot of places, and not just in the United States. They were expecting to see Jesus descending from the sky, 'coming with clouds,' as the scriptures say. I'm afraid they were disappointed. And Phaedrus, not to put too fine a point on it, but down there on the ground, in all that death and squalor, I believe you see the end of that cult, forever. We used to dream about that, Phaedrus. The greatest enemy that nature ever had is finally coming to an end. You used to call it exuberance, I think, the exuberance of nature. Maybe there's room for it now."

There was a huge sign overlooking the stadium. It said "Home of the Flames."

Phaedrus didn't reply to Henry. Jake studied Phaedrus' face for a moment, but Phaedrus' face was blank, his eyes distant as he looked out the helicopter window. Then Jake's eyes were drawn back to the death and indignity below.

Soon they were flying westward again, back toward the mountains. For a long time, no one spoke. Jake had seen only a tiny part of the world as the world now was. He couldn't help imagining such horror on a global scale, if that was even possible to imagine. Through his window he saw fields, and forests, and mountains to the west. From this altitude, it was possible to pretend that everything was normal.

Then Jake saw an object, moving fast, closing in on them from the northwest. It was at the same altitude as the helicopter. There was a chime, and Henry picked up the intercom. Henry looked out his window. Then Henry tapped Phaedrus, whose window faced south, and gestured toward a north-facing window. Phaedrus looked out the window, but didn't say anything. Jake didn't speak either, but he looked expectantly toward Henry. It was another alien spacecraft, not big this time, but small.

"Classified," said Henry, with an amused look on his face. "But I'll get that taken care of as soon as possible."

Now Jake looked toward Phaedrus.

"There's nothing to worry about," said Phaedrus. "They're harmless. In fact, they'll probably be pretty helpful. Did I say harmless? They're actually very nice."

Jake stuttered.

"Still classified," said Henry. "I promise we'll answer all your questions soon."

Jake eyes went back to the window. The craft was flying alongside them now. It was small and disk shaped. It was silent, and silvery, and strangely unthreatening. Like the black triangle, it had a light beam. A beam burst from the front of the vessel, pointing down and toward the west. The beam strobed, then went out. Jake glanced to west and guessed that the beam was pointed toward their destination, their little farm. Their little monastery. Then the vessel dipped an edge in a gesture like a salute, waggled in a gesture like a wave, and vanished straight up at an impossible velocity.

◆—◆

That evening, Jake and Phaedrus had planned a stargazing session in the upper field, because the moon was new. Mark excused himself, saying that it was a too cold to be out in the middle of the night. Phaedrus tried to encourage Joan to stay in by the fire, but she insisted on going along, though Jake had to carry her part of the way. Soon they stood on the usual hilltop, overlooking the farmhouse. With the absence of moonlight, the grid down, and all the old light pollution wiped out, the sky was spectacular.

"It's almost worth shutting down civilization for, isn't it?" said Jake. "I never thought I'd see a sky like this in my lifetime."

"It overwhelms," said Phaedrus. "Seeing a sky like this makes it so much easier to understand why the stars had such an effect on our ancestors. The stars become part of your world, a part of your daily experience. There is no impassable gulf, no real separation. 'As above, so below' becomes a credible proposition. Something happens when people are cut off from the stars. Their imaginations die. They're much more inclined to think only of themselves. But we'd better get a fire going. Joan needs the warmth. We'll have a nice, dark bed of coals by the time Ursa Major comes into view."

The brightness of their fire dimmed the stars. It gave them time to talk before they let themselves become silently absorbed in the sky, as was now their habit when stargazing.

"It all seems so radical," Jake said. "Surely there was a solution that wasn't so drastic, a solution that didn't involve so much death and destruction."

"What sort of solution?" Phaedrus asked.

"I don't know," said Jake. "New technologies? Democratic solutions? International agreements?"

"I'm glad in a way," said Phaedrus, "that I was here on this little farm and never had to have that discussion with the likes of Henry. I'm not sure what I'd say. But I can say one thing for sure, and that is that the nerds, as we've been calling them, came to the conclusion that there was no longer time to save the planet, and civilization, by any other means. I think they'd say that we're about thirty years too late for political solutions. I think they'd say that solving the problem with technology was only a utopian dream. And I think they'd say that once people started talking about a 'market' solution that the cause was truly hopeless. There just wasn't time."

"And the nerds killed all the billionaires," said Jake.

"They did. After all, why quibble over a few hundred billionaires in the context of 6.5 billion people dead? Apparently the billionaires didn't even see it coming. It's part of the price of hubris, I suppose. Rich people can't imagine that the world can revolve without them. But here we are, revolving."

"But if the smart people knocked off the billionaires, aren't the smart people billionaires now? And doesn't it come down to the same thing?"

"That might seem true, except that the two groups have different mind sets. The smart people are dreamers. They have imaginations. They tend to want change rather than the preservation of the status quo. Whereas billionaires see things another way. Oh, for sure there have been some examples of billionaires who used their money to do good. But that's not the rule. And economists have begun to understand that gross imbalances in wealth and income, just in themselves, have a destabilizing effect on societies. So the loss of the billionaires will make a difference, at least for a while. Eventually those people who want money and power will work their way to the top again, and a new status quo will form. But for a while, maybe even years, real change is possible. These people dream of a different sort of world."

"And these dreamers: did they share their dreams with you? Excuse me for laughing. It reminds me of a song. I'll explain later."

"Remember when we talked once about how monotheism is helpful to those who want to centralize power and use it to control a population? That centralized religious power always seeks to compete with centralized political power. In some times and places they may join up and make a show of working together, but a marriage between centralized religious power and centralized political power is always volatile. I'm beating around the bush. Here's a quicker way to say it. The nerds who are now running the world are pretty sure that they don't want any competition from centralized religious power, now that they've eliminated the super-rich."

"What's the alternative? Lots of gods?"

"That was what the Celts had – diffused, localized religious power, with many gods. In that kind of world, our little hilltop here might have its own little god. And the spring one ridge over that supplies our water might have its own little god, too."

"And how would we return to that kind of world?"

"That's the problem, isn't it? I'm afraid that it requires nothing less than the systematic repression of the dominant religion and its replacement with something else – partly through coercion and partly through persuasion. In other words, the same methods that the Roman religion always used to get rid of the competition. Except now these methods would need to be used against the Roman religion. And there is justice in that."

"It sounds messy. Are the nerds serious?"

"It would be messy. And the nerds are serious."

"And they want you to help?"

"They want me to help," said Phaedrus.

"I see why you have a lot to think about."

For a long time they were silent, alternately studying the sky and the coals of the fire and trying to make sure that Joan was warm. All of Ursa Major was now in view but for the tip of the tail. Jake spoke.

"Ever since I met you, Phaedrus, I've been trying to puzzle out what makes you tick. I think I've figured it out."

"Oh?"

"You're not like the billionaires, or even the nerds. You're not motivated by power and money. If you were, you wouldn't be here, living the way you live. No. Your issue is something else entirely."

"And what would that be?"

"Love. But I really should say the scarcity of love, or the poverty of love in some people's lives. And you're angry, I think, because some people are rich with love, and others are poor, through no fault of their own. Some people get love easily, but others never really do, no matter how hard they might try. And unlike wealth, love is something that you can't just steal, something that you can't exploit people for. All a person can do is put love out into the world, and hope that it comes back. But sometimes it just doesn't. It's all very clear to me now. I knew someone like you once."

"Who was that?"

"Jamie. I'll tell you, but you owe me a story too. Remember?"

"I remember," said Phaedrus. "Will you go first? Would you tell me about Jamie?"

"Jamie was the best friend I ever had. Maybe the only friend I ever had, until now."

"Was? Where is Jamie now?"

"I think," said Jake, trying to keep his voice from breaking because of the lump in his throat, "that I should start from the beginning. I've never told anyone the whole story. I hope you won't think less of me. I was young. I was stupid. I'd known Jamie since he was ten. I was a year older. We used to spend most of our free time together. Jamie was devoted to me. He was so small, so vulnerable, so girlish in a way. I always looked out for him. And he always looked up to me. It was like he was my mascot. It was strange, but no one ever teased me for having a best friend like Jamie. And no one ever teased Jamie, or bullied him, because everyone knew I looked out for him. I was probably the only person who really knew how smart Jamie was, because we talked. He'd go stargazing with me, actually. We'd sit under the sky, just like this, and he'd think up all these questions. Sometimes the questions were about why the world is the way it is. And sometimes the questions were about me. It was as though I was some sort of fascinating mystery to him. He'd always ask me what I was thinking. I'd tell him, usually. And sometimes we'd play a game in which he'd guess what I was thinking. He was generally pretty close.

"I'd have girlfriends, but he didn't much seem to mind. I guess it was because my relationships with girlfriends were so shallow, nothing like my friendship with Jamie. And somehow he understood that. Girls never much cared what I was thinking. Girls never saw me as some sort of mystery to be studied and understood. Girls would find my flaws, soon enough. But Jamie never tried to change me. He never tried to fix me. It was more like he thought he needed to earn being my friend, to deserve me. I liked the attention, I guess. But I never really understood.

"Then I went off to school. Spring semester, he asked if he could come visit, and of course I said yes. But all of a sudden he seemed so serious. I realized that he was in love with me, and that we weren't twelve years old anymore. I didn't know what to do. I didn't know what to say to him. He still never demanded anything, never expected anything, never even asked for anything. But I knew. I could see it in his eyes when he looked at me. I loved Jamie. Of course I did. But I didn't know how I could ever give him what he wanted. I was afraid I would make him unhappy, that it would screw everything up. I was trying to figure out how to buy time, I guess, and figure things out, without breaking his heart.

"One night we were drinking, and this girl I was seeing had an idea. She said why don't we let Jamie come in and catch us making out, and then he'll understand that he's wrong about you and that he should stick to his own kind. I went along with her. I don't know why. If only I hadn't been drinking so much that night. Jamie opened the door, and then he closed it. And I never saw him again."

Phaedrus waited silently until Jake was ready to continue.

"A couple of days later, I found out that he had hanged himself. He wrote me a note. His parents almost burned it, but they had to give it to the police. Jamie loved sappy songs. He said he must be in the wrong world, otherwise how could I give my love to someone else and share my dreams with him. He said that he was sure that he would see me again somewhere in a different world, and that someday there would be a place for us. I knew all the old songs, because he'd played them for me a million times. I knew that Jamie was in love with me. There had to have been a better way of working it out. But I got it wrong."

"Jake, I'm so sorry."

"How could I ever have thought that Jamie, my friend Jamie, was somehow of a different kind? The girl I was seeing, was she my kind? We were together for what, five months? She dropped me and got a guy with blond hair and a nicer car. There would have been more justice in the world if she'd caught me making out with Jamie. And so I began to see how unfair the world is. I began to see how it's just the same with love as it is with money and power. Some people have a lot, and some people don't. And some people may never really have much love no matter how hard they work. I already knew that, from Jamie.

"And so I saw, Phaedrus, that really you're just like Jamie. You're much tougher. You lasted longer. Jamie was fragile. You did it in a different way, but you turned your back on the world, too. I think you did it for the same reason. It was because no matter how hard you tried or how much love you put out into the world, it didn't come back to you. I just want you to know that I can see that. And I'm sorry."

They were silent for while.

"And now," said Jake. "You owe me a story. But I think I know what your story is."

"What's that?"

"My father broke your heart. It was the last straw. And so you became a hermit."

"That's about it," said Phaedrus.

"Do I remind you of him?"

"Yes," said Phaedrus. "You do."

The flames were gradually dying down, but the coals were still warm. Jake leaned toward Joan and scratched between her ears.

Then Jake heard the buzzing. He put his hands over his eyes for moment while the vision possessed him, as complex as a fugue, but over in an instant. The final chord seemed to reverberate from galaxy to galaxy. It was a major chord: as comforting as home, as optimistic as a kitten, as familiar as a lover. Then his head cleared, and he looked up into the night. A brilliant meteor flashed across the sky. It was so bright that it appeared to survive all the way to the treetops, where it burst into scattering sparks like fireworks.

"Wow," said Jake. "Did you see that? That was the best one I've ever seen. Jamie would have loved that. He had a knack for seeing them. He always made a wish."

"Why don't you make a wish?" said Phaedrus.

"I already have. You know what? For a second, I felt I was in a place where I have never been before, never in my entire life."

"And where was that?"

"The center of the universe. But it was just for a second. It was like we're all backstage in a play, waiting to go on, going over our lines. But most of the time we don't know it. It was like we're reading from a script. We pretend we don't know what's going to happen, but really we do. Does this sound strange? And it was like there is no such thing as a god. There's just us, and somehow we all wrote the script together. Still, how'd we get here in the first place? Jamie had a definition of god, you know. He said that god was whatever made the stars, and music, and all the little animals."

"I like that definition of god."

"Isn't that a monotheistic definition, though?"

"Not necessarily," said Phaedrus. "Perhaps one god made the stars, and another made music, and yet another made all the little animals."

Jake smiled up at the stars and scratched Joan's head again.

"Aha," said Jake, "I just figured out your real objection to monotheism."

"What's that?"

"A single god is not redundant. If god lets you down, you have nowhere to turn to. That's an existentially ugly place to be, as my mother might say."

"Precisely. And now you're very close to my definition of a heretic."

"What's that?"

"A heretic is a person who is not afraid to tell a god to go to hell."

Jake laughed.

"I get it. If god screws up, see if you can find a better one."

"That's right," said Phaedrus. "You're left with something to turn to. The god of music might keep us alive if the god of love has let us down. And all the little animals, they help, too."

"But there has to be a bigger god or two, doesn't there? I mean, not just any little god – little gods like us, and even like Joanie here – could make something as vast as the stars. And what about the other people out there? Other civilizations? Wouldn't there need to be a god or two big enough that his – or her – jurisdiction includes an entire galaxy, maybe more?"

"I suspect that your theology is sound."

"So there really are?" asked Jake.

"Really are what?"

"People out there."

"Yes, there are," said Phaedrus.

"You implied that you've met them."

"I have."

"And?"

"I promise we'll talk about it soon. Henry will get clearance, and then I won't have to beat around the bush. Besides, we've been through a lot down here on earth. Maybe we should try to deal with all that first. Different planets, same story."

"Phaedrus, are you being metaphorical? Or are you teasing me again?"

"I suppose I am too fond of metaphors," Phaedrus said. "But I don't recall ever teasing you."

Jake couldn't think of anything to say. So they sat silent for a while, looking up at the stars. Finally Jake spoke.

"So, Phaedrus, will you do what Henry wants you to do? Join the culture team?"

"I need to think about it. But yes, probably."

"Would you have to leave?" Jake asked.

"That's one of the hard parts. This place is a much nicer home than it used to be, with you and Mark here. But yes, I'd have to go away at times. I think that things could be arranged so that, most of the time, I'd be here at our little monastery. But you wouldn't have to stay here all the time, either, you know? I could use your help."

"I think you're just trying to flatter me, Phaedrus. I don't know how I could help you."

"But you could. You already understand what needs to be done. All that's needed is a plan. A script. The devil is in the details. There will be lots of devils and lots of details. Plus, you know how young people think. That's very important. I'm not sure I can model that anymore. You're open to change, to new ways of thinking, new ways of being. And there can't be just one monastery, Jake. Eventually there would need to be more monasteries if we want to keep the lights on and pull the world out of this new Dark Age. It would be good work for you, Jake. That is, if it's what you wanted. Things might move really fast for a while. I can't say about the center of the universe, but we'd certainly be pretty close at times to the new lords of this little planet and maybe even to the lords of some others. That can be a dangerous place to be. But how often do you get a chance to help write the operating system for getting out of a Dark Age? How often do you get to reseed the earth, to re-wild its land and seas, to rethink its cultures?"

"How strange to be talking about things like this. How did this happen? I'm just an architect, a pathetic architect from the suburbs. Sometimes – I shouldn't tell you this, Phaedrus – sometimes I'm still afraid of the dark. I don't have a clue. And yet I'm sure I felt it, the center of the universe, I mean. It moves so fast. It was here only for a second. And then I lost it again. I think it went back to Ursa Major. What is it about Ursa Major? I hope I can hold on to what it felt like, Phaedrus. It felt like … like a story. It felt like millions of people were watching us, to see what we will do."

Joan coughed, and her body stiffened.

"Oh, no," said Phaedrus, reaching out for her. "She's having a convulsion. Not tonight, Joanie, baby. Please, not tonight."

But it was over quickly. And soon Joan's body lay limp and warm and still, with Phaedrus bent over her and Jake caressing her front paw. They remained that way while the coals dimmed and Ursa Major rotated into position precisely overhead. Phaedrus sat with his head bowed. Jake looked up, took a deep breath, took hold of

Phaedrus' hand, let go of the old world order, and fell down, down, down into Ursa Major. As he fell, he could still feel the warmth of Phaedrus' hand and the softness of Joan's furry front paw.

Acknowledgments

Many thanks to the friends and old colleagues who read early drafts of this story: Ken Ilgunas, Dean C. Smith, Pamela Brunger Scott, and James-Michael Gregg. Ken, in particular, a fellow storyteller, story lover and resident of Acorn Abbey, honored me with many hours of discussion about many details of this story.